Best Regards
Dorien Grey

DORIEN GREY

HIS NAME IS
JOHN

ZUMAYA BOUNDLESS

2008

D1069993

This book is a work of fiction. Names, characters, places and incidents are products of the author's imagination or are used fictitiously. Any resemblance to actual persons or events is purely coincidental.

HIS NAME IS JOHN
© 2008 by Dorien Grey

ISBN 978-1-934841-04-4

Cover art and design by Martine Jardin

All rights reserved. Except for use in review, the reproduction or utilization of this work in whole or in part in any form by any electronic, mechanical or other means now known or hereafter invented, is prohibited without the written permission of the author or publisher.

Zumaya Boundless is an imprint of Zumaya Publications LLC, Austin TS.
Look for us online at http://www.zumayapublications.com

Library of Congress Cataloging-in-Publication Data
Grey, Dorien.
His name is John / Dorien Grey.
    p. cm.
ISBN 978-1-934841-04-4 (trade pbk. : alk. paper)
1. Spirits--Fiction. 2. Chicago (Ill.)--Fiction. I. Title.
PS3557.R48165H58 2008
813'.54--dc22
                    2008023255

Dinner went well...

Rick brought a bottle of wine, and they sat at the dining room table for nearly two hours, talking and relaxing. Elliott skipped the wine since he was on medication.

Rick was a social worker with one of the city agencies, and though it was a grueling and often depressing job with a lot of pressure, he always managed to focus on the lighter side, and had an endless string of funny stories of life within a bureaucracy.

Realizing it would be both awkward and uncomfortable, given Elliott's shoulder, for Rick to spend the night, neither of them mentioned it directly. Rick left around eleven, saying he'd call in the morning to see if Elliott needed anything.

Elliott turned out the lights and, more tired than he'd realized, did not, as was his custom, stand at the window and survey the jeweled galaxy of the city, spread out before him, prior to turning in. Instead, he just managed to get undressed and eased into bed.

— *He's nice.*

The thought-voice jerked Elliott back to near-consciousness. Was that John's assessment of Rick, or his own?

— *My name is John.* The sensation of frustration was overpowering. Elliott thought of a stroke victim, struggling to communicate but unable to find the words.

— *I know.* And with that he sank into a deep and dreamless sleep.

"You don't believe in me," observed the Ghost.

"I don't." said Scrooge.

"What evidence would you have of my reality, beyond that of your senses?"

"I don't know," said Scrooge.

"Why do you doubt your senses?"

"Because," said Scrooge, "a little thing affects them. A slight disorder of the stomach makes them cheats. You may be an undigested bit of beef, a blot of mustard, a crumb of cheese, a fragment of an underdone potato. There's more of gravy than of grave about you, whatever you are!"

Charles Dickens, *A Christmas Carol*

CHAPTER 1

❧❀❧

Waking up with a splitting headache and a throbbing shoulder, Elliott had no idea where he was. After he clamped his eyes shut and reopened them, he realized he was in a hospital room, with no memory how he'd gotten there.

He did know someone sat in the chair beside his bed, watching him. Yet when he managed to turn his head to see who it was, the chair was empty. He was alone in the room. Except he wasn't.

He drifted in and out of consciousness, roused with annoying frequency by nurses waking him up to do whatever nurses find it necessary to wake people up to do. Mostly, they said nothing and achieved their objectives with expressionless faces. Whenever he woke, he glanced over at the chair where whoever wasn't there watched him.

He gradually became aware that whoever was not in the chair's name was John, that John was dead and that John was, to say the least, confused and unable to grasp that he *was* dead. Elliott also sensed that John not only hadn't a clue as to how he died but no idea who he had been when he was alive.

Of course, on the subject of being confused, Elliott was hardly a poster boy for sharp thinking himself. He had no idea why he was in the hospital or, for that matter, which hospital. It wasn't until he saw Norm Shepard, an ER nurse who lived in his building, standing over him that he knew he was in St. Joseph's.

Norm smiled when he saw Elliott had noticed him.

"Welcome back to the world of the living," he said.

Elliott glanced over at the chair. John, he sensed, was not amused.

"I had to come up to this floor for some charts," Norm went on, "and thought I'd check in to see how you're doing."

Elliott opened his mouth to talk, but somebody else's voice came out; and Norm quickly raised a hand to silence him.

"No talk just yet," he advised.

✤

Over the next few days, every time he looked at the chair Elliott knew John was

1

there, watching him. When visitors stopped by—his sister Cessy came by a lot, as did several of his friends and Rick Morrison, a guy he had begun dating a few weeks before the accident—most stood by the side or at the foot of the bed. When anyone sat down, Elliott knew John wasn't in the chair—apparently, even though he was now noncorporeal, he didn't like being sat on.

At such times, Elliott would sense him by the window, looking out at the traffic on Lakeshore Drive. He never got the impression John was particularly interested in whoever else was in the room.

How he had ended up in St. Joe's he learned in bits and pieces. He was told he had been crossing Sheridan Road at Wellington a few blocks from the hospital around eleven o'clock at night, on his way home from dinner with friends and had been clipped by a car speeding around the corner. He'd hit his head on the curb, although fortunately his left shoulder had taken the brunt of the fall. He'd been unconscious then heavily sedated for several days, and was cautioned that he'd look a bit like a monk for a while after his release—they'd had to shave part of his head to stitch up a rather nasty cut on his scalp.

He did his best to convince himself that the concussion from the head injury accounted for John, and that "he" would just go away after a while.

But he didn't, and Elliott didn't dare mention him to anyone lest they decide to transfer him to the psychiatric ward for observation. He was nothing if not practical and logical, and John's intrusion into his life was neither. So, they kept their own counsel, John and he.

He still had the overwhelming sense that John was utterly confused over his current state and how it had come about. He also felt that, since he was the only one who was aware of John, John looked to him for help, though Elliott had no idea of what he could do for him.

Then, one night just before he was scheduled to be released, Norm Shepard stopped by again after his shift. Since his first visit, some vague memories of and after the accident had begun to return.

"I think I remember seeing you in the ER when I was brought in," Elliott said. "I guess I was in pretty bad shape."

"We weren't sure there for a while whether or not there was any bleeding into your brain, but there wasn't. You're a lucky guy."

Elliott sighed. "Considering the alternative, I guess you're right." Again, he was aware that John did not appreciate his humor. "But I vaguely recall they brought somebody in right after me, and you took off. I guess the other guy was in worse shape than I was."

"Yeah, you could say that. He didn't have a chance. Shot six times. It's a wonder he even made it to the hospital."

"Sorry about that," Elliott said, and meant it. "Who was he? Did I see a couple cops come in with him?"

"Yeah, they brought him in. Found him in an alley less than two blocks from here. No ID on him, and he died without fully regaining consciousness."

"So, did they find out who he was?"

2

"I have no idea," Norm said. "We admitted him as a John Doe."

✻

John Doe! Was the presence in the chair the guy from the ER? He sensed no particular reaction from the direction of the chair; but if it was the same guy, had he somehow made some sort of link with Elliott in the few minutes before he teetered over the threshold between life and death?

Or, more likely, it was Elliott who had made the link. Maybe this whole thing really *was* just a psychotic episode his mind had created for reasons of its own. When he got home from the hospital, back in his own world with his own things around him, "John" would probably just fade away.

Although he prided himself on logical, linear thinking, Elliott found his thoughts in the hospital skipping over the surface of his mind like a flat stone thrown onto a calm pond. He'd start off pondering one thing and end up somewhere totally unrelated.

Contemplating his conviction that the presence in the chair was named John, he convinced himself he must have subconsciously heard someone in the ER referring to the "John Doe." From there, his thoughts inexplicably segued to the fact that names had always intrigued him, possibly because "Elliott" was not a name he would have chosen for himself. When he was a teenager, he liked to think of himself as more of a Tom, or perhaps a Mike. He always suspected that his mother, whose maiden name had been Von Eck, had chosen a high-gloss first name like "Elliott" as a way of compensating for his primer-coat last name—Smith.

But, being a very adaptable sort, he had grown used to it. He in fact prided himself on both his adaptability and his practicality, though he took a certain pleasure in his few minor idiosyncracies. He collected trivia, for example, the way black pants collect cat hair. In addition to a penchant for remembering interesting but relatively useless information from everything he read, he enjoyed using his own observations to accumulate even more. He knew, for example, the height in stories of every building he passed regularly; he knew the number of steps between floors in any building in which he had occasion to use the stairs.

Now, bringing his thoughts back to the name John, he knew it as the second most common name for American men—more than four million—just as Smith was the most common American surname. He could bring to mind at least half a dozen Johns he knew personally.

Although his last name might have been common his resources were not. He had always been a little embarrassed that, by sheer chance, he was born into an extremely affluent family, not one member of which had done a real day's work in his or her life. He was hardly foolish enough to turn his back on the family money, but had done his best to avoid its pitfalls.

Possibly as an offshoot of his fascination with trivia, he had always had the innate ability to look at something and intuitively see how a minimum of effort and investment could produce the maximum results. It subsequently came naturally to him to support himself by buying, renovating and reselling small apartment buildings around the north side of the city, though he made an occasional concession to his wealth by retaining a few he couldn't bear to part with. It kept him busy, and he enjoyed it.

That night, and every night thereafter that he remained in the hospital, experiencing vivid technicolor dreams he could not remember later, there was one thing he could not forget, one thought accompanied by a sensation of sorrow and loss that repeated over and over.

My name is John!

❉

He convinced his doctors to release him on Friday so that he wouldn't have to spend the weekend in the hospital. Rick offered to take time off from work to take him home, but Cessy insisted she would pick him up and drive him in her new SUV, a combination thirty-fourth birthday and birth-of-a-third-grandchild present from their parents ("Now that you have three children, Cecilia, you need a larger, more dependable vehicle.").

Brad, Cessy's police detective husband, wasn't too happy about the gift, though he acknowledged it was a practical one. He had put his foot down, though, when the parents wanted to buy a new Steinway for their granddaughter Jenny when she began taking piano lessons at age seven. Brad was an extremely proud man; and while he never talked about it, Elliott knew reminders that Cessy had more money than he'd make in several lifetimes really bothered him.

Their—Cessy's and Elliott's—mother had, perhaps not surprisingly, been far less than pleased with Cessy's choice of a husband but knew her daughter well enough not to make her displeasure too evident. Cessy was a lot like Elliott in her attitude toward the family fortune, though her practical side had no problem with using it if she needed to. But out of deference to Brad, she was pretty restrained.

Having gotten Elliot safely home, and after making him promise about a dozen times to take his medication, rest and not do anything strenuous—he did manage to dissuade her from putting him to bed and tucking him in—Cessy left to attend a parent-teacher affair at Brad Jr.'s school. She said she would return later in the afternoon with some groceries—Elliott's kitchen cabinets were full, but after being gone for almost two weeks, he needed a few perishables like milk.

After Cessy left, he took a pill to forestall the onset of his recurring headache then spent a few minutes just looking around the apartment. He was glad to be home. Noticing that Ida, his cleaning woman, had obviously forgotten to water the plants on the balcony off the living room, he went into the kitchen to fill the watering can.

Doing everything with just one hand proved not to be as easy as he had hoped. He opened the sliding glass doors, having to set the can down first; he from experience that any too-sudden or too-sharp movement of his upper torso hurt like hell. Stepping outside, he watered the plants then stood looking at the city. He'd bought his 35th-floor condo specifically for its unobstructed south view of the city and the Loop.

It was a perfect just-before-summer day, with cotton-puff clouds gliding slowly across an incredibly blue sky. The lake, immediately below to his left, reflected the color of the sky, and was lightly flecked with whitecaps. He never got tired of looking at it.

Going back inside, he considered removing the sling the doctor had insisted he wear; he found it more cumbersome than helpful and was sure that, as long as he was careful not to move his arm too swiftly, he could do just as well without it. However, his practical side won out, and he decided he had better keep it on.

Sitting in his favorite chair near the window, he picked up the stack of mail Cessy had extricated from his full mailbox and left on the glass-topped coffee table. Opening it with one hand was even harder than filling the watering can had been; and when he did have it all opened, he determined that, other than a postcard from his parents, who were on a passenger freighter plying the islands of the Philippines, there was nothing that needed his immediate attention. Maybe it was all the medication, but as he sat in the sunlight with a nice breeze coming through the open balcony doors, he dozed off.

— *My name is John.*

— *Yes, I know. Tell me something I don't.*

— *I can't.*

Elliott woke up, feeling unexplainably very sad.

He had hoped, or rather assumed, that he'd left John at the hospital—he'd always heard that ghosts hang around the place where they died. Obviously, that was just one of those old-ghosts' tales. He had read somewhere that newly hatched ducks and geese imprint on the first thing they see when they're born, and he wondered if perhaps John, if he were not just a figment of the imagination, had somehow done the same when he died. The question now was, what was Elliott going to do about it? What *could* he do about it?

In the back of his mind, he still nurtured the very strong likelihood that all this was just a result of his head trauma, and that as he got better, John would just fade away. He had initially supported that theory because of John's having no clue who he was, which would be reasonable if Elliott had created him. Then it struck Elliott that, if he couldn't remember the details of his own accident, the trauma of being murdered could certainly make one unable to remember things clearly. On the other hand, he'd have thought the act of dying might have clarified things a bit. Obviously, it hadn't.

He considered that John might be experiencing some ectoplasmic form of total amnesia. Maybe just being dead produced it, which would account for the relatively few reports of ghosts. But, whatever the reason for John's lack of personal information, given the brief exchange of sleep-submerged conversation, he reluctantly came to accept that John might, in fact, be real and simply not know who he was.

❉

The afternoon passed with phone calls and the sisterly fussing of Cessy, who returned with the milk plus an entire bag of things he didn't really need but which she insisted would be good for him. He had never been overly fond of things he was told were good for him.

He was tempted to remind her that she was his sister, not his nurse, but resisted, knowing she was just trying to help.

The door had no sooner closed behind her when the phone rang.

"Elliott Smith," he said, reaching it just before the third ring.

"Elliott, I called the hospital and they said you'd been released today."

He recognized the voice of Larry Fingerhood, a real estate broker with whom he frequently worked.

"Yeah," he replied, "I got home just after lunch."

"Is it okay to talk business? I don't want to bother you if you're resting."

"No, I'm fine, thanks. What's up?"

"Just wanted to let you know I'm afraid we lost out on the bid for the Devon building. Evermore upped our offer by ten thousand, and because the owner didn't know how long you'd be in the hospital, he didn't want to wait and accepted it."

"Damn! But I guess I shouldn't be surprised." This was the second building he'd back-and-forthed on with—and lost to—Evermore Properties in the past month, and it was getting old. Fast.

"I'm really sorry, but I didn't have the authority to counter again."

Elliott sighed. "That's okay. You're right, and I understand. It's a nice building with a lot of potential, and I hate to lose it, but..."

Evermore Properties, which was primarily a development firm, had recently been taken over by Al Collina, whom Elliott had known and disliked since childhood and whose family had for a time lived next door to the Smiths in Lake Forest. The Collinas had come into their wealth during Prohibition by means everyone knew but no one openly talked about. By the time Elliott's generation came along, the source of the Collinas' wealth was just an interesting bit of Chicago folklore.

Elliott's passion was preservation of Chicago's past. Evermore, especially with Al Collina at the helm, was interested only in bulldozing whatever was there and throwing up expensive high-rise condos—though the phrase "expensive condos," when used in Chicago, was redundant.

"I know," Larry said, calling Elliott's attention back to the moment. "But you can't save every building with character in the city. When it comes down to altruism versus profit, profit nearly always wins. It's the old bottom line, and that line says that throwing up a high rise is a lot more profitable than renovating a much smaller building."

They'd had this conversation before, and Larry was right. One of the principal reasons Elliott had gotten into property renovation in the first place was out of a love for the feel, the flavor, the architecture of older buildings. Elliott Enterprises, his official business name, specialized in restoring and renovating four- to twelve-unit apartment buildings built in the 20s and 30s. He felt they had a charm many of the newer buildings lacked. They were part of Chicago's history, and he wanted to preserve as much of that as he could.

It wasn't that there was any particular shortage of potential properties, but every now and then, a building came along that especially interested him; the Devon building had been one of them. What disturbed him most was that losing the bid would disrupt his "flow," as he thought of it. He only concentrated on one building at a time, and had established a pattern—whenever the building he was currently working on was nearly done, he'd start looking for another, timing it so that he could smoothly move from the end of one job to the beginning of the next. He envisioned it as being rather like Tarzan swinging through the jungle from vine to vine, reaching out to the next just before he let go of the last. He'd planned on the Devon building being his next vine.

While he had, to the consternation of his parents, taken out a contractor's license, and often did much of the renovation work himself, he relied on a team of licensed independent subcontractors—primarily a plumber, a carpenter and an electrician—for any work that required the meeting of building codes. He also had contacts with other small, specialized subcontracting firms for things like roofing, carpeting, wood restoration, heating equipment and window replacement.

His most recent project, a classic ten-unit on Granville, had been nearly finished and almost ready to go on the market when he'd had the accident. He knew there would be another, but losing out on the Devon property broke his rhythm, and he resented it.

Shortly after he hung up, the phone rang again.

"Hello?"

"Elliott, it's Rick. You got home okay? How are you feeling?"

"I'm doing fine, Rick, thanks." Actually, he was developing a headache and realized he'd forgotten to take his medication.

"Think you might be up for a little company later? I thought I could bring some dinner over so you wouldn't have to worry about trying to cook. I won't stay long."

"Sure," Elliott said, his spirits picking up just on hearing Rick's voice. "That'd be fine. I was just going to have a TV dinner—that I can do with one hand."

"Any preferences?" Rick asked. "Chinese? Pizza? Something from The Bagel? Stella's?"

Elliott grinned, realizing as he did so that he hadn't done much grinning in some time. "Ya think Stella's might have meatloaf today? That or Salisbury steak? Something I don't have to use both hands to cut?"

"I'll find out," Rick replied. "What time should I come over? Seven?"

"Seven's fine. Thanks."

"No problem. Anything else I can bring you?"

"Not that I can think of. I'll see you at seven."

He called the lobby to alert the doorman that Rick was expected and to just let him come up without calling first.

Dinner went well. Rick brought a bottle of wine, and they sat at the dining room table for nearly two hours, talking and relaxing. Elliott skipped the wine since he was on medication.

Rick was a social worker with one of the city agencies, and though it was a grueling and often depressing job with a lot of pressure, he always managed to focus on the lighter side, and had an endless string of funny stories of life within a bureaucracy.

Realizing it would be both awkward and uncomfortable, given Elliott's shoulder, for Rick to spend the night, neither of them mentioned it directly. Rick left around eleven, saying he'd call in the morning to see if Elliott needed anything.

Elliott turned out the lights and, more tired than he'd realized, did not, as was his custom, stand at the window and survey the jeweled galaxy of the city spread out before him prior to turning in. Instead, he just managed to get undressed and eased into bed.

— *He's nice.*

The thought-voice jerked Elliott back to near-consciousness. Was that John's assessment of Rick, or his own?

— *My name is John.* The sensation of frustration was overpowering. Elliott thought of a stroke victim, struggling to communicate but unable to find the words.

— *I know.* And with that he sank into a deep and dreamless sleep.

Cessy called at nine-thirty the following morning, asking about his health, if he'd slept well, had he had breakfast, did he need any help around the apartment, to which he replied "fine," "yes," "yes" and "no."

"Well," she said in her don't-even-think-about-refusing voice, "you're coming to dinner this evening. Brad will pick you up around six. Be waiting in the lobby."

Though Cessy was four years younger than he, she often treated him as though he were the younger—by far. And though he would never tell her so, she at times reminded him strongly of their mother. He also knew that if he pled not feeling up to the outing for whatever reason, she would assume he was having a relapse and insist on coming over and playing Florence Nightingale. Their mother would have sent a nurse, and Elliott was glad she and his father were, for all intents and purposes, incommunicado. As far as he knew, they weren't even aware of his accident.

"I can catch a cab," he said. He knew far better than to suggest he could drive over.

"Nonsense!" Cessy said. "It would cost a fortune."

"I have a fortune," he teased. "Remember? So do you."

8

"Well, just because you have it doesn't mean you have to spend it," she said flatly. "Brad Junior has swim practice this afternoon from three to five-thirty, and they'll come by and pick you up right after."

"Yes, ma'am," he agreed with a heavy sigh.

"I can tell you're feeling better," she said. "Your sarcasm's coming back."

✳

Rick, true to his word, called shortly after Elliott got off the phone with Cessy. They talked for awhile and tentatively agreed to get together the next day for Sunday breakfast. Rick said he'd come pick him up, but Elliott insisted he could just take the bus, and that's how they left it.

He spent the day puttering and, in a rather grudging acknowledgment of the fact he still wasn't quite back to normal, napping. Around four, he began to get ready to go to Cessy and Brad's.

Although he wasn't particularly fond of hats, he decided he'd feel a little less self-conscious about his partially shaved head if he wore one. His selection was limited mainly to winter caps, but he did have a baseball cap with a small rainbow logo he'd picked up in Boys' Town at the last Pridefest, so he pulled it out of the closet as he was leaving the apartment. It wasn't until he casually slipped it on that he was reminded just how sore that part of his head still was to the touch.

He quickly took the hat off and went to the bathroom to check to see if any of the stitches might have been pulled out. Reassured that they hadn't, he very carefully put the hat back on and left the apartment.

He was standing in front of the main entrance when the SUV pulled up the ramp, made a U-turn in front of the garage entrance and stopped in front of him. Twelve-year-old Brad Jr. — BJ — hopped out of the front passenger's side and got in the back, pausing only long enough to say "Hi, Uncle Elliott." Since it was one of those no-elaborate-response-expected type of greetings, Elliott gave none, other than a short "Hi, Beej" — his nickname for his nephew — as he climbed into the front seat.

"You doin' okay?" Brad asked as Elliott fumbled on his seatbelt one-handed.

"Yeah, I'm fine."

"Sorry I didn't get by the hospital more often while you were there," Brad said, driving down the ramp and stopping at the street to wait for a break in traffic.

"No problem. I wasn't in much of a visitor mode for most of it, anyway."

He really liked his brother-in-law; they'd gotten along well since the first time they'd met. Brad wasn't much of a talker, and BJ pretty much took after his dad in everything — interests, build, skin coloring, hair. Only his facial features more closely resembled Cessy, including the Smith blue eyes.

Jenny, BJ's eight-year-old sister, was a carbon copy of Cessy at the same age. Jenny's principal joy seemed to derive from bedeviling her brother, who took it with far more patience and maturity than Elliott remembered he had exhibited

9

with Cessy.

The baby, Sandy, was too young at eight months for Elliott to be able to tell who she would more resemble as she got older.

The family lived in a typical well-kept single family home in Rogers Park, complete with a small front porch with a carved-wood sign saying "The Priebes" beside the door. The minute he walked in, he was greeted by Bozo, the family's golden retriever, and Jenny, who ran to him, wrapping her arms around his waist in a big hug.

"Uncle Elliott! I've missed you! They wouldn't let me come see you in the hospital."

Returning her hug, conscious of his shoulder as he did so, he said, "I missed you, too, Ladybug." He used the nicknames only when directly addressing the children, never when referring to them with anyone else. It was something special just between him and them.

The removal of his hat prompted immediate and rapt attention from both Jenny and BJ, though BJ tried not to make his fascination obvious.

"Does it hurt?" Jenny asked.

"Only when I laugh," he replied, eliciting no response from the girl but getting a grin from her brother.

While Cessy fixed dinner and BJ and Jenny were in their rooms doing homework—Elliott was surprised that Jenny, only in third grade, had homework— he sat with Brad in the living room having a beer and watching the news.

As a homicide detective and career cop with the Chicago Police Department, Brad wasn't fazed by very much, and had accepted Elliott's being gay as a matter of course. While it wasn't a subject they talked much about, neither did Elliot feel he had to avoid it. His sexual orientation had always been a non-issue with Cessy, who, in typical sisterly fashion, was continually questioning him about his social life and encouraging him to find someone and settle down.

He was rather surprised to find himself asking, during a commercial break in the news, "Brad, can you do me a rather odd favor?"

Brad looked over at him. "What do you need?"

"The day I was taken to the hospital, they brought another guy into the ER at almost exactly the same time, a gunshot victim with no ID. He didn't make it, and I understand they just listed him as a John Doe."

He was rather puzzled, both as he asked the question and on reflection, that he had never sensed a reaction from John when Norm had mentioned the John Doe. Perhaps the possibility that he might have been the other man in the ER just hadn't registered.

Brad tilted his head up once to acknowledge he understood the reference. "Yeah, Ken and I got that one, as a matter of fact. I wasn't aware you were in the ER at the same time. We weren't called in until a later, and I didn't find out you were in the same hospital until after. Anyway, what about him?"

"Have you identified him yet?"

Brad took a sip of his beer. "I'm afraid not."

"Do you know exactly what happened to him?"

"Other than that he was shot six times? Only that a nine-one-one call came in reporting gunshots in an alley between Surf and Diversey, just a couple blocks from St. Joe's. Responding officers found the guy on his back beside a Dumpster, barely alive. They called for an ambulance, but they didn't think he'd even make it to the hospital. He did, but only just."

"Do you think it was a robbery?"

"Possible, but I doubt it. Robbers don't usually bother taking stuff they don't want. This guy was left with nothing—they even tore the labels off his shirt and pants and took his shoes. That's pretty extreme. It was obvious they didn't want to leave anything at all that might help identify him. That all adds up to a premeditated hit."

"How come there was only one nine-one-one call, do you suppose? There are apartments all around there."

"There was a small fire about that same time on Pine Grove. The sound of the firetrucks may have covered the noise. It doesn't take long to pull off six shots."

"Christ!" Elliott said. "The poor guy. So, you think it was gang-related? Or Mob? Or a drug deal gone bad?"

Brad shook his head. "No way to know for sure. The guy was clean, not a trace of drugs of any kind. Given his age, the fact that he was a white male, and the area where he was killed, gang activity isn't likely. This guy was shot six times, and none of them to the head. We're willing to bet it was a hit, though pros don't usually waste bullets—one shot to the back of the head would be more their style. But we're checking into every possible angle."

"So, could you tell anything at all about him?"

Brad finished his beer and set the empty bottle on the floor beside his chair.

"Mid-to-late thirties, five-eleven, hundred-seventy-five pounds, brown hair, brown eyes. The only thing we're pretty sure of is that he wasn't from around here, since no one's reported him missing. That, of course, makes identifying a body even tougher."

"Do you get a lot of John Does?

"Quite a few—this is a big city." Brad said. "But there are more Janes than Johns. Most are identified within a week through missing persons reports, dental records, scars, birthmarks, tattoos, fingerprints or DNA, but since a lot of the Jane Does are prostitutes and a lot of the John Does are drifters, it isn't easy.

"Nobody's reported this guy missing. He had perfect teeth—not so much as one cavity—no tattoos, no scars, not a blemish on his body other than the bullet holes and some facial bruising. We figure he hit the ground face-first and then whoever shot him turned him over to clean out his pockets. There were no fingerprint or DNA matches. And the more time that passes, the less likely we are to be able to give the guy a name."

Elliott shook his head, feeling another odd wave of sadness. "So, where do

11

you go from here?"

"Follow up on any leads that might come along. We've already canvassed most of the residents of the buildings siding the alley and within sight of it, but nobody admits to having seen or heard anything other than the fire trucks. We took some postmortem photos, which is standard when the body is recognizable, and have shown them around the area, but again, nothing. Unless someone comes along looking for him, we're pretty much stymied at the moment. But it's an ongoing investigation, and we'll keep looking."

"Isn't there some sort of national clearing house for helping to identify unidentified bodies?" Elliott asked.

Brad shook his head. "There's the FBI's National Crime Information Center, but that has a list of more than fifty-two hundred people who've never been identified—that's one hell of a lot of dead bodies to sort through when you're looking for one specific person. And it's been estimated that number is only about fifteen percent of the actual total, largely because there aren't any laws requiring police to enter the information. We put your John Doe in, of course. Nothing's come up, but at least he's there.

"Some local agencies and jurisdictions have their own limited databases, but most agencies shy away from posting photos on the internet because there are too many pervs out there who would be swarming over the site just for kicks. And those jurisdictions that do post photos usually go to the trouble of opening the bodies' eyes or touching them or the photos up in some way to make it look like they're alive."

"Now, that's downright gross!" Elliott said.

Brad shrugged. "Maybe so, but that's the way it is. And then there's The Doe Network, which isn't affiliated with any governmental agency, but they don't post photographs, just sketches. They're on the internet, and it's their policy not to display postmortem photos publicly out of respect for the victims and their families. I personally don't believe any sketch is as accurate as a photo, but it's their call, and we're stuck with it."

Elliott shook his head in disbelief. "Incredible."

Brad repeated his shrug.

Cessy interrupted the conversation with a "Dinner's ready" call from the kitchen. Reluctantly, Elliott got up, quickly stepping out of the way of the kids, who came pounding down the stairs and through the living room. He followed Brad into the kitchen.

"Can we talk about this a little more sometime?" he asked.

"Sure," Brad agreed.

❧

Dinner with the Priebes, as Elliott called his frequent visits, went well, as always; and it was a comfortable evening despite the subject matter of his interrupted conversation with Brad. As always, Jenny insisted that he sit beside her. Unlike her brother, who seldom volunteered any information on anything, she provided a running commentary on everything going on in her life.

"I have a new teacher," she announced.

"Oh?" he said. "Is she nice?"

"Very nice. I really like her. Her name is Sister Marie. Mommy used to know her."

He looked questioningly at Cessy, who nodded, waiting until she had swallowed a forkful of salad before saying, "You know her, too, Elliott. She used to be Marie Collina. I haven't seen her since we were kids, but I recognized her immediately from that wine-stain birthmark on her forehead."

The Collinas again! Marie Collina was Al Collina's adopted sister. He hoped for Jenny's sake she had turned out nothing at all like her brother. He remembered Marie as being very self-conscious about her birthmark, and almost painfully shy.

Much of the rest of dinner was spent discussing the family's plans for their upcoming and long-anticipated Florida vacation, and Elliott volunteered to come by every day while they were gone to look after Bozo, though it would require two trips a day to feed him and let him into the fenced-in backyard in the morning, and bring him in at night.

At around nine-thirty, Cessy, despite his protests that he could easily call a cab, drove him home. He watched a little TV then, exhausted, went to bed.

He dreamt, not in visual images but in emotions, the primary one being confusion. Did he have a sister? Did he have any family at all? Did anyone love him? The next morning he realized with a mixture of fascination and mild horror that the dreams had not been his.

13

CHAPTER 2

O ver the next several days, Elliott spoke with Cessy but heard nothing from Brad. There had been no repeat of the strange dreams, though he knew John had not gone away. Every night, at some point, he was subtly aware of John's presence. Even when he could not clearly sense him, he felt that John had only withdrawn momentarily to sort things out and to come to terms with his situation, and that he would be back.

Elliott concentrated on his recovery, and was relieved at his next doctor's appointment to be told he could stop wearing the sling if he promised to be careful of his shoulder. As if he had to be reminded—any sudden movement did that for him quite effectively.

The doctor specifically advised him against doing any physical labor, but he spent a large amount of time checking with his crew on the progress of his nearly completed current project. The question of his next project was resolved subsequent to a phone call from Jim Brewster, a guy with whom he'd had a casual but very pleasant relationship several years before. Jim worked for Central Property Management & Realty, one of the oldest and most respected Realtors in the city. Elliott had bought a building or two from them in the past, which was how he'd met Jim. They hadn't been in touch in quite a while.

"Jim! It's good to hear from you. What's up?"

"That's what I'd like to talk to you about," Jim said, a little cryptically. "Could you meet me for a drink after work? Gentry on State, maybe?"

"Sure." Elliott had not really been out much since the hospital, and not at all to a bar. "What time?"

"Five-fifteen, five-thirty be okay?"

"Great! I'll see you there." They exchanged goodbyes and hung up, leaving Elliott mildly curious about the reason for the call.

❊

His hair was starting to grow back in the shaved area. He'd thought about having his entire head shaved to match but decided against it. The scar and the whole side of his head were still sensitive to the touch, and he didn't want a

14

barber, however careful, to go running around them with a pair of clippers. So, when the time came to leave to meet Jim, he put his baseball cap back on.

Jim was already there when he arrived. Elliott extended his hand as Jim got up, to forestall the possibility of a hug, which Jim began to give him anyway until he noticed Elliott wince. He backed off quickly, a look of mild surprise on his face.

"Something wrong with your shoulder?" he asked as they sat down.

As he waited for his drink, Elliott quickly sketched the details of the accident, neglecting, of course, to mention John; and he again wondered whether John's name really was John. If unidentified bodies were referred to as Heathcliff instead of John Doe, he'd have had a better idea.

"I'm really sorry," Jim said, sounding as though he meant it. "I'd have come to visit you if I'd known. You doing okay now?"

Elliott grinned. "I'm fine, and I appreciate your concern. I'll be good as new in no time."

His drink arrived, and he slipped a bill across the bar to the bartender, who took it with a nod. Elliott waved him off as he started to return with the change.

"So, what," he asked, turning his full attention to Jim, "has been going on with you?"

"Well, I'm leaving Central, for one thing."

Registering his surprise, Elliott said, "How come? It seems like you've been with them forever. What happened?"

Jim took a long drink then fished out an ice cube, which he crunched loudly and swallowed before answering. "My boss is selling the company. I hear they'll be cutting the staff in half."

"That's too bad, but you shouldn't have to worry too much. I'd think the new owners would want to keep the most qualified employees, and you're one of the best."

"Thanks, but I don't think I'd want to work for them. You know Evermore, I assume?"

Elliott winced mentally. Evermore again!

"Evermore's buying you out? No wonder you're leaving. I just lost a property to them."

"And do you know the guy who owns it?"

"Al Collina. Yes, I've known him since I was a kid. His family lived right next door to my folks."

"Evermore used to be a class outfit until Collina took over and started gobbling up properties all over town, especially in the older, close-in areas."

"Yeah," Elliott agreed. "He's apparently out to make himself Chicago's condo king. So, when's this all going to happen?"

Jim signaled the bartender for another drink. "I'm not sure, but the boss has called a staff meeting for Monday morning. The only way I know about what's going on is that I've got a friend at Evermore—Grant Tully. You know him?"

"The name sounds familiar," Elliott said, searching his mind for any specifics

15

as to who Grant Tully might be and failing.

"Grant called me last night to give me a heads-up. He could get himself fired if anybody knew he told me. I started looking for a new job today."

"Well, I'm really sorry to hear that, Jim," Elliott said. "But you shouldn't have any trouble with that, and I'm pretty sure you've been stuffing your commissions under the mattress for years. You'll be okay."

Jim grinned. "Yeah, I suppose. But change is always a little hard." He reached into his wallet for a bill and slid it across the bar to the bartender before continuing. "My employment woes aren't the main reason I called, though. I've got a tip for you that you might want to follow up on."

"Ah?"

"I don't know if you're in the market for another building right now, but I know how you like the older ones with character. We've been managing a twelve-unit on Sheffield for some time now. The owner lives there, but after his wife died, he didn't want the hassle of managing it himself. The minute I saw it, I thought of you. It's been in the owner's family since it was built in the mid-twenties, but he's getting older and his kids want him to move to Florida—you know the story. It's been one of those 'I want to sell/I don't want to sell' deals.

"Anyway, he's finally decided to sell, and I've got an appointment with him tomorrow morning to list it. I know it would be perfect for you. As I said, it's twelve units, a nice courtyard, kind of rundown at the moment, but it has a lot of potential and a lot of history, from what I understand. I was going to call you about it anyway."

"Fantastic!" Elliott said. "There are several buildings on Sheffield I've had my eye on over the years. What's the address, if you can tell me?"

"I can do better than that," Jim said. "Did you bring your car?"

Elliott shook his head and indicated his left shoulder. "I'm trying to avoid driving for another couple of days."

"Well," Jim said, "my aunt's having me over for my monthly 'you need a good meal' dinner tonight, and she lives relatively close to you, so if you'd like, I can give you a lift home and we can drive by the place so you can have a quick look at it."

"That'd be great!" Elliott said.

"I know damned well Evermore is buying us out mainly to get our listings," Jim continued. "They want our name and our reputation, and they'll run both right into the ground. Because we specialize in older buildings, they think that buying us out will let them con the owners into selling to Evermore. I think one of the things that finally convinced this particular owner to list with us was that somebody from Evermore actually approached him about selling. He turned them down because he knows they only buy to tear down.

"And now I'm sort of between a rock and a hard place. He doesn't know about Evermore buying us out, and ethically, I can't tell him. But I'd feel rotten if he lists with us, and Evermore takes over before it's sold. Evermore's bound to find a way to get it, and I'd hate to see that happen. I just thought it would be nice if I could yank something out from under them before I go."

"A truly noble thought," Elliott replied. "They just outbid me on a building on Devon, so I'm definitely in the market for another one. I really appreciate your thinking of me."

Jim took another sip of his drink and said, "The minute I get the owner's signature on the listing papers, I'll tell him I know of someone who might be interested and try to set up an appointment to have you go through the place as soon as possible. Maybe tomorrow, even?"

"That'll be fine. I can't guarantee it'll be what I'm looking for, of course..."

Jim gave a quick nod. "Understood," he said. "But I really do think this place would be perfect for you. If you agree, it's a win-win situation for all of us."

"I could use a win," Elliott said. "Give me a call as soon as you can. I'll stick around the apartment until I hear from you."

Jim glanced at his watch and emptied what little was left of his drink in one gulp. "Damn! Look at the time. Are you about ready to go?"

Elliott drained his glass and got up. "Yep."

❋

The building was on Sheffield a few blocks south of Fullerton, and Elliott recognized it immediately. He'd actually had it on his "keep-an-eye-on" list for some time, and had on more than one occasion toyed with the idea of trying to find out who owned it and if they would be willing to sell.

"Serendipity lives," he remarked to Jim as they stopped momentarily in front of the building to give him a better look.

He didn't ask the listing price; he was already pushing his luck by having Jim tip him off on its availability. He had a general idea of what other properties in the area were going for and figured that, unless the seller's demands were too far off base, he could handle it. He also had faith in Jim's skills in guiding the seller to a realistic asking price, and in his own at making the best possible deal.

As he looked across the courtyard to the building's entrance, he suddenly felt an odd tingle—a flush of anticipation and excitement not unlike he felt cruising someone across a crowded bar. He often got a feeling of anticipation when he first saw a prospective new property, but this was different, more intense. He credited it to a certain perverse pleasure in knowing that if Al Collina were aware of what was going on he would be mightily pissed. It might be only one building, but from what he knew of how Evermore was being run, and what he could remember of Al from his childhood, he had no doubt the man would take Elliott's depriving Evermore of it personally.

For the rest of the ride to his condo, he managed to juggle a casual conversation with Jim with resurfacing memories of Al Collina and the Collina family. Despite living next door to one another, the Smiths and Collinas had had little contact. Vittorio Collina, the family patriarch, was rockbound first-generation Sicilian, having come from Sicily to Chicago as a teenager. It was rumored he had been high up in Capone's bootlegging operations, though he

17

had never been convicted of a felony. He married relatively late in life and it lasted only three years before his wife, Al's mother, died. Al was two, and Vittorio was already nearly sixty. His second marriage, contracted less than a year later, produced another son, Johnny. They subsequently adopted the daughter of one of Vitto Collina's closest associates after the man and his wife both died in an automobile accident.

Whereas many first-generation immigrants were eager for their children to assimilate, Vittorio gave his two sons old-country names—Alfonso and Giovanni—and insisted they be called exactly that in his presence. But Giovanni was always Johnny to Elliott.

They were twelve years old when they met; and though the Collina children attended strict Catholic schools, he and Johnny managed to become fast friends. Al was four years older than Johnny, and Elliott's limited memories of him were distinctly unpleasant.

At sixteen, Al was already a hypocrite and a bully, making life miserable for his younger brother and sister, raising general hell when his parents weren't looking and instantly becoming the perfect, pious son when they were. He was a tyrant and a liar, and tormented both Johnny and Marie endlessly. He was, in fact, exactly like his father and, not surprisingly, was Vittorio's favorite child.

Elliott found it interesting that Marie Collina had become a nun. He remembered Al teasing her mercilessly about her birthmark, and he never let her forget she was adopted.

Elliott had had almost no contact with their father, but remembered him as a dark, brooding old man with an always-furrowed brow and a look of constant suspicion. He'd seen a photo of Vittorio as a teenager, and was struck by how much Johnny had looked like him. Johnny's mother Sophia was much younger than her husband, and his exact opposite in looks and personality. Elliott had liked her.

It was with Johnny he had first discovered sex. Once having discovered it, the two boys spent every possible moment practicing it, coming perilously close to being caught on several occasions. Their testosterone fest continued until they were sixteen and the Collinas moved to an estate on Lake Geneva, just over the border in Wisconsin. They exchanged a few letters at first, and then gradually lost track of one another.

Elliott still had a framed photo of himself with Johnny when they were about fourteen. The last he had heard, Johnny, always a free spirit, had quit college to join the Peace Corps. Vitto Collina, he remembered having heard, had died three or four years later in a fall down the stairs at the family home.

All this was just bits and pieces of information Elliott had filed in his mental trivia drawer under "Collina." A succession of other partners had taken Johnny's place in Elliott's expanding world, and had Al Collina not re-entered the picture with his purchase of Evermore Properties, the whole family would have just faded to those bits of trivia.

He now vaguely recalled that, only a couple of days before his accident, he had read of the death of Sophia Collina. She had become well known for her various philanthropies, and her death made all the local papers. And while these reminders of the Collinas made Elliott curious as to what had become of Johnny, he had no desire to approach Al to find out.

Having been lost in his thoughts, Elliott was almost surprised when Jim drove up the ramp to his building. Jim dropped him off at the front entrance, saying again that he would call, as soon as he had officially obtained the listing, and set up an appointment for Elliott to see the property.

He had a quick dinner then used the den phone to dial Brad's number. BJ answered with a teenager's bored "Hello?"

"Hi, Beej. Your dad home?"

"Yeah, just a sec...*Dad!*"

Elliott winced at the volume of the shout.

"It's Uncle Elliott."

A moment of silence was followed by "Hi, Elliott. What do you need?"

Obviously, Brad knew him better than Elliott gave him credit for.

"Do you have a minute to talk before dinner?"

"Sure."

"I've been thinking about this John Doe thing. I'm curious as to what happened to his body? What's the process? Where does he eventually wind up?"

"Unclaimed bodies from the City of Chicago are held at the morgue, and if they're still unclaimed or unidentified, they're then sent to Woodlawn Gardens in Woodlawn for cremation. We keep whatever information we have on the body on file, just in case, but..."

"So, he ends up in a Potter's Field," Elliott said, instantly depressed.

"I'm afraid so," Brad replied.

Elliott's mind automatically opened his trivia file, where the origin of the term *potters field* was neatly stashed away from the time he'd had to look it up for a college term paper on WWI. It was from the Bible—Matthew 27:7—and referred to the priests using the thirty pieces of silver returned by a repentant Judas "to buy the potters field as a burial place for foreigners." It was not called *potters field* because a potter owned it, but because the land was worthless for growing crops and used only by potters to dig clay. He'd found the thought depressing when he first learned it, and he still did.

"And there's been no new information on this particular one, I assume," he said, bringing himself back to the moment.

"Unfortunately not."

"What a hell of a way for anyone to end up."

"I agree."

"I don't know why I've gotten so hooked on this thing," Elliott confessed, "but it's almost like I feel some sort of connection to the guy. He died right next to me, and I just hate the idea of nobody knowing who he was."

"I understand," Brad said. "But we've done everything we could. The positive side, if there is one, is that there's no statute of limitations on murder, and your guy is listed several places. There's always a chance he'll be identified, and his killer or killers found."

"But not much."

Brad sighed. "Not much," he admitted.

They chatted for a few more minutes until Cessy asked to talk to him, to update him on the latest status of their vacation plans. Then she insisted on a full report on his current condition, whether he was sleeping well, eating properly, etc. He assured her everything was fine, and at last she excused herself to go put dinner on the table.

As he took frozen lasagna out of the freezer, put it in the oven and went into the den to watch television, he felt depressed reflecting on John's fate. For anyone to end up in a potters field, regardless of what it was called, was sad beyond words. Maybe he could pay to have the body buried in a regular cemetery—he could afford it. But there still would be no information to put on a tombstone, and then what happened if John were later identified and his family wanted his remains?

No, he realized, it was a noble thought, but not a very practical one. Maybe, if no one had come along after a year or so, he could reconsider it.

He sat in front of the TV, his eyes and ears functioning but his mind disengaged. He felt himself nodding...

— *My name is John.*

— *Oh, God, I know. Why don't you just go toward the light, or whatever it is you're supposed to do?*

— *I don't know what I'm supposed to do. There is no light.*

— *What do you expect me to do about it?*

— *I don't know.*

— *What do you know?*

— *Nothing.*

And again, the sadness.

The soft ding of the oven announcing the lasagna was ready woke Elliott with a start, feeling overwhelmed by confusion and frustration that were further compounded by his uncertainty as to whether the feelings were his or John's—or if there was a John at all.

He got up from his chair and went into the kitchen, contemplating seeking professional help. He made a small salad, returned to the den to set up a TV tray, went back to the kitchen for the lasagna and a glass of milk, all accomplished with a minimum of conscious thought. His mind was on John, and on himself. If there was a John, and if all this wasn't just some sort of game his mind was playing with him, how could John not know anything at all about himself? Again, Elliott thought of a stroke victim, wanting to speak but unable to make speech and mind connect.

From their exchange during his nap, it seemed John was finding his voice, if not his memory. Why had John chosen him for help? Well, that link was obvious if John were, indeed, the guy from the ER and not just some mental aberration.

20

But if that were true, logic would further dictate that Elliott should have sensed some reaction to or verification of the few details Brad had been able to provide regarding the body and its disposition. Yet, there had been nothing.

Of course, the bottom line of logic would be that there are no such things as spirits and ghosts.

Elliott was not a psychic, or a medium. He'd never had his palm read or been to a seance, or even seen a real deck of tarot cards. He'd never tried to foresee the future by staring into tea leaves at the bottom of a cup or examining the entrails of an owl, nor had he ever understood why anyone would want to do so. He'd never, in short, been very big on the paranormal, and had never given much thought to the subject of ghosts or spirits one way or the other.

Though not given to long periods of introspection, he recognized that John's unsought intrusion into his life was leading him down paths within himself he'd never previously taken. As he sat eating dinner, staring at but not really paying any concerted attention to the TV, he decided against seeking professional help for the moment. He'd always been able to work through his own problems, and couldn't see any particular reason why he couldn't handle this one, as well. If John were a side effect of the accident, chances were good that he would simply go away eventually. In the meantime, Elliott would just deal with him.

He did find it interesting, and not a little disturbing, that John was now conveying thoughts other than "My name is John." On the other hand, as long as John was not warning him that people were out to get him or encouraging any type of bizarre behavior, he could afford to give it all a bit more time to see what might develop. And in truth, as frustrating as he found the entire John situation to be, it was also oddly fascinating.

Nevertheless, he was rather relieved, on waking the next morning, to be unaware of having had any dreams involving John. The only one he could even vaguely recall had something to do with mountains.

❧

Jim had said his appointment to list the Sheffield property was at ten-thirty; so around half-past eight, Elliott took a walk up to the little diner tucked under the Thorndale el stop where he went two or three times a week, more from the power of habit than anything else. The food was adequate and abundant, but he doubted anyone had ever used the words *ambience* or *cuisine* in reference to the place.

He was back home by nine-forty-five and, disinclined by his still-sensitive shoulder to attempt to do anything around the apartment that might involve a lot of motion, opened the living room balcony doors wide and settled into his favorite chair with a book he'd started some time before his accident.

Jim called at eleven-fifteen to see if Elliott could meet him at the Sheffield building at two, and he readily agreed. Jim offered to come pick him up, but Elliott said he could just as easily take the el to Fullerton and walk from there. They agreed to meet in front of the building.

"Normally," Jim explained, "I prefer to show a property when the owner isn't around, but given the time element and the circumstances, I think having you talk directly to the guy might help. Do you mind?"

"Fine with me," Elliott said.

The prospect of a new project always excited him: going through a building, imagining it as it had looked when it was new and envisioning what it would look like when he'd finished; figuring out the proper balance between modernizing and retaining as much of the original character as possible—and finding ways to achieve the maximum effect with the minimum expenditure. For some reason, his attraction to this building was particularly strong.

He knew the thousands of convoluted details involved in such transactions could drive most people to distraction, but he handled them with aplomb. The questions of leases and relocations and what to do when and in what order he always dealt with methodically and, overall, with a minimum of difficulty.

Jim was waiting for him in front of the building as promised. He'd deliberately approached from the opposite side of the street so he could maximize his impressions of the building as it fit in with its surroundings. He was again favorably impressed.

As they crossed the U-shaped courtyard toward the entrance, Elliott instinctively noted areas that needed tuck-pointing, windows and frames that should be replaced, a few minor cracks in the foundation, a broken rain gutter. But all in all, he decided, the building—from the outside at least—appeared solid and in good shape for its age.

The small foyer was neat and clean, and he was pleasantly surprised by the quality of the materials that had been used during construction—they were actually a upscale for the area. He could tell that, beneath the several layers of paint on the paneled walls, the original hardwood waited for restoration. The mailbox doors appeared to be real bronze, and the door buzzer buttons were, he was pretty sure, ivory.

These were the kind of details he always looked for in a prospective building, and he thought of them as "gingerbread"—details either already present or that could be easily added to appeal to a prospective buyer when it was time for resale. Beamed ceilings, hardwood floors, big rooms, wood paneling—even arched doorways—were a definite plus, he'd found. In buildings with courtyards, landscaping of even a very small space could add to the building's overall appeal to both buyer and prospective new tenants.

Jim pressed one of the ivory door buzzers, which was followed by the click of the door lock being released, and they entered the first-floor hall. A stairway immediately to the right of the entrance led, Elliott assumed, to the top two floors. As he followed Jim to the first door on the left, he observed that, while everything was showing its age, the building had obviously been well cared-for. The carpets were worn but clean, the paint slightly mottled with age but not flaking or chipped.

Jim's knock was quickly answered by a pear-shaped man who looked to be in his late seventies, the stub of an unlit cigar clenched at the corner of his mouth. He quickly removed the cigar and stepped aside, opening the door wide.

"Come in, come in," he said, pleasantly enough, but without smiling.

When they'd entered the large, comfortable living room and closed the door behind them, Jim did brief introductions.

"Mr. Capetti, this is Elliott Smith."

The two men shook hands, exchanged the usual first-meeting formalities, and Capetti gestured them to a seat. Elliott took in as much of the room as possible without being obvious. Crown moldings. A real fireplace with fake logs—gas, he surmised. No obvious cracks in the walls or ceiling.

Gradually, and rather disconcertingly, he became aware someone else was in the room, and he had no doubt as to who it was. He didn't want to even begin to speculate what John was doing there, or why, and forced his mind and eyes to focus on Capetti, who had taken a seat on the large sofa across from him, leaning forward to drop the cigar stub into an otherwise clean ashtray.

"My wife made me promise to give them up before she died," he said, indicating the ashtray. "But every now and again..." He looked from Jim to Elliott and shook his head. "This is all going a little faster than I expected it to. I haven't quite adjusted to the fact that I'm actually selling."

Jim turned to Elliott. "The building has been in Mr. Capetti's family since it was built," he explained, though he had already mentioned it when he first talked to Elliott about the building.

Capetti nodded. "My father bought it in nineteen-twenty-six," he said. "I lived here since I was born, except for a couple of years in the army and when I first got married. My kids were raised here." He sighed. "It's hard letting go of the past."

"I can appreciate that," Elliott said, and he could.

"The most important thing to me is that I don't want to see the place torn down. I been approached a couple of times by people who made me a good offer, but who only want it for the land. I happen to know the same people have made offers on the buildings on either side of me. Well, I won't be part of it. Jim tells me you're a preservationist. That's what this town needs more of these days. Problem is, nobody gives a damn anymore. They changed the name on Marshall Field's, fer God's sake! A hundred and fifty years of history just wiped away like it was a runny nose! Macy's! Macy's is New York; Marshall Field's is Chicago!"

Realizing his passions were getting the better of him, Capetti stopped abruptly and got up from the sofa.

"Well," he said, "I expect you'd like to see the rest of the place."

Elliott and Jim followed him as he began the tour, starting with his own apartment.

"All twelve units are basically the same," he said. "Two bedroom, one bath. All the units on this side had working fireplaces, but they were closed off years ago or converted to gas, like this one. They could be reopened if anyone wanted to. Eleven of the units are occupied; the people in three-D moved out last week, and I didn't want to try to rent it out again until I knew whether I was going to sell or not. So, I can show you that one, if you'd like. It's a rear unit."

Elliott took mental notes throughout the tour, but what he saw pleased him. Hardwood floors throughout, lots of gingerbread already in place or that could be readily added. There were a lot of things that needed doing, of course. The kitchens and bathrooms would have to be modernized, the floors redone along with the wooden back porches, the single four-car garage torn down to allow room for uncovered but private parking spaces.

Distracted by his concentration on the building, he completely forgot about John's presence...until Capetti led them to the basement to show the laundry, utility and storage areas, which were divided by a center wall running the length of the building. The minute they entered the basement, John's presence began to fill him like water filling an empty glass. He tried to ignore it, concentrating on looking for signs of moisture, mold or other evidence of structural damage or weakness; but by the time they entered the laundry/utility half of the basement the feeling they were not alone was overpowering.

The front section of the space housed the furnace, boilers and electrical circuitry. He was pleased to note circuit breakers rather than fuse boxes. It was in the rear section, the laundry area, that he felt the weight of John's presence and, like dye slowly poured into a full glass of water, as the sense of that presence was gradually infused with confusion. It was only with great effort he was able to concentrate on the tour. Luckily, neither Jim nor Capetti noticed his distraction.

From what he'd seen, the building appeared to be exactly what he was looking for, and he considered the asking price reasonable. He'd have to arrange for his subcontractor crew to go through the place to verify his impressions of the building's structural integrity, but...

Leaving the building, he accepted Jim's offer of a ride home, which would give them time to discuss his impressions of the place and for him to look over a packet of fact sheets Jim had prepared for him on the property, taxes, insurance, utilities, a projected city sidewalk assessment and other financial information, plus a list of other recently sold comparable buildings in the area, with their asking and selling prices. Jim had obviously done his homework.

While he did his best to stay focused, Elliott had been disturbed on several levels by John's presence. What was he doing there? It *was* John—there wasn't a question about that. He didn't know how he knew, but he knew. That John seemed to be following him at will—John's will, certainly not his—was disconcerting. It reinforced his sense that the passage of time was not lessening his connection with John but increasing it.

While ostensibly looking over the pages of information, he searched for some indication John was in the car. There was nothing..

"Please understand, I'm not trying to pressure you," Jim was saying, "but if you are interested in the place, we really should act as quickly as possible. I don't want Evermore to get a whiff of this, and at this juncture, I have no idea what's going on at work, and how much Evermore already knows about our listings."

Elliott lifted his right buttock slightly to put the papers partly under him.

"I understand," he said, "and I'll go over all this information again carefully tonight. Right now, I'm strongly leaning toward taking it, but I can't make a snap decision. I'll give you a call in the morning. And if I decide to go with it, we'll have to set it up for my guys to go over the place carefully before I make an offer."

"That'll be fine," Jim said.

He spent the remainder of the afternoon reviewing the information Jim had given him, jotting down notes on things he'd thought of while going through the building, making lists of what definitely required work—cosmetic touches that would enhance the building's appeal to a future buyer—and making rough estimates of the projected costs of each based on his past experience. As he worked, he gradually became aware that John was unobtrusively present, as if observing him. But he also detected...What? An interest? An interest in what? What he was doing? That was a first, as was the very concept of John's being aware of anything other than his name and his understandable concern over his loss of identity.

Elliott was still ambivalent about whether or not he might be unconsciously creating this entire John scenario by projecting his own thoughts and feelings and crediting them as originating from John. However, that overwhelming sense of John's presence and...confusion...in the basement of Capetti's building? He knew he hadn't been projecting anything there. And he still had no idea of what it was all about.

He dreamt that night of the building, and of the basement, and of mountains; and the latter dream was filled with a longing he was well aware was not his.

✻

He awoke in the morning determined to make an offer on Capetti's building, contingent on the outcome of his crew's inspection. To act in such haste was very unlike him, and that troubled him. He once again reflected on whether the changes in his life since his accident were the result of John having an actual existence, or if it might be indicative of some sort of undiagnosed brain injury resulting from the accident that was also influencing other areas of his life, such as his judgment.

He was increasingly convinced that John was real, which he knew in and of itself might be evidence of mental malfunctioning. He also knew that people with serious mental problems almost never thought they had any.

He fought a rising tide of frustration and forced himself back to what he still felt confident was reality. As far as his judgment was concerned, he was looking for another property. The Capetti building was exactly what he'd been looking for, verified by his having had an interest in it long before the accident. The price was reasonable, and he was going to hedge his bets by making his offer contingent on an inspection by qualified people on whose opinion he could depend. So, it wasn't as though he were just suddenly taking wild risks.

John's intrusion into his life, he reassured himself, was still largely peripheral, and as long as it remained that way, he could handle it.

He looked up Jim's cell phone number and called.

✤

The offer was made and, as part of the eternal pas de deux of real estate sales, countered, responded to and accepted with, for a change, a minimal amount of hassle. The inspections went off without a hitch and revealed no unanticipated problems. Even Elliott was impressed by the uncharacteristic smoothness of the process.

Capetti had requested a sixty-day escrow to give him time to prepare for his move to Florida, but Elliott, through Jim, had convinced him to accept a thirty-day escrow with an up-to-thirty-day extension of Capetti's occupancy at no charge.

Elliott was, therefore, more than a little surprised when, shortly after escrow closed, he received a totally unexpected call at home.

"Elliott Smith?" the very male caller asked. He did not recognize the voice.

"Yes?"

The voice had no warmth, no particular expression. "This is Al Collina. We were neighbors in Lake Forest when we were kids."

Elliott tried not to let his surprise show in his tone. "Yes," he said, "I remember. What can I do for you?"

"I understand you just bought a property on Sheffield." Collina didn't wait for a reply. "I'd like to take it off your hands before you start renovations. I'll make it well worth your while."

Capetti had mentioned that the buildings on either side of his had been the subject of inquiries recently but hadn't known if they'd been sold. Obviously, they had; and it was, as Elliott had suspected, Evermore that had bought them. He also suspected Collina had known Central Management was handling the property even before he bought them out. He must, Elliott reasoned, have been one very unhappy real estate developer when he found it had been snatched out from under his nose.

"I don't want to see it knocked down for another concrete-slab high-rise," he said.

"Who said that's what I was going to do?" Collina protested. "It just so happens that building has sentimental value. My old man and Gus Capetti came over from the old country together. My dad loaned him the money to buy the place."

Sentimental value? To Al Collina? Elliott didn't buy it.

"That was very generous of him," he said. "But Mr. Capetti never mentioned your father. And I'm curious why you hadn't approached him before he put it up for sale."

"I didn't find out about it until just recently," Collina lied. "I just came across some of my old man's papers, and they mentioned it."

26

Elliott got the impression Collina was struggling to be civil, but wasn't fooled.

"How's Johnny, by the way?" he asked.

"He's dead. I thought you knew."

Despite the number of years since Elliott last set eyes on Johnny Collina, he felt a strong pang of sorrow.

"No," he said, "I didn't. How did it happen? When?"

"He joined the Peace Corps in one of those godforsaken African stinkholes," Collina said almost casually. "It must have been eight years or so ago now. He was crossing some lake on a ferry when a storm came up and capsized it. Only a couple people survived. Johnny wasn't one of 'em. They never found his body— they figure the crocs got it."

"God! I'm really sorry!" Elliott said, truly shocked. "I can't believe it!"

"Yeah, well, shit happens. Him and me never were very close anyway. My old man disowned him a long time before that. But then, you knew Johnny was a fag."

He could hardly believe his ears. Johnny was Al's brother! He wanted to know more, but felt his anger building and didn't want to let it show. And why had Collina felt it necessary to say that Johnny was "a fag?"

"So, about that building..." Al prompted after a pause.

"No, I'll keep it."

"Yeah, I figured you'd say that. But you think about it. You could make a damned good profit."

"Profit isn't everything."

He heard the sneer in Collina's voice. "You and Johnny always were two of a kind." His tone made it clear what he meant, and Elliott couldn't help but wonder if Al knew about his and Johnny's true relationship. It wasn't difficult to read between the lines to figure out why Vittorio had disowned Johnny. A fag in the family? In Vittorio Collina's family?

But he didn't want to pursue it, certainly not with Al. All he wanted to do at the moment was get off the phone.

"I'll call you if I change my mind," he said.

"Do that." Al hung up.

❀

As busy as he was with his new project, Elliott was seldom more than peripherally aware of John, except when he would awake in the morning with a dim recollection of recurring dreams of mountains. What they might mean, if anything, he had no idea.

His hair gradually grew back to the point it was hard for him to tell where the shaved area had been, and his scars were no longer sensitive to the touch. His shoulder gave him only occasional discomfort, mostly when he forgot that it had been injured and tried to perform some motion that quickly reminded him.

He had Dinner at the Priebes' twice, and Rick came by a couple times to spend the evening...and the night. Ever since they'd met several weeks before the accident, they'd hit it off both in bed and out.

The first time Rick stayed over following the accident, Elliott felt strangely self-conscious, keeping alert for any indication of John's presence. Being watched while having sex, even by a spirit, wasn't on his list of turn-ons. But John apparently believed in privacy, and Elliott was relieved.

He lay there for a while, listening to the subtle changes in Rick's breathing as he fell asleep and, shortly thereafter, followed him.

— *Do I have someone?*
— *I don't know.*
— *It would be nice to be missed.*
— *I'm sure you are.*
— *It would be nice.*

And then Elliott dreamed again of mountains.

CHAPTER 3

❧

By the time escrow had closed on the Sheffield property, Elliott had all his forces organized. The one thing he did not like about buying a building for renovation was the issue of what to do with the tenants.

Depending on the amount of work to be done, he was sometimes able to work around them. However, when that was not possible, as it wouldn't be this time, his other properties usually had sufficient vacancies for him to offer to relocate the tenants. He had even occasionally moved a tenant at his own expense, an act of generosity only someone in his financial position could afford.

But he didn't do what he did to make money, though he almost always did. It was the restoration of the property to its original glory that gave him a deep sense of satisfaction.

While his plumber, electrician and carpenter had been to the property several times, and Elliott had met with them either singly or jointly every couple of days, he had only made a few trips to the building to make some rough sketches of what he had in mind in the way of gingerbread. Their jobs were made relatively easier by the fact that all twelve units had basically identical layouts, so they were able to do all their measurements and estimates using the building's one vacant apartment as a model.

As always, after consulting with the appropriate contractor, Elliott chose the electrical fixtures, kitchen appliances, new toilets, sinks and tub/shower units for the bathrooms. The layout of the kitchens was to be changed slightly to allow for new cabinets and a dishwasher. Part of the wall separating the kitchen from the dining room would be removed to create a pass-through for a more open feeling. The hallways were to be repainted, recarpeted, and new lighting installed; the solid wood exit doors at the back end of the hallway would be replaced with full glass doors for better illumination and to reduce the claustrophobic nature of the space. The open wooden porches crossing the rear of the building were to be redone to give each rear unit a small private patio/balcony area flanking the center exit stairs. The kitchen window of each of the rear units was to be replaced by a doorway to the private balcony.

The basement, too, was to be redone, with the laundry room separated from the furnace and utilities area by a new wall. The storage area would remain largely unchanged, though with new paint, new tile and new doors for each of the twelve lockers.

The week of the escrow close, Elliott arranged for the required building permits then set up a Friday appointment to meet with his three contractors to finalize plans for the basement, which would be the first stage of the renovation while the final logistics of relocating tenants were worked out. He'd printed out rough sketches of his ideas and given copies to all three men for their input, arranging for his carpenter to make the final detailed to-scale drawings.

The minute he entered the building and moved toward the door to the basement, located under the back of the stairway to the second floor, he was aware of John's presence, but he was becoming used to it. He entered the laundry side of the basement to find the three contractors—Ted Swanson the plumber, Arnie Echter the electrician and Sam Bryte the carpenter—standing around a clothes-folding table in front of four washing machines on which was spread Sam's detailed drawing of the space. Elliott strongly sensed John was near the back wall.

After an exchange of greetings, he joined the men at the table. Ted and Arnie watched him closely as he studied Sam's drawing, doing their best to suppress grins. He looked from one to the other, puzzled.

"What?" he asked.

"Look closely," Arnie said, letting his grin break out.

He did. Arnie was right—something was wrong with the drawing.

"Sam's losing it," Ted said, poking Sam on the shoulder.

"Why aren't the two sides of the basement equal?" Elliott asked.

Sam sighed. "Because this side of the basement is three feet shorter than the other side," he said.

"See what I mean?" Ted hooted. "He's losin' it."

"I'm not losing it!" Sam protested. "I measured the damned thing three times. This side's three feet shorter than the other side. It's eighteen feet from the door to the back wall on the storage side, and fifteen feet from the door to the back wall on this side."

"How can that be?" Elliott asked. "I wonder if Mr. Capetti might have a copy of the original blueprints."

"He does," Sam said. "I asked him right after I took the measurements. He had 'em in a trunk in the storage area." He stepped over to reach behind the nearest washer, which had a faded handwritten "Out Of Order" sign duct-taped to it, and pulled out a rolled up sheath of obviously very old blueprints.

"Why the hell didn't you use these in the first place?" Arnie said.

"Because I didn't think I'd need 'em, and I wanted you assholes to have your fun before Elliott got here," Sam replied, untying the string that surrounded the roll.

He switched his drawing to one end of the table and spread the roll open, anchoring down the two sides with two one-gallon bottles of bleach. "They were in the trash," he explained about his paperweights. "I filled 'em with water."

"You're enjoying this, aren't you?" Ted asked.

Sam grinned at him. "Yep."

The basement blueprint was on top, and Elliott, reaching for Sam's drawings, saw that he was right. The laundry room half of the basement was now three feet shorter than on the original blueprints.

He glanced at the rear wall. Concrete block, just like the rest of the basement. Absolutely no discernable difference. A wall was a wall was a wall. The only thing different about this wall was it was three feet closer to the door than it was supposed to be—and it had John's intensely strong presence in front of it.

"I wonder what's behind it," Sam said.

Elliott, equally distracted by the puzzle of the three-foot discrepancy and John's unexplainable presence, shook his head.

"I haven't a clue." However, even as he spoke he sensed what he could only interpret as confusion mixed with distress emanating from the area immediately in front of the wall. The sense of confusion was familiar, similar to that he'd encountered his first time in the basement, but was now even stronger; the distress was a new and disturbing element.

He pulled himself back to the moment, sincerely hoping the other three men were not aware of his distraction. A glance at each of them showed they apparently were not.

"When was this place built, exactly?" Ted asked.

"Nineteen-twenty-six," Elliott replied.

"So, it was here during prohibition?"

"Yeah, so?"

"So, maybe they had a still in there or something," Arnie volunteered.

"In a three-foot space behind a solid wall?" Sam scoffed. "That doesn't make any sense at all."

"Well," Ted speculated, "a lot of gangsters lived in this area in those days."

"So, what could they put in a three-foot space behind a solid wall?" Sam asked.

Ted shrugged. "Who knows? Hide money, maybe? There might be a fortune back there."

"Uh-huh," Arnie said. "I always wall my money up and forget about it for eighty years."

Elliott said nothing, but the aura of John's confusion remained strong, and was blending with his own.

"Would an extra three feet of space make any difference to your plans?" he asked, trying to call the three men, and himself, back to reality.

Sam shook his head. "Not really. But three feet more is three feet more."

"Well," Elliott said, "we'll start down here on Monday, and we can punch a small hole in it to see if there's anything back there. If we don't really need the space I can't see taking the whole wall down."

A medley of nods and "okays" settled the matter for the moment, but John's presence remained by the wall, as did the confusion.

❧

Rick invited Elliott over for dinner that Saturday evening—a first in what he still wasn't sure could be considered a budding relationship. He realized it was much too early to even think about such things, and he wasn't sure what he thought about the prospect of an other-than-casual relationship at all.

He'd had three that he classified as such in his life, the longest lasting only four years. They'd all ended badly and left him with strong reservations about ever having a fourth. Rick, too, he'd learned, had a rather rocky history of relationships, the most recent being when a guy he had really thought was his "Mr. Right" suddenly and without explanation dropped him shortly before he met Elliott.

Still, Cessy might be right in insisting that it was time for Elliott, at thirty-eight, to start settling down.

He had been to Rick's apartment only once before, the night he'd picked Rick up at the Gentry on Halsted just before last call. They'd gone there and almost directly to the bedroom. Elliott had had a meeting early the next morning, and barely had time to get out of bed and get dressed before he had to leave; so he really hadn't seen much of the place, other than getting the general impression that Rick had talents that extended beyond the erotic.

He took a chance on driving over, stopping to pick up a bottle of wine, and was lucky to find a parking place within a few buildings' walk. His earlier general impressions were confirmed as the two settled in for a before-dinner drink.

When Rick excused himself to go check on dinner, Elliott idly surveyed the room and settled on a large coffee table book on a lamp table opposite him. Curious, he got up and went over for a closer look. It was titled *Moonrise*, and the cover photo was of a crescent moon hovered over what at first looked to be the ocean but on closer inspection was a sea of pine trees, some flecked with snow, which gave the illusion of whitecaps. He picked it up and carried it back to the couch, placing it on his lap and opening it with one hand as he retrieved his drink from the coffee table with the other.

There was no text, just full-page and double-page photos. The first picture he turned to was of a full, cream-colored moon rising above a stark, jagged black silhouette he realized were mountains. He was sure he had seen it before, and then realized that he had.

In one of his dreams.

Then, with the suddenness and intensity of an electric shock, John was there. Not just there but directly beside him on the couch, so close their calves surely would have been touching if John had been corporeal. It caught Elliott with such surprise his entire body involuntarily jerked, and he almost spilled his drink.

"Something wrong?" Rick asked as he reentered the room.

"No." Elliott hastened to close the book. "Just a twinge in my shoulder. It

32

happens every now and then."

Rick rejoined him on the couch, and John's presence subtly shifted to accommodate him.

"Ah," Rick said, then indicated the book with a tilt of his head. "Great book," he said. "You like nature photography?"

"Uh, yeah," Elliott said, still recovering from the shock of John's arrival.

"G. J. Hill," Rick said, again indicating the book. "Fantastic photographer. I've admired his work for years—at least, I think it's a 'his.' I hate it when people just use initials, and there's no information or picture of the author anywhere on the jacket or inside the book. But I guess it doesn't matter, it's the work that counts."

Elliott forced himself to reopen the book and thumb through the pages. John's presence was almost palpable as he did so.

The photos were extraordinary, each one featuring the moon in varying stages of fullness. In only a very few were there even the slightest evidence of human habitation. The instant he closed the book and set it on the coffee table, John's presence dimmed, like turning a rheostat from "bright" to "low."

It was only with extraordinary conscious effort that Elliott was able to regain his inner composure and allow himself to get on with the evening.

It was worth the effort. Rick, he was delighted to discover, was an excellent cook, and the entire evening, once he was able to put John's abrupt invasion behind him, went by far too quickly. When Rick invited him to spend the night, he was more than happy to accept. And when they finally got to sleep, he was aware of nothing at all except a deep sense of peace across which, like the shadow of a tree in bright moonlight, lay an indescribable sadness.

❈

Elliott had always prided himself that logic, order and willpower were key factors in his life. Yet driving home from Rick's on Sunday afternoon, he realized those very traits were counterproductive to dealing with the question of exactly who or what—or why—John might be.

The very idea that ghosts and spirits might exist was not logical; having one in his life was disruptive to his sense of order. Yet, using his willpower to hold John at arm's-length, as he had been doing, simply was not working. John wasn't going away. If anything, he was becoming more intrusive, and that was both disturbing and more than a little frightening.

He got the distinct impression that John, so recently transitioned from life to death, was not unlike a fledgling bird trying to figure out how to fly. Were John's appearances, for want of a better word, trying to communicate something? If so, what? What possible connection could there be between a basement and dreams and photographs of mountains? And how could John expect to tell him anything at all when the strongest message he had been able to convey was that he knew nothing except his first name?

The only things Elliott was sure of in connection with John were that, like it or not, John probably did exist, that he was almost certainly the unidentified man who had died in the emergency room, and that for whatever reason, he had sought out Elliott for help in discover who he was.

As he parked in his building's garage and took the elevator to his floor, his mind remained fixed on John. He most certainly did not want a repeat of the previous night, when he'd been caught totally unawares by John's intrusion, but he had no idea how to avoid it. He tried summoning John, reaching out to him with his mind like some necromancer and feeling not a little foolish in doing so, but there was nothing. His mental radar picked up no ectoplasmic blips. Obviously, when, where and how John made himself known was not up to Elliott, and that fact, too, distressed him.

He realized as he unlocked his door and entered his apartment that this was the first time he had seriously devoted himself to thinking of John as he related to his own life. Yet even as he did so, he remained conflicted. These were not the actions of a rational man, part of him pointed out. The rest of him was loath to disagree but countered that, as a man rooted in logic and order, he couldn't simply disregard whatever was going on without trying to understand it.

Though he vaguely sensed John's presence several times Sunday afternoon and evening, it was frustratingly peripheral. Despite concentrating as hard as he could each time he was aware of it, the only feeling he was able to discern was one something akin to bemusement. Whether it came from John or from himself he wasn't able to determine.

On the logical grounds that the only time John manifested other than as emotion was while Elliott was asleep, Elliott deliberately went to bed early, only to realize that one of the perversities of human nature is that few things are harder than *trying* to go to sleep. He finally just gave up on trying and eventually drifted off.

— *Sorry.*
— *For what?*
— *For being so difficult. I know you're trying to help.*
— *Why were you at Rick's?*
— *I don't know. I was just...there.*
— *Did it have something to do with the book?*
— *I don't know. I like the pictures.*
— *Did you recognize something in them?*
— *I don't know! They're nice pictures. They make me feel...*
— *You can feel?*
— *Of course I can feel! Not physically, but...*
— *How did the pictures make you feel?*
— *Calm. Comfortable...sad.*

Gradually, like static on a wandering radio signal, bits and flashes of totally unrelated dream images began intruding. Elliott fought to concentrate, even though he was aware he was dreaming.

— *How about the basement in the Capetti building. Why were you there?*

— I don't know.
— Did you feel anything there? Anything about that wall?
— I felt...odd.
— Do you know why?
— No.
— Are you trying to tell me something?
— I don't know.

The dream-static became more intrusive until it gradually drowned out his exchanges with John, and he simply gave up and let it take over.

❊

Donning his usual work uniform—sturdy seen-better-days jeans, battered work boots and a frayed long-sleeve shirt—for the first time since his accident, Elliott ate a quick breakfast of toast, cereal and coffee, made a sandwich for lunch, emptied the remainder of the coffeepot into a thermos and headed for his car. He kept his toolbelt, work gloves and a variety of tools in the trunk, and made his usual quick check to be sure he had everything.

He was at the Sheffield property a little before eight and was the first of his crew to arrive. He went directly to the basement, conscious of John's growing presence from the moment he started down the steps. By the time he reached the laundry room, he knew John was there, waiting, by the wall. There was no sensation other than that of presence—no confusion, no anxiety, nothing.

He resisted the temptation to immediately go to the wall and start punching a hole in it, gladly deferring to his willpower, which dictated that he wait for the others. In the meantime, he busied himself clearing a section of the utility area end of the room to make space for stacking the building materials he'd ordered for delivery sometime during the morning. That done, he disconnected the out-of-order washing machine—all four, and the dryers, were going to be replaced anyway—and moved it away from the wall to be taken upstairs for disposal.

He'd managed to walk the machine over to the door by the time Sam arrived.

"Lumber's here," Sam announced. "They pulled up just as I was coming in. Where do you want them to put it?"

"Have them bring it on down, and we can stack it right here," Elliott replied, pointing to the area he'd just cleared.

Sam nodded and went back up the stairs.

By the time Arnie and Ted arrived, the lumber was unloaded, and a number of other distractions had been dealt with, it was close to noon before anyone even thought of the wall. Elliott had been so preoccupied with work he was totally oblivious to John.

"So, when are you going to check that wall?" Sam asked.

The minute Sam mentioned the wall, John was back, if he'd ever left.

Elliott looked at his watch. "Why don't we break for lunch," he suggested, "and tackle it as soon as we get back?"

Like Elliott, the others customarily brought their lunch, and they all went outside to sit on the back steps to eat. When they'd finished, he went to his car and took a large hammer and concrete chisel from the trunk, and all four men returned to the basement. John's presence seemed stronger, though again Elliott perceived no accompanying emotion...except, perhaps, for the slightest sense of curiosity.

"You're going to cut us in on any cash back there, right, Elliott?" Ted asked, only half-joking.

"Sure," Elliott replied, running one hand along the wall at about shoulder height. Picking a spot almost in the exact center of the wall, he held the chisel in one hand and raised the hammer with the other. Carefully, so as not to destroy more than one concrete block, he chipped away until his target block was completely and cleanly removed.

Moving his head forward, he tried to peer into the darkness. He could see nothing except a section of the original wall behind the opening he'd just made. There was the strong odor of mold.

"Get me a flashlight," he said, and Arnie removed one from his belt and handed it to him. Shining the light through the hole, Elliott moved the beam around the space. Nothing. The hole was too small to let him put his head and arm in, and he really didn't want to make a bigger hole.

"Damn! I wish I had a mirror!"

"Hey, Ted," Arnie said, "lend Elliott your compact."

"Very funny," Ted replied. "But I can do better. Some asshole clipped the passenger's-side mirror off my truck last night. I've got it on the front seat. I'll go get it."

He left and returned a moment later. Though it was a little awkward, Elliott held the flashlight with his right hand and inserted it into the hole. Holding the mirror with his left, he put it just inside the opening and began shining the light around the space, trying to coordinate it with moving the mirror.

When he moved the light to the floor, he could see something there. It looked like a rolled-up rug. He choreographed the flashlight and mirror as best he could, moving the light from one end of the rug to the other, then stopped abruptly. At the top of the rug there was nothing. At the bottom of the rug was a pair of shoes.

They were not empty.

CHAPTER 4

The police arrived shortly after Elliott called them on his cell phone, and after only a few questions, during which he referred them to Capetti, they took his phone number and told him and his crew to go home. The stairway leading to the basement was blocked off with "Do Not Cross" tape.

Having little other option, Elliott sent Arnie, Ted and Sam home, telling them he'd call as soon as he found out anything. Then, resisting the temptation to hang around, he did likewise. He immediately called Cessy and, without telling her what had happened, asked her to have Brad call him as soon as he got home.

While the discovery of a body had distracted him, as soon as he got into his car and headed home, his thoughts turned to John and how he related to everything. As far as Elliott could tell, John was not currently present, though by intense concentration, not unlike squinting one's eyes to see something more clearly, he could get a very vague sense that John was somewhere nearby and a distinct impression he was deliberately trying to be unobtrusive. Elliott once again tried, by sheer willpower, to summon him and once again failed.

— *You knew about that body, didn't you?* he demanded..

There was no response.

— *Do you know who he is?*

Nothing.

— *Is it you?*

Nothing.

Even as he asked the last question, he was pretty sure that whoever the body behind the wall might have been, it wasn't John. It had obviously been there for a very long time; he seriously doubted John would have waited seventy-five years or more before making himself known.

But if the body wasn't John's, why had John been in the basement? Maybe he'd find out that evening since John's specific thoughts came only when he was asleep.

The discovery of a body in the basement of a building he'd just bought was a major monkeywrench thrown into his schedule. He had no idea how long the police might hold up his work team. He also had no idea in what shape the police would leave the wall, but it undoubtedly would have to be completely removed. It wasn't that he was insensitive to the fact that a dead human being was involved. Quite the contrary. But after seventy-five years or however long it might have been, the preserving crime-scene would not be as intensely pressing as it would have been if the body were more recently deceased. The urgency of needing to resolve the anxiety of grieving relatives would have long ago diminished.

Still, he very much wanted to talk to Brad to learn what the police may have discovered, and what they would do to determine the identity of the body.

✳

Along about five p.m., he briefly considered trying to take a nap, to see if perhaps John might have anything to say, but he thought better of it. John was already enough of a disruption to his life, and he did not want to make the situation worse by starting to cede time to seeking him out.

He cursorily watched the news at five-thirty, glancing frequently at the time, which, of course, only made it pass all the more slowly. With no word from Brad by six, he decided to make a quick check of his e-mail, which he hadn't done in a couple of days. He wasn't that much of a computer person, and didn't really have all that many friends he couldn't just pick up the phone and talk to.

He deleted thirty-seven spam messages and read only the few personal ones, none of which called for an immediate response. Then, without even thinking about it, he went to Google and typed in "G. J. Hill," immediately wondering whatever had possessed him to do so. Although Hill was the author/photographer of Rick's coffee-table book, *Moonrise*, the one that had elicited John's sudden and unexpected presence, he hadn't thought of the book since.

The search yielded several sources—a number of links to various bookstores and the titles of three books: *Moonrise, Sand Petals* and *Sea Dreams. Moonrise* was the most recent, *Sand Petals* had come out two years previously and *Sea Dreams* two years prior to that.

Even though Rick had mentioned that *Moonrise* had no author information included, Elliott was still rather surprised to find there was no indicated website for Hill, and no biographical or personal links. He went to the books section of Amazon and typed in the title *Sea Dreams.* The instant the cover appeared on his screen, he experienced the jolt of John's presence as suddenly and powerfully as he'd felt it at Rick's, and the hair rose on the back of his neck. John was so close behind him he was sure if he turned his head suddenly it would brush against a face.

Without turning, he took a deep breath and willed his composure to return.

— *I wish to hell you wouldn't do that!* he complained.

There was no response. He didn't expect one.

He enlarged the image and saw it was a nearly full-cover shot of a beautifully iridescent seashell partly surrounded by the froth of a receding wave. As he

38

stared intensely at it, he sensed a subtle wave of...pleasure. His or John's, he couldn't tell, but he had his suspicions.

He then went to *Sand Petals*, the cover of which was of a monarch butterfly on the opening bud of a cactus flower, and then to *Moonrise*. The appearance of each cover evoked a subtle but distinct pulse of pleasure. All three books, Elliott noted, were published by Retina Press of San Francisco.

The sound of the phone cut off any further speculation as to the link between the books and John, and Elliott hastily got up from the computer to answer it.

"Elliott. It's Brad. I just got home. What's up?"

Elliott got no further than mentioning the body in the basement than Brad interrupted him.

"Whoa! That was your building? I heard about it, and I knew it was on Sheffield, but I didn't realize it was your place. Jeez. Cessy says she saw something about it on the local news at five, but she didn't catch the connection, either."

"Yeah, it's mine. What else did you hear?"

There was only a brief pause before Brad said, "Not much, really. Apparently, the body's been there for years, maybe even a leftover from Prohibition days and the gang wars. Forensics has the body; they'll be able to get a better idea."

"Any idea on how long the police will be holding me up?" Elliott asked. "I've got a lot of work to do, and this is throwing me off schedule."

"I don't imagine it'll be long," Brad said. "As soon as they get everything they need, they'll turn the place back to you. I doubt there's much in the line of clues after all this time."

"Good." Elliott suddenly remembered his conversation with Al Collina. "There is something you might want to check out, though," he said.

"Yeah? What's that?"

"I told you at dinner one time that I'd had a call from Al Collina right after escrow closed on the building, wanting to buy it from me. He mentioned that his father had loaned Capetti's father the money to buy the building. Do you suppose there might be some tie-in there to the victim? And if so, I wonder if Collina might be aware of it? Considering that he made the offer before the body was discovered..."

There was a slight pause, then Brad said, "Interesting! We'll look into it. Thanks."

"If you hear anything else, will you let me know?"

"Sure. Here, hold on a second. Cessy wants to talk to you."

For the next ten minutes, he underwent a cross-examination on everything that had happened in the building that day—why he hadn't told her about it when he'd called, the state of his health, and everything he'd been doing since they last talked. She asked yet again if he was sure taking care of Bozo for the upcoming two weeks wouldn't be an imposition, and he reassured her yet again that it would not. It was only the immediacy of her getting dinner on the table that finally ended the conversation. He loved his sister, but there were times...

He wondered how she'd react if she knew about John.

After hanging up , he went into the kitchen to make himself a drink and to put a frozen pizza into the oven. Returning to the den, he deliberately turned his mind off and flipped on the TV. The evening passed.

He made a point of watching the local ten o'clock news; as he expected, there was a segment, complete with reporter standing in front of the building, about the discovery of "human remains" behind a false wall in the basement, and a bit of speculation that it may have been a mobster from Chicago's gangster days of the 20s and 30s.

When he first went to bed, Elliott attempted yet again to tune his mind in to John, with the usual negative results; At last, he just stopped trying and drifted off.

— *It's not me.*
— *How can you be sure if you don't know who you are?*
— *I might not know who I am, but I know who I'm not. I'm not him.*
— *That's what I thought. Do you know who it is?*
— *No.*
— *But you knew he was there.*
— *No.*
— *Then what were you doing there?*
— *I don't know.*

Elliott fought off the rising static of incoming dreams.

— *What about the books?*
— *I like the pictures.*
— *You've said that. But all three books are by the same photographer.*
— *I know. I can read.*

Again, Elliott was aware of a sense of bemusement.

— *Sorry. What does that mean to you?*
— *I don't know.*
— *Have you seen them before?*
— *I don't know. They're...familiar.*
— *The photos or the places?*
— *The photos are the places.*
— *What do you feel about them?*
— *I told you. Like I'm not alone.*

The static-filled dreams grew stronger.

And then Elliott was looking at the cover of *Sand Petals*, and the butterfly flew away.

✳

He drove over to the Sheffield property early Tuesday morning. No police cars, plain or marked, were around, but as he entered the foyer he could see the tape still blocked the basement door. Though he had a key and could have let himself into the hallway, he rang Capetti's bell.

"Yes?" a tinny-sounding voice asked from the small speaker set into the brass plate beside the buzzers.

"Mr. Capetti, it's Elliott Smith. Can we talk a moment?"

The buzz of the lock being released corresponded with a "Sure" from the speaker. Elliott entered the hall and went to Capetti's apartment. He was about to knock when the door opened.

"Come on in," Capetti said, and Elliott stepped into a room filled with boxes of various sizes and in various stages of being packed. "Excuse the mess. The movers will be here day after tomorrow, and I'm nowhere near ready. And then to have this..." He paused, moving a large box from a chair to the floor, obviously distressed. "This...yesterday business!"

He motioned Elliott to a chair then pushed a box aside on the couch to make room for himself.

"What can I do for you?" he asked.

"I wonder if you can tell me anything about the body in the basement."

Capetti reared his head back as if in amazement. "Good Lord, no! That wall's always been there. I didn't even realize it wasn't the original. I told the police all that yesterday."

"So, that would mean the wall was put up sometime before..."

"I was born in twenty-nine," Capetti said, "and as I say, as far as I know it's always been there. Whoever put it up must have done it while the building was being built. My father bought it the minute it was finished."

Elliott wasn't quite sure how to broach the subject without possibly insulting the older man, but he felt he had to know.

"The twenties were a pretty wild time for Chicago, what with Prohibition and all the gangland activity going on. I understand your father knew Vittorio Collina, who was involved with the Capone gang. Did your father have any—" He didn't have a chance to finish his question before Capetti interrupted.

"Mob connections? Just because we're Sicilian? That's nonsense. My father came here from Sicily when he was a boy, and he worked like a dog to support his family. He was as honest as the day is long, and he never had so much as a parking ticket!"

"I'm sorry," Elliott said. "I didn't mean to imply that he might. I'd just heard that he and Collina came over from Sicily together and were good friends."

"My father knew Vittorio Collina, yes. I'll wager most Italian immigrants from that time knew or knew of someone involved in bootlegging. They weren't proud of it, but it was a fact of life in Chicago. You can't paint everyone with the same brush."

"And I certainly didn't intend to," Elliott said. "It's just that bodies don't generally show up walled into basements. I'm sure your father had nothing to do with it, but since he knew someone like Vittorio Collina, perhaps..."

"I have no idea who the body is or how it got there. I'm positive my father didn't know, either."

After an awkward pause, Elliott changed the subject to general questions about the building.

✤

After leaving Capetti, he drove to the appliance warehouse to verify delivery dates on the new washers and dryers. He could just as easily have called, but it gave him something to do other than worry over the fact he was losing another full day of work.

Then, on his way home, and on what he first assumed to be a whim but later questioned, he found himself detouring to Unabridged Books on Broadway to see if they might have any of G. J. Hill's books. They had all three, and he bought them. Even as he did so, he had the very odd feeling that John was present but trying not to be. Elliott had the distinct impression the fledgling spirit was getting better control of his wings.

Driving back to his condo with his purchases on the seat beside him, he found himself angry, though he wasn't sure at whom. At himself, for increasingly behaving as if something that could still very well be a creation of his own mind were real or, if there were truly such things as ghosts and spirits, at John for possibly trying to manipulate him.

This fight between his intuition that John was real and his logic that John was some sort of mental aberration resulting from his accident had been going on ever since John first appeared in the hospital. The more convinced his conscious mind became that John was real, the more strongly his logical nature rebelled, protesting—well, logically—that he was becoming more seriously deluded and delusional.

As he was going from the garage to the elevator, his cell phone rang.

"Yes?" he said, after extricating it from the pouch on his belt.

"Elliott Smith?" a voice he did not recognize asked.

"Yes."

"Mr. Smith, this is Sergeant Kreuger of the Chicago Police Department. I just wanted you to know we've finished our investigation of your building on Sheffield, and you're free to resume your work."

"Thank you," Elliott said. "May I ask if they've identified the body?"

"Not yet," Kreuger said. "He's been in there a very long time. But we will."

"Well, thanks for calling," Elliott said, and heard the click of the receiver at the other end of the line.

When he got to his apartment, he set the three books on the coffee table and, deliberately ignoring the growing cognizance of John's anticipatory presence, called Sam, Arnie and Ted in turn and told them to come to work in the morning. He then went into the kitchen to make a cup of coffee, not allowing himself to even look at the books as he passed.

But in the kitchen, he knew John was near the books, and a definite feeling of impatience.

He poured his coffee and took his time adding the sugar, opening the refrigerator to take out the half-and-half, pouring and stirring, then replacing the carton and closing the refrigerator door. By the time he was done, the impatience was almost palpable. But was it John's, or his?

— *All right, all right!* he thought in exasperation. He still refused to allow himself to speak to John aloud. That would be a concession his logic, willpower and concerns for his sanity would not let him make.

He took his coffee into the living room, picked up *Sea Dreams* and, specifically avoiding the couch, carried it to his favorite chair. He set his coffee cup on a coaster on the end table and sat down. Instantly, John was there, descending on him like a gigantic downfilled quilt, the sense of his presence so all-encompassing Elliott couldn't pinpoint his exact location.

He opened the book, carefully looking for anything to indicate who G. J. Hill might be. There was a brief glowing introduction by another noted photographer, but it addressed the quality of the work without saying anything about the individual who had created it.

When he turned to the first photo, a naked child running along the edge of the waves, he experienced a vague feeling—a gentle surge and ebb of something he could not define but that struck him as being not unlike a small wave lapping at the shore. This same sensation occurred each time he turned to the next picture.

He couldn't quite put his finger on what there was about the photos that gave them their power—the lighting, the composition, the suggestion that each was part of a larger, largely unrecognized story waiting to be told but suspended forever in time.

And exactly what, he asked himself, did all this have to do with John? How did it relate—how could it relate—to some poor guy dying in an emergency room, or to a body walled up in a basement for more than three-quarters of a century? There were the sensations and emotions he attributed to John, but where were the details of what they represented? If John was telling him these things were significant, how could he, at the same time, be incapable of conveying what they were significant of? Why, after all these...clues, if that's what they were...didn't John seem to be getting any closer to recalling his identity?

Elliott felt strongly that the books and the photos might be somehow relevant, but he could not comprehend how, or what the body behind the wall might have to do with anything.

Concluding that there was just too much going on in his head at the moment, when he reached the last photo of *Sea Dreams*, he closed the book and set it aside, resisting the temptation—whether his or John's didn't matter—to move immediately on to the next.

As he went through the on-autopilot motions of making dinner, he was still mildly irked at himself over the degree to which he had allowed John to intrude on his life and his wavering between accepting John as real and getting on with helping him find out who he was, or picking up the phone and either calling his doctor to discuss checking him more closely for neurologic damage or finding a good psychiatrist.

The evening passed uneventfully, with the usual phone call from Cessy and a call from Rick inviting him to go see a new movie they'd talked about. TV filled the rest of the time between dinner and bed.

— *I apologize.*
— *For what?*
— *For being such a bother.*
— *Why did you pick me?*
— *I didn't. You were just there.*
— *Are you the guy from the ER?*
— *I don't know. I can't remember anything before I saw you lying in that bed.*
— *Why are you so drawn to those photo books?*
— *I told you. I like the pictures.*
— *But why them?*
— *I don't know. Why not them?*
— *You said they were familiar to you. Had you seen them before? Did you live around where they were taken?*
— *I don't know. They make me feel comfortable. And sad.*
— *Do you know who G. J. Hill is?*
— *Yes. His name is on the books.*
— *So, you know Hill is a man?*
— *Yes, he's a man. I'm not sure how I know, but I know.*
— *Do you know him?*
— *I don't know.*

Elliott felt a sense of profound frustration. How much of it was his and how much John's he couldn't tell. He suddenly and chillingly thought of Chang and Eng, the original Siamese twins.

— *Are you real?*
— *Yes. Aren't you?*

❋

Over the next several days, Elliott poured himself into his work, concentrating entirely on what he could see and touch. He was aware of John frequently, but it was as if John were trying to keep out of his way, and he appreciated it. Even at night, John remained largely silent, though Elliott still dreamed of mountains, and so could not delude himself John had gone away.

The basement at the Sheffield building was largely finished; there was no evidence of the knocked-down wall behind which the body had been found. The space was now occupied by a long table for folding clothes flanked by two tiers of small lockable storage bins where each tenant could keep laundry supplies. The washers and dryers were waiting to be installed as soon as the tile floor was replaced. The new wall between the laundry and furnace areas needed only painting and the hanging of the door. Work had begun on the storage-area half of the basement.

Details boring to most, but Elliott took comfort in preoccupation with them.

He'd spoken to Brad a couple of times about whether anything had been found out about the body in the basement. Brad said he wasn't aware of anything, other than that they had checked with Al Collina about what he might know of his father's connection to the building. Aside from restating that his father and the elder Capetti had been friends, Collina claimed to know nothing at all; and with Vittorio Collina dead, there wasn't too much they could do to prove otherwise.

The more Elliott thought about it, the more he tended to believe that Al Collina might not have had any knowledge of the body's being behind the wall. If he had, it was unlikely he would have even mentioned his father's association with the building; he could have just relied on the profit pitch to try to get Elliott to sell the building to him. He probably figured Elliott, being a "fag," might buy into the "sentimental value" angle as a ploy, however weak and transparent.

Brad told him the medical examiner still had the body and had not yet made a final report, but that they had determined the victim to have been a Caucasian male about five feet, seven inches tall, approximately forty-five years old, and that he had died as the result of a gunshot wound to the back of the skull. The homicide squad was going back through records starting in 1926, when the building was built, through 1933, which was Capetti's first recollection of being in the basement. He'd been adamant that it had never been altered since that time.

Capetti, it turned out, still had records of everyone who had lived in the building since it opened; and while it wasn't likely the victim had been a resident, the police were going over the names of the tenants from those years for a possible lead.

Since it was not at all unusual, during Chicago's gangster era, for mobsters to routinely disappear, even if Vitto Collina had been involved in this particular murder, trying to put together the puzzle of who the victim might have been would involve a lot of time. And after all these years, the identification had a rather low level of priority. Still, Brad was confident they would keep at it until they had the answer.

DNA had been extracted from the remains, he said, but no familial link had been found—not surprising considering how relatively few people have their DNA on record.

"Your John Doe from St. Joseph's being a case in point," he added.

"Speaking of that, is there anything at all new on him?" Elliott asked.

"Not that I've heard. And as I said before, the more time that goes by the less likely we are to ever identify him. But there's always hope."

"You said they'd taken some postmortem photos."

"Yeah. They get the face, plus any tattoos, marks or scars. This particular John Doe didn't have any distinguishing marks at all. I've seen the headshot that was circulated to all the detectives just in case someone might have run across him before in relation to a crime."

Elliott realized Brad would undoubtedly question his mental stability, just as he had, if he asked his next question, but he didn't feel he had a choice.

"Could I see them?"

There was a rather obvious pause before Brad asked, "Why would you want to do that?"

He did some fast mental tap dancing then went with a lie he hoped might work. "Well, although I only got a quick glimpse of him in the ER, it's occurred to me several times since that I might have recognized him from somewhere."

"Why didn't you mention this before?"

"Because I wasn't sure...still aren't...but I've been thinking about it, and..."

Brad didn't sound totally convinced when he said, "So, nobody specific?"

"No, or I'd have mentioned it right away," Elliott assured him, "but if I did see him before, maybe seeing his photo might remind me. It's worth a shot."

Another distinct pause. "Well, I suppose you're right. I'm sure I can pull a copy, but it'll probably have to wait until we get back from vacation."

Elliott felt a wave of relief. "Any time you can will be fine. Thanks, Brad! I appreciate it."

He had hoped that mentioning the photo might provoke some strong reaction from John, but other than the usual vague sense of his presence, there was nothing. John might not still fully accept that he was dead and therefore was not relating a photo of a dead body to himself. But if he was the John Doe from the ER, perhaps seeing his picture might, as with amnesia victims, bring back some knowledge of who he was.

❧

The two weeks of Brad and Cessy's vacation passed rapidly, with work on the Sheffield Building and taking care of Bozo occupying just about every minute of Elliott's time. John's presence was constant but subdued, and there were dreams and bits of conversation in the depths of sleep; but for the most part, Elliott got the distinct impression John was trying not to be too intrusive. It occurred to him, too, that the dead might well have very different concepts of the importance of time.

He was able to get together with Rick a couple of times the first week—a movie one night, dinner and a stay-over on a Saturday—but realized the following Thursday that they'd not even talked for several days. He felt increasingly comfortable with Rick, as Rick seemed to feel with him; but it was as though they had an unspoken agreement not to rush things.

Though he never mentioned it, Elliott could tell Rick was still carrying the torch for his last affair, and while he was naturally curious as to what had happened and why, prying was not in his nature. He had pieced together that the guy, who came from an ultra-conservative fundamentalist background and had apparently come out only recently, still had not yet totally broken free from his past.

So, although he chose not to speculate, not having heard anything was unusual; so he made a point to call him Thursday night after dinner. He got the answering machine and left a message.

A cool wind off the lake was blowing through the open balcony doors, and as he returned from closing them, Elliott was drawn to the photo books neatly stacked, thanks to Ida, on the table where he'd left them. He picked up *Sand Petals* and took it to his favorite chair. Turning on the lamp, he sat down and opened it.

The immediate strong sense of John's presence was not unlike a sudden gust of wind, as if the balcony doors he'd closed had burst open again.

The book, as the title suggested, was comprised of photos of the desert in spring. Each photo had, as those in *Moonrise* and *Sea Dreams*, a unique feel to it, creating a separate atmosphere of combined beauty and starkness—of desolate isolation and promise. Amazing blooming cactus. A long shot of endless waves of sand with one small flower visible halfway up a dune that drew the eye like a magnet. Carpets of spring flowers spread across the desert floor, bringing it to vibrant life. Elliott was both impressed and absorbed, and he was aware John was, too.

It struck him that there was a common theme in all three books—waves. Waves of trees and mountains in *Moonrise*, waves of sand in *Sand Petals*, and of course *Sea Dreams*. Each book evoked a sense of power, of ebb and flow—and of life itself.

He speculated that G. J. Hill quite likely lived in California, which provided easy access to the subjects of each book.

And who was G. J. Hill? John had maintained Hill was a man, and Elliott tended to agree, though he had no facts on which to base such a conclusion. If John did know Hill personally, how could he find out for sure? He toyed with the idea of trying to contact Hill through the books' publisher then realized that, even if he did manage it, he would have no idea what to ask. "Do you know someone named John?" Who didn't? But this John would likely be someone Hill had not seen or heard from in a while.

Not having a last name was the problem. Of course, if he had John's last name, he wouldn't have to contact Hill at all. Confusion led to more confusion, which led to even more confusion, until he slammed the book closed in exasperation, tossed it back onto the coffee table and pushed himself up from the chair. He strode into the den, plopped heavily on the loveseat, picked up the remote and flicked on the TV.

His frustration had segued again to anger, and he wasn't exactly sure why. Anger at whom? At what? At himself, he realized, for being pulled ever deeper into the quagmire that John represented, and at his inability to either just step away from it or know what to do to resolve it.

❉

He was still angry when he went to bed and, finally, to sleep.

— *I'm sorry.*

— *Yeah, you've said that.* Even in sleep his anger was still with him. *Why don't you just go away?*

He instantly regretted the thought when an overwhelming sense of fear, like being immersed in ice water, came over him. The fear, he knew, was John's.

— *Where would I go?*

The fear was replaced by a feeling of sorrow and loneliness so intense Elliott wanted to cry.

— *I didn't mean that. I'm sorry. It's just...*

— *I understand. It's very hard.*

— *But what do you want of me? What can I do?*

— *Help me.*

— *How?*

— *I don't know.*

A flush of anger returned briefly, but he forced it away.

— *That's just it—you don't know! Anything! How can I help you if you don't know?*

— *Help me to find out.*

He was aware of his own sigh, even through the depth of sleep.

— *I'm not doing a very good job of it.*

— *Yes! You are! You've helped me feel things. I don't know what they mean, but they have to mean something. Why do we dream of mountains?*

Instantly, Elliott was wide awake.

— *We?*

CHAPTER 5

᯾

He glanced at the digital clock on the nightstand. Five-fifteen. Too early to get up, too late to go back to sleep even if he could, which he doubted. That single dreamed word *we* had totally unnerved him with the shock of realizing that it was true. If John existed, or ever had existed, outside Elliott's own mind, he was John's only hope of finding out who he was and what had happened to him.

And even if John was only a figment of his imagination or some side effect of his accident, what could he lose by looking into it? The fact remained that a man had died in his presence in the hospital emergency room, and that man deserved the dignity of an identity. Someone, somewhere, knew him. He had to have family, friends—a partner, perhaps—who wondered where he was and what had happened to him.

As for his own family, he'd received a letter from his parents saying they had decided to extend their vacation with a side trip to Bali, which would delay their return home by several more weeks. He loved his parents, but they had always led their own lives quite separate from his. Cessy, Brad and the kids had returned from Florida on Saturday, and he spent Sunday afternoon with them, hearing all about their adventures and generally catching up. He didn't mentioned John Doe's photo, figuring Brad deserved not to be reminded of work on his last day of vacation; and he was relieved that Cessy, for a change, did not press him on his social life.

However, Monday morning he got up, went through his morning ritual and waited until seven o'clock, when he knew Brad and Cessy would be up, then reached for the phone.

"Hello?" Cessy's voice didn't betray any curiosity over who might be calling at seven a.m. As a policeman's wife, she was used to calls at all hours, day or night.

"Cessy, hi. Sorry to bother you so early, but is Brad around?"

There was a slight pause before: "Yes, he just got out of the shower. Is something wrong?"

He hastened to assure her that everything was fine, but that he just needed to talk to Brad for a moment. He heard a hand-over-receiver-muffled "Brad? Elliott wants to talk to you" followed by "He'll be right here. Are you sure everything is okay? You seemed a little distracted yesterday. I worry about you."

He resisted the temptation to say "So I've noticed," and settled for "I'm fine, really. I've just been very busy working—as I told you, the new building has been taking up all my time."

Apparently making up for her lapse the night before in not inquiring about his private life, Cessy asked, "Have you been dating at all? I didn't get a chance to ask you yesterday, but that doesn't mean I'm not curious."

Her question reminded him he'd still not heard from Rick.

"Not really," he said. "I'll start up again when this project is a little further along."

"Well, I don't want you to become a monk. I...Oh, here's Brad. I'll talk with you soon."

There was the shuffling sound of the phone changing hands, then, "Hi, Elliott. You still want that photo, right? I'll make a point of getting it today."

"No problem," Elliott said. "But I would appreciate it."

"Hey," Brad said, "it would make my job easier if more people would take an interest in trying to find John and Jane Does."

"I guess most people just aren't aware of them."

"That's true. But people go missing all the time, and for all sorts of reasons. Most disappear voluntarily and show up eventually. Very few of them, over all, end up dead. And for those who do, well...the very fact that someone's a John Doe often indicates he's not from the area where he was found, and anyone who might be looking for him just doesn't know where or how to look."

"That sucks," Elliott said.

"That it does, but that's the way it is." He paused for a moment, then said, "Well, I'll make a point of getting it for you today. But right now, I've got to run."

"Sure," Elliott said. "I've got to get going myself. Thanks a lot, Brad."

"I'll give you a call tonight."

✻

Work on the building was going along well. He'd subcontracted the tearing down of the garage and blacktopping of the new parking area while he and his regular crew concentrated on the kitchens and bathrooms of the two empty apartments at the rear of the building, which included replacing the kitchen window with a doorway to what would be the private patio. There were an infinite number of logistical details to be juggled all at once, and Elliott thrived on them.

He had always taken pride in knowing that when he worked, he worked. He kept his mind focused on the job immediately at hand and didn't allow it to go wandering around looking into things that might distract him and thereby slow him down. To Elliott, time was not so much money as it was productivity. He was now always aware of John's presence, but he had accepted it to the point where he was able to pretty much ignore it.

On the drive home, though, he began to think of both Brad's anticipated call and of the fact Rick had yet to contact him. He found it interesting that, of the two, it seemed to be Brad's call that concerned him most.

He found a message from Cessy waiting for him on his machine.

"Elliott, your cell phone must be turned off. Call me as soon as you get in. Brad called this afternoon and mentioned he was bringing home something for you. If I'd known that this morning, I'd have invited you over for dinner tonight then. You men just never think. It's five o'clock now, so plan on coming over for dinner and you can kill two birds with one stone. Call me."

Checking his cell he saw that it had, indeed, somehow been turned off. He then glanced at his watch—it was five twenty-eight—sighed and picked up the phone to call his sister. He'd just had dinner with them the night before, but at least he wouldn't have to wait for Brad.

Assuring Cessy he'd be over shortly, he took the time to give Rick another buzz. He didn't expect him to be home yet, and was surprised to hear the phone picked up and a voice he'd never heard before say "Hello."

Thinking he might have gotten a wrong number, he said, "Is Rick in?"

"No," the voice said. "He's still at work. He should be here shortly. Do you want him to call you?"

"No, that's okay. I have to be leaving in a minute. Just tell him Elliott called."

There was a slight pause, then: "Oh. Okay. Elliott, huh? I'll tell him."

Elliott, huh? He wondered what that was supposed to mean, and who was answering Rick's phone. He had a feeling he knew, and he was mildly irritated. If, as he suspected, Rick's ex had re-entered the picture, he felt Rick should have had the courtesy to let him know. As he hung up, he felt a surge in John's presence, and a strange sensation of empathy.

Quickly washing up and changing clothes, he headed out the door for another Dinner at the Priebes'.

❉

Arriving shortly before six-thirty, he found Cessy in the final preparations of dinner and the kids in their rooms doing homework. There wasn't enough time for him and Brad to have their usual pre-dinner beer, but as he settled into his favorite chair, Brad left the room, returning a moment later with a manila mailing envelope.

"Sure you want to look at this before dinner?" he asked, only half-jokingly. as he handed it over.

"Sure." Elliott opened it to extract an eight-by-ten photo, which was facedown. John's presence nearly overwhelmed him. He turned the photo over and looked at the handsome but badly bruised and unmistakably dead face. A small mugshot-type sign on his chest identified him as John Doe #147.

He was not prepared for the tsunami of emotion that swept over him, sorrow so overwhelming he became lightheaded and felt his eyes misting over. He had to blink rapidly to clear them.

"You okay?" he heard Brad ask.

He nodded. "I'm fine."

51

At the same time, he was fully aware that, though he didn't recognize the man in the photo, John did.

Luckily, Brad was distracted by Cessy.

"Dinner's almost ready," she said. "Five minutes."

She turned back into the kitchen. Brad returned his attention to Elliott.

"So, do you recognize him?" he asked.

Elliott shook his head to clear it and tried to pull himself together. "I definitely recognize him from the ER," he said, "even though I only saw him for a moment and was pretty much out of it myself. As to other than that, it's really hard to say."

Fighting his lightheadedness, he pretended to study the photo more carefully for a long moment. Short-cropped dark hair—brown, Brad had told him—a neat, short-stubble beard of the kind seen frequently in the bars and in TV commercials.

"Now that I got a better look at him, he does look familiar somehow." He was mostly lying. "I think I might have seen him in one of the bars." That wasn't true, but it was the first thing that came to his mind. That John had obviously recognized himself was the primary thing. As to Elliott's recognizing him, the face shared too many qualities with any number of good-looking men seen in the bars and on the streets every day. True, he might have seen him before, but...

"The bars? So, you think he might have been gay?" Brad asked.

"I'm not sure." Elliott pulled himself back into the moment. He hated misleading his brother-in-law, and he had nothing other than his assumption to go on that John might be gay. But he needed an excuse for his next question. "I was wondering if I might keep this."

He was aware of Brad's immediately raised eyebrow.

"Why? If you think he might be gay, we can take it around to the bars to see if any of the owners or bartenders recognize him. It might give us a lead."

Elliott regretted ever having asked, but now that he had, he felt he had to follow up on it.

"That's a good idea," he said. "But if I could keep this one, I might be able to ask some of my friends if they've ever seen him. It couldn't hurt to cast a little wider net."

Brad thought a minute. "Well..."

"You know I'll be discreet," Elliott hastened to add, "and as I said, it might turn up something."

Brad pursed his lips and stared at him, making him even more uncomfortable. "I suppose," he said, "but you'd better be *damned* discreet. The department likes to keep pretty close control on its evidence. But like you say, it couldn't hurt if the guy *was* gay. You can get around in the bars easier than we can."

Elliott was sliding the picture back into the envelope when Cessy appeared again in the doorway.

"Ready," she said, and Brad and Elliott rose from their seats, Brad going to the stairway to the second floor to call the kids.

✤

John's presence weighed on Elliott like a thick winter coat throughout dinner and all the way home. He couldn't imagine being in John's position—to see himself...dead.

The gigantic wave of sorrow that had swept over him when he first looked at the photo had ebbed but not vanished, replaced by John's apparent resignation to the fact that he was, indeed, dead. But there was also an element of hopelessness. John had recognized himself but still, apparently, had no idea who he was.

As soon as he got back to his condo, Elliott took out the photo again and studied it carefully, in case either he or John might somehow be able to tell something more. *Had* he ever seen John in a bar? It was possible, but as Brad had said, the fact that John was a John Doe indicated he was not from the immediate area. Which again begged the question as to whether "John" was his real name.

Brad had said the man's eyes were brown. The face was expressionless in death, and there were ugly dark bruises and swelling on the cheek, jaw and neck, although none was disfiguring. John was without question a good-looking man, probably very close to Elliott's own age; and the harder he stared, the stronger he felt there was something familiar about him.

Probably just his imagination, and imagination could be misleading. He knew full well that staring long and hard enough at anything—even at a word like *the*—could play really strange tricks on the mind. The chance he might actually ever have seen John before the ER was too remote a possibility to be seriously considered.

He once again questioned his own mental state. He still could not comprehend how, if John were a real, albeit non-corporeal, entity—how he could not know who he had been in life. In fairness, Elliott reasoned, he had no idea what it was like to be dead and what that might do to memory.

Yet, while his logical nature strongly preferred the latter to continue to believe John some lingering effect of his accident, his heart and instincts clung to the belief John was real. So, he once again resolved to go along and see what developed. If John were truly a lost soul, Elliott felt an obligation to help him find himself.

The ringing of the telephone ended further speculation, and he hastened to answer it.

"Elliott?" Rick asked, as if he might have doubts. "It's Rick. I really want to apologize for not having gotten back to you sooner."

"No problem. I assumed you were busy."

"Well, yeah, I have been, actually. I..." There was a long pause, then: "Look, can I come over for a few minutes? I know it's getting late, but I really want to talk to you about something, and I don't want to do it over the phone."

Elliott glanced at his watch. It was nine-forty-five, and tomorrow was a workday. Still, he could tell from Rick's voice that it was important to him, even though he was pretty sure he already knew what it was about.

"Sure," he said. "Come on over."

"I'll be there in a few minutes."

He called downstairs to tell the doorman Rick was expected then carefully returned John's photo to the envelope and carried it into the den to set it on the desk. He didn't want to think any more about it just then.

Rick arrived shortly after ten, and Elliott suspected he'd probably called from his cell phone while already on the way over. He looked uncomfortable as Elliott led him into the living room.

"Like a drink?" he asked.

"No, thanks," Rick said. "I don't want to keep you too long."

Gesturing him to a seat, he noticed that Rick perched on the front edge of the couch, bent forward, elbows on his thighs, hands clasped between his spread knees. Elliott sat in his favorite chair and leaned back.

"So, what's up?" he asked.

Rick took a deep breath before saying, "Joel's back."

"So I gathered. He answered the phone when I called earlier."

Rick looked up, surprised. "Really? He didn't tell me."

Elliott suppressed a wry smile and reserved comment. "No big deal," he said.

"Well, he was getting ready to head back to DeKalb. He's doing some post-grad studies at NIU. He...Well, he called me about a week ago and said he'd thought the whole thing over and that he was wrong to have broken it off between us, and wondered if maybe we could get together again. I really don't know what to do! I mean, I met you, and we seem to get along really well, but we haven't known one another long enough to tell where we might be headed, or if we're headed anywhere at all, and I sure as hell don't want to screw over your life, and..."

Elliott realized that if there had been no accident—and subsequently, no John—he very well might be viewing the situation somewhat differently.

"That's okay," he said, trying to find a balance between giving Rick the impression it didn't really matter at all to him and coming across as being bravely noble. It did matter—he was really quite fond of Rick, but they hadn't reached the point where the issue of whatever their relationship might have become would have a too-serious or long-lasting effect.

Besides, Elliott reasoned, his life was much too busy at the moment for Rick's possible absence from it to leave an unfillable void.

"It's *not* okay," Rick insisted. "I really like you and enjoy being with you, and I feel like a real shit just cutting it off. But I never did get over Joel, and if there's a chance...But, hell, who knows? He dumped me once. What's to say he won't do it again?"

Elliott smiled. "Hey, Rick, it's *okay*. You have to do what you think is right. If you want to try it with Joel again, fine. And if it doesn't work out, I'll most probably still be around, and we can think about picking up where we left off."

"Jeez, Elliott, I really appreciate your saying that. I was afraid you might be angry with me, or hurt, or..."

"I understand," Elliott said. "Really. I could always tell how you felt about Joel, and if you think it can work this time, go for it."

✿

Rick left a few minutes later, and Elliott got ready for bed. He was rather pleased with himself for taking the entire situation so much in stride. He was also glad Joel had re-entered the picture now rather than six months from now. Rick wasn't his first aborted relationship, and he'd be surprised if he was the last.

Elliott had always enjoyed dreaming. It helped balance his more practical, awake side, and he was lucky enough to be able to remember at least the gist of his dreams. He particularly enjoyed the ones in which he could fly, or run down a street or descend long flights of stairs without his feet touching down.

Occasionally, he dreamt not in thoughts or pictures but in concepts—reams of paper or boxes or random shapes. He didn't enjoy those, since they were devoid of both logic and emotion.

He awoke sometime that night with a distinct impression of weight, as though he were sleeping under a gigantic mound of blankets or had several mattresses piled on top of him. He willed himself back to sleep.

— *Sorry.*

— *You don't have to keep saying that.*

— *But I am. For weighing you down.*

— *What do you mean?*

— *I've been thinking of that photograph. I know it's me, but I still have no idea of who I am.*

Elliott was aware of the gentlest of breezes, and identified it as John's equivalent of a sigh,

— *Or, rather, of who I was.*

— *You're John.* He was aware that even in sleep he was trying to be conciliatory.

— *Yes, but John who?*

He sank into a deeper level of sleep, where there was no awareness. He had no idea how long he was there, until...

— *The picture books.*

Elliott rose to just below the surface of sleep.

— *What about them?*

— *The mountains and the desert, and the ocean. I'm sure they mean something.*

— *I wish I could help you, but if you don't know, how can I?*

— *They're... familiar.*

— *These particular pictures, or just pictures of deserts and mountains and oceans in general?*

— *I don't know. They're the only pictures I've seen.*

55

Even for a dream, Elliott was aware that was an extremely odd statement. Feeling a mild wave of frustration, he released his grip on semi-consciousness and let himself sink back to the depths of oblivion.

❉

One significant thing about his conversations with John, he thought as he stood, coffee cup in hand, waiting for the toaster to disgorge his English muffin, was that he remembered most of them clearly and, on reflection, recognized in them a slow but definite development of John's awareness.

John had come to him a totally blank slate, knowing only that his name was John, and Elliott realized he had become a conduit through which John was, like sketching out a complex mathematical formula, linking together individual bits of information that would enable him to solve the equation of who he was. For whatever reason, it was only through him that John was able to gather these bits of information.

If the photos in Hall's books triggered a sense of familiarity and feelings of connection in John, even though he didn't yet know why, it was through Elliott the connections had been made.

It was after Elliott had obtained the autopsy photo that John recognized himself.

On the other side of the coin, had he not felt John's presence so strongly in the basement, would he ever have bothered knocking a hole in the wall to check what was behind it? He could not imagine what the body behind the wall might have to do with anything, other than to provide another blurred glimpse into whatever plane of existence John was in. So, was it any wonder, he thought, that John had used the word *we*?

He ate breakfast, pulled a chicken breast out of the freezer for dinner, packed his lunch and drove to work on autopilot, his mind still largely on John, interspersed with a few thoughts of Rick. Once at work, his self-discipline kicked in, and he immersed himself in the details of what had to be done for the day.

On the way home, however, his thoughts returned to John, and he deduced that he was more than just a simple conduit through which to help John find his identity. He was, as near as he could tell, the only means John had for becoming aware of anything on any level. When John told him the photos of mountains, the desert and the sea in Hall's books were the only photos he'd ever seen, he meant it literally—because they were the only photos Elliott had looked at since John's arrival. He knew only what Elliott, in effect, presented to him.

The weight of the responsibility for finding answers that might lead to John's identity teetered on the oppressive, especially when Elliott realized he had no exact idea of what questions to ask.

The recurring element in the puzzle was G. J. Hill's photos, but he couldn't be sure whether it was specifically those photos that triggered John's fascination and sense of familiarity or if mountains, desert and the sea were generic clues to where John came from. Chicago, of course, had neither mountains nor deserts, but as he considered it he realized he was often conscious of John's presence either at the windows overlooking Lake Michigan or on the balcony. Maybe, he thought, being so high in a building reminded John of being on a mountain.

So, it was quite possible, as had occurred to him before, that John was from California, which offered easy access to all three elements. The fact G. J. Hill's publisher was also located in San Francisco might underscore a California connection.

By the time he reached his condo, Elliott had determined to look for more general pictures of mountains, deserts and the sea to try to narrow down whether John was responding to general geographical features or specifically to those in Hill's photos. If, as he suspected, it was the latter, he'd then think about contacting Hill's publisher or possibly Hill himself. Maybe having more specific information about exactly where the photos were taken might give him—and, though he thought it unlikely at this stage, maybe John—a general area to start zeroing in on. If he could come up with that, he or Brad could send a copy of the photo to the local police to see if anyone matching John's description had been reported missing.

Since he wasn't planning on leaving home that evening, after changing out of his work clothes and washing up, he threw on a comfortable pair of old pants and a faded T-shirt. He didn't bother putting on socks or shoes. Grabbing a beer out of the refrigerator and checking to see that the chicken breast was completely thawed, he wandered into the den to watch the evening news.

During a commercial break, he glanced at the bookcase beside the TV and noticed that, in the stack of old magazines on the bottom shelf, there were several back issues of *National Geographic*, to which he once had a subscription. One thing about *National Geographic* was that there was never a shortage of pictures of mountains and deserts and oceans. Still, he resisted getting up to retrieve them and instead concentrated on the news. Aftewards, he returned to the kitchen to start dinner, and only after putting it in the oven did he go back to the den to take the *National Geographics* from the bookcase.

He detected in the surge of presence that John knew what his objective was, and he got the impression John was as curious as he to see what his reaction might be.

The cover of the top magazine on the stack listed an article on "Secrets of the Kalahari," and he opened it immediately. Impressive photos, as expected, and a wide variety of subject matter, but he perceived no particular reaction from John. Searching through the other issues, he found articles featuring a number of mountain ranges and ocean vistas, but again sensed no particular spiking of the intensity John's presence or interest.

Having gone through all of the magazines with no reaction from John, and with a sigh that caught him rather by surprise, he got out of his chair, put the magazines back in the bookcase and went into the kitchen to check on dinner.

✽

— What now?

The mental voice, like a commercial break in a TV show, interrupted a dream in which he and Rick were exploring an old house, finding new rooms where no rooms should have been.

— I'm not sure. You didn't react to any of the photos.

— They were just pictures. There was nothing to react to.

— So, what were you reacting to in the other photos?

— I'm not sure.

— Perhaps because you've been there?

— You asked that before.

— And you said you didn't know. But that was before you saw those other pictures. Do you know now?

— I'm still not sure. But perhaps. I wish I knew.

Elliott once again sensed and shared John's desperate frustration in grasping for things just beyond his reach. But it was clear to him, even in the fog of sleep, that Hill's photographs were the key.

❀

The next evening after work, he went directly to his computer. He assumed Retina Press, the publisher of the G. J. Hill books, would have a website, and he was correct. He learned the company was devoted exclusively to producing high-quality art and photography books, publishing only two or three titles a year since its founding in 1991. G. J. Hill was one of only a dozen or so artists it represented.

Again, there was no indication of a website for Hill, or any biographical information. *Moonrise, Sand Petals* and *Sea Dreams* were Hill's only books, which verified the results of Elliott's earlier Google search.

Returning to the home page, he looked for a "Contact Us" link and wrote asking if there were some way, as a fan, he might directly contact G. J. Hill. He didn't hold on to any real expectation of a response, but he figured it was worth a try. If Hill could tell him the exact areas his photos were taken...

He'd just hit the "enter" key to send his note off to Retina Press when the phone rang. He hurried to answer it and was a little surprised to hear Brad's voice.

"Elliott, hi. Just thought you might be interested to know we have an identity on the body in your basement."

"Wow." He was impressed. "That was fast. From what you'd said I thought it would probably take forever."

"Well, normally it probably would have, but with your pointing us toward a connection to Vitto Collina, we were able to cut more to the chase, as it were. We have a guy in administration, Chet Green, who is our resident expert on Chicago mobs and gang activity during the Prohibition days. When he heard about the body and I mentioned Collina, he started going through his files. It seems that one of Bugs Moran's top lieutenants, Little Joe Donnelly, disappeared in February of nineteen-twenty-nine. His body was never found.

That in itself was a little unusual, since mob murders were often pretty much public spectacles—gangs used hits like telegrams to send a message to their rivals. But Donnelly was one of the relatively few gangsters to just vanish without a trace. What zeroed Chet in on Donnelly was that one of the people the police questioned was a woman named Patricia Cargill, who was rumored to be a mistress of one Vitto Collina. Donnelly was apparently trying to make a move on her. And guess where Patricia Cargill lived?"

"I suspect I don't have to guess," Elliott said.

"Yep," Brad continued. "Her address was given in a newspaper article at the time. We verified it by checking Capetti's rent receipts from 1929."

"Interesting, indeed." Elliott was aware of John and wondered what in Brad's story might account for it. He still couldn't imagine what interest a murder more than three-quarters of a century old might hold for someone so recently murdered himself—other than, of course, for the fact of murder itself.

He did not have time to reflect on the possible relationships of the dead because Brad's voice brought him back to reality.

"So, that wraps that one up."

"Collina killed Donnelly—or had him killed—and walled him up in his girlfriend's basement?"

"No way to be sure of the details, but exactly who killed him and why really doesn't matter after all these years. Everybody directly involved is now long dead. The main thing is that we identified the body and notified what family we could find. It does leave the little question of, if Capetti's father was as clean as his son says he was, exactly how someone could have used his friend's basement to wall up a body without his knowing about it.

"Anyway, the case is closed now, and I just thought you'd like to know."

"Well, thanks, Brad. I'm really glad you told me. That makes one less John Doe in the world. Maybe there's hope for mine."

"We'll keep workin' on it," Brad said. "Based on the possibility he was gay, we've been showing the photo around at several of the bars and other gay places along Halsted, but nothing yet. Have you had a chance to show it to anyone?"

"I haven't been out at all," Elliott admitted, "so I haven't really had a chance. I may make it a point to go out this weekend, though, and see if I can find anything."

"Okay," Brad said. "Keep me posted. Do you want to talk to Cessy? She's in the kitchen, and I don't think she knows I'm talking to you."

"Uh...that's okay. I don't want to interrupt her." He loved Cessy, but really didn't want to go through another sisterly interrogation.

"Okay. Talk to you later, then."

"Thanks again, Brad. Bye."

❊

— I'm glad.

   — About what?

   — That they found out who that man was. Now his family will know.

— I'm afraid most of them are dead now, too.
— Still, I'm glad. Names are important. Families are important. I wish...
— I know. And if you have a family, we'll find them.
— You think so?
— I'm sure.
— That would be nice. I hope you're right.
— I am. Trust me.
— I do.

❖

Elliott wasn't much of a bar person. When he did go out, it was either with friends or with the specific purpose of finding a partner for the evening. To go out by himself with a purpose other than cruising was new to him, and not particularly appealing. Still, he'd gotten John's photo from Brad on the understanding that he'd show it around to people he knew at the bars, and he was a man of his word.

So, Friday night, after eating dinner and watching a little TV, he took a quick shower and got ready. Not wanting the hassle of trying to find a parking place on Halsted on a Friday night, he walked up to the el station, got off at Belmont and went east toward Halsted, the main street of Boys Town. He found it interesting that he sensed John was with him.

He knew he couldn't possibly hit all the bars in one night, or even in several. His trivia file told him there were at least eighteen on Halsted and another twelve on Clark, with perhaps five on Broadway. He felt a bit strange, realizing just how long much time had passed since he'd been out by himself; and while he wouldn't be averse to picking someone up, John's presence made him feel slightly guilty about even considering it. Even though he was increasingly convinced John was not from Chicago, he had no way of knowing how long he might have been in town before he was killed. He was also was increasingly convinced, with no basis, that John had been gay. It was possible someone might have seen him.

His first stop was at Spin, at the corner of Belmont and Halsted. He walked in to find a typical Friday night crowd. Spin was one of what he called his "mood" bars—he either felt immediately comfortable and had a great time or couldn't wait to leave, and he never really knew until he got inside the doors which mood would prevail.

Going to the bar, he ordered a weak bourbon-and-Seven, thinking that if he was going to be hitting several places, he needed to make sure he didn't let alcohol get the better of him. As he surveyed the crowd, he spotted several guys he knew and a couple he decided he wouldn't mind getting to know, but the reason why he'd come kept him in check.

He was about to start approaching the guys he knew when someone said, "Elliott! Good to see you out and about!" He turned to his left to see Danny Sable, an old acquaintance who had been at the dinner party the night of the accident.

"Sorry I didn't get to stop by the hospital to see you," Danny said, leaning toward him to be heard over the general din of the music and the crowd, "but I didn't even hear about it until a couple of days later."

"That's okay," Elliott said, raising his voice and tilting his head toward him. "It was no big deal."

"Well, you were lucky. It could have been a lot worse."

Elliott thought of John, and agreed.

"What's with the envelope?" Danny asked, gesturing with his glass.

"Glad you asked." Elliott set his drink on the bar then opened the envelope and removed the picture. "I was wondering. Have you ever seen this guy before?"

Danny took the photo and looked at it, tilting it toward the light. "Can't say that I have," he said. "Jeezus, who beat the crap out of him? Nice-looking guy other than that, but what happened to him? He looks a little..."

"Dead," Elliott said, to Danny's automatic recoil.

Danny quickly handed the photo back, and Elliott replaced it in the envelope.

"Well, I hope you'll excuse my asking," Danny said, "but where the hell did you get a picture of a dead guy, and why are you carrying it around with you? I didn't know you were into that sort of thing."

Elliott merely smiled and turned to pick up his drink.

"Long story," he said, "but this is a guy was brought into St. Joe's ER the same time as I was, except he didn't make it. He had no ID so they listed him as a John Doe. I told my brother-in-law, who's a homicide detective, that I might have recognized the guy from somewhere, and he managed to get the picture for me on the grounds that if he happened to have been gay somebody from the community might recognize him." Aware of John's presence, he felt a little uncomfortable talking about him so casually.

"Did you recognize him?" Danny asked.

"I'm not sure," Elliott lied. "But I figured it would be worth showing his photo around, just in case. He has a name, and an identity, and probably people who are looking for him somewhere. I hate the idea of their never knowing what happened to him. He deserves better."

Danny shrugged. "Yeah, I suppose," he said. "Well, like I said, he was a nice-looking guy, and I'm sure I'd remember if I'd seen him before."

"It was just a long shot," Elliott said. "But thanks."

They exchanged a few more words, Elliott looking around the crowd until Danny nudged him and pointed toward a tall, thin blond just approaching the bar with an empty glass in his hand.

"Have you talked to Alex?" he asked. "He knows everybody, plus he's got a photographic memory. I'll bet he can tell you the name, address and phone number of just about every guy in town. If anybody'd remember seeing your guy, it'd be him."

"Thanks," Elliott said. "I'll do that. Excuse me, will you?"

Danny nodded, and Elliott moved down the bar to where the blond was waiting for his drink. He had seen him frequently in various bars over the years, but had only actually spoken to him two or three times.

"Excuse me, Alex," he said, moving next to him.

The blond turned and gave him a big smile. "Hi, handsome. Elliott, right?" he said, as though they were good friends who'd seen one another the day before. "I haven't seen you around much lately. Been out of town?"

"No, just busy. I was wondering if you can help me."

Alex grinned. "I thought you'd never ask!" he said. "Your place or mine?"

Elliott knew he was joking.

"We can try the bathroom later," he quipped. "I wouldn't want to take you away from your evening."

Still grinning, Alex said, "Well, I am with someone, as a matter of fact, although there's always room for one more. But what can I do for you at the moment?"

Elliott set his nearly empty glass on the bar again and opened the envelope, taking out the picture. "Do you know this guy?"

Alex glanced at the photo, then his eyes widened in surprise. "Is he..."

"Dead, yes."

"Jesus, what a shame! He was good-looking under all those bruises! What are you doing with his picture?"

Elliott gave the same basic explanation as he'd given Danny while Alex continued to stare at the photo. Finally, he handed it back and shook his head slowly.

"I'm sorry, Elliott, I've never seen him before. You think he was from around here?"

"Apparently not." Elliott returned the photo to the envelope. "But that's what I'm trying to determine. I thought if anyone might recognize him, you would."

Alex turned to the bartender to pay for his drink then turned back. "Yeah, I'd think so, too. But I really don't think I've ever seen him."

"Well, I appreciate your looking at it."

"No problem," Alex said. "I wish you luck in finding out who he was." He glanced across the room and nodded at someone. "Well, I'd better get back," he said. "But I'll take a rain check on that bathroom thing, okay?"

They exchanged grins, and Alex moved off into the crowd.

Elliott was debating whether to order another drink or leave when he heard "That's nice of you," and turned to the stool on his right to see an extremely good-looking Hispanic in his early thirties looking at him.

"I'm sorry?"

The man indicated the envelope.

"I couldn't help overhearing your conversation," he said then smiled. "Though it wasn't exactly easy with all this noise. It's nice of you to want to find a name for someone who doesn't have one. Obviously, you're a romantic."

That struck Elliott as strange. While he considered himself many things, a romantic had never been one of them. He took quick stock of the guy as he talked; though he was sitting down, Elliott estimated him to be about his own height and weight, with black hair, intense dark eyes and perfect teeth. But it was the color of his skin that most drew Elliott's attention. He had always been attracted to Hispanics, and especially to those with this guy's coloring, a cross between a soft olive and coffee-with-cream, as though he'd been born with a perfect tan.

"I'm Steve," the man said, extending his hand. "Steve Gutierrez."

"Elliott," Elliott replied, taking it. "Smith."

Steve gave him a quick raised eyebrow but said nothing.

"So, did you see the picture?" Elliott asked.

"Not really. But then, I'm just new in town and don't know all that many people yet."

"Ah? Where are you from?"

"California," Steve said. "I was born and raised in Barstow, and most recently lived around Big Bear."

"What brings you to Chicago?"

"I'm a commercial artist. A good job came up here, so I took it."

"How do you like the place so far?"

"I like it. There's a lot going on. But I don't know how I'm going to feel about the winters."

Elliott laughed. "You lived in Big Bear; you'll get used to them." He turned to signal the bartender for another drink.

CHAPTER 6

✾

*H*e awoke in the night, hearing the sound of Steve's breathing beside him. He
had become so accustomed to nightly, if brief, conversations with John that
not having one had awakened him. It was rather like someone accustomed to the
loud ticking of a clock suddenly being aware that it had stopped.

He didn't know if John was unhappy with him for not having devoted the
entire evening to his search, or just being discreet in leaving him and Steve to
their own devices, as had been the case with Rick. Part of him did feel guilty, but
the rest was relieved that John had not totally taken over his life.

He closed his eyes, concentrated on listening to Steve's regular breathing
and went back to undisturbed sleep.

In the morning, while he was in the kitchen making coffee, Steve wandered
into the den, where Elliott found him looking through the pages of *Moonrise*.
John was instantly there.

Steve looked up at him and grinned. He was wearing one of Elliott's robes,
open to the navel, and it took all of Elliott's willpower to resist dragging him
back into the bedroom.

"So, you're a Hill fan, too!" Steve said. "I knew there was something I liked
about you."

Elliott walked over beside him and laid his hand on Steve's shoulder. "A
recent convert," he said, "but I do like his work."

Steve tapped the open book on his lap. The page featured a shot taken from
a hilltop across a valley to another ridge of hills where the moon hung just over
the highest peak. The valley floor was sprinkled with the lights of a small town.

"We have a lot of the same stomping grounds, Hill and I, and we're both into
landscapes. This was taken not twenty miles from where I lived in Big Bear," he
said. "I can even tell you exactly where he took the shot—I did a painting from
almost the same spot, only in daylight. I recognize a lot of these places, even
though they were taken at night."

He indicated *Sand Petals*, lying on the table beside him, with a nod of his
head. "That one has a couple shots of places I know from around Barstow; most
of them are of the Mojave and Death Valley."

64

"Yeah, I kind of thought they must have been taken around there," Elliott said. "Did you ever meet Hill?"

"No, never," Steve said. "I gather he's something of a recluse."

"Aren't all you artist types?" He grinned, and Steve returned it.

"No, just the photographers. All us painters is party folk."

"I'd like to see your paintings sometime," Elliott said, knowing as he said it he wanted to see them not only for himself but for John.

Steve reached up and put one hand over Elliott's. "I left most of them with my folks when I moved," he said, "but I have a few you're welcome to see any time."

"I'd like that," Elliott said. "Now what say we go have some coffee?"

❊

Driving home after dropping Steve off at his apartment and accepting his invitation to come over for dinner that night, Elliott reflected on the serendipity of having met him, with its implications for a possible lead to John's identity. He was now certain that John was from California, and Steve's verification of the locale of the photos meant he might not have to pursue contact with G. J. Hill, from whose publisher he had received no response.

His mental trivia file included bits of geographical data, among which was that both Barstow and Big Bear were in San Bernardino County, the largest county in the contiguous United States—larger than nine states—and that while Barstow was in the high desert and Big Bear was in the mountains, they were only about fifty miles apart. He could ask Brad to contact the local police jurisdictions and send them John's photo. He had no way of knowing what sort of set-up San Bernardino County or Barstow or Big Bear might have regarding missing persons from their areas, but it would certainly be worth checking into. Exactly how he was going to go about convincing Brad to do this without having his sanity questioned, he had no idea.

He was a little surprised that he'd sensed no intensification of John's presence during these deliberations, and he wondered what that might mean. That he was totally off-base? That John didn't make the same connections he'd made? However, most troubling was the sudden and unwelcome recurrence of the idea that there was no John at all and he was just playing some weird mental game with himself.

He remembered that when he was in about the sixth or seventh grade he had looked at a map of the stars and realized he could draw a straight line from any star to any other star. He'd considered this a profound scientific discovery until he disclosed it to his teacher, who explained that any two points, anywhere, could be connected by a straight line. He wondered if that was what he was doing now—making connections between random, unrelated points.

He forced his mind off the entire situation by busying himself organizing a briefcase full of paperwork on the current financial status of the Sheffield project, and comparing completed expenditures with projected costs for the remaining work. He was pleased to find they were almost exactly on budget.

After the evening news, Elliott changed clothes and headed for Steve's, arriving shortly before seven. Steve lived in an attractive new six-unit building on a corner lot on Diversey, and Elliott, who had been admired the location when he'd dropped him off, was even more approving when Steve showed him into his second-floor apartment.

An impractically small balcony, hardly deep enough to stand on, spanned the glass-fronted living room, which was both sparse and comfortable at the same time. The walls were hung with what he assumed to be Steve's own work, mostly landscapes and still lifes, with display lights over each picture. He imagined using them as the room's primary source of illumination at night would be very effective.

"I'm impressed," he said, as he surveyed the room.

"I'm glad you like it." Steve was obviously pleased.

"And these are all yours?" Elliott indicated the pictures.

Steve grinned. "They're all mine, but not all of mine. As I said, I left most of them with my parents."

Going over to one, a study in greys and browns of a row of sagging and dilapidated wooden buildings against a mountain backdrop, Elliott was entranced. Like Hill's photos, Steve's paintings seemed to be much more than simply a realistic depiction of the subject matter. There was something elusive he didn't feel sufficiently knowledgeable about art to grasp, but there was the definite suggestion that each brush stroke was like a sentence in a long and fascinating story.

"Calico," Steve explained, anticipating his question. "A great old ghost town in the hills not too far from Barstow." He pointed to another painting on the opposite wall that depicted the shell of a four-story concrete building clinging to the side of a mountain. "That one's Jerome, Arizona. I guess you could say I have a thing about ghost towns."

"Not too many of those around Chicago," Elliott said, "but I can understand your interest. I've always been intrigued by them, too. Actually, I think my folks took me to Calico when I was a kid. Maybe that's where I caught the fever."

The subject of desert ghost towns made him alert for John's presence, but he noted no particular spiking of John's interest as he viewed the pictures. There were a few more paintings of desert landscapes and mountains reminiscent of Hill's photographs and apparently done in the same general region.

Steve pointed to the painting next to the one of the abandoned building in Jerome. It looked familiar.

"This is the one I told you about—Hill took a photo from the same spot." While Hill's photo had been at night, despite the painting's vibrant blue sky and the vivid greens of the trees, the shape of the mountains that formed the skyline was identical.

"So, maybe there's a chance Hill might be from around Barstow, then?" Elliott asked.

Steve shrugged.

"It's possible," he said, "The whole area kind of lends itself to people who like their privacy. There are a lot of places to get lost in. It's got a lot of advantages for artists and writers, being both pretty isolated and yet relatively close to LA and San Diego."

After looking at the rest of Steve's paintings, Elliott followed him on a tour of the apartment. Besides the long living room, one end of which was a dining area, there was a small windowless kitchen, a bath and two bedrooms, one set up as a combination studio and den. On an easel near the window was a painting in progress, which Elliott recognized immediately as Belmont Harbor—more specifically, a popular gay area known as "the rocks."

Returning to the living room, he took a seat on the small sofa while Steve went into the kitchen, coming back after a moment with a tray on which were a bottle of wine, two glasses and a plate of cheese and crackers. Elliott was pleased to think that Steve had gone out of his way to impress him. He had succeeded.

"I hope you like Mexican food," Steve said as he put the tray on the coffee table in front of the sofa and sat beside Elliott.

"I love it," Elliott said, and Steve smiled as he poured the wine, handing him a glass.

"Good," he said. "If you didn't I'd have had to fall back on ordering in a pizza or Chinese. But I had the urge to make enchiladas—my grandmother's recipe, though I went easy on a couple of the spices. You can add more if you want them."

They clicked glasses in a silent toast. After taking a sip, Elliott set his glass down and reached for the cheese and crackers.

*

When he got home around one o'clock Sunday afternoon, he noted two messages on his machine, both from Cessy. The first was from the night before, the second had come about an hour before he'd gotten home. She said she was wondering why he hadn't returned her first call, where he was, if he was all right, and so on. He decided he'd better get in touch before she called again.

The phone rang three times, and he was about ready to hang up, figuring they must be gone, when he heard the receiver being picked up, and Jenny's voice.

"Hello?"

"Hi, Ladybug," he said. "Is your mom home?"

"Yes. She's out in the yard with Daddy. We're planting a tree."

"Oh, well, don't bother her, then," he said. "Just tell her I called, okay?" He knew Cessy would call him back the minute she got in the house.

"Okay. Bye, Uncle Elliott."

"Bye, Ladybug."

He headed for the bedroom to change clothes. Though he'd showered at Steve's, he'd not taken along a change of clothes and didn't like wearing the same ones, especially underwear, two days in a row—one of the reluctant legacies inherited from his somewhat obsessive-compulsive mother.

As he changed, having resisted the impulse to shower again, he reflected on his evening with Steve. It had been memorable on several levels, not the least of which was the determination that John was from the same general area as Steve, and that there was some definite link between John and G. J. Hill.

Was it conceivable, he wondered, that John *was* G. J. Hill? That would be a real stretch, he knew—John had given absolutely no indication of it. Of course, one of Elliott's primary frustrations with the whole question of whether John was real or not was that John had provided him with no concrete information on his own. The only way he could determine for sure what John's link with Hill might be was to contact Hill directly, but he wasn't sure how to accomplish that unless he heard from the man's publisher.

The ringing of the phone just as he was putting on his socks sent him semi-hopping into the den to answer it.

"You're home!" Cessy said.

"Yes, Mother, I'm home," he replied, not quite sure whether to be amused or irritated by her keeping constant track of him.

"Well, I was beginning to get worried. Why do you bother having a cell phone if you never turn it on? You had a date?"

"I went to a friend's for dinner and stayed over."

"Do I know him? You have so many people coming and going in your life, I do wish you'd pick one and settle down."

Ignoring the last part, he said, "No, you don't know him. But I promise I'll keep you posted, and when I do decide to settle down, you'll be the first to know."

"I'd better be!" she said. "But the reason I called is to ask you over for dinner tonight. I've got a pot roast on, and there's enough food for an army. Would you like to bring your friend?"

He wasn't sure if she was serious or just teasing, but knowing his sister...

"Jeez, Sis, I just met the guy! I don't want to scare him off by parading him in front of the relatives so soon. Nice of you to ask, but no." He had the sudden mental image of being at a dog show, trotting Steve in front of Cessy and her family like a prized whippet. She had never been quite so pushy before, but perhaps she was becoming desperate for him to find someone.

"It doesn't hurt to ask," she said. "So, can you make it? Around six-thirty?"

"Sure," he replied, and she rang off.

Normally, he would have begged off—he felt he was practically living there recently—but knew it would give him another chance to talk with Brad. He still didn't know exactly how to approach him about sending John's photo to the San Bernardino County police, though. While he was now fairly confident John was from that area, he had no way of knowing whether John had gone missing from there or had merely moved away, in which latter case contacting the police there would be all but pointless.

Fighting off a rising tide of frustration, he went into the den, grabbed Hill's three books and strode into the living room, where he plopped down on his favorite chair and, with all three in his lap, determinedly opened the top one— *Sea Dreams*—and began staring intently at each photo, as if doing so might force John to reveal something. He was perversely aware that the act might very well increase his frustration rather than lower it.

Although the sense of John's presence intensified, as it always did whenever he went near Hill's books, he wasn't quite sure what he expected to accomplish. He knew from experience that he couldn't expect anything but sensations, at least not while he was awake, but he hoped that, by concentrating very hard on each photo, he might sense something that would provide a clue as to what he should do or where he should look next.

He made his way all the way through *Sea Dreams* and moved on to *Moonrise*. The fact that he still found each of the photos captivating, and noted new detail in nearly every one, made him almost forget his objective. John's presence remained steady but unwavering.

When he came to the photo looking out over the valley—the one Steve's painting duplicated in daylight—he paused even longer than usual; he had no idea why. Staring intently brought out some details he'd missed on earlier viewings, but nothing he considered significant.

A few pages further on was a photo of a lone tall pine tree on a rock outcropping, silhouetted against the sky with the full moon showing through its branches, which again held his attention longer than normal. A few pages beyond that there was a shot of a new moon balanced on the deeply shadowed outline of what appeared to be a sagging barn roof, as if the lunar weight were causing it to bend.

Elliott picked up an opened envelope from the table beside his chair and tore off pieces to make bookmarks for the three photos. He'd ask Steve if he might recognize exactly where they had been taken.

Finishing *Moonrise*, he set it aside and picked up *Sand Petals*, but even with the same intense study, none of the photos stood out as had the three from *Moonrise*. He was again frustrated—if John were trying to tell him something by means of those three photos, why had there been there no fluctuations in the intensity of John's presence?

The soft chiming of the grandmother's clock in the dining area made him look up; he was startled to find he'd been sitting there for nearly three hours. Once again mildly exasperated with himself, he got up and carried the books back into the den.

✻

He arrived at Cessy and Brad's just before six to find Brad and BJ engrossed in a football game on TV. Elliott had never been a very big sports fan, and was always grateful to his father for not pushing him to be. As a matter of fact, having little or no interest in organized sports, he had never really figured out what the fuss was all about, or cared. One night at a bar he had told an obnoxiously sports-oriented acquaintance, "If you're so wild about football, put down the beer and get off your dead ass and go out and play it."

After a brief exchange of greetings, he picked Sandy up from her playpen beside the couch and followed Cessy into the kitchen. As always, he was intrigued by the baby's flawlessly soft skin, crystal-clear blue eyes and that indefinable but distinct "new" smell that all babies share. He held her with her head on his shoulder, one hand supporting her upper back and rocked her gently back and forth.

"Don't you ever miss not having children of your own?" Cessy asked, taking a stack of plates from the cupboard.

"Oh, I suppose, sometimes," he confessed. "I love kids. I just don't want to go through the details of making one."

"Well," Cessy said without looking up from dealing the plates onto the table, "maybe when you settle down you can adopt. A lot of gays are doing that now, I understand."

He grinned. "Yes, that's what I understand, too."

Cessy looked up quickly to see how he meant the comment and, seeing his smile, returned it.

"We'll see what happens," he added.

Dinner was delayed until the end of the game, and Elliott and Cessy sat at the kitchen table talking. Jenny wandered in and out of the room with various things she wanted to tell or show Elliott, and each time he gave her his rapt attention. Sandy had fallen fast asleep, and he had returned her to her playpen.

Cessy filled him in on their parents' continuing adventures; their mother kept in close touch with her, sending detailed accounts of their travels. She seldom wrote Elliott other than the briefest of notes—probably, he surmised, on the not totally unfounded assumption that men didn't care for nonessential information in a letter. They were planning to return to Chicago at the end of the month in time for some annual charity affair with which they were associated.

He had never spent too much time reflecting on his relationship with his parents. It wasn't that they were bad parents, it was just that they always had a lot of other things to do. Neither was particularly demonstrative, though neither he nor Cessy doubted they were loved to the best of their parents' interpretation of the word. He was an adult before he realized one day that he could not recall ever having addressed them as "Mom" and "Dad"—they were always "Mother" and "Father"—and that he didn't consider that the least bit unusual. It was simply the way of things—they were, after all parents, not friends. Perhaps that was one reason he and Cessy were so close.

The kids had been excused from the table, and the three adults were sitting drinking coffee when Brad brought up the subject of John, or, more accurately, "Elliott's John Doe."

"You never found out anything from the picture, I assume," Brad asked, freshening his coffee from the carafe Cessy had brought to the table.

"I'm still working on it," Elliott said. "I took it to a bar the other night but

70

didn't really have a chance to talk with that many people."

He noted Cessy's raised eyebrow and knowing smile.

"But I haven't given up, by a long shot."

Cessy shook her head. "I really don't understand your fascination with all this," she said. "I'm afraid it might not be healthy for you to dwell on it."

"Well, I'm hardly dwelling on it," he said, knowing even as the words left his mouth that he was lying. "It's just that the idea of someone being robbed of their very identity really, really bothers me. Somebody knows this guy; somebody misses him. I'd be a pretty poor excuse for a human being if I didn't do whatever I can to help."

Cessy gave him a small smile. "But there must be so many John Does out there. You can't find names for them all."

"No," he said, "but this is a guy who died lying on a gurney right next to me. That makes him special."

Brad nodded in agreement. "I understand," he said. "It's frustrating for a lot of us in law enforcement—we do whatever we can with every John Doe case, but there are so many other, more urgent things to deal with that, after the initial investigation, we just don't have the time."

Elliott reached for the carafe and poured himself more coffee. "I don't suppose you found out anything more about...What was his name? The guy in the Sheffield basement?" he asked.

"Joe Donnelly," Brad said. "And, no, not really. We're convinced that Vitto Collina was behind it, but the whole thing is kind of moot now. So, while there's no statute of limitations on murder, Vitto's death effectively put an end to pursuing the matter."

"Vitto Collina? Vittorio Collina?" Cessy asked. "Our next-door-neighbor Collinas? I never realized. No wonder Marie became a nun!"

Elliott nodded. "If I had a brother like Al and a father like Vitto, I'd probably have become a nun, too." He caught Brad's quickly raised eyebrow and suppressed smile, and grinned.

Cessy, oblivious, continued. "So, we lived next door to a murderer? And they seemed like such a respectable family!"

"I'm afraid 'respectable' isn't a word many people would ever use to describe Vitto Collina," Brad said. "He was a gangster and an inveterate womanizer...and those were his good qualities."

"Poor Marie! It must have been terrible for her." Cessy shook her head and stared into her coffee cup. "And you and...Johnny, was it?...were best friends. He seemed like such a nice boy. I don't remember much about Alphonso, but I know I didn't like him. He used to make Marie cry just for the fun of it."

"That's Al, all right," Elliott said. "And I don't think he's mellowed with age. I was telling Brad that Al called me the other day to try to con me into selling him that property I'd just bought on Sheffield."

"And Johnny? What became of him?" she asked.

Again, Elliott felt a strange wave of sadness. "He died in Africa several years ago, while he was in the Peace Corps," he said. "Al mentioned it...and I do mean mentioned it. He might as well have been talking about losing a phone number. It was obvious he couldn't care less. After all these years, he's still a bastard."

❦

He talked with Steve several times over the next week, but they didn't have the chance to get together, largely because Elliott was so preoccupied with completing the Sheffield building. Work was going along well—was, in fact, ahead of his projected timetable. The back porch/patio project was completed, and four of the six apartments redone. Elliott had not forgotten about the three photos from *Moonrise*, and wanted to ask Steve about them as soon as he could, even though he didn't sense any pressure from John to do so.

He had learned not to project anything onto John in the way of anticipating what he could or should expect. It was as frustrating as thinking his intense concentration might produce some specific response. It never did. John communicated what and when he wanted or was able to communicate, and Elliott was powerless to change it. He had gradually rejected the idea that John was deliberately concealing information, and resigned himself to the fact that John was truly as much in the dark as he was.

He had always been one to prefer action over excessive contemplation. He was used to thinking about something long enough to lay out what he considered to be a workable plan of action then following his plan. But that was in his dealings with the real world; it didn't necessarily apply to John. Having largely accepted the idea that John was real and not something his mind had created, he was not comfortable with all the speculation that seemed to accompany that acceptance. Why John did not respond or react in a logical manner was a primary source of frustration, but he recognized that he had no idea how being dead might affect one's perceptions, thought processes, responses or reactions. He just took it on faith that both he and John were doing the best they could.

He continued to have dreams, but it was almost as though, having convinced Elliott that the dreams meant something, John had relented a bit on their intensity. But he was always aware, in his dreams, of a sense of confusion and loneliness and longing.

On Friday evening, he called Steve to ask him over for an impromptu order-in-pizza on Saturday, and Steve agreed. He told Elliott he had just received some potentially good news he was anxious to share but would wait until they got together. Elliott was, of course, curious, and had a mental flash that the news might involve an old flame returning to Steve's life as had happened with Rick. He then wondered why he would even think such a thing and chose not to pursue it.

❦

Steve arrived promptly at six carrying a six-pack of imported beer.

"Pizza's not pizza without beer," he explained, and Elliott agreed. He already had two six-packs of domestic beer in the refrigerator in anticipation but didn't say anything, figuring they would serve as a back-up if needed.

He called in the pizza order after checking with Steve on his preferences, which he was pleasantly surprised to find matched his own, right down to the anchovies. Taking two beers out of the carton, he put the rest in the refrigerator and returned to the living room, where Steve stood at the window enjoying the view.

"Mind if I come over sometime and do some sketches from your balcony?" he asked.

"Be my guest," Elliott said, uncapping the beers and handing one to him. They stood side-by-side looking out over the city.

"Amazing," Steve said. "I love the view from mountaintops. California's got tons of them. Chicago's flat as a pancake, but you can get the same effect from the thirty-fifth floor of a condo."

"Never thought of it that way," Elliott replied, grinning. Actually, he'd had the same impression when he sensed John at the window or on the balcony.

They sat next to each other on the sofa and small-talked for a while until Elliott said, "So, tell me your news."

Steve took a long swig of his beer. "A gallery wants to show my work! I'd been in touch with a couple galleries before I moved here, and Thursday night I met with one of them. They liked my portfolio and said they'd like to put me on their schedule of featured new artists."

Elliott reached over and laid a hand on Steve's leg. "That's fantastic!" he said. "I'm really glad for you. Where's the gallery?"

"It's in the...What do they call it?...the River North area, on Superior near Wells. A really nice place. Needless to say, I'm excited about it. I never expected things to happen so fast."

"Did they give you a date yet?"

Steve shook his head. "No, not yet. Probably won't be for a couple of months, but hey, I can wait! We'll have to work out what paintings to show, and I'll have to send for some from my folks. I don't know if you're into art galleries, but maybe you'd like to go down there with me sometime before the show to take a look at the place."

"Sure," Elliott replied, "I'd like that." He did like and appreciate art, but he hardly considered himself an art connoisseur; and he couldn't remember the last time he had actually been to a real gallery. Since his mother had given up trying to stuff culture into him like cornbread dressing into a turkey when he was a teen, most of his gallery experience had been with art displays at street fairs.

He'd just sat down again after getting them another beer when the front desk called to say the pizza man had arrived. Elliott okayed his coming up and went to the front door, fishing out his wallet on the way. They ate at the dining room table, which was the only concession to formality. Paper towels, the opened pizza box and fingers substituted for napkins, plates and silverware; neither used a glass for their beer. Steve seemed as comfortable with the arrangement as

Elliott was.

As they ate, they exchanged information on family backgrounds. Steve's dad had been career military, and he'd spent most of his early years bouncing from country to country. Like Elliott, he had a younger sister, but also a younger—and gay—brother, which Elliott found interesting, since he'd always wished he'd had a brother, no offense to Cessy. Steve's dad was now retired, his mom ran a small beauty shop in Big Bear; his sister was married with three kids of her own, and his brother lived in LA and had been HIV positive for six years.

"He's doing really well," Steve said. "You'd never know he was positive to look at him, and his meds have everything under control. But I do worry about him. Probably more than I should."

"Hey," Elliott said, "he's your brother. You're entitled to worry."

Though Elliott had a couple of HIV positive acquaintances and had known several more who had died of AIDS over the years, he'd never been really close to anyone living with the disease, and couldn't fully comprehend how hard it must be for Steve...or his brother.

The conversation turned to Elliott and his family background, and as always, Elliott played down his family's wealth and connections. He talked instead about Cessy and their upbringing by parents who were gone much of the time and generally preoccupied when they were not.

"Did you miss that?" Steve asked. "The closeness to your family?"

Elliott shook his head. "Not really. Cessy and I are really close, and it's not as though our parents didn't...don't...care about us. They were just busy with other things."

Steve wiped his mouth with a paper towel then took another piece of pizza from the box. "I guess I was really lucky," he said. "My whole family is really close. They know about Manny and me, but we don't talk about it much. They just accept it, and they've been incredibly supportive, especially of Manny."

Before Steve arrived, Elliott had brought *Moonrise* from the den and laid it on the coffee table. When they'd finished eating, they returned to the living room with their beer, and Elliott tapped it with an index finger as they sat down.

"I've been meaning to ask you," he said, very aware of John's presence. "I came across a couple photos in here that really interested me, and I was wondering if you might be able to figure out where they were taken."

Steve grinned, reaching over to pick up the book. "I can try," he said. "But no guarantees."

Elliott returned the grin. "None expected," he said.

"Which photos, exactly?"

"I marked them." He indicated the three pieces of torn envelope sticking from the book.

Steve gave a nod and opened the book to the first tab.

"I know that first one was in the same spot as your painting," Elliott said, "but I was wondering just where it was? Near Barstow? Or Big Bear?"

"Big Bear," Steve replied. "If you turned around from where this was taken, you could see Big Bear Lake." He moved on to the second photo, the single pine tree on the rock outcropping.

"I know there are a hell of a lot of trees out there," Elliott said, "but…"

Steve grinned. "Well, I don't recognize this specific tree, but I know there are some interesting bluffs and rock formations near Fawnskin—that's a really small town just on the other side of Big Bear Lake from Moonridge —and it could have been taken around there."

Elliott looked at him with a raised eyebrow. "You're not making these names up, are you?" he asked. "Fawnskin? Moonridge?"

Steve raised his right hand. "Swear t'God," he said. "Fawnskin's got maybe four hundred people, and Moonridge's a comparative metropolis with almost three thousand. How they can stand to live in such close quarters I'll never understand." He grinned. "I'll bet you've got that many living in this building alone."

"Not quite," Elliott said. "This block—close."

Steve shrugged and returned to *Moonrise* and the final tab, the photo of the new moon balanced on the sagging roof.

"This one I'll bet I know," Steve said. "It's just off Highway Thirty-eight going into Fawnskin. I'm into barns, and I always wanted to paint this one but never got around to it." He looked at Elliott closely. "Interesting that you should pick out three photos taken so close to one another. Are you sure you haven't been there?"

Elliott shook his head. "Coincidence," he said.

"Uh-huh."

"I know this sounds a little odd, but could you check and see if you can tell if any others might have been taken in the same area?"

Steve gave him a sidelong glance, pursed his lips and went back to the first page of the book. He picked out half a dozen other photos he was pretty sure were taken within ten miles of Big Bear Lake; and when he'd finished, he closed the book, set it on the table, looked closely at Elliott again and said, "Mind telling me what this is all about?"

Elliott felt not unlike a kid caught with his hand in the cookie jar, and he hoped he wasn't blushing.

"You know that picture I had of the guy from the emergency room when I had my accident? The one I was trying to see if anyone recognized?"

"Yeah."

"Well, I'm pretty sure he was from the same area as Hill photographed."

"Based on…?"

Elliott was positive he was blushing now, which disturbed him, since he was not the type to blush. "I don't know. I just feel it."

Steve grinned at him again. "Maybe he's trying to tell you something."

"Hill? What would…?"

"Not Hill. The guy from the ER."

"He's dead."

75

"So you said. But there are more things 'twixt heaven and earth, as they say. I never really did get a very good look at his photo. If you think he might be from around Big Bear, maybe if I could see it again..."

"You wouldn't mind?" Elliott said, getting up even as he spoke. He hurried into the den and took the manila envelope from between two books where he'd stashed it, removing the photo as he returned to the living room. He handed it to Steve, who looked from it to him.

"Nice-looking guy," he said. "A real shame he's dead. How did he die, do you know?"

"Murdered," Elliott replied. "Shot six times and left in an alley, with no ID."

Steve sighed, shook his head and studied the photo more carefully.

"Have you seen him before?" Elliott asked, and Steve furrowed his brows as he studied John's face.

"Geez, it's really hard to say. I could have. He looks like a lot of guys I've seen. But I don't actually know him. If I've seen him, it was just in passing, maybe in a store or at a gas station. An awful lot of people come through Big Bear all the time."

"So, you don't think he lived there?"

Steve shook his head slowly. "Of course, I didn't know everybody who lived there, but I'd guess if he did it probably wasn't right in town—not Big Bear City, anyway. It's possible he lived in the town of Big Bear—they're all of five miles apart, but I think I know most of the locals. And of course, a lot of city people have cabins in the area and just come up from time to time. As I told you, there are a lot of places around there for people to lose themselves if they want to."

"I wonder why he'd want to."

"Beats me," Steve said. "Everybody's got a story—who knows what his might be? The fact that he ended up getting murdered might be a pretty good indication that he had one."

"Point," Elliott agreed.

Steve returned the photo, and Elliott put it back in the envelope.

"Well, I wish you luck in finding him. What do you do now?"

"Since my brother-in-law is a homicide detective, I'll ask him if he can send it to the various police jurisdictions in the Big Bear area. It can't hurt."

"It's a reach," Steve said.

"I know. But better something than nothing."

Steve stifled a yawn then gave him an embarrassed smile. "Sorry," he said. "It's not the company. I got up at dawn this morning, and the beer didn't help. I'd better get going."

"You have to go? I thought you could spend the night."

Steve grinned. "Well, I didn't want to be presumptuous."

Elliott, still standing, extended his hand to pull Steve off the couch. "Consider it an open invitation," he said.

❋

76

— *I'm really not trying to be difficult,* the soundless voice said from the blackness of sleep.

— *I know.*

— *And I know you want me to know more than I do, or to react to things that I have no basis for reacting to. It's hard.*

— *I understand, but I'd think you'd be able to make associations more easily. Why is it that I get such a strong sense of your presence when I go through the Hill photographs, yet Steve's painting of the same area elicited no response?*

— *I don't know. They're just...different.*

— *Are you G. J. Hill?*

— No!

Elliott was startled and baffled by the same sudden, strong charge of emotion as he had felt when John recognized himself in the photograph.

— *How do you know?*

— *I told you before—I may not know who I am, but I do know who I am not. I am not G. J. Hill!*

CHAPTER 7

❦

He awoke in the morning to find Steve propped up on one elbow, watching him.

"Good morning," Elliott said, wiping his hand across his eyes.

Steve grinned down at him. "Do you know you talk in your sleep?".

"I do?" Elliott was both shocked and mildly embarrassed.

Steve nodded.

"About what?"

"Pictures," Steve said. "And G. J. Hill. I didn't catch it all."

Elliott reached with one hand and ran it across Steve's smooth chest, fascinated as always by the color and feel of his skin. "I'm really sorry. I had no idea I talked in my sleep. Have I been doing it all along?"

"This was the first time I was aware of it." Steve reciprocated the caress.

"In a hurry for coffee?" Elliott asked.

"Not particularly."

"Good."

✽

It was early Sunday evening before he had a chance to call Brad. He waited until after seven, when he was pretty sure the big game of the day was over. When they didn't have company over, the family usually ate on TV trays in front of the set while they watched the game, so he didn't worry about possibly disturbing their dinner.

Cessy answered the phone, which tied him up for a good five minutes before she transferred him over to Brad.

"Hi, Elliott, what's up?"

"I'm pretty sure I might have a lead on our John Doe," he said.

"Really? That's great! Who do you think he is?"

"I don't have a name," he admitted, "but I ran into a guy in one of the bars who just moved here not long ago from southern California—the Big Bear area. He's pretty sure the guy in the picture is from there. He recognized him right away." He was lying, but hoped Brad couldn't tell. He kept going. "I know, it's a

78

real coincidence, but the gay world is pretty tight-knit, so it's worth checking out."

"Big Bear, huh?" Brad asked.

"Yeah. It's in San Bernardino County, which is a pretty big area. But maybe if you could get it to the county sheriff and the local law enforcement agencies around Big Bear—Big Bear, Big Bear Lake, maybe even Barstow—there's a chance he might be recognized even if he hasn't been reported missing. The fact he was murdered might mean he'd been in some sort of trouble out there, too." He knew he was stretching, but he was willing to try anything.

Brad was silent a moment before saying, "Well, I suppose it wouldn't hurt. There's still been nothing on him from this end. I'll see what I can do."

"Great! I really appreciate it. I just want to give this guy a name, and let his family know what happened to him."

"Yeah," Brad said, "me, too."

❦

Elliott checked his computer for messages after he got home from work Monday and felt a surge of excitement to find one with "G. J. Hill" in the subject line. He quickly opened it.

> Mr. Smith,
>
> Thank you for your inquiry regarding G. J. Hill. As is our policy, we have forwarded it to Mr. Hill for his possible response.
>
> We appreciate your interest in Retina Press.

There were three other messages, none of them from G. J. Hill. Actually hearing from Hill wasn't as important as it had been before he'd met Steve, but considering John's attraction to Hill's work, it would be nice to see if there might be some direct connection between the two.

Checking his e-mail again on Tuesday, he found a message titled Automated Response that said,

> I'm currently on assignment but will respond to your message as soon as I return. Thanks. G. J. Hill.

Elliott wondered about the "assignment," but it was the date the message was posted that caught his attention—roughly two months earlier. Whatever the assignment Hill was on, it was obviously a long one.

And he was more than a little disturbed when, for the first time while he was awake, he heard John's silent voice, somewhere in his mind, saying, *I am* not *G. J. Hill!* The fact he had expressed himself as strongly only once before—when he recognized himself in the morgue photograph—was clear evidence that while John might not be G. J. Hill there was a strong connection to him.

79

But with Hill not available to clarify matters, Elliott had few options other than to wait to see what Brad turned up.

Still, on the far outside chance that Hill might return soon, or that he might be checking his e-mail from wherever he was, Elliott used the address on the automated response to send off another note. For the subject line, in an effort to catch Hill's eye among all the other messages undoubtedly awaiting him, he chose *Seeking John*.

> Mr. Hill,
>
> I am looking for information on a friend or acquaintance of yours whom you've not seen or heard from since about the time you left on your last assignment. His first name is John, and he may have told you he was coming to Chicago. I regret to report that he was murdered here and, because we have no last name for him, was listed as a John Doe. We have strong reason to believe that he had some direct association with you. Any information you can provide would be most appreciated.
>
> Thank you,
> Elliott Smith

He rather hoped that the use of the "royal we" would imply some connection to a governmental agency, which might elicit a response more readily than a note from a private citizen. He looked the note over, then sent it. If Hill was the only one to use his computer and had no way to check his mail while on assignment, the message would sit there until he returned, but at least Elliot felt he'd tried. He wasn't sure how, if anyone did respond, he was going to explain how Hill's name had come up in the first place, or on what basis he assumed a connection. He decided he'd handle that when and if the time came.

The next couple of days passed quickly. He talked to Steve on Wednesday, and to Cessy both Wednesday and Thursday, but heard nothing directly from Brad and didn't want to press him. There was no response to his e-mail to Hill, other than a duplicate of the automated "I'm not available" response he'd gotten the first time.

He had become so accustomed to John's presence—constant but low-key— that he now seldom thought of it. The exception was when he had to go into the basement at the Sheffield Building on Thursday and was aware of a strong surge of that presence, which puzzled him. Why should that place still elicit such a response? Perhaps, he thought, this time it was his *own* general reaction to the whole incident.

But that night, shortly after falling asleep...

— *There's more.*

— More to what?

— To the basement.

— What do you mean?

— I don't know. I just know there's more, somehow.

Elliott was never quite sure why or how it was that, with few exceptions, each morning after having had a conversation with John, he was usually able to remember it so clearly, whereas his memories of other dreams were seldom so detailed. Nonetheless, he left for work earlier than usual Friday morning to spend some time in the basement.

John's presence was clear in the laundry-and-equipment half of the room, though at nowhere near the intensity of before the discovery of Donnelly's body, and not specifically concentrated in any particular area. Elliott had no idea what he might be looking for. The building's blueprints showed there were no other false walls, and the entire basement had been totally redone since he took possession. After a while, he gave up in frustration and left.

On returning home from work later, he found a message from Brad asking him to call. He did so immediately, and after the usual five-minute buffer conversation with Cessy, Brad came on the line.

"Brad! Anything?"

"I'm afraid not," Brad said. "I faxed the photo and his physical description to the San Bernardino Sheriff's Office and to the police departments in Barstow and every town around Big Bear big enough to have a police department. Nothing. So, either he wasn't from around there or he kept a very low profile and never had a run-in with the law. There was one missing-persons report filed with the sheriff's office by someone in San Luis Obispo on a guy who roughly fit John Doe's description, but there was no photo. They said they would check it out, but..."

Elliott sighed. "Well, it was worth a shot," he said. "I really appreciate your going to all this trouble."

"Hey, no trouble," Brad replied. "We want to give this guy a name as badly as you do. I'll let you know if anything else should come up."

"Thanks, Brad. Tell the kids hi for me."

"Will do. See you later."

His spirits followed his arm's downward arc as he hung up the phone. All the doubts he had thought he had resolved about John and the question of his reality came flooding back. He thought back on his sleep-talks with John, and the fact that he had "heard" John while awake. Was John becoming more communicative, more real, or was his own mental stability deteriorating at an accelerating rate? How could he possibly know?

He'd been so sure John was from the Big Bear area, only to find—well, he told himself, John still could be from that area and Brad was right that he just hadn't had any contact with the police. The thought provided less comfort than he would have preferred.

He found himself going into the den to turn on his computer, figuring he might as well become totally depressed while he was at it.

The minute he saw the name "G. J. Hill" in his inbox, his spirits shot skyward, and he immediately clicked on it.

> Mr. Smith,
>
> While checking G. J.'s mail, I came across your note. Please tell me more about this John Doe, and describe him. As G. J.'s partner, I might be able to help you.
>
> Sincerely,
> Rob Cole

Without a second's hesitation, Elliott hit "Reply" and began typing.

> Mr. Cole,
>
> Thanks for your reply...I assume Mr. Hill is still on assignment.
>
> The man in question was murdered on March 22 on Chicago's north side. He was 5'11" tall, 175 lbs, brown hair and brown eyes, and somewhere in his mid-to-late 30s. He had no scars or tattoos, and perfect teeth with no cavities. I have a post-mortem photo which I can send if you think he sounds familiar.
>
> Could you please let me know one way or the other?
>
> Thanks again.
> Elliott Smith

He considered sending John's photo along with his e-mail but thought better of it; he'd wait for Cole's reply first. He realized, of course, that except for the detail of having perfect teeth , John's description would easily fit any number of people. Still...

He tapped the enter key.

So, he reflected as he sat staring at the screen, G. J. Hill had a partner. He wondered if Cole meant that strictly in a business sense. Somehow, he doubted it, which meant G. J. Hill *was* gay. He also found it interesting that Cole referred to Hill by his initials. He was a little surprised by his sense of anticipation, and wondered briefly how much of it might be John's.

Finally pulling himself back into the moment, he got up to go to the kitchen to see about dinner.

❦

The nice thing about TV dinners was that they didn't require dirtying many dishes, but the dishwasher was nevertheless loaded with silverware, cups and glasses; so after he'd tossed the empty carton and rinsed his silverware and glass, he put them and powdered detergent into the machine and turned it on.

Returning to the den, he picked up the TV remote, but as he passed his computer leaned over the keyboard and moved the cursor to his email icon. Once again, the name "G. J. Hill" and Hill's return address leapt off the screen. He quickly put the remote aside and sat down at the computer to open the message. It was brief and to the point.

> Mr. Smith,
>
> Please call me immediately when you get this. I need to talk with you about your message. 805-896-7897.
>
> Rob Cole

Elliott immediately took his cell phone from his pocket and punched in Cole's number. The phone rang three times before he heard the receiver picked up and a singularly expressionless "Hello?"

"Rob Cole? This is Elliott Smith. You asked me to call."

"Yes. You say you have a photograph of an unidentified body? Could you send it to me?"

The man's tone struck Elliott as being remarkably casual, and he was a little curious as to why Cole didn't ask more about what John Doe looked like before asking to be sent the photo. Still, he felt a rush of anticipation mixed with an unexpected sense of apprehension.

"So, you think you or Mr. Hill might know who this guy is?"

There wasn't a second of hesitation before: "I'm afraid it might be G. J. He went missing sometime between March sixteenth and the twenty-first."

The anticipation vanished, but the apprehension expanded to take its place. John had been adamant in saying he was not G. J. Hill, but that Hill had disappeared within days of John's being murdered couldn't possibly be coincidental.

"I'm sure it couldn't be him," Elliott said. "The man I'm looking for is named John."

"That's why I didn't say anything in response to your first message," Cole explained. "I couldn't allow myself to think it might be G. J. But then I realized that I don't know of anyone named John who disappeared, and I'm sure G. J. didn't, either. But G. J. *is* missing.

"I left here on the sixteenth to visit my parents, and when I got back on the twenty-third, I found a note from G. J. saying he had to be gone for a few days, but that he'd be back on the twenty-fourth. But he wasn't, and I haven't heard a word from him."

Elliott, still totally confused, said, "Did you contact the police?"

He heard a deep sigh.

"Not right away. G. J. does this—just goes off for a while—every now and then. He'll get an assignment to do a shoot in Brazil, and he'll just take off. I've gotten used to it. But he's always told me when and where he was going, and this time he didn't. After two weeks, I contacted the police and filed a missing persons report."

That he'd waited two weeks before reporting Hill missing struck Elliott as more than a little unusual, until he remembered the report Brad had mentioned, with the guy fitting John's general description. But that had been from San Luis Obispo.

"Where do you live?" Elliott asked. "I see you've got an LA exchange."

"Yes, but it's a cell phone. We actually live in our motor home, and we're always on the move. Right now we're—I'm—in Northern California, near San Luis Obispo. G. J.'s doing a book of photos of the coast along US-One. I took the car, and G. J. was going to spend the time here going over proof sheets."

Elliott was trying to make some sense out of the whole thing. "You and G. J. are lovers?"

"Yes, and business partners. We've been together two years now."

"Well, I really don't mean to offend you, but is it possible G. J. might have been seeing someone else?"

"I don't think so. I'd have known, I'm sure. Of course, he could have met someone while I was gone, but..."

From what Cole was saying, and from his overall attitude, it struck Elliott that his relationship with Hill was something less than a storybook romance.

"And you have no idea where he went, or why?"

"No. And he didn't take his camera equipment, which was unusual. He always takes his cameras. I should have called the police sooner, but as I say, he's done this before and he's always shown up eventually."

"You contacted his family, of course," Elliott said, realizing he was making assumptions.

"He doesn't have any family."

"What about friends?"

"We travel so much, we're never in any one place long enough to really make friends."

Again, Elliott was struck by Cole's casual tone. And he thought again of John's denial of being G. J. Hill.

"I'm curious why you didn't provide a photo when you filed your missing persons report."

"Because I don't have one," Cole said. "G. J. refuses to be photographed. Ever. I know, that's pretty strange for a professional photographer, but I guess we all have our little quirks."

Elliott thought it strange, too, but didn't say so. "Well, don't jump to any conclusions until you see the photo," he said instead. "I'll scan it right now and send it to you as an e-mail attachment. I'm sure it isn't G. J., but please let me know if you recognize him anyway."

"I will. Thanks."

84

"Okay, it'll be coming along in about five minutes."

"Thanks again."

He heard the click of the call being disconnected.

Getting up from the computer as he returned his cell phone to his pocket, he went for John's photo. He was still in a very strange and unusual state he couldn't really describe, but he was now clearly aware part of whatever he was feeling came from John.

Scanning the photo, putting it into a file and e-mailing it took slightly longer than the five minutes he'd promised, so he didn't bother including a message with the photo. He sent it and sat back, waiting—which he realized was foolish. There was no way he could expect an instant response.

He turned the sound up full on the computer so he could hear the "ding" of an incoming message and got up to turn on the TV. He had no idea what he was watching, and kept looking at the clock every several seconds. Nothing. After an hour, he got up to look, in case he'd missed an incoming mail notice. There was none, of course, and he was mildly irked for having worked himself up into such a state. This was definitely not like him, and he rationalized that it had to be John's influence.

An hour passed, then two; and with every passing minute Elliott, to his dismay, became more and more impatient. The impatience turned gradually to anger. John wasn't G. J. Hill, but either Cole recognized him or he didn't. If he didn't, why didn't he have the courtesy to call and say so?

Suddenly realizing he hadn't given Cole his phone number, he was strongly tempted to call him back but thought better of it. If Cole had recognized John, he'd have e-mailed.

Elliott's spontaneous dislike of Cole grew.

The more he thought about it, the stranger his conversation with the man seemed. Either Cole was amazingly good at concealing his emotions, or he was a pretty cold fish. Of course, Elliott had no way of knowing what Cole's and Hill's relationship may have been like, but he felt strongly that if he had a lover who had gone missing, he'd have been just a little more emotional about it than Cole seemed to be.

Cole said he hadn't responded immediately to Elliott's first message because he didn't think John could have been G. J. Hill, but the coincidence of the date of John's murder and Cole's returning from his trip had piqued his interest.

And even if Hill did disappear from time to time for photo assignments, when Cole saw he hadn't taken his camera equipment, wouldn't that have rung a very large bell? Why would he wait two weeks before filing a report? It hadn't been until Elliott mentioned the photograph that Cole seemed to show much concern.

Strange, indeed.

Just before he went to bed, against his better judgement and chalking it up to John's influence, he sent another e-mail to Cole.

85

Mr. Cole,

I'd rather hoped to have heard from you regarding the photograph, and would appreciate your dropping me a note even if you did not recognize him.

Thanks
Elliott Smith

Still abnormally and inexplicably agitated, he went to bed.

❊

— *Why didn't he answer you?*
   — *I don't know. He probably didn't recognize the photograph.*
Elliott sensed John's deep disappointment.
   — *I don't like him.*
   — *Any specific reason?*
   — *No. You don't like him, either. Do you have a reason?*
   — *No.*
   — *Will we ever find me?*
There was apparently something about the mind's workings during sleep that made it impossible for Elliott to lie.
   — *I don't know. I hope so. Are you absolutely sure you're not G. J. Hill?*
   — *I am not G. J. Hill. I know it.*

❊

Though he normally did not turn on the computer before going to work in the morning, he did so the next morning, on the basis that California time was two hours earlier than Chicago's, and Cole could have replied after Elliott had gone to bed. He hadn't, and Elliott went off to work feeling both disgruntled, and angry at himself for being so. And the more he thought about it—though he tried very hard not to—his anger shifted from himself to Cole. The least Cole could have done would be to have given him the courtesy of saying "You're right. It's not G. J." But nothing at all?

Thursday morning, he was helping steady the last of the porch/patio doors as Sam jostled it into position when his cell phone rang. Bracing the door with one hand, he fished out his phone with the other.

"Elliott Smith."

"Elliott, this is Brad. I thought you'd like to know we have an ID on your John Doe."

The sudden force of John's presence was like opening a door to a hurricane-force wind. It was so powerful Elliott nearly lost his grip on the door.

"You do? How did you find out? Who is he?"

"We got a call this morning from the San Luis Obispo police. The guy's name is G. J. Hill."

86

CHAPTER 8

❧

That's impossible," Elliott blurted. "How can they be sure?"

"Did you send the photo I gave you to Hill's partner?"

"Yes, but...it can't be G. J. Hill."

"Well, his partner says it is, and he should know. You sent the guy the photo—and I'm going to want to talk to you about how and why you picked out this Hill guy in the first place."

Elliott was well aware he was teetering on the edge of a very steep and slippery slope. "I sent it because I had reason to believe Hill might have known him. It can't be Hill himself."

There was a slight pause, then: "So you said. But I want to know how you can be so sure."

"Well, I can't, of course," Elliott admitted. "Look, can I call you tonight when I get home? I'm right in the middle of a project here, and..." And he needed time to think.

"Sure, but be sure you do. I've got the feeling there's something going on here I'm not aware of."

Elliott could not have agreed more, but said nothing except "Later, then," and flipped off his phone.

He stood with the phone in one hand, propping the door with the other, totally confused. He had never before in his life experienced anything similar to his—or was it John's?—reaction to Brad's call. But whomever's reaction it was, he was totally unprepared for it.

He became aware that Sam was looking at him strangely. "You okay, Elliott?"

He nodded and put his cell phone back in his pocket. It took all his willpower to turn back to the task at hand. He felt as though he were a salmon trying to swim upstream through the force of John's presence. His own confusion and frustration were compounded and amplified, he was sure, by John's similar reaction. There were no words in his head, but the John's powerful turmoil combined with his own was overwhelming.

He managed to get through the day, but the minute he got into his car for

87

the ride home, the floodgates of his mind opened; and John's presence came rushing back, one thought in particular—John's—coming through loud and clear,

— *I am not G. J. Hill!*

Elliott was now well beyond confused. Cole had identified John's photo as being G. J. Hill. How could that be possible? John was adamant he wasn't G. J. Hill, but if Hill's own lover said he was...

Elliott's mind was spinning out of control. The whole mystery reminded him of a popular mind-teaser game he had played in his college days that involved a detailed mystery story known only to one of the group, who took the role of guide.

The guide sketched in only the roughest of background information, and the rest of the players had to figure out the entire story by asking questions to which the guide could only answer yes, no or "not relevant."

In this case, Elliott was in the position of trying to solve the mystery of John's identity only through finding answers to his specific questions. Unlike the game, however, there was no guide. While John was the key to everything, he was as much in the dark as Elliott, though he could recognize and acknowledge the things Elliott got right. He could also let Elliott know when he was totally off-base, such as thinking John might be G. J. Hill, but without knowing details as to why. He had more than once, since waking in the hospital, had the distinct impression he was doing a high-wire act without either a balance pole or a net. It was not a pleasant sensation.

Once again came the unacceptably disturbing thought that he was basing everything on his total acceptance of John's existence. But if he didn't—if, after all this time, he turned out to be only a figment of Elliott's imagination—the implications of that never ceased to frighten him.

He suddenly realized he was gripping the steering wheel so tightly his knuckles were white, and forced himself to relax, pushing his doubts of John's existence back into the dark corner from whence they'd come. There were simply too much evidence, ephemeral and elusive as it might be, supporting his conviction that John was real.

Which returned him to one basic question. If John was real, and was not G. J. Hill, why would Rob Cole say he was?

Even though he'd never set eyes on the guy, there was something about Cole he instinctively disliked. He didn't know how much stock he could put into the fact that John appeared to share his impression.

Letting his mind sort through what little he knew of Hill and Cole, he found an admittedly wild scenario taking shape. Hill, from everything he knew, was pretty much a recluse. That he lived in a motor home and therefore might not have a permanent address made being reclusive a bit easier. But would a recluse have a live-in lover?

Cole had said Hill refused to have his photo taken, and his books contained neither a bio nor a photo. What would prevent Cole from saying John's photo was Hill when it wasn't? He could just show the photo of a John Doe—conveniently supplied by Elliott—to the police and claim it was Hill.

But why would he do that?

The only plausible reason would be if Hill were dead and Cole knew it, had maybe even been involved. Fingerprints from the motor home or anything Hill owned would verify John's contention that he—the man in the photo—wasn't Hill, but what were the chances the police would bother to take fingerprints on a simple missing persons case? Slim to none.

So, if Hill was by some chance dead and Cole was responsible, being handed a photo of a John Doe who died a thousand miles from California would provide him with a solid alibi, especially if he could prove he'd been in California at the time John was murdered.

But then why, Elliott asked himself, would Cole even have bothered to report Hill missing? He could have just driven off in the motor home—no one would know.

No. Elliott took a mental step backward. Someone would have had to know Hill had disappeared sooner or later. The motor home's license would come up for renewal, or Cole would have tried to sell it. And Hill's publisher would eventually have become curious enough to start looking around. So, reporting him missing was a logical thing for Cole to do. Especially if he had done something with Hill's body to guarantee it would never be found.

With no idea of what Hill's and Cole's relationship might have been like, it was quite possible, from what he had picked up of Cole's attitude, that the man had seen Hill as nothing but a meal ticket.

He forced his mind away from his wild speculations. Even the concept of deus ex machina had its limits.

The adrenaline of the speculations faded, and rationality took over once again. Elliott, John's presence notwithstanding, still considered logic to be the cornerstone of his life. There had to be some logic to everything, and there was none here. People didn't just go around killing their partners and then conveniently being handed a photo of some far-off John Doe to be used as an alibi. Life was strange, but not that strange.

And how was he going to explain all this to Brad?

The one thing of which he was absolutely sure was that John was beginning to border on an obsession, and taking up far too much of his life.

✳

He got home and fought off the urge—whether his or John's he couldn't tell—to call Brad the minute he walked in the door. It was time, he decided, to retake control of his life and the situation.

He deliberately went into the kitchen to fix himself a drink—a strong one—then into the den to watch the news—or rather, to stare in the general direction of the TV—and to think about what he was going to tell Brad. He wasn't the least bit hungry, but he waited until he was fairly sure Brad had finished dinner.

He was just reaching for the phone when it rang.

"Hello?"

"Elliott," Brad's voice was that of a policeman, not a brother-in-law. "I thought you were going to call me."

"I was waiting until I figured you'd finished dinner," he protested, feeling more than a little guilty. "I was just picking up the phone when you called."

"So, are you ready to tell me what's going on? Who is this G. J. Hill? How do you know about him? What makes you think there's any connection between him and this particular John Doe? And why, since Hill was reported missing and his partner claims John Doe is Hill, are you so convinced that it's not?"

Elliott took a deep breath.

"Okay," he began, "I know this is going to sound really strange, and I can't possibly explain it rationally, so I hope you'll give me a little leeway here."

"I'm listening."

"G. J. Hill is a photographer. He's published three books of photos of the deserts, mountains and seashore around southern California. I told you I'd shown the photo you gave me to a guy from around Big Bear, who said he recognized him and that he thought the guy was a photographer without my having mentioned it."

He hated lying, and especially to a police detective who was also his brother-in-law, but he had no choice. The part about John's being a photographer was a way to shore up an incredibly flimsy story. He just prayed he could get away with it and avoid having to give Brad reason to think he was totally crazy.

"I just took a really wild swing and thought I'd try to contact G. J. Hill on the far outside chance that he might possibly know some other photographers in the same area. I had no idea at all that Hill himself was missing, but when I got in touch with his...partner...something just didn't sound right."

"I can agree to that," Brad said, and Elliott wasn't sure if he was joking or serious, so he just forged ahead.

"Look, my gut feelings, however strange they may have been, led me to Hill, and the fact that Hill happened to be missing is admittedly an almost unbelievable coincidence. But the same feelings tell me that, regardless of what his partner says, our John Doe is not G. J. Hill."

Brad's skepticism was clear in the tone of his next comment. "Based on what evidence?"

Elliott sighed, feeling as though he were a male Alice descending into the rabbit hole. "Look, I know it sounds crazy, but..." and he proceeded to outline the scenario he'd devised in his car.

"I realize this is asking a hell of a lot," he concluded, "but would it be at all possible to check with the San Luis Obispo police to see just how carefully they looked into this guy's story? If they're just taking his word for it, could you ask them to look just a little further, or get some verification other than his word that the photograph is Hill?"

There was a long, uncomfortable silence from Brad's end of the line, then: "I really don't know, Elliott. That story is pretty farfetched, though admittedly interesting. Our main objective is to solve one murder investigation, not to open up the possibility of another two thousand miles away. I'm not sure how the San Luis Obispo police would react to our questioning their thoroughness.

"Identifying our John Doe is all well and good, but this is a murder investigation, after all. We want to know who killed him."

"Well, the two things are hardly mutually exclusive," Elliott pointed out.

"Of course not," Brad agreed. "Identifying him would certainly let us know where to start looking for his killer or killers, but finding out who killed him would probably be just as effective a way of telling us who he was."

"So, how is that part of the investigation going?"

"Not well, I'm afraid. One of the first things we do is to compare the markings on the bullets used in a crime to see if they might match those from previous crimes. In this case—nothing, other than that all the bullets came from the same gun.

"It's pretty obvious this wasn't just a coincidental robbery-shooting. The fact that Doe was stripped of anything that might help to identify him is a pretty clear indication that whoever did it knew he wasn't from around here. They seemed pretty confident that by stripping him of everything, we'd never be able to find out who he was—which also leads us to believe that he probably didn't have any sort of criminal past that we'd be able to trace."

"So, finding out who he is moves up to top priority, then, I'd assume," Elliott said.

"Yeah, I guess you're right."

Another long pause followed. Finally, Brad broke the silence.

"You really feel that strongly about this Hill thing?"

"I do."

"Well, if by some chance it isn't Hill, that would mean we can't close the case. I suppose it couldn't hurt to be absolutely sure."

Elliott sighed in relief. "Thanks, Brad! I know it's crazy, but if there's any chance at all that John Doe isn't Hill, and this guy Cole is up to something..."

"I'll check it out. And Cessy's standing here at my elbow wanting to talk to you, so I'll turn you over to her."

"Okay, Brad. Thanks. I owe you."

There was the shuffling sound of the phone changing hands, then Cessy's voice. "I wanted to tell you that Mom called from Singapore. She and Dad will be back next weekend. It seems as though they've been gone forever."

He realized she was right, and felt a little guilty that he hadn't thought much about his parents in several weeks.

"And do you have any plans for two weeks from Sunday?" Cessy continued.

"Uh, not offhand, that I know of. Why? The folks planning something?"

"Well, not with us. They've got a benefit for the Chicago Symphony to go to. It's amazing. They aren't even back in town yet, and already their social calendar is filled for the next month. But Jenny's school is having a recital that same day, and we want you to come."

"Did you mention the recital to Mother?"

"Yes, but they'd already committed to attending the benefit, so..."

Elliott couldn't tell from her voice whether she was hurt that they would prefer the Chicago Symphony over their granddaughter's grade-school recital, but if she was, she didn't let it show. She was used to it.

"Sure, I'll be there. What time?"

"The recital is at three, but we can have brunch somewhere first. Would you like to invite your friend? It would be on neutral territory, and he wouldn't have to feel like he was being trapped into anything."

He suddenly realized he had not talked with Steve in a while. "Uh, it's nice of you to offer, but I'm not sure. He might be busy. Let me get back to you. And he's *a* friend...I have several."

"That's the problem. But you knew which friend I meant. That's a good sign."

She was good, Elliott had to admit that, but he wasn't sure if that was reassuring or not.

✻

The issue of not having heard from Steve was resolved shortly after he hung up from talking to Cessy and went into the kitchen to make a sandwich. He'd just opened the refrigerator door when the phone rang. He was pleased to hear Steve's voice.

"Hi, Elliott! How's it going?"

"Fine, Steve. Sorry I hadn't called for a while."

"That's okay. I should have called, but I've been really busy. I figured you were, too. Anyway, one of the reasons I'm calling is to see if you'd like to go down to the gallery with me on Saturday. I've got to drop off some photos of the paintings that are still at my folks' house to see if they want to show any of them. It's not a formal meeting. I just have to leave them for the owner."

"That'd be great," Elliott said, grateful for the chance to pull himself away from work and his obsession with John for a day. "What time?"

"I was thinking of early afternoon. And maybe, if you have the time afterward, we could go down to Navy Pier. I've never been there."

"Sure! And have you ever been to Pizzaria Uno or Due? Maybe we could make a day of it and end up there. Fantastic pizza!"

"It's a date. You think we should drive or ...what?...takethe el?"

"The el's good. We can meet at the Fullerton el stop, say around one-thirty?"

"Looking forward to it," Steve said. "Later, then."

"So long," Elliott said and hung up. For some reason he felt much better about life than he had in a while. Maybe Cessy was right after all.

✻

Friday was spent installing a new iron fence and gate in front of the building, and buying landscaping materials and lighting for the small courtyard. Tuck-pointing had been done, all the windows either painted or replaced, the foyer woodwork completely restored—the building was almost ready for showing, and Elliott was giving thought to his next project. The entire job had run well ahead of schedule and only slightly over budget, and he was more than pleased with the results. He'd call Larry Fingerhood within a couple of weeks to talk about listing it as soon as he had done all the financial calculations—basically, purchase price plus materials and labor—necessary for him to come up with a realistic asking price and profit.

He spent Friday night doing just that, and even began looking through the paper for a prospective new project. He tried very hard not to think of Rob Cole or G. J. Hill or what might be going on in far-off California. That was totally out of his control; and despite a steady sense of curiosity and concern, which he ascribed to John, he refused to get caught up in speculation.

✣

— What will they do?

   — What will who do?

   — The police. In California.

   — I have no idea. I do hope they'll look into Hill's disappearance more closely.

   — I don't trust him.

   — Who? Cole?

   — Yes. He's...not nice.

   — Why do you care?

   — I don't know.

   — Do you know anything about Cole or Hill or their relationship?

   — I'm not sure...I can't say.

   — Can't or won't?

   — Can't. There's something, but I don't know what it is or what it means.

   — Do you know if Hill is alive?

   — I don't...I...no, he's not.

Elliott awoke with a start. Looking at the digital clock on the nightstand, he saw it was quarter after three.

Hill was dead? But more important by far was that this was the first time John had ever stated something definite, other than his denial of being Hill, in response to a question. Was his memory coming back? If it was, John had to have known Hill.

Then he realized it could merely be evidence of some form of intuition or knowledge to which the dead are privy that is not shared by the living.

Whatever it was, it was yet another solid sign that John was evolving and moving toward...something.

Knowing from experience that there are few things less likely to succeed than trying to will oneself back to sleep, Elliott let his mind meander between full consciousness and the threshold of sleep until shortly after six, at which time he gave up trying and got out of bed. Pulling a pair of sweatpants out of the dresser drawer, he stumbled awkwardly into them, fully aware of his body's displeasure over his mind's having deprived it of needed rest.

He stood in front of the coffeemaker impatiently while it, oblivious to his glare, hissed and burbled and took its own good time. Tearing himself away, he put a bagel in the toaster and went to the refrigerator for a bottle of V-8 juice and a container of salmon-flavored cream cheese, wishing he had some real lox.

Drinking a glass of juice in the time between slathering the bagel with the cream cheese and filling his coffee cup, he carried his breakfast through the living room and, sliding the patio doors open, stepped out onto the balcony.

The sun hadn't gotten too far above the horizon, but the day was already warm with a moderate, steady breeze. He stood leaning against the railing, looking out at the lake. There were a few people walking along the shore, and in the small park directly below, several dogwalkers wandered about, pulled from place to place by their pets. A few had ventured onto the sand. Officially, dogs weren't allowed there, but no one seemed to pay attention to the rules.

Wiping a dab of cream cheese from the tip of his nose after taking a too-large bite of his bagel, he set his coffee down on the small glass-topped table and sat down, staring off beyond the light Saturday-morning traffic on the Lakeshore Drive to the towers of the Loop.

So, Hill was dead. He found it interesting that he had reached the point of accepting John's word. Hill was dead and John was dead, and John was not Hill. Therefore...what?

He gradually loosened his control on his thoughts, letting them wander around like sheep let out to pasture. Was there a connection between the two deaths? Or was John's knowing Hill was dead just some sort of spiritual-plane thing Elliott could not comprehend? John had always said he didn't know if he knew Hill or not. John had been killed on March 22. Cole had said he'd been out of town for a week and returned on March 23 to find Hill missing. So, if Cole had anything to do with Hill's death, it probably meant Hill was killed sometime around the sixteenth, before Cole left for what might have been an alibi-establishing trip. Kill Hill on the fifteenth, dispose of the body somewhere it was fairly certain not to be found—where or how Elliott had no idea.

Of course, if Hill were dead, it wasn't axiomatic that Cole had killed him. Cole, he speculated, could have deliberately left the door open to the possibility that Hill might have met someone while he was away. All Elliott really knew about Cole was what he'd gathered from their brief phone conversations, and just because he didn't like the guy was no reason to make a quantum leap to his being a murderer.

His mind kept churning out thoughts and possibilities, few of which had much basis in logic, and none of which he had any way of pursuing easily. It wasn't until the ringing of the phone startled him out of his reverie that he realized his bagel was gone and his coffee was cold. He hurriedly got up and went inside to answer the phone.

"Elliott, hi. It's Steve. I hope I didn't wake you."

"No, I've been up quite a while. We still on for this afternoon?"

"That's what I was calling to check on. One-thirty at the Fullerton stop, right?"

"Right. I'll be on the first car, so if you're there, watch for me. If you're not, I'll get off and wait."

"Good plan. I'm looking forward to it. And—" A shrill whistling interrupted him. "Damn, the tea kettle's boiling. I'd better go. Later."

"Later," Elliott echoed, and they hung up.

❖

Leaving his condo at exactly ten minutes to one, Elliott walked to the Thorndale el station. A train pulled up just as he reached the top of the stairs, and he was able to hurry to the first car and step on without breaking stride.

Not seeing Steve as the train pulled up at Fullerton, he got off. As he waited, he indulged his fascination for trivia. As a Brown Line train pulled in, he idly reflected that there were twenty-eight stops on the Brown Line route, thirty-three stops on the Red Line. He hadn't taken the Purple, Blue, Green, Pink and Orange Lines often enough to have made a stop count on them. That he considered himself a practical man yet was addicted to information that had little or no practical value didn't detract from the pleasure he took in it.

Seven trains later—one southbound and two northbound Brown Line, two northbound and two southbound Red Line—a southbound Brown Line pulled up to the platform and Steve got out, a large manila envelope in one hand.

"Sorry I'm late," he said. "I hope you weren't waiting too long."

"Not at all," Elliott assured him as a southbound Red Line pulled up on the other side of the platform.

❖

They got off at Chicago and walked the three blocks to the gallery. Classic renovated "Old Chicago" exterior, all chrome, glass, high ceilings and polished hardwood floors inside—it was exactly what Elliott had mentally pictured. Aside from a very stylishly dressed woman in a business suit and a couple he took, from the camera around the man's neck, to be tourists, the place was empty. They entered to a smile of recognition from the woman, directed at Steve, and went directly over to her, Steve extending his hand as they approached.

"Miss Brown, it's nice to see you."

"And you, Mr. Gutierrez," she replied warmly, taking his hand.

Steve turned to introduce Elliott. "This is my friend, Elliott Smith."

They exchanged "Pleased to meet yous" and a handshake. Miss Brown's gaze subtly moved back and forth between Steve and him, the eye movement accompanied by a small, knowing smile.

Extending the envelope, Steve said, "I've brought these for Mr. Devereux. If he'd like to give me a call when he's had a chance to look at them..."

The tourist couple moved toward the door with a smile and a nod to Miss Brown, who returned them with a pleasant "Thank you for coming by." When the couple had left, she turned her attention back to Steve.

"Thank you so much for bringing them by. Mr. Devereux is sorry he couldn't set up a definite appointment to look at them with you, but his schedule this week is just so...full."

"I understand," Steve said, giving her a dazzling smile. "I'll look forward to hearing from him."

Glancing out the window, Elliott noticed a stretch limo pull up to the curb. The passenger-side rear door opened and a woman resembling a young Katherine Hepburn, complete with slacks and a sweater tied casually across her shoulders, emerged. She turned briefly, bending to say something to the driver, then shut the door, and the limo moved off. As she approached the gallery door, Miss Brown, who apparently missed very little, laid her hand lightly on Steve's arm.

"Would you excuse me?"

Steve gave her another smile and said, "Of course."

As she started for the door to greet the new arrival, she turned slightly to say "Please do look around, if you have the time." Then she hastened away, free hand extended to the new arrival.

Steve gave Elliott a grin. "You want to take a minute to check out the place? They've got some really great things."

"Sure," Elliott said, beginning to really pay attention to his surroundings for the first time.

At first glance, it appeared to be just the one large room with perhaps twenty paintings carefully placed on cloth-covered walls. What appeared to be a large opening on the back wall actually led to a number of smaller partitioned areas. Whoever had designed the lighting had done a great job. Whereas the main room primarily relied on light from the huge front windows, the back areas were far more intimate, each picture individually and dramatically lit.

They wandered around, first in the large room, where Miss Brown and "Katherine Hepburn" were in deep conversation in front of a Georgia O'Keefe-style still life of a brilliant red anthurium in a translucent blue thin-necked vase, then moving to the back. None of the paintings bore any indication of their cost, but he could imagine. Steve was right—there were some truly beautiful works on display, and he was aware of Steve watching him as he studied the various pieces.

At one point, in one of the farthest partitioned areas, Steve stepped away from him long enough to look out into the main room, where the two women were still engrossed in their conversation. Then he came back to Elliott, took him by the shoulders and kissed him, catching him totally off-guard but hardly displeased.

Finally, Steve broke the kiss and backed away, looking at him with a grin into which Elliott read volumes.

"Hey, what can I say?" Steve asked. "Art turns me on!"

They left the gallery a few minutes later after exchanging waves and smiles with Miss Brown who, with her prospective client, had moved on down the wall to a huge abstract that looked to Elliott like it had been done by a chimpanzee with a paint roller. He had a general rule when it came to art, which he did not relay to Steve—if he couldn't tell what it was supposed to be, he wasn't interested.

"Impressive place," he said as they left the gallery. "And if you can land a couple of buyers like the limo lady, you'll have it made."

Steve grinned and shrugged. "Well, it isn't quite that easy, I'm afraid. Though it sure would be nice if it were."

When they reached the corner of LaSalle and Superior, Elliott said, "You want to catch a bus, or shall we walk part of the way? It's over a mile to the Pier, but we can catch the free trolley on Michigan Avenue."

"Sure," Steve said. "It's a nice day, won't hurt us to walk."

Their conversation was interrupted by the ringing of Steve's cell phone. Fishing it out of his pocket, he flipped it open, giving Elliot a quick "Sorry."

Elliott noted with bemusement that he and Steve had identical phones. Though he tried not to listen, he gathered the call was from Steve's brother, and from the conversational tone of Steve's voice, he gathered it was nothing urgent. Steve cut the call as short as he could and returned the phone to his pocket.

"Sorry about that," he repeated. "Manny and I try to talk a couple of times a week."

"How's he doing?" Elliott asked.

"Great. He just got back from the gym."

Elliott wondered again what it must be like to have a brother, and especially one who was HIV positive.

They continued their zigzag route from Superior and Wells to Michigan and Ohio, where they caught the free trolley to Navy Pier.

"So, this is your first time to Navy Pier?" Elliott asked as the bus traveled along Michigan Avenue.

Steve nodded. "Yeah, I'm anxious to see it. I've heard a lot about it."

"Biggest single tourist attraction in Chicago," Elliott said.

Steve raised an eyebrow. "Really? No Navy there, though, I gather?"

"Not since nineteen-forty-seven," he replied, unable to resist dipping into his trivia file. "Now the only sailors you'll see are from the Great Lakes Naval Training Station in North Chicago. And lots of commercial tour boats."

They got off the bus at the main entrance and started along the more than half-mile of shops, restaurants, concession stands and various other enterprises designed to part the tourist from his or her money. Elliott made sure they stopped at the large stained-glass window exhibit, though, and Steve, as an artist, was duly impressed.

By the time they'd traversed the length of the pier and back again, stopping for some overpriced coffee, which they drank at their leisure at tables along the edge of the dock, it was nearly five o'clock. All in all, a great afternoon, he thought. Steve was funny and sharp and obviously had more than a passing interest in him. And though he knew John wasn't far away, he was spared any overt reminders of G. J. Hill, Rob Cole and his search for John's true identity.

"So, where to now?" Steve asked as they left Navy Pier's main entrance.

"Well, it's a little early for dinner, but by the time we get there and have a drink, it might be time, if you don't mind eating early."

Steve shook his head. "Hey, I can eat anytime. How far away is the place we're going?"

"Pizzaria Uno. It's on East Ohio—not all that far, but we've already done our share of walking for the day." He glanced up at the sky and the increasing number of grey-bottomed clouds moving in from the west. "Besides, it looks like it might decide to rain."

Steve shrugged. "I don't mind a little rain, but I'm a pretty good cloud-reader, and I can almost guarantee you we don't have to worry about it."

Elliott gave him a skeptical look, then said, "If you say so. How about we compromise—take the shuttle back up to Michigan then walk the rest of the way? It's only about three blocks from there."

"Deal."

❊

Even at five-forty-five, the restaurant was nearly full. He led Steve to the menu posted by the door then gave his name and their order to the girl in charge of the seating. Informed there'd be at least a half-hour wait, they moved into the relatively small dining area and found two seats at the far end of the bar.

"What'll you have?" he asked Steve, who furrowed his brows as if in deep thought.

"Hmm. I'm not sure. Something pink and frothy with a slice of pineapple and an umbrella in it, I think."

"Great idea!" Elliott replied. "I'll just sit over there until you're finished."

"Ah, the body and the mind of a truck driver."

Elliott punched him lightly on the arm as the bartender came over to them.

"Bloody Mary," Steve said.

"Make it two," Elliott echoed.

"So, did you ever find out anything more about that guy in the photo?" Steve asked as they waited.

Well, Elliott thought, so much for not thinking of Hill today.

"Sort of," he said. He wasn't sure just how much he should or could tell Steve without risking painting himself into a corner.

Steve looked at him quizzically. "Well, that was cryptic," he said. "I withdraw the question."

"No, no, that's okay," Elliott said. "It's just that things are getting pretty complicated. I don't want to bore you with a long story."

The bartender bought their drinks, and they went through the ritual reaching-for-the-wallet routine, which Steve won. Handing the bartender a bill, he turned back to Elliott.

"I don't mind being bored every now and then," he said with a grin. "But I don't want to pry into your affairs."

Returning the grin and picking up his drink, Elliot said, "That's a big part of it. It's not my affair, really. I just sort of stumbled into it through the side door." He took a long drink from his Bloody Mary, immediately noticing the bartender had been a bit too generous with the tabasco.

They were both quiet a moment until Steve said, "Okay, you've got me. Is there more?"

Flagging down the bartender for a glass of water and waiting until he'd put out the fire in his mouth, he nodded.

"I wrote to G. J. Hill to see if he might know the guy. It seems Hill himself is missing."

Steve edged closer. "Aha! Interesting! How did you find that out? And do you think your John Doe might be G. J. Hill?"

"I emailed Hill on a whim, saying there was a John Doe here in Chicago he might possibly know. I got a reply from his lover, who struck me as someone I don't think I'd care to get to know much better, asking for more details. It turns out they live in a motor home that's in San Luis Obispo at the moment. The guy told me he'd gotten back from a trip on the twenty-third of March and Hill was gone. He hasn't been heard of since. John Doe was murdered on the twenty-second. I sent him a copy of Doe's picture and...he says it's Hill. I don't believe him."

Steve's face reflected his puzzlement. "I don't understand. Why wouldn't you believe him? The guy sure as hell should be able to recognize his own lover. From what I remember of the photo, the guy was pretty banged up but hardly unidentifiable."

"I know," Elliott said, "but..." And he proceeded to lay out the same scenario he'd presented to Brad.

"Wow!" Steve said when he had finished.

They were on their second round of drinks—Elliott had switched to a gin and tonic—when a waiter came up to them.

"Your table's ready," he said with a smile.

They followed him then sat in relative silence, enjoying their drinks, until Elliott looked up to see Steve watching him.

"What?"

"I was just thinking of something," Steve said. "You said Hill lived in a motor home?"

Elliott nodded. "That's what Cole told me."

Steve continued to stare at him, lips pursed, brows again furrowed. After a moment, he said, "Well, this may sound odd, and I'm sure it doesn't have anything to do with Hill's disappearance but...I was just thinking of the time in Big Bear I got picked up by a guy in a motor home."

Elliott was immediately curious. "Ah?" he said. "Tell all!"

Steve gave him a small smile, and Elliott, who had been surprised by a small flash of totally uncharacteristic jealousy when Steve mentioned another guy, hoped he was not reading his mind.

"Well, I was in a grocery store in Big Bear about a year ago, and this guy kept cruising me—not subtly, either." His smile broadened into a grin. "Hey, I'm only human! So, he goes through the checkout line and leaves while I'm still shopping, and when I leave the store I see this huge motor home with California plates sitting in the lot, and this guy's standing in front of the open door. When he sees me come out, he gives me a heads-up 'come hither' nod, so..." He shrugged. "I'd never done it in a motor home before. Kind of exciting, even if the guy was a kook.

"Anyway, the reason I brought it up is that I remember noticing there was a glass-fronted cabinet on one wall with a lot of camera equipment in it. While we were getting dressed afterwards, I asked him if he was a photographer, and he said no, but the guy he was traveling with was. He said he'd left him out in the woods while he came into town to pick up supplies. Do you suppose there might be any chance...?"

"Good question," Elliott responded. "You said the guy was a kook. How so, if I'm not prying into your bedroom secrets?"

Steve chuckled. "No, not a kook that way. More subtle. He asked me to take my shoes off as soon as I got in the door, for one thing, and when I did, he lined both our pairs up just so. There wasn't a gnat's eyebrow out of place, that I could see. When we got undressed, he folded his pants carefully over a chair and smoothed out the wrinkles, then did the same with his shirt. It was a T-shirt, fer chrissakes! Then when we got out of bed he spent five minutes remaking it. I realized then that he was probably doing more than 'traveling' with the guy he'd left in the woods and didn't want him to know he was out trolling for tricks the minute the guy's back was turned. But still, given everything else..."

"He sounds like a real winner," Elliott said, feeling his adrenaline level building. "Did you get the guy's name?"

Steve shook his head. "It wasn't exactly a name-exchange situation," he said. "But when you said Hill had a motor home—the guy said it was his own, by the way—it just all sort of fell into place, and a motor home might explain how Hill could spend so much time in the area without living there. And if the guy was Hill's lover, he's not only a neat freak, he's also a real prick. I don't like guys who lie, and guys who cheat on their lovers piss me off."

Elliott couldn't agree more. And he was somehow pretty sure Steve may very well have had a run in with Rob Cole.

CHAPTER 9

❧

They emerged from the restaurant to find the streets and sidewalks glistening with reflections of streetlights, headlights and neon signs on the glimmer from a recent downpour. He grinned at Steve and nudged him with the back of his hand.

"So much for cloud reading," he said.

Steve shrugged. "So, maybe Illinois clouds are different from California clouds. Besides, the rain's stopped, so I was right—we didn't have to worry about it."

Heading for the subway, Elliott said, "It's still early. What do you feel like doing?"

Steve gave him a suggestive smile. "How about you?"

Elliott could recognize a double entendre when he heard one, but he deliberately sidestepped it.

"I was figuring maybe we could go over to my place and watch a video."

"PG or X?"

"Your choice."

Steve grinned again. "Did I mention that pizza has the same effect on me as art?"

"Ah, so that's what turned you on the night you came over to my place."

"Well, hardly, but it didn't hurt."

Elliott returned the grin. "I'm beginning to suspect the phone book would do the same."

Steve sighed. "Well, I am partial to the Yellow Pages."

"So, I guess I'd better start going back to my SA meetings?"

"SA?"

"Sexaholics Anonymous—though that always strikes me as being redundant."

They descended into the subway and headed for Elliott's condo.

❈

He woke before Steve, who lay with one arm across Elliott's chest. Rather than make a move that might wake him, Elliott watched him sleep—his hair tousled,

101

mouth partly open, breathing quietly. The movement of his eyes beneath the lids indicated they were following the action of a dream. Once again he was fascinated by the coffee-with-cream color of Steve's flawless skin.

He'd heard nothing from John the entire night, which he chalked up to John's discretion, although he sensed a subtle underlying something akin to a mental aftertaste he couldn't define—disappointment? sadness? resignation? *He* certainly felt none of these things. Quite the contrary, as he watched Steve sleeping beside him, he was downright content.

Lost in his thoughts, he grew aware Steve was awake and watching him.

"Morning," Steve said, moving his arm to wipe the sleep out of his eyes.

"Good morning. Sleep okay?"

"Oh, yeah. Always."

Elliott grinned. "We should have pizza more often."

Steve returned the grin. "Don't say I didn't warn you."

"Hardly what I'd consider a warning."

Throwing back the sheets, Steve sat up and swung his legs off the bed. "If you'll excuse me for a second, the bathroom calls."

Echoing the movement on his side of the bed, Elliott said, "I'll put the coffee on while you're gone." Not bothering to put on a robe, he padded into the kitchen.

❧

They had toast and coffee on the balcony, Steve in one of Elliott's robes and Elliott in a pair of sweats and a T-shirt.

"God, I envy you this," Steve said, indicating the view with a slight gesture of his coffee cup.

"I'd trade it for your talent," Elliott replied, only half-joking.

They were quiet a moment. Then Steve said, "I had a dream last night about Hill and that asshole lover of his."

Elliott instantly switched into full-alert mode. "Really?" he said, hoping his voice didn't show the intensity of his interest. "What was it about?"

Steve shrugged. "I can't remember it now, but I think it had something to do with Hill's being dead. You told me you thought he was, but in the dream I knew it."

"Probably just the anchovies from the pizza," Elliott said, and Steve grinned; but he couldn't help but wonder why Steve had dreamed about Hill at all, let alone about his being sure Hill was dead. That was something only he and John knew.

"Maybe," Steve said. "But if Hill is dead and his lover had anything to do with it, I hope to hell Hill comes back and haunts the shit out of him."

"You believe in ghosts?" he blurted before he could catch himself. He didn't know if this was a conversation he wanted to pursue.

Steve took another sip of coffee and looked at him. "Sure. Don't you?"

"Uh, I don't know," he dissembled, having no idea what else he dared to say and feeling equal parts interested and uncomfortable.

"We had one when I was a kid," Steve said casually. Elliott didn't know whether to take him seriously or not.

"You had a ghost?"

"Yeah. Really. His name was Robert. Or at least, that's what we called him. He was pretty cool. I was never afraid of him for a second."

"Do you think he wanted you to be?"

"No. My folks rented this old place near Fort Hood in Texas while my dad was stationed there. I guess it used to be Robert's. Anyway, like I said, Robert was cool. He loved classical music and bedrooms, the one my brother and I shared especially. Maybe it used to be his. Maybe he was gay—who knows? We never saw him, but we'd always know when he was around."

"So, what happened to him?"

"You mean after we moved? I don't know. I assume he's still there, if the house is." He gave Elliott a raised-eyebrow grin. "You think I'm nuts, huh?"

Elliott shook his head. "No, of course not. It's just that I..." He had no idea how to finish the sentence, so he just let it trail off.

"Well, as I think I said before, there are more things 'twixt heaven and earth..." Steve began,

"...than are dreamt of in your philosophy, Horatio," Elliott finished the quote. "And I guess you're right." He felt another surge of discomfort and got up from his chair. "More coffee?" he asked.

"Sure."

Taking Steve's proffered cup, he went back inside. What he really wanted was a chance to recoup. The talk of ghosts and Steve's dream had really disconcerted him.

His hands refilled their cups and added cream and sugar while his mind tried to figure out what was going on. Was it possible Steve was being influenced by John? Why else would he dream of Hill and Cole? Most likely, he told himself, it was sheer coincidence, and not all that unlikely, considering they had been talking about the Hill situation. He was having enough problems dealing with John as it was. He didn't need or want Steve involved.

They took their time over coffee then decided to go to brunch. Steve wanted to stop by his apartment to change clothes first, having discovered a previously unnoticed but large spot of undetermined origin on the front of his pants.

"Well, I'll start getting ready," Elliott said. "You want to join me for a shower?"

Steve looked at him and grinned. "Uh, no, I don't think that's a good idea if we actually plan to have brunch before four this afternoon. You go ahead, and I'll shower at home before I change, okay?"

Elliott shrugged. "You don't know what you're missing."

"I know exactly what I'm missing," Steve replied. "But there'll be plenty of time for that later."

As he was lowering his head into the spray to wash the shampoo out of his hair, Elliott heard his cell phone ring, and a moment later heard Steve's "Hello?" He finished showering, dried off and padded into the bedroom to get dressed. Steve was sitting on the edge of the bed facing away from him, putting on his socks. He partially turned to look at Elliott when he realized he was there.

"Sorry," he said, indicating the two identical cell phones side-by-side on the bed. "Your sister called. I didn't realize we had the same phone until it was too late."

Elliott mentally rolled his eyes at the ceiling as he sighed. "I'm the one who's sorry," he said. "I imagine she dragged out the rubber hose?"

Grinning, Steve said, "It wasn't quite that bad. She sounds really nice, if just a bit...uh...curious."

Elliott went to the dresser to extract socks and a pair of shorts. "That's Cessy," he said. "She's always treated me like I was the younger of us two. She can't wait to start picking out china patterns for me."

"I kind of got that impression," Steve said. "Maybe I should have told her I like Wedgwood."

Luckily, Elliott could tell he was joking.

"I told her I'd have you call her as soon as you could. She said to remind you about the recital."

Elliott knew full well that was Cessy's way of prodding him to invite Steve, and he knew that, now she had talked with him, she was going to be relentless until she met him.

"Thanks," he said, hoping Cessy had not gone further into the recital thing. However, knowing her, and not wanting to simply ignore it in case she had directly asked Steve and he was being diplomatic in not saying so, he felt obliged to bring it up.

"My niece is having a recital at her school a week from next Sunday," he explained as he selected a pair of pants and shirt from the closet. "I'd mentioned that I'd met you, and she jumped on it. She wants me to invite you to come to the recital with me. I told her I was sure you'd have better things to do with your time."

Steve got up from the bed, putting on his shirt and stained pants. "I don't mind recitals," he said, and Elliott turned to look at him.

"You don't? I mean, I'd be happy to have you come with me, but you really don't know what you'd be letting yourself in for. If you thought she was curious on the phone, just wait until she gets into the same room with you."

"Well, I'll leave it up to you," Steve said. "I certainly don't want to put you in an awkward position."

He was already in an awkward position but didn't want Steve to know it. It was precisely because of Cessy's curiosity that he hated telling her any more than he absolutely had to about anyone he was seeing. Usually, it didn't matter, since he seldom saw the same guy more than a couple of times, and never got anywhere near being serious about any of them. Rick was out of the picture before he had a chance to know if anything substantial might have developed or not. And Steve was really too recent an entry into his life for him to have given much thought to where it might go.

But he did really like Steve, and perhaps it might be time to seriously think of settling down. If he decided he wanted to have someone share his life, he didn't want to push it off until he was seventy to do it.

"Well, sure," he said as he buttoned the last button on his shirt, "if you're brave enough to step into the lion's den, I'd really like to have you go with me."

Steve smiled and slipped into his shoes. "Okay, then. Thanks. But if the pressure gets a little too heavy, please feel free to withdraw the invitation at any time, with no hard feelings on my part."

By the time they'd stopped by Steve's so he could shower and change clothes, it was nearly one-thirty, so after they had debated on where to go for brunch, Steve suggested IHOP, which served eggs benedict all day. Elliott was actually rather pleased by the further evidence that Steve had his feet pretty firmly on the ground in not opting for someplace more trendy.

❋

It wasn't until early Sunday evening, back home, that he realized he'd not returned Cessy's call. Surprisingly, there was no message from her on his machine, and she'd not tried his cell. It was unlike her, but perhaps she was just trying to give him some quality time with Steve. He knew that, when he did call, he'd be in for a long interrogation, and decided just to let it go and enjoy the respite.

Besides, he rationalized, Brad would not have had time to contact the San Luis Obispo police with his concerns, if he would contact them at all. He didn't want to ignore Cessy but determined to see if he could hold off calling until Monday evening.

He watched the ten o'clock news, still with no call from Cessy, and went to bed.

— *I am not a ghost.*
— *What are you, then?*
— *I am a human being, just as I was...before.*
— *And you still have no idea who that human being was?*
— *No. But...*
— *But what?*
— *I'm not sure. So many...things. It's confusing.*
— *Exactly what do you know?*
— *My name is John.*
— *Yes, we've established that.*
— *I am not a ghost.*
— *If you say so.*
— *And I am not G. J. Hill.*
— *Then why did you identify the photo as being you? Cole says it's Hill.*

105

— *And you believe him? The picture is me, but I know I'm not G. J. Hill! Why do you always doubt me?*

He felt a flush of embarrassment, even in sleep, knowing John was right.

— *I'm sorry. Really. It's just all so confusing, and I'm trying to understand.*

— *I know. So am I.*

Aware of a mounting and mutually shared frustration, Elliott released his grip on semi-consciousness and sank below the level of dreams.

❖

Arriving for work shortly before eight, he heard the sounds of demolition. A huge commercial Dumpster was in the street directly in front of the building next door to the north. He had been peripherally aware, over the past week or so, of several moving vans coming and going, but it had never occurred to him that the building was being vacated in preparation for demolition. A perfectly good building with character and, in his eyes, charm, another piece of the fabric of Chicago's past with decades of practical use ahead of it, was being sacrificed to what he considered nothing but greed. Evermore at its worst.

The thought that the building he was currently putting such great care and effort into restoring would soon be sandwiched between towering, featureless slabs of concrete infuriated him. Recognizing that his anger was irrational and disproportionate did not make him any less angry.

His mood was not materially lightened when, as he went out to attach a brass plate with the building's street number to the new front gate, a late-model Mercedes pulled up into the fire zone in front of his building and parked next to the hydrant. The moment the driver got out, Elliott recognized him, though he had not seen him in more than twenty years—Al Collina.

Beefy, with crankcase-oil hair, spotless white shirt with the cuffs rolled up, expensive sportcoat slung over one shoulder, Collina totally ignored the hydrant and the yellow curb. It wasn't that he didn't know they were there, Elliott knew; he just didn't give a damn.

Collina paused long enough to light up a cigarette then strode past the Dumpster and disappeared into the courtyard of the building being demolished.

Elliott couldn't decide whether he should call the police for the parking violation or simply go get a screwdriver and puncture the car's tires. He opted for a third solution and went to his car for his digital camera, which he used frequently on the job. It had a feature that marked the time and date the photo was taken in the lower right corner. He snapped several pictures of the car, the yellow zone and the fire hydrant.

"What the fuck do you think you're doing?" a voice demanded just as he took a shot of the front license plate. He turned to look into the no-nonsense face of Alphonso Collina.

Though the years had been less than kind, Elliott could see the sixteen-year-old bully clearly behind the man's narrowed eyes.

"Guess," he replied, closing his camera and sticking it into his shirt pocket.

106

Collina's eyes narrowed further as he studied Elliott's face. "I know you," he said after taking a long drag from his cigarette. "You're Elliott Smith."

Elliott said nothing.

Collina indicated Elliott's building with a jerk of his head and a wave of his cigarette. "This is the place you pulled out from under me. You realize you cost me one hell of a lot of money by not taking my offer. I had to totally redo my plans for this whole block, and I figure you cheated me out of the profit from the twenty-four condo units I'd have put up in this space."

"Cheated you?" Elliott was incredulous. "Now, that's a novel way of looking at it."

"That's the way I see it," Al said.

Elliott shook his head and turned back toward the building. "I've got work to do. Nice talking with you."

He walked through the gate and into the courtyard without looking back.

❖

As he expected, there was a call from Cessy waiting for him on his answering machine when he returned home. He had planned to call after dinner but thought better of it. Cessy's patience for indulging her big brother's inattention had its limits, and there was a chance Brad might be home so he fixed himself a drink and went into the den.

"Hi, Ladybug," he said, recognizing Jenny's "Hello?" "Is your mom home?"

"Just a minute, Uncle Elliott...*Mom! It's Uncle Elliott!*...followed by, "You're coming to my recital, aren't you? I've been practicing really hard."

Jenny had been taking piano lessons since she was six, and while he doubted she'd ever have a career as a concert pianist—or want one—she was pretty proficient for her age and enjoyed playing.

"I wouldn't miss it for the world," he said, and meant it.

"Good! Here's Mom."

"He's very nice," Cessy said.

"Good lord, woman! I don't get a 'hello' before you start in on me?"

"What are you talking about? I just thought that Steve seems like a very nice guy, and I thought you'd appreciate that I share your opinion of him." She paused. "That is your opinion of him, isn't it?"

He laughed. "Yes, he's a very nice guy. And he says he thought you were nice, too. But cool it, please. I've only known the guy a couple of weeks. Don't start making things complicated just yet."

She sighed. "I've never understood you, Elliott Smith, and I don't think I ever will."

"Baloney!"

"So, did you ask him to the recital?"

"I asked him. He says he'll try to make it. It's still nearly two weeks away. A lot can happen in two weeks. He's a busy guy."

"He'll make it. He likes you, I can tell."

107

"We really have to get you a life, Cessy," he said gently. "So, is Brad home yet?"

"No, he called and said he'd be a little late. Do you want me to tell him to call you?"

"Yeah, if you would. I just have a quick question."

"I'll tell him as soon as he comes in."

"Thanks, Sis, I appreciate it."

Cessy spent another five minutes filling him in on what each member of the family—including Bozo—had been up to since they last talked. The conversation only ended when BJ called down from the top of the stairs to ask what she'd done with his backpack and Cessy excused herself to go and find it for him.

❊

After watching the news, he remembered the steak he'd taken out of the freezer and put in the bottom drawer of the refrigerator before he left for work that morning. Going into the kitchen to retrieve it, he first located a large baking potato he'd bought his last trip to the store. Washing it, he stabbed it with a fork several times then slathered it with olive oil, inserted two aluminum spikes to hasten baking and turned on the oven. He'd broil the steak once the potato was done.

He debated having another drink but thought better of it and returned to the den to see what was on TV. The phone rang just as he sat down.

"Elliott. Brad. Cessy told me you called."

"Yeah, I was just curious if you'd had a chance to contact the San Luis Obispo police today."

"I did, but I don't want to press them too hard—these guys are professionals, they know what they're doing, and I didn't want to imply otherwise. I didn't ask them how deeply they'd looked into the partner, but I sent them our John Doe's fingerprints for comparison and further verification. If they hadn't done a fingerprint comparison before, maybe they will now. I told them we have some DNA information if they need it."

"That's great, Brad. I really do appreciate it. Will you let me know if you find out anything more?"

"Sure. You're really a dog with a bone on this one, aren't you?"

He forced himself to laugh. "I guess so. Still don't know why, but thanks for going along with me."

"Well, when we're talking about a murder investigation, it never hurts to go a little out on a limb if it might help the case."

❊

Work on the building kept him totally occupied Tuesday and Wednesday, and the gutting of the building next door proceeded apace, though he did not see Al Collina again. He'd decided against making an issue of the illegal parking, though he told himself that if it happened again he definitely would, and he kept his camera handy just in case.

Tuesday night, he talked to Steve briefly. Steve hadn't yet heard from the gallery, but while he was obviously anxious about the forthcoming show, he didn't seem overly concerned.

On returning home from work Wednesday, Elliott was surprised to find a message on his machine from his mother—it was the first time he'd heard her voice in more than four months.

"Elliott, this is your mother," the message began, as if he wouldn't know. But it was typical of her, and he just shrugged it off. "Your father and I will be returning to Chicago Friday afternoon. We'd like to have you and Cecilia and her family join us at the club for dinner, say around seven-thirty? We look forward to seeing you. I've got to run, they've just announced our flight. Until Friday..." And she hung up.

She hadn't said whether she'd talked to Cessy, though he was sure she had, but just to be sure he dialed his sister.

The phone had barely rung when Jenny answered.

"Hi, Ladybug," he said. "Your mom around?"

"She's changing Sandy," the girl answered.

"Ah, okay. Will you just ask her to call me when she gets a chance?"

"Okay. Grandpa and Grandma Smith are coming home!" she announced. "We're all going to have dinner with them on Friday. Are you going to come?"

"Yes, I'll be there. And I just wanted to ask your mom if Grandma had called her. Obviously, she did, so she doesn't have to call me. I'll talk to her later, okay?"

"Okay. And you're coming to my recital, too, aren't you?"

"Of course I am. A week from this coming Sunday. Are you practicing every day?"

"Oh, yes! I want to be good."

"You'll be fantastic," he assured her. "So, tell BJ and your dad I said hi, and kiss Sandy for me."

"Okay. Bye now."

Given that he had never called—or ever been encouraged to call—his parents anything but "Mother" and "Father", he wondered how they felt about Cessy's kids calling them "Grandma" and "Grandpa." He was pretty sure they were a bit uncomfortable with it but probably held their tongues lest they risk alienating Cessy, as they certainly would. He found it rather significant that while they called Brad Sr. "Brad," the children were "Bradley," "Jennifer" and "Sandra." It was, Elliott was sure, their way of dealing with the fact of their own children's disregard for family protocol.

As he expected, not ten minutes passed before Cessy called him back.

"I told Jenny you didn't have to call," he explained. "I'd only wondered if Mother had called you about Friday."

"Yes, they're not even back in the country yet and she's busily arranging things. Still, it'll be nice to see them after all this time. I wonder if mixing with the common folk all over Asia might have mellowed them a bit."

He couldn't help but laugh. "Right!" he said. "That'll be the day. And going from luxury hotel to luxury cruise ship to luxury resort could hardly be considered 'mixing with the common folk.' The only common folk they know are you and me—though they'd rather die than admit it."

Cessy laughed, too. "My, we have been a burden on them, haven't we?"

"Not really," he said. "That's what our nannys were for. So, you're looking forward to dinner at the club?"

"Actually, I rather am," she replied. "I'd never say it to Brad, but sometimes I do miss some of the perks of being rich. I'm sure he would prefer dinner at Red Lobster, but he's such a wonderful sport about things like this. And they don't happen all that often."

"True," Elliott agreed. "It should be interesting."

"Would you want to ride out with us? We have plenty of room, and maybe you shouldn't drive all that way so soon after your accident."

"Cessy," he said patiently, "it's all of twenty-seven miles, and I'm fully recovered from my accident, thanks. I appreciate the offer, but I can take my own car. You'll have your hands full with the kids."

"If you insist," Cessy replied, her displeasure evident in her tone. There was a slight pause, then her mood switched and she said, "Well, since you're driving yourself, why don't you invite Steve along?" she asked. "That would really liven things up!"

He laughed again. "I'm sure it would, but I'd never subject anybody I was seeing to a night at the club with my parents. Talk about cruel and unusual punishment!"

While he had not the slightest doubt his parents were fully aware he was gay, it was a subject that had never come up; and until and unless there was a real necessity to mention it, he was quite sure it never would.

He had just finished lunch and returned to laying linoleum in the last of the Sheffield building's bathrooms on Thursday when his cell phone rang.

"Elliott? Brad."

He was instantly aware of John's strong presence, which alerted him to the reason for the call.

"Hi, Brad. What's up?"

"I heard from the San Luis Obispo police just now. Hill purchased a round-trip ticket to Chicago on March twenty-first, leaving for Chicago on the twenty-second with a scheduled return for the twenty-fourth. The return ticket was never used.

"Tracking Hill's itinerary hasn't been easy. From everything they've been able to determine—which isn't very much—he was a real loner. How he ended up with a partner is anybody's guess. They're doing a thorough check into the partner, too. They're verifying his alibi of being in Reno at his parents' at the time, but right now he's shaping up as a prime suspect in Hill's disappearance."

"Based on anything specific?"

"Nothing that I know of. But all the pieces are there. Apparently, everything is in Hill's name, though Cole seemed pretty possessive of them—kept referring to things as 'our' or 'my.' He and Hill had a joint bank account that Cole's dipped into pretty heavily since Hill's disappearance, and they're looking into any other possible financial ties or irregularities.

"But the fact that Hill was killed in Chicago makes for a pretty good alibi for Cole, especially if he can prove he was with his folks. I suppose it's possible he somehow arranged for Hill to be killed here, but that's pretty unlikely."

"Cole told me he and Hill were business partners. Did the police look into that?"

"Yeah, he told the police the same thing. Apparently, he considered sleeping with the guy and cleaning up the place qualified him as a 'business partner.'"

"I still can't believe it's Hill," Elliott managed to say. "Did they check the fingerprints you sent?"

"That's another mark against Cole. They tried, but it seems Cole has OCD—how recent a condition this might be they don't know. He was polishing the chrome on the motor home's bumpers when they got there and didn't stop puttering the whole time. He even asked them to take off their shoes before going inside. He agreed to let them check for fingerprints, but they didn't find any. None. Not on the steering wheel, or the dashboard, or door handles, or in the bathroom, or on any of the surfaces most likely to have them."

"What about Hill's personal things? His camera equipment?"

"Nothing. So, either Cole is a neat freak, or he's trying to cover something."

"So, it's still possible Cole just used the photo I sent him to claim it was Hill."

"Normally, I'd just give you a flat no. But the more we find out about Cole, the more weight I tend to give to your scenario, even though it's more than a little farfetched," Brad said. "If he's just *claiming* our John Doe is Hill, he can't get away with it forever. He doesn't strike me as being the brightest button in the jar, and if he's lying, we'll find out.

"But the fact remains that, until and unless we can prove otherwise, we have to go on the assumption that our John Doe is G. J. Hill."

Despite his confusion, Elliott forced himself to concentrate. "So, what happens now?"

"They'll keep looking into Cole, and try to see if anyone in the area might know anything at all about Hill, or be able to recognize the photo. The problem with the photo is that, other than the bruises, Doe has what we call a generic look—the kind of guy who'd be hard to pick out of a lineup. There are an awful lot of guys who look enough like him to confuse people.

"So, they'll do what they can from their end, but since Doe was killed in Chicago, and as far as we know Hill flew to Chicago that same day, that lets San Luis Obispo toss the case back in our court. We'll start with the airport. We've got the flight number and arrival time, and we've started checking the car rentals, shuttle services and cab companies. Maybe we can get an idea of where he was staying."

"Did Cole have any idea at all what Hill might be doing in Chicago?"

"No, other than that he read the Chicago papers regularly. So, maybe he had some connections here."

Elliott was slowly getting a grip on his thoughts.

"You might check the City Suites Hotel on Belmont," he said, having no specific reason other than it was well known in the gay community and popular with gays visiting Chicago. "I'd imagine that, since no one here reported him missing, he probably wasn't staying with friends or relatives. And since he was gay, he might well have made reservations there."

"Hmm," Brad said. "I'm sure we showed his picture there and nobody said anything. But we didn't have a name at that time, either, so we'll definitely be rechecking all the hotels in the area. We'll start with the City Suites. Thanks for the tip. Maybe you should consider a job on the police force."

Elliott laughed. "Thanks, but no thanks. One cop in the family is enough." He paused, then said, "I know it's a lot to ask, but would it be possible for you to keep me posted what you find out?"

"Well, since without you we never would have put a name on Hill, I think that can be arranged. We'll have to start checking for his family, too. Cole said Hill told him he didn't have one, but that doesn't mean he didn't. They may not be local, but we'll check it out."

"Thanks, Brad."

"No problem. Now I've got to get back to work."

"Yeah, me, too," Elliott said, but he was lying.

He really struggled to keep his mind on the business at hand, but it was as though he were trying to run while waist-deep in molasses. He was successful in fighting off his thoughts but not his emotions. He was weighed down with a combination of confusion, frustration and anger. And, while he felt nothing specific from John, he was well aware of his presence, and of emotions as strong as his own. He refused to let himself even formulate what he knew were all-too-obvious questions.

He once again managed to make it through the workday, but the minute he stepped into his car the tsunami of thoughts came rushing in. Anger rose to the top of his feelings, and while he tried to direct it at John for possibly lying to him, it was instantly re-channeled against himself for ever having believed so firmly that "John" was anything more than an aberrant creation of his own mind.

— I am not G. J. Hill!

"Go away!" Elliott snapped—and was immediately distressed to realize that he'd said it aloud. It was the first time he had ever done so, and only the second time that John had said anything while he was awake. It again made him think that he had no alternative but to seek professional help to get rid of his delusions once and for all.

❋

He uncharacteristically had three drinks before tossing a TV dinner in the oven and staring sullenly at the television. Such a foul mood was uncharacteristic of him, and it took his full concentration to keep his thoughts caged. It was rather like trying to close a suitcase that had far more items than it could contain.

When the phone rang as he was finishing his third drink, he let the answering machine take the call, but when he heard Steve's voice, he picked up the phone.

"Hello?"

"Elliott, hi. How are you doing?"

"Lousy, thanks," he replied sullenly, immediately sorry he'd said it. He had no reason or right to drag Steve into his problems.

"Uh-oh, sorry!" Steve said. "Anything you can talk about, or do you want to call me back when you're in a better frame of mind?"

Elliott sighed. "I'm sorry, Steve. It was just a bitch of a day, a long story I don't want to subject you to right now. I'll be okay."

"Hey, you're entitled. I'm just sorry you had to go through whatever it was."

"Thanks, me, too. But you didn't call to hear me bitch. What's new with you?"

"I heard from the gallery. They've scheduled the show for next month, the fourteenth through the twenty-first."

"That's great!" Elliott was relieved to find that Steve's good news was able to pull him a few inches out of his mental cesspool. "I'm really glad for you!"

"Thanks," Steve said. "I'm going to meet with Mr. Devereux at the gallery Saturday evening at eight to discuss exactly what pictures they'll want to display. I know it's short notice, but I was wondering if we might be able to get together tomorrow night to celebrate—if you're up to it. My treat."

"I'd love to, but my folks just got back into town and they've set up a family-dinner thing. But maybe we could do something Sunday, if you're not busy."

"Sunday'd be fine. Call me when you get up in the morning."

Feeling considerably better, he said, "I'd rather nudge you, but reality rears its ugly head."

Steve laughed. "Reality does that a lot," he said. "But we'll survive."

"Good luck at the gallery," Elliott said.

"Thanks. And I'll look forward to seeing you Sunday. I hope you're feeling better by then."

"I'm sure I will. Later, then."

Though Steve's call had raised his spirits considerably, he had to fight off a slow slide back into depression as he ate his dinner in front of the TV, letting the images on the screen flow past his eyes without filtering them through his brain. As a new show started, he realized he couldn't remember the name of the one he'd just watched.

He deliberately forced himself to stay up well beyond his bedtime, even though Friday was a workday. He didn't want another conversation with John. He considered having another drink to dull his brain but decided against it and reluctantly went to bed at eleven-thirty.

— *I'm not G. J. Hill.*

— *Damn it, go away!*

— *I can't. We've come so far!*

113

— *What the hell is that supposed to mean?*

— *I mean we can still find me. I know it. We're getting closer.*

— *The only thing I'm getting closer to is being fitted for a straitjacket.*

— *That's not true, and you know it. Trust your instincts. They led you to G. J. Hill. Don't give up on them now. There's more. I know it.*

Elliott swam toward the surface of consciousness then relaxed, sinking back down past the level of conversation and into the depths of dreamless sleep.

CHAPTER 10

❦

He awoke still in a foul mood. He didn't want to go to work. He didn't want to go back to bed. He didn't want to just sit home all day and sulk. He didn't want to do anything.

One of the most disturbing of the various negative thoughts he'd been having the past couple of days was that, collectively, they all were signs of weakness, implying he had no control over his own life. Such a concept was both alien to him and totally unacceptable.

Forcing himself through the workday wasn't easy. Ted, Arnie and Sam, sensing his mood, pretty much stayed out of his way. That the day actually went fairly well helped him feel a bit better, and as always, he was grateful for his ability to largely lose himself in his work. He even reminded himself to contact Larry Fingerhood about listing the building once it was ready—he estimated two weeks—and to go through the paper when he got home to check for potential properties for his next project. He could devote part of Saturday to driving by any that seemed interesting.

He arrived home in a much better frame of mind than he'd been that morning, and even discovering that his cell phone had again been turned off at some point during the day did not bother him.

The light on his answering machine was blinking as he walked into the den. One message. From Brad.

"Elliott, tried to reach your cell but no answer. I'm on lunch break, but thought I'd tell you we confirmed that Hill arrived at O'Hare at eight-forty-five p.m. on the twenty-second. We also checked the City Suites, and sure enough, he had a reservation but called the day he was supposed to show up to cancel it. That leads us to believe that someone—I wouldn't be surprised if it was whoever killed him—picked him up. But where he would have gone, and why, we have no idea. We're not overlooking any possibility. Next we start checking for any paper trail that might link him to Chicago, and we're working with the San Luis Obispo PD on that one. Just wanted to let you know. See you tonight."

His mind and body continued on their separate ways as he got undressed and stepped into the shower to get ready for dinner with his parents. What, he wondered as he worked shampoo into his hair, would happen to John once he learned who he was? Would he do whatever lost spirits are supposed to do when the thing that kept them earthbound was resolved? He was still fluctuating between questioning and being sure of John's existence, and was currently in the latter mode. He was also rather surprised to realize that, in that mode, he'd actually miss him.

John was, as usual, present during these reflections but, also as usual, unobtrusive. Elliott wondered if John would miss him, too. He quickly abandoned that line of thinking; he wasn't comfortable with too much sentimentality.

Splashing on some Old Spice, mostly because he really liked it but partly because he didn't give a damn if other people, including his mother, thought it was totally déclassé. He pulled a never-worn dress shirt from the dresser, pricking his finger on one of the 499 straight pins the manufacturers always use when packaging new shirts, and went to the closet to extract a custom-made dark-blue suit he'd only had on twice. He seldom wore a suit, and had this one only because it had been a Christmas gift from his parents—actually, they had simply made an appointment with his father's tailor and instructed Elliott to show up for a fitting and put himself in the tailor's hands.

He picked out a blue-and-burgundy silk tie Cessy had gotten him for his last birthday. He disliked getting so dressed up, but ritual was ritual, and this evening's dinner definitely fell into that category.

❉

The evening rush hour was pretty much over as he drove up I-94 to the Milwaukee turnoff, following it to the Lake Forest exit. As he turned off Skokie Valley Road onto Vine and entered the country club's parking lot, he saw his father's Lincoln Town Car, which would have been lost among all the other town cars except for the license plate: "Smith 1." There was no sign of Cessy and Brad's SUV.

Entering the club, he was tempted to go to the bar and wait until he saw Cessy and Brad come in, but he had to pass the doorway to the dining room, where he saw his parents at a table for eight by the fireplace. The maitre'd spotted him and, though he hadn't seen him in at least two years, smiled broadly.

"Good evening, Mr. Smith. Your parents are right this way, if you'll follow me."

This ceremony always amused Elliott. He could clearly see his parents and would have had no trouble joining them, yet he dutifully followed as though he were being guided through an impenetrable jungle.

His father, a large, robust man with a full head of pure-white hair, rose and extended his hand. "Elliott. Good to see you."

Elliott shook his hand, said "Good to see you, too, sir." He then moved to his mother and bent over so she could give him a peck on the cheek.

"Mother."

"Elliott." She pulled her head back slightly and said, "Why do you insist on

116

wearing that awful fragrance? Didn't I get you a bottle of Perry Ellis for your birthday?"

Taking the seat next to her, he smiled. "Yes, you did, and I usually wear it. But I was in the mood for Old Spice tonight."

She gave him a slightly raised eyebrow and a small smile. "I'm sure you were."

The waiter came by for his drink order. He ordered a Manhattan, and his father asked for another vodka gimlet.

"So, how are you both?" he asked. "I want to hear all about your trip, but will wait until Cessy and Brad get here with the kids."

They filled the ten minutes until Cessy and her family arrived with general small talk, mostly his mother's critique of the various hotels, cruise ships and airlines they'd had occasion to utilize. Elliott noted the Priebes were dutifully dressed for the occasion, Cessy in a very striking blue dress, Brad in his best suit, BJ looking mildly uncomfortable in an obviously new sportcoat and sharply creased black pants, Jenny in a white dress with ruffles at the collar and on the sleeves and Sandy in a frilly pink dress with a matching bow in her hair. Elliott was aware of his mother's discreet scrutiny as, he was sure, was Cessy.

Greetings exchanged—handshakes between Brad, BJ and the elder Mr. Smith, and Brad and Mrs. Smith; cheek pecks and small hugs between Mrs. Smith, Cessy and the children—a high chair was brought to the table for Sandy, and everyone was seated. With that, the evening officially began.

✳

He was back home shortly after ten and watched a little TV before going to bed. The evening, he decided, had gone quite well. His parents had enthralled BJ and Jenny with stories of their travels, and Elliott had been reminded about his father's dry wit, which was often at the expense of Elliott's mother, who had the innate ability to completely overlook things with which she had no experience or in which she had no interest.

They had traveled through some of the most squalid regions of southeast Asia, yet his mother seemed sincerely oblivious to the very real suffering that had been around her, as though it all was part of some movie studio's backlot.

He went to bed around eleven-thirty and was asleep within minutes.

— *I wish it was easier.*

— *So do I. But what, specifically, are you referring to?*

— *For you to really believe in me.*

— *You don't exactly make it easy.*

— *I know, and I'm sorry.*

— *But you still don't know who you are?*

— *No. There are more…things…now, but…*

— *But what? What things?*

— *It's hard to say. I've never been dead before. It's like a blind man becoming vaguely aware of colors.*

— *Are you playing games with me?*

117

— No! I swear. You're not dead; you have no idea what it's like.

— You're right, I don't. What is it like?

— It's...different. Confusing. Like being a newborn baby. I have no words to explain.

And then Elliott was a small boy, lying on his back on the bright-green grass on his parents' front lawn, looking up at a sky full of puffy clouds in which he could clearly see whales and elephants and sailing ships.

❄

The ringing of the phone jarred him awake, and he was amazed to see, as he fumbled to answer it, that it was nearly eight-thirty—the latest he had slept since he was in the hospital.

"Hello?"

"Elliott. Did I wake you?" Steve asked.

"No, that's okay. I had to get up to answer the phone anyway...That's a joke, son," he hastened to add.

"Pa-da-pum!" Steve shot back. "But I am sorry I woke you. I figured you'd be up by now."

"Yeah, I usually am, but I'm glad you called. I wasn't expecting to hear from you until tomorrow."

"Just thought I'd check in. How did the family gathering go?"

"Not bad, really. Everyone was on their very best behavior, though as usual my mother took advantage of every possible opportunity to let me know—she majored in subtlety at Sarah Lawrence—that what I do for a living is unworthy of the family. I delight in reminding her that Smith is the most common surname in America. She somehow fails to see the humor in that."

"What about your brother-in-law being a cop. Does she ride him, too?"

"Ohhh, no! Cessy is the apple of both my parents' eyes. Brad is strictly off-limits. Mother knows Cessy would up and walk out of the family. Besides, I think both my parents, however grudgingly, like Brad. But me, I'm the ne'er-do-well son, so I'm open game." He paused and laughed. "It isn't nearly all that bad, of course. I just like to make a play for sympathy every now and then."

"You're entitled," Steve said.

"So, you're going to the gallery tonight at...what?...eight?"

"Yeah, and I have to spend the day getting ready for it. They've asked me to bring along my full portfolio, just in case they might want some other ones. It's in pretty good shape, but I'll have to take out some that I've already sold before I moved here. What's on your schedule?"

"The day's pretty open. I'm going to go through the paper looking for a possible next project, and if I find anything that looks interesting, I'll take a drive by to check it out."

"You don't go through a broker or an agent?"

"Oh, yes, but no one agent knows everything that's out there. Some of the best buys come from owners trying to sell their own properties. Besides, I get a kick out of it. So, you still want to get together tomorrow?"

"Sure. Why don't you call me when you get up? That way I don't have to risk disturbing your beauty sleep."

Elliott laughed. "I don't think you have anything to worry about there, but yeah, I'll call you when I get up. Anything special you'd like to do? There's still a lot of Chicago you haven't seen."

"Well, if you wouldn't mind, maybe we could consider the Museum of Science and Industry? I've always wanted to go there. That's the one with the mammoth in the entry, isn't it?"

"No, that's the Field Museum. But we can do whatever you want. We can think about it and decide later."

"Okay. Well, I'd better get busy. Talk to you tomorrow."

"Good luck tonight."

"Thanks. See ya."

❧

Elliott took his time over his morning coffee, carrying it onto the patio along with the newspaper and a highlighter. Settling into a molded plastic chair, he noted that clouds were creeping across the western horizon, apparently hoping no one would notice, hinting of rain for later in the day. From his vantage point, however, the sun was shining brightly along the lakeshore; and several people, oblivious of the incoming clouds, already were wandering around the beach, while the white triangles marking sailboats were visible a mile or so offshore.

Taking out the classifieds and laying the rest of the paper on the table, using a large potted geranium from near the railing as a paperweight to keep it from blowing away in the ever-present breeze, he settled back and opened the paper to the real estate section.

But like the approaching clouds, thoughts about John and G. J. Hill began encroaching on the periphery of his mind. Even if Cole had, for his own reasons, claimed falsely that John's photo was Hill's, exactly how had Elliott been drawn to Hill, and why? There had to be a reason—John's reaction to Hill's photos was too strong for there not to be. It had to go beyond just an association with the places in the photos.

But surely Cole couldn't be stupid enough to think he could really get away with claiming John was Hill if he wasn't. Everyone leaves traces of themselves somewhere. Even if Cole had done his very best to eradicate Hill's fingerprints from the motor home, there had to be some he missed. Even if, as Cole claimed, Hill had no family, somebody else had to have known him. And the more suspicious the police became of Cole, the harder they'd look until they found something.

Which was all well and good, but where did that leave John? He tried again to imagine what it must be like for him—being dead, existing in two worlds at once—and to no surprise, he couldn't. Where, he wondered, was John when he wasn't aware of him? Did the dead have any concept of time?

He forced his mind back to the classifieds, and lacking his usual

119

concentration, he almost randomly marked a couple potential properties on the near north side. When he'd finished his coffee, he put the geranium back in its regular spot and carried the paper back inside then headed to the shower.

❧

As he got ready for bed Saturday night, he felt a sense of mild frustration not associated, for a change, with John. The day had been largely a waste, and he deeply resented wasting days. His property search had produced nothing, nor had just driving up and down side streets on the chance of finding anything of interest. As a sign of his desperation to wring some sense of accomplishment from the day, he had, on returning home, done the laundry—a task Ida normally handled—then gone back out to the grocery store for some things he really didn't need.

The evening had been spent in front of the TV. He briefly considered calling a couple friends to see if they'd like to go out for a drink but then decided he didn't really want to.

His dreams, that night, were his own.

❧

Whereas Saturday had been not much more than a cipher, Sunday was thoroughly enjoyable. He called Steve at eight and, when Steve suggested they have breakfast, picked him up at nine-thirty. They ate at a small family diner near Steve's apartment, taking their time and talking.

Steve's meeting with the gallery owner had gone well, he said, and though he tried to be casual about it, Elliott could tell he was hyped at the prospect of his upcoming show.

They spent the bulk of the day at the Museum of Science and Industry. Steve was fascinated by the architecture of the sprawling Beaux Art structure, which Elliott's trivia file reported had originally been built as the Palace of Fine Arts for the World's Columbian Exposition of 1893. Though he'd been there often, he always enjoyed it, and took pleasure in watching Steve's first-visit reactions. They had, at Steve's insistence, their pictures taken in a vintage open roadster on the Yesterday's Main Street exhibit, walked through the U-505, a WWII German submarine, and visited all of Elliott's favorite exhibits.

After an early dinner at one of Elliott's favorite Chinese restaurants, Steve suggested they go over to his place for a little show-and-tell, to which Elliott readily agreed. However, because they both had to work the next morning, they didn't make it a sleepover, and he left for home around eleven.

❧

The next week passed quickly and busily. On Thursday, he called to verify that Steve still wanted to go to Jenny's recital on Sunday. He wasn't sure he'd want to go to a similar affair if the situation were reversed.

"You're sure you don't mind going?" he asked yet again. "I'm just afraid you might be bored out of your mind. This isn't exactly the Chicago Symphony."

120

Steve laughed. "I don't mind if you don't. But I've been thinking. From what you've said of Cessy, is she going to assume that just because you show up with a guy there are wedding bells in your future?"

"Of course, she will," Elliott replied. "She assumes that when I have the pizza boy do a delivery. She'll get over it."

"Well, I just don't want to put you in an awkward position."

"If anybody might be put in an awkward position, it'd be you. Cessy means well, but she'd make a great prison camp interrogator. But if you can handle it, I do want you to come."

"Well, if she gets too pushy, I'll just pull out the videotape of our last session."

"I do assume you're kidding," Elliott said.

Steve laughed again. "Yes, I'm kidding. Though it might be fun sometime."

Elliott sighed in relief. "Yeah, it might. But let me know first, okay?"

"Promise. So, do you want to give me a call Saturday to let me know what time Sunday and where we should meet?"

"Sure." He resisted the temptation to suggest they get together either Friday or Saturday night. He didn't want Steve to think he was trying to rush the relationship. Meeting the family was pressure enough.

And then he was rather surprised that thought had even occurred to him. He wasn't much of a relationship-pusher, and he recalled a couple of times when he'd met nice guys who had driven him away by coming on too strong and too fast. He didn't want to do that to Steve.

There was a rather long pause before Steve said, "Okay, I'll talk to you on Saturday, then."

Elliott wondered if perhaps Steve might be thinking along the same lines, and hadn't mentioned getting together for the same reason. He sensed bemusement at the thought, and knew it was neither his nor Steve's. John, apparently, was slowly finding an identity, even if he didn't yet know whose identity that might be.

❃

— I've been thinking...
   — That's a good sign. Thinking about what?
   — Just thinking. It's as though I'm learning how all over again.
   — And have you come up with anything about your identity?
   — Not much. I feel we're getting close, but...
   — But what?
   — But you're still my only window to the world. I only know what you know.
   — That's not quite true. You knew your name.
   — Yes, but that was...the beginning. It was all I knew. It still is, basically.
   — You recognized yourself in the photo.
   — You recognized me first. I merely confirmed it.
   — This is confusing as all hell.
   — If you think you're confused, try it from this side.
   — So, what now?

— Keep doing what we've been doing. We're getting there...I feel it. We just don't know where "there"' is yet.

❄

Cessy called early Saturday morning to tell him that Brad's mother was coming for a visit, though she wouldn't make it in time for Jenny's recital. Elliott had met Marcella Priebe several times over the years and really liked her. She was a native Italian who had married Brad's father when he was stationed in Naples during his stint in the Navy. The family settled in New York, where Brad grew up and his mother still lived. Brad's father died when Brad was a teenager.

Though she spoke with something of an accent, she had refused, when Brad was younger, to teach him Italian.

"You're an American," she told him. "You should speak American."

When her grandchildren came along, though, she had relented a bit on the language issue, teaching BJ and Jenny a few common Italian words and phrases.

"Your grandma likes you better than she liked me," Brad would tease her when the kids would repeat something she'd taught them. "I wasn't smart enough to learn Italian." And she would invariably, if close enough to him, slap him lovingly on the arm and say, "You're so silly!"

"How long will she be here?" Elliott asked, hoping he'd be invited over for one of Mrs. Priebes' lasagna or ravioli dinners.

"Just a week this time," Cessy said. "So, you'll have to set aside some time for her. She likes you."

"I wouldn't miss it for the world," he said.

❄

He held off calling Steve until around noon, for no reason other than that he really didn't want to give Steve the impression he was too eager about developing a relationship. It registered at that moment that John's entrance into his life had changed him. Never much given to introspection, he'd always managed to view relationships with a certain detachment—whatever happened, happened. He neither had nor particularly wanted any specific control over them, which, he realized now, might partly account for why he had never really had one that lasted.

Partners came and went, as Rick had, and it was all the same to Elliott. Probably the same would be true with Steve, but for the first time he was behaving as though it might matter where the relationship went, and at what speed.

Aside from the fact that he really liked Steve as a person, a lot of his attraction to him, oddly, had to do with Steve's skin. Not only the color, but the feel, the exciting sensation of velvet over steel. Steve had—to Elliott, at any rate—the most beautiful chest he had ever seen, neither flat nor having the Butterball-turkey pecs of a muscle builder. Like Baby Bear's porridge, it was "just right."

And that he would associate a word like *beautiful* with a man's chest was

122

another first for him. Chests were sexy, or hot, but he'd never considered one beautiful until he met Steve.

With Steve, as with John, he concluded, he had no real idea of what was going on, and for someone as self-disciplined as he was, that was a source of considerable frustration. Reverie was not a state in which he felt comfortable, and he forced himself out of it and reached for the phone.

"Hi, this is Steve," the answering machine dutifully announced. "I obviously didn't hear the phone, but please leave your name and number so I can get right back to you."

Mildly and again uncharacteristically angry with himself for not having called earlier, he hung up and went into the kitchen to get something for lunch. He was just slicing the tomato for a BLT when the phone rang.

"Elliott, hi! Sorry I missed your call. I just ran down to the mailbox. What's up?"

Obviously, Steve's machine had caller ID.

"Nothing much," Elliot replied. "I just wanted to confirm where and when for tomorrow."

"Great! Name it."

"The recital starts at two, and there's some sort of reception afterwards, but I wondered if you'd like to have brunch before we go."

Cessy had suggested they all get together for lunch before the recital, but Elliott had made an excuse not to—he didn't want to overdose Steve on togetherness with the family just yet.

"Sure, that'll be fine. Oh, and what's the dress code?"

Elliott laughed. "I don't think there is one. I'll check with Cessy just to make sure, but I assume it's pretty casual. I'll let you know if it isn't. And why don't I pick you up at eleven-thirty? That should give us enough time." Then, without thinking, and cursing himself immediately after for doing so, he heard himself saying, "So, what are you doing for the rest of today?"

"Laundry and chores this afternoon, then I'm going out with some of the other illustrators from work. A mostly straight crowd, but it should be okay."

"I'm sure you'll survive," Elliott said.

"Yeah. I almost called you last night to see if you wanted to go for a drink, but then I thought better of it."

"Better of it?" Elliott asked, puzzled.

"No, no." Steve hastened to add, "I didn't mean it that way. It's just that I've been taking up a lot of your time lately, and I don't want to wear out my welcome."

Elliott felt his mood improve markedly. "No worry about that happening," he said, not allowing himself to add that he'd resisted doing the same thing, for the same reason.

"Good," Steve said. "So, I'll see you eleven -thirty tomorrow, then."

"Okay, and have a good time tonight."

"I'll do my best. Later."

— *I like him.*

   — *Steve?*

   — *Yes. I like him.*

   — *Do you know anything about him that I don't?*

   — *No. But I like him.*

   — *What about G. J. Hill? And Rob Cole? Anything else on them?*

   — *No...although...*

   — *Although?*

   — *There is something there. I have no idea what it is, but something. Just...feelings. Maybe it's just part of being...where I am now.*

   — *But you feel some connection to them?*

   — *It's so hard to explain. Everything is new to me. I don't know anything, but I feel things.. I wish I had a better way to explain. I know I'm not G. J. Hill, and I know I don't like Rob Cole, but I have no idea why.*

   — *What do you feel about Hill...other than you're not him?*

   — *Confused. Sorry. Sad. Rob was not nice to him. He wanted out of the relationship.*

   — *Rob did? Or Hill?*

   — *Hill.*

   — *Did Rob kill him?*

   — *I don't know. I know he's dead, but I don't know how I know. I'm...learning.*

They arrived at Jenny's school shortly before one forty-five. Elliott had carefully timed it to give him time to introduce Steve but not time enough for Cessy to start asking too many questions. They had agreed to meet at the front entrance, and Cessy, Brad and BJ were standing on the steps when they arrived.

Though Cessy had assured Elliott casual dress was fine, he noticed Brad was in a coat and tie, probably at Cessy's insistence because Jenny was on the program. Cessy herself looked very nice in a yellow dress Elliott had not seen before, and had obviously just had her hair done. BJ, dressed a bit more casually in sport shirt and slacks, was obviously not overjoyed at having to spend a Sunday afternoon at a school recital, sister or no.

The introductions went smoothly, with Brad shifting Sandy from one arm to the other in order to shake hands with Steve. They smalltalked for a minute or two, Elliott vastly relieved to note Cessy's restraint, though he did catch her glancing frequently from him to Steve. Steve gave no indication that he noticed, though Elliott was sure he had.

They made their way into the school auditorium and found seats, Cessy next to Elliott. Leaning slightly forward so she could address herself to Steve, she said, "What do you do for a living, Steve? Elliott has been very secretive about you, I'm afraid."

Steve and Elliott exchanged a glance, and Steve smiled and said, "I'm a commercial artist."

Suddenly embarrassed that Steve might not fully understand the reason behind his secretiveness with his sister, Elliott felt obliged to step in.

"Steve's being modest," he said. "He's an exceptionally talented painter with a gallery showing coming up shortly."

"How wonderful!" Cessy said sincerely. "Will it be open to the public?"

"Of course," Steve said, "and I'd be pleased if you might want to come and see it."

"We'd love to!"

At that point, the lights dimmed, and a diminutive nun walked out in front of the closed curtain into the oval of a single stationary spotlight.

"Welcome to St. Agnes's annual student recital," she said. "We're delighted you could come, and we hope you'll enjoy the performance."

Cessy leaned toward Elliott. "That's Sister Marie," she whispered, "our neighbor from Lake Forest."

Looking more closely, Elliott could make out a red wine-stain birthmark starting an inch or so above her left eye and disappearing beneath her wimple. He remembered how mercilessly her brother Al had teased her about it. A real shit, that Al Collina.

The program consisted of several pieces by the school's orchestra and chorus, separately and together, interspersed with solos by a number of students with varying degrees of talent. When it was Jenny's turn, after applauding enthusiastically as she walked across the stage to the piano, Cessy took both Elliott's and Brad's hands nervously.

Jenny, looking very much the young lady in a new green dress, her hair in a ponytail tied with a matching green ribbon, sat down and began a Chopin etude, which she executed flawlessly. Elliott glanced over at his sister and brother-in-law, whose pride clearly showed on their faces. BJ, sitting on the other side of his father, looked mildly bored, and Sandy slept through the whole thing.

At the end of the recital, Sister Marie came out again to thank the audience and praise the students, then announced that coffee and cake would be served in the gym across from the auditorium. Brad sent BJ out to the car for the camera, and they waited for Jenny to come out from backstage before going to the gym. Steve was gracious and sincere in his praise of Jenny's playing, and Elliott could see he had won Cessy over totally—even Brad seemed pleased. Hearing praise from someone other than a family member obviously meant a lot.

When Jenny came out, there were hugs all around and an introduction to Steve, who instantly charmed her as well. They'd just left the auditorium and were crossing the hall when BJ returned with the camera. The group paused while Brad took a couple photos of Jenny, and Steve volunteered to take a picture of the whole family, thus endearing himself further to Cessy. She then insisted that she get a shot of Steve and Elliott together, and Steve deliberately put an arm over Elliott's shoulder, pulling him close and grinning broadly as he did so. Ellott knew it was totally for Cessy's benefit but rather enjoyed it.

Most of the audience was milling around noisily in the gym, at one end of which a number of tables and chairs had been set up. Coffee urns and cups, cartons of milk, Saran-wrapped pieces of cake on paper saucers and paper plates piled with cookies were spread out on two buffet tables against the wall to the left of the doors, overseen by two nuns. Several of the school's faculty, including three or four other nuns, formed the nuclei of little clusters of parents and students.

BJ split off and headed immediately for the food. As the rest moved to follow, Jenny said, "Oh, look! There's Sister Marie. Don't you want to go say hello?"

Before anyone could answer, she caught the sister's eye and waved, causing her to move in their direction.

"Mr. and Mrs. Priebe." She extended her hand as she approached. "You must be very proud of Jenny." She took Cessy's hand as Jenny beamed and Brad put his free hand on his daughter's shoulder. "You did very well today," she said, to the girl's obvious delight.

"Sister, I'm sure you remember my brother Elliott. And this is his friend Steve."

Shaking hands with both men, Sister Marie smiled broadly. "Of course I remember Elliott!" she said. "You and John were the best of friends."

"I can't tell you how sorry I was to hear of his death," he said. "We hadn't seen one another in many years, but I always remember him fondly. And please accept my condolences on the death of your mother."

Sister Marie's smile dimmed a bit with sadness but soon regained its full power. "Yes," she said. "I miss her terribly, but she's with the Lord." She reached out and touched Elliott's arm. "And do you know, she would never allow herself to admit that John was never coming home. She never removed him from her will, and despite Alphonso's insistence that she do so, she even refused to sign the papers necessary to declare John legally dead. You remember Alphonso, and I'm sure you can judge his reaction." She gave a small smile. "It may be uncharitable of me to say, but I'm glad she didn't. She was the only one in the family, other than John, to ever stand up to him." She sighed. "Well, they're together now in heaven."

As though suddenly realizing she'd been talking of personal matters to relative strangers, she pulled herself up to her full five feet, six inches and said hastily, "Well, I must go say hello to some of the other parents. It's been very nice talking with you. Nice seeing you again, Elliott, and nice to meet you, Steve. Jenny, I'll see you in class." And with a warm smile all around, she turned and left.

The fact that she'd referred to her brother as Alphonso—a name Al detested but which his father insisted he be called—was not lost on Elliott, and he felt it spoke volumes about Marie's feelings toward her one surviving brother. It also struck him that, with Sophia Collina now dead, there was no one to block Al's

126

efforts to file the papers that would undoubtedly bring him even more money than he already had, in the form of his half of John's portion of the estate.

They moved to the refreshment tables then joined BJ at an empty table. He'd already polished off most of his cake and a carton of milk. Looking up as his parents approached the table and attempting to ward off an expected rebuke, he said defensively, "Hey, I was hungry, all right?" As everyone else sat down, he got up to get another piece of cake.

"Leave some for everybody else," his father said.

"I'll just take a small one," BJ promised and hurried off before Brad could say anything else.

In the twenty minutes or so that they sat at the table with their cake and coffee, Cessy managed to get pretty much all of Steve's life story. Her subtle interrogation was somewhat deflected when, upon mentioning that he liked fishing, he and Brad got into a side discussion on the subject.

❄

"Thanks for putting up with all this," Elliott said as they pulled out of the parking lot. "You're a brave man."

Steve laughed. "No problem. I enjoyed it. You've got a really nice family. I've been feeling a little homesick lately, and being around a real family helped. Too bad about your friend."

Elliott looked over at him. "Johnny? Yeah. We were really close. He died in Africa some time ago, and I hadn't seen him since we were teenagers. Still, I do think about him from time to time and think of what a waste it was for him to die so young."

They rode in relative silence until they turned left on Peterson Avene. Elliott's building stood out on the horizon nearly two miles away.

"I don't suppose recitals have the same effect on you as art galleries and pizza, do they?"

Steve grinned and put a hand on Elliott's leg. "However did you know?"

Returning the grin, he put his free hand over Steve's. "A wild guess," he said.

CHAPTER 11

꧁꧂

Cessy called Sunday night just after he'd returned from taking Steve home to give her official stamp of approval.

"So," she said, "are you two getting serious?"

"Cessy, I've only known the guy for a couple of weeks. It's way too early to think in terms of serious."

"But you like him."

"Of course, I like him. I wouldn't have brought him to the recital if I didn't like him."

"And he likes you," she said. "I could tell. You make a really nice couple."

Even though she couldn't see it from the other end of the phone, he shook his head. "Cessy, are we back in fifth grade again? 'He likes you. I could tell.' Come on!"

"Well, you can joke about it all you want, but I think you've got a good thing going there, and I just want you to be happy."

Recognizing her sincerity, he mellowed. "I know you do, sis, and I do appreciate it. But let's just take it slow, okay?"

He heard her sigh. "Okay. Well, Sandy is crying, and I'd better go see what the problem is. Talk to you later."

❉

Around noon on Monday, as he was going out to his car for a tool, he heard a commotion out in front of the building. Curious, he went down the narrow walkway between his building and the one being demolished next door. A towtruck was in front of his building, removing a car parked by the fireplug—Al Collina's car. Al was in the street, yelling at the towtruck driver, who ignored him and drove off.

Although Elliott hadn't noticed the car's being illegally parked again, apparently one of the neighbors had called the police. When the towtruck pulled away, Al noticed him standing there. His eyes narrowed and his brows furrowed in an expression of pure fury.

"You cocksucking, motherfucking fairy!" Al yelled, his face livid with rage.

Elliott was sure he was going to come at him, and he prepared himself for a physical confrontation. Instead, Al glared at him then shook his head menacingly, pulled out his cell phone and stormed back to the demolition site.

Al clearly assumed it was Elliott who had called the police, given the earlier incident where he'd caught him taking photos. Well, that was Al's problem, not his.

✳

On Wednesday, Elliott called Larry Fingerhood to talk to him about listing the Sheffield property. He was delighted with how the renovation had turned out, and had toyed with the idea of adding the Sheffield to his collection of buildings he couldn't force himself to sell. However, practicality dictated he couldn't keep them all. They made arrangements to meet at the property on Saturday.

Thursday morning, on his way from the bathroom to the kitchen to start breakfast, he made his usual detour to the den to turn on the morning news. He had just turned toward the door when he heard, "...North Sheffield, where a massive explosion has destroyed a vacant apartment building undergoing renovation. Flames spread to an adjacent empty building. Firefighters are still working to..."

Elliott spun around to see his building in ruins, water streaming from firehoses through a third-floor window, smoke pouring from the roof and out the front entrance. He felt physically ill and sank into a chair, forcing himself to concentrate on what was being said.

"Police and fire department investigators are on the scene, hoping to determine the exact cause of the blast, though a nine-one-one call just prior to the explosion reported the strong smell of natural gas. And in other news..."

He remained motionless as the picture on the set switched back to the studio, paying no attention to what was being said. As the shock slowly began to wear off, his first thought was gratitude that apparently no one had been injured. His second impulse was to jump into his clothes and race to the scene, but he realized there was nothing he could do there, other than to answer questions, and he wanted to be fully pulled together before he did that.

He pushed himself up from his chair and deliberately made his way back to the bedroom to get dressed.

✳

Sheffield was still blocked off when he arrived, and he had to park two blocks away. A fire truck remained in front of what was left of the building, flanked by two police cars. Officers were stringing "Do Not Cross" tape across the width of the property at the curb. Barricades blocked the sidewalk. There was still a sizeable crowd of onlookers.

Elliott could see as he approached that, while the front of the building was largely intact, looking up through a shattered third-story window revealed the roof was gone; and as he got closer, he saw the entire back third of the building was missing. He again gave thanks it was vacant—the chances of anyone in the rear units surviving a blast that powerful would have been slim to none.

129

He'd called his crew on the way over to tell them what had happened and not to come to work. Walking up to a policeman just tying the end of the warning tape to one of the barricades, he identified himself and was directed to two men standing near the front entrance, one in full fire gear, the other in plain clothes. Hesitating only a moment and taking a deep breath, he squared his shoulders, ducked under the tape and went through the open front gate to meet them.

The rest of the day was a blur. He spent a good forty-five minutes with the on-scene investigators, assuring them that, while he and his crew had occasion to have been from one end of the building to the other, including the basement, numerous times every day, they had not noticed anything out of the ordinary, and most specifically no odor of escaping gas. The most logical place for a gas leak was in the laundry room in the basement, where the main gas lines came into the building from the alley. It was also where the four gas dryers were located. The investigators agreed that was probably the origination point of the explosion, but that the collapse of the rear of the building had eliminated any possibility of a positive determination until the debris was cleared away.

He noticed the damage to Collina's building next door appeared to be relatively heavy, and was glad it, too, had been empty. Calls to the insurance company and his lawyer—he had no doubt whatsoever that Collina would find some excuse to file suit for the damage to his building even though it was in the process of being demolished—filled out the rest of the day.

It was only when he got home and fixed himself a drink that his adrenaline levels began to return to normal and he could allow himself to consider the possible cause of the explosion. Actually, as far as he was concerned, there was only one possibility that made sense: Al Collina. It wasn't just the confrontation over the towing of Al's car, though he wouldn't be surprised if that hadn't precipitated it. It was that Al wanted the property. Now that it had been destroyed, he probably felt Elliott would be more than willing to sell it to him. He might well use the threat of a lawsuit as a bargaining chip.

He had no doubt the destruction of his building had been in Al's mind ever since Elliott had first refused his offer to buy it, but he had deliberately waited until Elliott had invested the maximum amount of time and money into the project. However, waiting until it was in another owner's possession would have taken the pleasure out of destroying it. Impractical and illogical as that might sound to others, he knew it would be typical of Al Collina.

The evening news once again mentioned the explosion, and less than two minutes later the phone rang.

"Elliott!" Cessy's voice reflected her shock. "Was that your building I saw on the news just now?"

"Yes, I'm afraid it was."

"Why didn't you call me? Are you all right? Is there anything I can do?"

Despite his frequent mild impatience with her, he decided that a sister who cared was a nice thing to have.

"No, sis, there's nothing you can do, but thanks. I feel bad about losing it, but no one was hurt and it was insured, so it's not the end of the world."

"I can't understand how you can be so calm about it," she said. "All the time and money you put into it..."

He allowed himself a small sigh. "I know," he said. "But when something happens that you have no control over and can't change, you just have to accept it and get on with your life. I'll be fine."

"Have you talked to Steve?"

The question caught him by surprise; he realized he hadn't even thought of calling Steve yet. As far as he knew, he'd never even mentioned the Sheffield building specifically.

"Not yet," he said. "I'll call him later." He didn't add that he had no intention of mentioning the explosion when he did call. He couldn't see any point in dragging Steve into things that didn't involve him—a decision made more out of consideration for Steve than a desire to keep him at arm's length. In Elliott's mind, mentioning it would seem too much like he was looking for sympathy, and he didn't want that.

"Well, I..." Cessy began, then stopped. "Just a second, Elliott. Brad just came in."

He heard muffled voices as she covered the mouthpiece to talk to Brad, then: "Here's Brad."

Another brief silence.

"Elliott. Cessy just told me about your building. I heard something about it at work, but I never realized it was yours. That sucks. They said something about a gas leak?"

"That's what they said."

"You don't sound convinced."

"Oh, I'm pretty sure it was gas. But I'll wait until after the investigation before I say anything to anybody about my suspicions about the how."

"Well, I won't press you, but if you think it wasn't an accident, you should say something."

"Yeah, I will. But like I said, I think I should wait until after the investigation results come in."

"Whatever. But I'm here whenever you want to talk."

"I appreciate that, Brad. I just don't want to go opening up cans of worms before I'm sure it wasn't an accident."

"Understood. Keep me posted on what they find out, okay?"

"Okay...and anything new on John Doe?"

"Yeah, a couple of things. We checked the cab company records for O'Hare pick-ups around the time Hill's flight got in. I'd told you we'd learned that he called to cancel his reservation at the City Suites, which lends weight to the idea that somebody—possibly his killer—might have met him when he got in. I told you the San Luis police weren't able to get any fingerprints, but they did take Hill's toothbrush and a hairbrush that might yield DNA evidence we can compare with what we got from our John Doe. It would have been easier for

131

them to run a DNA test from their end, but they apparently didn't want to go to the expense, so they're sending them to us so we can do it here." Brad paused, then said, "You still convinced Hill isn't our John Doe?"

"I'm as sure as I can be without having any facts to prove it."

"Well, this whole case has a hell of a lot more conjecture and circumstantial evidence than I'm comfortable with, but we can't ignore anything. I do have to admit Cole seems to be setting himself up as a prime suspect in Hill's disappearance. But until we get Hill's DNA to compare it to our John Doe, we'll just have to assume they're the same guy.

"To play it safe, we're running Hill's Social Security number through the system—the San Luis police had to get it from his publisher. For having been his partner, Cole didn't seem to know much about him; he even had to look in one of Hill's books to find the publisher's name."

❁

Talking with Brad about the John/Hill situation had momentarily helped divert his mind from the loss of his building and the certainty that Al Collina was responsible for it. Once the conversation ended, his anger against Collina re-emerged, and he had to fight to control it. But he knew one thing with a cold, hard certainty—there was no way in hell Collina was going to get his hands on that property. He'd level the building and leave it as an empty lot until hell froze over first.

He briefly flashed on the idea of turning the lot over to the city for a mini-park until he realized that, while that might well foil Al's plans to build on it, a park would only enhance the value of whatever Al threw up immediately adjacent to it. Collina would come out ahead no matter what Elliott did, and that thought infuriated him. Eventually, however, he convinced himself to just step back and give the whole thing time to simmer down. Nothing had to be done or decided just yet.

❁

Friday was filled with loss-related details—filings, paperwork, a visit to the site, innumerable phone calls, meetings with his insurance representative, two concerned calls from Cessy checking on how he was doing, and too many other things for him to remember in detail later. Somewhat against his better judgment, he called Steve's home phone and left a message asking him to call when he got home from work. He very much felt the need for a little relaxation, and Steve came immediately to mind. Maybe dinner out, or a round of the bars—anything to take his mind off his problems.

He still didn't want to drag Steve into it all, but knew he'd have to tell him about it eventually. He promised himself he'd do his best to keep it as casual as possible.

Around four-thirty, shortly after he returned home, his phone rang.

"Elliott. Brad. I've been trying to get you on your cell, but your line's been busy."

"Yeah, it's been a busy day. What's up?"

"We got Hill's toothbrush and hairbrush from San Luis today. We've sent it to the lab, but it will take some time before we know anything."

Going into the kitchen for a glass and some ice cubes after the call, he returned to the den and poured a stiff drink. He'd downed about half of it when Steve called. Elliott did his best to engage in a few seconds of small talk before losing his battle with temptation and saying, "Are you doing anything tonight?"

"Just laundry. Why? You sound a little strange. Is everything okay?"

"I'm fine," Elliott lied. "I just really feel like going out tonight, and thought we could have dinner and go to a movie or hit the bars. I apologize for the short notice, and if you don't feel up to it, I'll understand."

"No, that's fine," Steve replied. "Out's fine. But are you sure you're okay?"

"Yeah. I'll tell you all about it when I see you. Seven o'clock okay?"

"Sure. I can make it by then. Where shall I meet you?"

"I'll pick you up."

"You're sure?"

"I'm sure. I'll see you then. And thanks."

"No thanks necessary," Steve said. "I'll be out front."

To forestall the possibility of any more thinking, Elliott downed the rest of his drink and headed to the bathroom for another shower, removing his shirt as he went.

✿

True to his word, Steve was standing in front of his building when Elliott pulled up.

"Cornelia's okay for dinner?" he asked as soon as Steve got in.

"Sure," Steve said, fastening his seatbelt.

"Sorry to keep you from your laundry."

"It'll wait." Steve glanced at him out of the corner of his eye.

They rode in silence for a couple of blocks until he realized Steve was waiting for him to say something. Maybe it was just part of his mood, but he'd deliberately not said anything to see what Steve's reaction would be, and he was pleased that Steve seemed to understand.

"My building blew up," he said calmly.

Steve turned to look at him fully. "That was *your* building? On Sheffield? I saw it on the news. I had no idea it was yours. I'm so sorry!" His voice reflected his sincere concern, but he was obviously trying to follow Elliott's lead and not make too much of it.

Elliott shrugged, only mildly disgusted with himself for saying anything at all. "Yeah, it was really a great old building, and we'd put a lot of work into it. But I'll be okay."

"Do they know how it happened?"

"Gas leak, most likely," he said, foregoing further detail. "They won't know until their investigation is complete."

"Well, I'm really sorry. I wish there was something I could do to help."

Reaching his free hand over to put it on Steve's thigh, he smiled. "You're

133

doing it," he said.

❀

Dinner was exactly what he needed. He hadn't really been aware of how tense he had been over the last two days until he felt it slowly draining away. As they talked, he had a quick mental image of ballroom dancers, with Steve taking the lead in guiding him effortlessly around the conversational floor.

After dinner, they left the car near the restaurant and walked down to a couple of the Boys' Town bars on Halsted. It was nearly midnight by the time they got back to Steve's apartment, where he was more than happy to accept Steve's offer to spend the night.

❀

He opened his eyes to see the digital clock on Steve's nightstand telling him it was 8:03 a.m. Granted, they hadn't gotten to sleep until nearly two, but even so, he was surprised that he'd slept so late. He turned over to find the other half of the bed empty, and as sleep faded, much as the tension had the night before, he realized that he had heard nothing from John during the night.

He'd been sure his conversation with Brad would sparked some strong reactions from John, but there'd been nothing, and that at first puzzled him. Then, remembering John's tendency, when Elliott was with someone, not to intrude, he was grateful to have had some uninterrupted alone-time with Steve. In any event, his puzzlement was balanced with something akin to relief.

"Ah, you're awake."

He hadn't noticed that Steve, wearing only a pair of sweatpants, had entered the bedroom carrying two cups of coffee.

"Yeah," he replied with a grin. "You been up long?"

Steve moved to Elliott's side of the bed and waited while he adjusted his pillow so he could sit up against the headboard, then handed him his coffee. "Not long. I hope I didn't wake you."

Taking a sip of coffee, and pleased Steve remembered that he took both cream and sugar, Elliott shook his head. "Not at all. I was really out of it."

Steve sat on the bed beside him. "I figured you needed the rest."

He felt a flush of warmth as he—subtly, he hoped—studied Steve. It took all his willpower to keep from reaching out and running his hand all over that beautiful, perfect skin.

"I had an interesting dream last night," Steve said, and immediately all of Elliott's thoughts of skin disappeared in a rush of adrenaline. He looked up from his coffee.

"Yeah? About what?"

"About your John Doe, oddly enough. I don't remember the details, but like I said, it was interesting. Something about motor homes and mountains. Did you ever find out anything more about him?"

Elliott reached over to set his coffee cup down on the nightstand. He didn't trust himself to hold it.

"As a matter of fact,..." he began.

134

He told Steve everything he'd heard from Brad, being very careful never to mention John as other than the object of the investigation. He didn't want to speculate on the content of Steve's dream or the implications of his even having had such a dream.

"Wow, that's really interesting," Steve said when he had finished. "And to think all this came about because you cared about some guy you never met. I'm sure he's grateful to you for trying to help him."

Elliott had no idea how to take that remark.

"He's dead," was all he was able to say.

Steve nodded. "I know, but that doesn't mean he doesn't know." He gave Elliott an embarrassed smile. "You probably think I'm a nutcase," he said. "But I told you about Robert, and I really do believe there's a lot more out there than we know about."

Taking Steve's coffee out of his hand, he set the cup beside his own on the nightstand. Pulling Steve down to him, he said, "You're not a nutcase. I know. Trust me."

❧

It was not until he was on his way home that he allowed himself to give any thought to Steve's dream. Was it possible John was reaching out to Steve, too? If so, why? What did he hope to accomplish? It could all be just coincidental, of course, but he somehow knew it wasn't.

The respite of his time with Steve aside, he was still tired from the stress of the past few days and went to bed relatively early, for him.

— *He really does like you.*
— *I like him, too.*
— *I know. I told him.*
— *So, he knows about you?*
— *Not really. Not yet. It's not my place.*
— *You want me to tell him?*
— *That's up to you. Not until you're ready.*
— *What do you think of this Hill thing?*
— *I'm not G. J. Hill.*
— *I know. You keep telling me.*
— *The DNA will tell you.*

❧

Sunday morning, as he sat on the balcony with his coffee reading the paper, Cessy called to invite him to BJ's soccer game that afternoon and dinner afterwards.

"Thanks, Sis, I appreciate it, but..."

"No buts about it. I'm not going to have you sitting around that apartment moping and worrying."

He laughed. "Where did you get the idea I was sitting around moping and worrying?"

Cessy's response was firm. "Well, I would be if I were you. I think you should

135

get out of the house."

"I've *been* out of the house."

"Oh?" Her voice perked up. "You've seen Steve?"

"Yes, I've seen Steve."

"Is he there now? Why don't you bring him to the game, and to dinner?"

Elliott sighed. "Cessy, I keep telling you, we're just seeing one another. We're not joined at the hip."

"Well, you could still invite him to the game."

"I could, but I won't. Nothing kills a relationship faster than a choke hold."

"But you'll come anyway? BJ would really like to have you see him play."

"Okay, I'll come. What time and where?"

"Why don't you come by here at around two. The game starts at three, no sense in taking two cars."

"Two it is," he said. "I'll see you then. Bye." He returned to his paper.

❊

Monday morning, he realized that, for the first Monday since he was fully recovered from the accident, he didn't have a specific job to look forward to. The day was still filled with details surrounding the loss of the building, including a call from the fire inspector he'd met at the site. They'd been able to get into the basement; and though the explosion had obliterated just about everything in the laundry area, it was evident it had originated near the dryers, all but confirming the gas leak theory. Whether the leak had been accidental or deliberate was yet to be determined. Elliott once again assured the inspector there had never been a problem before, that the dryers were new and had been professionally installed.

He talked briefly with Larry Fingerhood; the explosion had made their previous appointment moot. Larry's job was switched from listing the property for sale to trying to find a new project.

"You're sure you're ready to get right back on the horse?" Larry asked.

"I'm ready," Elliott said. "And the sooner the better."

He was not, however, ready for Brad's call, which came at about three-thirty.

"We got the DNA results," Brad said. "Our John Doe is G. J. Hill."

CHAPTER 12

✿

Elliott had no idea what he said in response, and was only aware of ending the conversation and hanging up. Dizzy and feeling physically ill, he plopped down onto the chair beside the phone and tried to pull himself together. The weight of John's presence again pressed on him like a stack of heavy blankets on an uncomfortably hot night, and he slowly realized that his reaction was being compounded by John's.

How could it be? How could John deny being G. J. Hill when his DNA said he was? DNA doesn't lie. Maybe John had an identical twin? His mind was a maelstrom of shortcircuited thoughts, flashing and sputtering and throwing off sparks. Everything he knew or thought he knew about John was called into question, even to the point of wondering again if John wasn't some sort of a tumor on his imagination. That was a thought that truly frightened him.

He made it through the rest of the evening somehow, and was reluctant to go to bed. He didn't want to have another talk with John, so he sat in his chair and stared at the television until, despite his best intentions, he fell asleep.

— *I'm not G. J. Hill.*

Even asleep, Elliott felt his frustration.

— *Yes. you are, damn it! DNA doesn't lie.*

— *No, it doesn't. The DNA is mine, but I'm not G. J. Hill.*

— *What in the hell is that supposed to mean?*

— *I...I'm not G. J. Hill!*

— *Then who the hell are you?*

— *I still don't know. It's closer, now. I feel it. But I still don't know. Please stay with me—I can't find out without you!*

— *What do I have to do with it?*

— *I don't know that, either. I told you, I'm learning. The only thing I knew when I came to you was that my name is John. And then I knew I was not G. J. Hill, but I never would have learned that if you hadn't found my books.*

— *So, they are your books. Then you are Hill.*

— *No, I'm not. I...I...They're my books. I know now that I took the pictures. But it's so hard to explain...or to understand. It's so close. You're the key to the answer. I only learn through you. Help me.*

In total frustration, Elliott let go and sank into unconsciousness.

✻

Tuesday morning was a morass of conflicting thoughts and emotions, which he fought to bring under control. How the hell could John be G. J. Hill and not be G. J. Hill? If John wasn't Hill, who was he?

The only possible logical explanation he could come up with was that John had for some reason changed his real name to G. J. Hill—or had it changed for him. If John *had* changed his real name, it might well be a direct link to why he was killed, and maybe to who had killed him. Could John have been in the Witness Protection Program, perhaps?

His immediate impulse was to go to the phone and call Brad, but he quickly discarded it, at least for the moment. Suggesting Hill was not the victim's real name would open the door to far too many questions as to how he might have come to that conclusion. It was, he decided, probably preferable to sit back and wait to see if the police could figure it out on their own. Brad had said they were checking on Hill's Social Security number. Surely, that would reveal something. Maybe then they could track backward to the point where the name change had occurred, and from there...

By that afternoon, he eventually got back to his own life, immersing himself in paperwork and details and phone calls. Cessy called to announce that Brad's mother was arriving Friday, reminding him again to set aside some time for her.

After Cessy's call, he phoned Ted, Sam and Arnie, assuring them that he was looking for a new building, and that, in the meantime, he would try to keep them busy with small projects at his other properties.

Late in the afternoon, he'd pulled himself sufficiently out of the morass to drive by the few potential properties he'd seen in Sunday's paper. He could, of course, just wait until Larry found something for him, but he was too impatient.

Only two—a four-flat on a corner lot on Elmdale, a couple blocks off Broadway, and a ten-unit on Montana just west of Halsted—looked promising because he liked their neighborhoods. He drove by the ten-unit first. It was in the center of a block of mid-nineteen-twenties buildings of a similar style, and was being offered by a realtor he was not familiar with. He would have liked to park and take a walk-by for a closer inspection, but couldn't find a parking place—not a good sign. He circled through the alley to see it from the rear and check on garage space. There was a two-car wooden garage and a concrete ramp only large enough for three other cars at most.

The four-flat had no sign in front. That usually meant the owner was trying to sell it himself, which could be either a positive or a negative from the standpoint of a potential buyer It was a raised three-story set on a corner lot. He assumed the half-basement constituted the fourth flat, though it was difficult to tell from the outside. Finding a parking place on the street paralleling the side of the building, he got out for an inspection, first walking down the alley behind the property to see it from the rear. He then moved up the side to the front. From what he could see, it appeared to be in basically good shape. It stood out from its neighbors primarily for its arched windows and other subtle but important gingerbread elements he always looked for. He put great stock in small details that indicated the builders had put some extra care into their construction.

He made a mental note to call the numbers given in the ads for both properties.

❊

By the time he got home, he was feeling considerably better. He was grateful to John for keeping in the background and giving him some space. Having seen two prospective new properties had helped. Even if nothing came of it, he felt like he was accomplishing something. About the Sheffield building, he adopted a stoic attitude. His lawyer would handle any lawsuit that might arise, and his insurance would pretty much cover the financial losses.

He was having a drink and watching the news when Steve called to see how he was doing, and to invite him to a play Friday night—he had been given tickets by a friend at work who was unable to use them. Elliott readily accepted the invitation.

He and Steve were, he decided, developing a very nice unspoken understanding. He sensed that neither of them wanted to push the relationship too far too fast, so they seemed to be taking turns in initiating their get-togethers. If either of them should want a little extra space, he could just hold off on his next "turn." It hadn't happened yet, but Elliott was grateful the option was there.

He'd just hung up and was ready to see about dinner when the phone rang again.

"Elliott, Brad. We've got a new problem with our John Doe."

Puzzled by the reference to "John Doe" instead of "G. J. Hill," Elliott said, "What do you mean? What kind of problem?"

"Well, San Luis ran a check on Hill's Social Security number, and it seems there is no such person."

John was right! He had insisted he wasn't G. J. Hill, and he wasn't. G. J. Hill didn't exist. He never had.

"So, we're back to square one," he heard Brad saying. "San Luis found the number had originally been issued to a George Joseph Parsons, who's been dead since 1989. A new Social Security card was issued to someone claiming to be him in 1998."

"How can that happen?" Elliott asked, though he knew identity theft was common.

"Going through a cemetery looking for someone with a similar birthdate then contacting Social Security to request a new card under that person's name is one of the oldest tricks in the book, and I'm amazed it still works, but sometimes it does.

"Actually, when you consider the size of the Social Security bureaucracy and

139

the number of requests for new IDs they get every year it's inevitable that things like this fall through the cracks. Especially after nine-eleven, when they tightened security.

"But whoever our John Doe is took it one step further. Once he had the card, he filed papers for a legal name change from Parsons to Hill. He kept Parsons' initials."

"Why wouldn't he just have kept Parsons's whole name?"

"Probably to try to put one more step between his real identity and the chance of anyone finding out he'd stolen Parsons name."

Elliott shook his head. "I still can't imagine anyone getting away with it."

"Maybe you can't, and maybe I can't, and maybe he was just damned lucky all the way around, but the fact is that he did do it and he he did get away with it. The bigger the bureaucracy, the more holes there are in it."

"So, what happens now?"

"Well, there had to have been a reason for him to be in Chicago. And since the nature of Doe's murder suggests premeditation, that means his killer or killers knew he was in town. We'll have to coordinate more closely with the San Luis police to try to figure out what he was doing here.

"Hill's publisher said he had no idea, said he was supposed to be working on a book of photos of the California coast. He did take some freelance magazine assignments, so it still might have been something to do with his work, but who knows? Cole might still be involved, but there's no use speculating, at this point. We'll check it all out, anyway."

❀

Brad was right, they were back to square one—"they" being the police, Elliott and John.

Knowing that "G. J. Hill" was an assumed name both solved a mystery and created a new one. John now had an identity, but it wasn't the right one. He still had no idea of what it was like for John, on whatever plane of existence—or nonexistence—he inhabited. The bottom line, still, was that he had not been deceiving Elliott; he wasn't G. J. Hill.

He'd also said several times that he was "learning"—learning what, Elliott had had no idea, until he realized that John meant it literally. He had started out knowing nothing at all except his name. Everything presented to him since his death was new to him. He still conveyed his thoughts in fairly simple terms. It was as though he were trying to move back and forth across a bridge between two worlds and didn't yet know how to do it easily. He knew he was not G. J. Hill but was unable to convey the complexities of living as Hill without *being* him.

❀

The rest of Elliott's evening was uneventful, and when he went to bed, he dreamed again of mountains.

— *They aren't mountains, they're hills.*
— *Does it matter?*

140

— I don't know how to explain it. But it's important.

— Does it have something to do with your real name?

— Yes! I don't know what, but I know we're very close!

— Were you in the Witness Protection Program? Is that why you chose the name G. J. Hill?

— I don't think so. Wouldn't I have had to have done something wrong to be put there?

— Not necessarily. But it might explain why you were...what happened to you.

— Oh. No, I think I'd sense it if I might have been.

Even asleep, he noticed that John knew what the Witness Protection Program was, indicating that his general knowledge of the world was expanding rapidly.

— I can only imagine how confusing all this is for you.

— Oh, you have no idea!

✻

Thursday morning he got a call from the fire marshal asking to meet him at ten o'clock at the rear of the Sheffield property. He had deliberately avoided even driving by the ruins since the day of the explosion, and didn't want to spend any more time there than he had to. Rather than driving down Sheffield past the front of the building, he went directly to the alley behind it.

An official-looking car was pulled up parallel to the security tape that cordoned off the property. Pulling up behind it, he recognized the man in it as the same one who had been at the scene the morning of the explosion. He remembered the man's name was Swans, partially because the marshal, a heavy-set, florid-faced man in his mid-fifties, was to Elliott's mind anything but swan-like.

After a handshake and exchanged greetings, Swans led past the cordon tape to what remained of the back steps. The entire back third of the building was gone, with only the north side wall and a section of the back southwest wall rising above a mountain of rubble. He could see that the southeast corner of the basement had been somewhat cleared out to expose what little remained of the laundry area.

Pointing into the hole, Swans said, "That's the flashpoint," he said. "You can see what's left of one of the dryers. It was right there."

"How can you be certain?" Elliott asked, immediately feeling stupid to have asked.

"Can you see the gas connector hose going into the back of the dryer?"

He nodded.

"Well, you can also see that the coupling is all but undamaged. Which means that one dryer, at least, had been disconnected from the gas line. But we found the valve to the line was in the on-position."

"So, someone uncoupled the dryers but left the valves on?"

"Yep. Definitely not an accident. You got any idea who might have done this?

Or why?"

Elliott glanced over at Collina's building, which had also received damage in the blast, though it was hard to tell because the presence of a large end-loader indicated they had reached the stage of pulling down the walls.

"As a matter of fact, I've got a pretty good idea," he said, "though I don't know how to prove it."

Swans looked at him, nodding slowly. "Well, why don't you just tell me what you think, and we'll take it from there."

Elliott did.

As they returned to their cars, Swans said, "So, when are you going to start razing it? Now that our investigation's completed, the city will want it down as soon as possible. It's too much of a safety hazard the way it is."

Elliott looked back through what had been the bedroom of one of the second-floor front apartments. "Yeah," he said. "I'll get on it tomorrow."

❀

The play Friday night turned out to be a musical comedy revue that, while Elliott doubted it would ever make it to Broadway, gave him the chance to laugh, which he'd not done much in recent days. He'd accomplished quite a bit during the day, most of it taken up with making arrangements to have the building demolished. However, he also called the numbers for the two buildings he'd checked out Wednesday and set up appointments to see both Saturday.

Being with Steve was a major factor in lightening his mood. And, as always, he was aware of John's presence on the periphery of his consciousness, although he had begun to detect some subtle difference ever since the explosion. Confidence?...Purpose? He couldn't put his finger on it, but it felt as though John was definitely becoming more sure of himself.

They spent the night at Steve's and, though Elliott couldn't remember who suggested it first, agreed to have dinner later. Returning home Saturday morning to change clothes and get ready for his property-viewing, he found a message from Cessy.

"I didn't want to bother you on your cell phone. I figured you might be with Steve. Just wanted to tell you Marcella's here and wants to have you come over Monday night for dinner. She's fixing lasagna just for you. Give me a call as soon as you can. Bye."

The reference to Steve didn't escape him. Cessy was bound and determined he was going to settle down, or she'd die trying. And he knew that Mrs. Priebe—only Cessy called her Marcella—wasn't going to all that trouble just for him, although he thought it was nice of her, or Cessy, to pretend she was. He immediately called to confirm.

❀

Whenever he looked at a property represented by a Realtor he'd not dealt with before, he always played the naïf, as though the particular property being looked at was his first venture into real estate. He could tell a lot from how the Realtor presented it—what was emphasized and what was not, what was mentioned and what was not, which questions were addressed head-on and which danced around.

The female agent for the ten-unit on Montana was one of the bubbly "isn't-everything-just-wonderful?" types he could not abide. Any potential problem he pointed out was greeted with an "oh, look over there!" deflection.

It was when the issue of selling price came up that he definitely turned off. The one quoted in the paper had struck him as more than a little on the high side, but he knew there was always room for negotiation. However, when he asked her, in his role of not knowing much about real estate, how much she thought the owners would take, she looked at him as though he should not be allowed to handle sharp objects.

"Oh, it's worth every penny of the asking price!" she said. "Of course, I'm obligated to present any offer you might make, but I've had several other people looking, and if you're really interested in the property, the more closely you come to the asking price, the better."

He resisted adding *And the higher your commission.*

But while her attitude and presentation were a sufficient turn-off, it was the condition of the interior on which he based his decision. Unlike the Sheffield building, it had not been well maintained. He went through it with a mental calculator, noting what absolutely had to be done, what changes could be made to increase its value, and how much those changes might cost. The ceilings in the top floor hallway showed evidence of water damage—a strong indication the roof probably required significant work, if not complete replacement. The work that needed to be done throughout the building went far beyond the cosmetic.

He thanked the Realtor for her time and made a note of the agency's name for future reference. He didn't think he'd bother looking at another of their listings anytime soon.

The four-flat on Elmdale was another story. He could tell that a minimum of effort would greatly increase the property's value. It was a typical raised-three-story post-WWI Chicago-style and originally had been a three-flat, with each apartment taking up an entire floor. As he'd noted on his walk-by earlier, though it didn't look like it from the outside, the raised basement was now considered a fourth flat.

The owners were a pleasant middle-aged couple who lived on the first floor but were in the process of buying a condo in Evanston. They had arranged with their tenants to let him do a walk-through, and he was favorably impressed. There were several nice gingerbread elements which, though largely hidden in the course of several minor renovations, could easily be restored or replaced.

As to the basement being a "flat," he found that, sometime in the early 1950s, the front two-thirds of the basement had been turned into a small, currently unoccupied three-room apartment, which didn't technically qualify as a true flat. Still, he could see how, with relatively little work, it could be turned into a much larger sunken garden-style apartment and still leave enough room for a compact laundry and utility area in the rear.

The asking price here was also a little high, but he was sure they would negotiate. Part of the game was never appearing overly eager, so he told the owners he would give it careful consideration and get back to them early the following week to arrange to have his crew go through the building. The owners were amenable, and he left feeling fairly confident he had found his next project.

❋

When he called Steve to see about dinner, Steve suggested that, instead of going out, they get a bucket of carry-out chicken and rent a movie, which was fine with Elliott. He really wasn't a going-out-a-lot kind of guy, and was pleased to learn that Steve also didn't feel the necessity to be always on the go. He volunteered to stop for both food and film on his way over, and Steve left the selection of movie to him.

On a whim, he took along one of his own favorite porn videos—not that they needed one, but from what he knew about Steve, he was pretty sure how the evening would end up and figured it would be fun for them to duplicate the on-screen action.

He was right.

❋

Sunday, Steve fixed breakfast then replained he wanted to spend the day painting, so Elliott headed home, where his own day was spent jotting down notes and ideas on the Elmdale four-flat—estimating rough costs, time involved, making some preliminary sketches based on what he remembered of the building, and a myriad other details.

He had by now become so accustomed to John's presence that, like the faint sound of the el trains three blocks away, he was no longer conscious of it. He had the sense that John was waiting patiently for whatever lay ahead, but there was also that growing emanation of confidence he assumed was a combination of John's growing awareness of the world beyond himself, of accommodating himself to his current state, and the fact that Elliott and the police were on track to discovering who the man behind G. J. Hill might have been.

❋

Monday evening on his way to Brad and Cessy's he stopped at a small Italian grocery store and picked up a large tin of Amoretti Biscotti, which he knew Mrs. Priebe loved and which he also knew wouldn't last through the evening with Brad and BJ around.

It was, for him, one of those evenings when he was truly grateful for the gift of family. Part of it might have been the reserve of his relationship with his parents in contrast to the warmth and sense of inclusiveness he got from Cessy and her family, but the feeling of truly belonging was one he treasured.

Brad's mother, too, was a delight. Warm and funny and affectionate, she adored her son and her grandchildren and treated Cessy as though she were a daughter rather than her daughter-in-law. And she'd always been very kind to Elliott on those rare occasions when he had the chance to see her.

Elliott, of course, flattered her at every opportunity, but he felt the flattery was justified. In addition to her other sterling qualities, she was a superb cook, and he ate more at that one meal than he usually ate in a day. Luckily, anticipating the appetites of three men—BJ ate like a ranch hand—Mrs. Priebe had made two huge pans of lasagna.

After dinner, as Cessy and Mrs. Priebe cleared the table and brought in coffee and the tin of biscotti, he asked Brad if there had been any further developments on tracking down G. J. Hill's true identity. He was a little surprised at himself, since he didn't like to drag Brad's work into family time.

Mrs. Priebe, who had just returned to the table with Cessy, said, "What's this about?" and Brad filled her in briefly on the case and its complexities, and Elliott's role in it.

"So, the only thing we know for sure is that Hill is not the victim's real name," he concluded

"You do have a fascinating life," she said with a smile.

"I like names that are things," Jenny volunteered. She turned to her mother. "I found out that Kathy Montagna's last name means *mountain*." She then turned to her grandmother. "Grandma, what's the Italian word for *hill?*"

Mrs. Priebe smiled at her. "*Collina,*" she said.

CHAPTER 13

꧁꧂

He managed to say "Excuse me a moment" before heading for the bathroom. He closed the door behind him and sat down on the toilet, his head between his hands. He felt so dizzy he was afraid he might pass out. He had no idea what part of his reaction was his, and what part was John's, but the combination of the two produced a sensation he had never before in his life experienced, and it terrified him.

He didn't know how long he was in there before there was a rapping at the door.

"Elliott, are you all right?"

"I'm fine, Sis. I'll be right out."

He pulled himself together and got up to splash water on his face. He patted himself dry with a towel then flushed the toilet and left the bathroom. Cessy stood in the hall, waiting for him.

"Are you sure you're all right? We were all worried about you. You turned pale as a ghost!"

"I'm sorry," he replied, ignoring the irony of her comment. "I've been a little under the weather the past few days," he lied, "and I guess I just ate too much too fast."

They returned to the table, where he made his apologies and repeated his excuse. He noticed Brad looking at him, and knew he didn't buy it.

He left shortly after, assuring Cessy he was fine to drive and taking, at Mrs. Priebe's insistence, a large dish of lasagna "for when you're feeling better."

Despite his lightheadedness and the indescribable turmoil going on in his head, he made it home. He resisted the urge to go directly to bed, knowing that he'd be hearing from John and wanting to take a little while to sort out his own thoughts first.

John Doe was John Collina, who had not, as his brother Al had said and as his sister Marie believed, died in Africa. Elliott had no idea what the real story was; but now that John knew who he was, perhaps it might restore his memory, and he'd be able to explain it all—as well as identify his killer, although Elliott was pretty sure he already knew.

Shortly after ten, he gave up on his attempt to watch the news when he realized he hadn't heard a word of what had been said. He'd just gotten up to go into the bedroom when the phone rang.

"Elliott, it's Brad."

He knew full well who it was and wondered why Brad insisted on telling him.

"So, I gather from your reaction at dinner that you think our John Doe...G. J. Hill...whoever... is a Collina?"

"Not just *a* Collina," Elliott replied. "He's John Collina, Al's brother."

"I see." Brad sounded as if he did no such thing. "And how does this get around the fact of John Collina's having died in Africa eight years ago? You want to tell me what's going on? What haven't you told me?"

"That's just it. There's really no proof that John died in Africa. No body was ever found. I think he just used the ferry capsizing to disappear for good. It..." He paused, trying to gather his thoughts so they'd make some sense. He didn't want to mention John's current status if he could avoid it. "It's a long story," he continued. "Are you sure you want to go into it now?"

"I waited until the kids were in bed, and Cessy and Mom are in the kitchen talking. Yes, I want to go into it now. Something about this whole thing has been strange from the very beginning. What's going on?"

Elliott opened the floodgates, carefully controlling the flow to avoid mentioning John's presence.

"Look, John never got along with either his dad or Al. Al told me Vitto had disowned John for being gay. I think he joined the Peace Corps to put as much distance as he could between himself and Vitto and Al. The ferry capsizing gave him the opportunity to cut his ties to the family once and for all. He returned to the States, where he took...Parson's...name. He probably couldn't force himself to give up his own name totally, so he disguised it by changing it to Hill. He might have decided to keep Parson's initials, G. J., because they could also stand for Giovanni, his birth name, and John, the name he preferred—though that's just a guess."

"Why in hell would he go to all that trouble? Why would he want to disappear in the first place?"

"Well, for one thing, can you imagine being gay and having a father like Vitto and a brother like Al?"

"Yeah, but that was a pretty rotten thing to do to his sister and mother."

"Granted. But knowing Johnny, I'm sure he must have had a very good reason, though I can't guess what it might be."

"That's it?"

"That's not enough? Well, I'll also bet Al found out John wasn't dead—I have no idea how or when."

There was a slight pause before Brad said, "Interesting, if pretty unlikely, theory. But theories don't stand up well in court. If Al knew John didn't die in

Africa, why wouldn't he have said so?"

"Because Al wanted him to stay out of the way. Once he found out John was still alive, he probably kept as close track of him as he could, which John didn't make easier by moving around all the time. I don't know if he knew Al was aware he was alive or not, but he probably didn't want to take any chances."

"Okay, so, if he disappeared because of his old man, why didn't he resurface when Vitto died?"

"Al was still around. And by that time, he probably thought his mother and sister couldn't or wouldn't be able to forgive him for letting them think he was dead. Knowing Al, when Vitto died, I'd guess he pretty much took over as much of the family affairs as Sophia would let him get away with. He certainly wouldn't want John coming back and creating problems."

"So, what was John doing back in Chicago?"

"I'll bet he came back for his mother's funeral. I'm not sure of the exact date she died, but if you check it out, I think the funeral was the twenty-third or twenty-fourth—Cole told me John had left a note saying he'd be back on the twenty-fourth, and I don't imagine he would have planned on staying in Chicago any longer than he had to. You said the San Luis police found he had a return ticket for that date."

"Okay, then, how did Al know he was coming back? And why, if Al wanted him dead, didn't he do it as soon as he found John was still alive? He could have done it anytime."

"I think Al was pretty confident John wanted to keep his distance. But when Sophia died, Al probably knew John would try to make it to the funeral, and he decided to kill him before he got there."

"I still don't see what reason he'd have. He could just have let John come back."

"Marie told us at the recital that Sophia had refused to sign the documents that would have declared John legally dead, even though Al had been after her to do so. She also apparently never changed her will, which means John was entitled to a third of her estate. Al's a greedy bastard, and killing John before he had a chance to resurface—and making sure no one would be able to identify his body—would mean he could then file the papers to have John declared legally dead and thereby get his portion of John's share of Sophia's estate."

There was another long pause; then Brad said, "This is all conjecture and speculation, but it would be a pretty solid motive. I suppose we could talk to him. But there's still one major problem."

"What's that?"

"Despite everything you've said, and as plausible as it may be, we'd still need proof positive that our John Doe is John Collina."

"You have John's DNA. Can you get a sample from Al?"

Brad laughed. "If I'd just killed my brother and tried to destroy his identity, I sure as hell wouldn't volunteer to give a DNA sample!"

"Well, would it hurt to ask? If he refuses, that'd be another pretty good indication that he's hiding something."

There was another long pause. "Well, I'm not sure. Let me think about all this. We can't go running off accusing people—even a shit like Al Collina—of murder if we're not sure of who the victim is. It still could be possible that our John Doe is someone else entirely."

"Trust me, he's not. He's John Collina."

"I admire your conviction, Elliott, and I might agree with you, but I don't *know* that he is, and unless you know something you're not telling me, you can't, either. You've made a good case in theory, but again, theory isn't the same as fact. Is there anything else? Anything you're not telling me? "

"No," Elliott lied. "I'm just absolutely positive that I'm right, and if I am, we can't let Al Collina get away with it."

"No argument," Brad said. "But I'm walking on pretty thin ice here. As I say, let me think on it and figure out how to handle it, okay?"

"Sure. Thanks, Brad. I don't know what I would—or could—do about all this if it weren't for you."

"No problem. We'll talk later. G'night."

"Night."

❋

Elliott had no doubt, when he went to bed, that he would be hearing from John. But trying to will himself to sleep, of course, had the opposite effect, and his growing impatience made it even worse. The last time he remembered looking at the clock, it was twelve-fifteen.

— *I'm John Collina! John Collina! I have a name!*

Elliott could feel the relief.

— *You're sure? It's not just because I say you are?*

— *No! No! I know it, now. But I couldn't have known it without you. Thank you, Elliott!*

John had called him Elliott! It was the first time John had ever acknowledged him as an individual human being, and not just a window through which he was looking in an effort to find himself. To Elliott, it was a seminal moment.

— *But...*

— *But what?*

— *Did you and I know each other...before?*

— *Yes.*

— *Were we friends?*

— *Yes, we were friends. What do you remember about...before?*

— *Bits and pieces...like fragments of dreams, but I know they weren't dreams. It's so hard to describe. But there are more of them all the time. It's all coming together, but not fast enough!*

— *Do you remember your family?*

— *Yes, I...sort of, but again, not clearly, not fully. I know I do not like my father. Do I have a sister? I think I do.*

— Marie.

— Yes, Marie. I like Marie.

— And you have a brother, Al.

— Al. Isn't Al my father?

— No, your father was Vittorio.

— Oh. I'm...I'm getting...confused. Can we stop now?

— Sure.

And when he next looked at the clock, it was seven forty-five.

❧

He could not recall the last time he had felt so good. It was as though he had just been separated from a Siamese twin. There was a sense of mild euphoria knowing John had made a giant step toward what Elliott could only think of as independence.

He had rather hoped that once John learned who he was his entire memory would immediately return, including the details of his murder and the knowledge of who killed him. But he resigned himself that, as in any case of retrograde amnesia, John had to rediscover things at his own pace.

He found it both interesting and ominously significant that John had his brother and his father confused. Hardly a surprise, though, considering how much alike Vittorio and Al Collina were. He thought it a little odd, though, that John had not mentioned his mother.

A call from the demolition company informed him they had received the necessary permits and that the work would begin Thursday. Finishing up some final calculations, which confirmed that the Elmdale four-flat could be a worthwhile investment, he called the owners to set up a Wednesday meeting to discuss the selling price, after which he believed he would be able to make an offer contingent upon an inspection by his crew.

Feeling a bit guilty about his behavior the previous night at dinner, he made a point to call Cessy and, after verifying that Mrs. Priebe would be leaving Sunday, invited her and the family out to dinner Thursday night. Cessy thought it was a great idea and told him she'd check with Brad and get back to him.

"I hope you'll ask Steve to come along," she said, never passing up an opportunity to push her brother down the aisle. He grinned to himself, but said nothing.

❧

As he was having his before-dinner drink and watching the news, the phone rang.

"Elliott, Brad. Dinner Thursday's fine, though you don't have to."

"I know I don't, but I want to see your mom again before she goes back, and I don't want Cessy to have to feed me two times in one week. I figured we could go to Castlemare—I think your mom would like it."

"That'll be great," Brad said. "We can arrange the logistics later. I just wanted to let you know that we'll be seeing Al Collina tomorrow afternoon at two o'clock at his office. We won't even bring up the Sheffield incident—that's up to the fire department's arson squad—but at least we can get a feel for what he might know about his brother and some of the other things we talked about. I'll give you a call to let you know how it went."

"I really appreciate that, Brad. I know you're going way beyond the call of duty on this."

"Well, John Doe was murdered. He had a real name when he was alive. Whether he was John Collina or not, and whether Al Collina had anything to do with his death or not, we owe it to him to check out every possible lead."

"Our John Doe is John Collina, and Al Collina killed him. I have never been more sure of anything in my life."

"I admire your conviction," Brad said. "So, we'll talk later."

Elliott hung up the phone with a new appreciation for his brother-in-law, and realized that maybe they were both more sentimental than they cared to let on.

❧

— *Is it true?*

  — *Is what true?*

  — *What you said to Brad. About my...brother?*

  — *I'm afraid so. Do you remember anything about him?*

  — *No. But I don't think I like him very much.*

  — *Do you know why?*

  — *I've been trying to remember. Really. But...he was not nice to...Marie. When we were children...That's when you and I were friends, isn't it?*

  — *Yes...Can you remember anything at all about your childhood?*

  — *No. Just feelings. But they're strong feelings. Do you really think my brother would kill me? How could he do that?*

  — *I really wish I could tell you.*

  — *Maybe it would be better if I don't remember.*

  — *No! You've got to remember, if you can. Keep trying.*

  — *I will. I have been.*

❧

Wednesday passed quickly. He had set up a ten-thirty meeting with the owners of the Elmdale building. Somewhat to his surprise, they had a lawyer—the wife's brother—present. The lawyer's presence didn't bother him as much as the fact that the sellers had not mentioned he would be there. Still, he could understand their natural concern, and had gone through enough negotiations himself to know what he was doing. He was confident he could spot anything suspicious or not totally aboveboard.

He quickly determined the lawyer was just there as silent reassurance for the owners, and actually was grateful for his presence when he was able to resolve a couple of questions on which they might otherwise have been confused without the man's expertise.

Although by the end of their meeting Elliott knew exactly how much he was going to offer, he did not want to appear too eager, so he told them he would get

151

back to them later in the day. He ran some errands, stopped at Unabridged Books to pick up a mystery Steve had recommended to him then went across the street for coffee at the Caribou, where he ran into a couple of friends he'd not seen in a while and spent some time catching up. Returning home around two, he called the owners of the four-flat to initiate the offer-counteroffer dance. They told them they'd talk it over and get back to him with an answer.

He'd just hung up from a check-in call from Steve when Brad called.

"Things are starting to move in our John Doe case." he began.

Elliott noted Brad still was not totally convinced of his story or fully accepted that John Doe was John Collina.

"We met with Al Collina this morning, and showed him Doe's photo. He denied that it was his brother, and of course, he flatly refused our request for a DNA sample. He's got a pretty solid alibi for the night Doe was killed—he was at his mother's wake in Lake Geneva with his wife and daughter. Which doesn't mean he didn't have someone else do it for him.

"And there's been another really interesting development. Remember Little Joe Donnelly, the body in your basement?"

"Hard to forget a body in the basement," Elliott said.

"Yeah, well, the cause of death was pretty obviously a gunshot wound to the head, and forensics found the bullet still inside the skull. Other than determining it was from a thirty-eight, it was too distorted to even try to trace it to a specific weapon. But there was also a second bullet, lodged between two vertebrae in the spine, they apparently hadn't bothered to check. Maybe they figured that, after all this time, it didn't matter.

"It did. When they were preparing Donnelly's remains to return to the family, someone realized that no comparison had been run on the second bullet, which was largely intact, so they finally checked. And guess what? The gun that killed Little Joe Donnelly in nineteen-twenty-seven also killed our John Doe."

"How can they possibly know that? The same gun used in two murders nearly eighty years apart?"

"Every gun has a unique bore pattern which is etched onto the bullet when it passes through the barrel. As soon as they put the Donnelly bullet in the computer system, it kicked out a match to the bullets found in John Doe."

"But the same gun? After nearly eighty years? Is that possible?"

"A gun's just a piece of metal—or several pieces—after all, and with the proper conditions and care, there's no reason one can't last almost forever."

"What does this mean?"

"It's all circumstantial, of course, but since Vitto Collina was implicated in Donnelly's death, it's not impossible that he might have had the gun hidden somewhere, and that Al found it. Al probably didn't even knew about Donnelly, and he might have figured that a gun that old couldn't be traced."

"So, what's the next step?"

"We're going to show Doe's photo to Sister Marie, to see if she recognizes him, and ask her for a DNA sample."

152

"Ah, I'm afraid that won't help."

"Why not?"

"Because Marie was adopted. She's not genetically related to Al or Johnny."

"Damn! I didn't know that—or had forgotten, if I did! Well, if we want DNA, we're just going to have to find a way to get it from Al. We'll see what she says about the picture."

"Good luck!"

"Thanks. Nobody said police work was easy. So, we'll see you tomorrow? Do you want to meet us here, or shall we just meet at the restaurant?"

"Why don't we meet at Castlemare at around seven-thirty? I'll call for reservations as soon as we hang up."

"Sounds good. We'll see you there."

✻

— I told you.

   — Told me what?

   — About the man in the basement. That there was more. I just didn't know what it was.

   — Did you know about the gun?

   — No. I don't like guns. I don't like to think about them.

   — Of course. I'm sorry.

   — Don't be sorry.

   — So, no more thoughts or memories about your...about Al Collina?

   — No. I don't like to think about him, either.

   — Well, Marie will recognize you.

   — I don't want her to see that photo. I don't want her to see me...that way.

   — I understand that, too, but without her identification...

   — I know. But maybe you can ask Brad not to show it to her. Maybe it's enough that I know who I am.

   — You can't believe that! It's not enough! You deserved more!

   — We all deserve more. What happened to me happened. It can't be changed.

   — No, it can't be changed, but whoever did this to you has to pay for it. He took your life!

   — And his will end, too, someday. I still can't believe my brother could have done this. I don't want revenge.

   — But justice would be nice.

   — Yes, it would.

   — And you'll get it, I promise.

✻

Thursday morning he took a drive down to the Sheffield property to see if the demolition crew had arrived. He entered the alley intending to park in the area behind the building, but a large bulldozer, a smaller end-loader and a dump truck had taken up all the space. Going around to the front, he saw several workers carefully taking down the new fence he'd put up in front of the building,

153

which apparently the demolition company intended to salvage for resale. A larger end-loader, engine running, sat halfway on the sidewalk waiting to move closer. The sight gave him a sinking feeling in his stomach.

He found a parking place a block or so north and started back to the site. He noticed Collina's building was all but entirely leveled, and that the building on the north side of it was now in also in the demolition process. Apparently, Collina's condo complex plan was going on as planned. He saw Al's car, though Al was nowhere in sight, which was fine with him.

He'd reached his own property and was about to find and speak to the foreman of his demolition crew when he heard his name called. Turning around, he saw Al Collina approaching, cigarette in one hand, can of soda in the other.

"Smith! I want to talk to you!" He strode over like a bantam rooster.

"What can I do for you?" Elliott vowed not to let the bastard rattle his cage.

"How about calling off your boys here?" Al said. "I've already got a crew on my site. What say you let me take the whole thing off your hands, save you a ton of money, and I'll buy it all flat out. You walk away with no worries and a nice piece of cash."

He quoted a figure, and Elliott just stared at him.

"Very generous of you, Al," he said, "but I'm thinking of having the property rezoned for commercial use and putting in an auto junkyard."

Collina looked at him, not sure at first whether he might be serious, then took a long drag on his cigarette and shook his head.

"Last chance," he said. "You won't get a better offer."

"I'm not looking for an offer," Elliott replied.

Taking a last swig from his cola, Collina dropped his cigarette butt into the can and tossed it casually onto Elliott's property.

"You always were a pain in the ass," he said, then turned and strode away without looking back.

Elliott smiled and went over to pick up the discarded pop can.

❧

Castlemare, though small and relatively new, was fast developing a reputation as one of the best Italian restaurants in the city, and it lived up to that reputation. Even Mrs. Priebe was impressed, which was, to Elliott, the ultimate sign of approval.

On the way out of the restaurant, after handshakes and hugs goodbye, Elliott asked Brad to wait a moment while he went to his car. Returning with a small paper bag, he handed it to him.

"What's this?" Brad asked.

"A pop can and a cigarette butt," Elliott replied, "and Al Collina's DNA."

❧

"Can I ask you a really stupid question?" Steve asked as they lay in bed after another Saturday night get-together.

Elliott turned on his side to face him and propped himself up on one arm.

154

"Sure," he said, a bit puzzled.

Steve sighed. "Please don't take this the wrong way. I'm not trying to get anything out of you, but I was just curious. How come every time I ask you to do something, you always say yes?"

Elliott laughed. "Well, that is an unusual question. What made you ask it?"

Steve shrugged, looking a bit embarrassed in the dim light coming from the partly open bedroom door. "You didn't answer me."

"Well, the answer is, why wouldn't I?"

"Questions don't answer questions," he said. "What I'm wondering is...don't you date other people?"

Elliott wasn't quite sure he understood—or wanted to understand—what Steve was getting at.

"I'm a one-at-a-time dater," he said. "I've never been good at juggling three or four guys at the same time. Why? How about you? You a juggler?"

Steve's face clearly reflected that he wished he'd never brought the subject up.

"No, I'm not a juggler. I guess I'm pretty much like you in that regard. It's just that I feel like I've been taking up a lot of your time, and I don't want you to feel...well, obligated."

Elliott shook his head slowly. "I don't feel obligated to do anything. I could easily have asked you the same question and said the same thing. If you want to see other guys, I sure can't stop you—I left my handcuffs and leg shackles at home. You're a big boy, and you can do what you want." He said it with a lot more assurance than he felt, and mentally began preparing himself for the other shoe to drop.

Steve scooted over closer to him. "Jeez, no. That's not what I meant at all! Damn! I knew I wasn't going to say it right, and I didn't. All I wanted to say was that I don't want to put you in a stranglehold. I'm not seeing anyone else because I don't want to see anyone else. I was just trying to find out if we're on the same page on this."

Elliott grinned and reached to slide his hand over Steve's chest.

"We're on the same page," he said.

❋

Having had a call on Saturday morning from the owners of the Elmdale property, countering his offer at only slightly more, Elliott had agreed, contingent on the inspection. On Monday, he called Ted, Arnie and Sam to coordinate on a time then called the owners to confirm.

As always with an impending new project, he was energized by the prospect and began going over the notes and rough sketches he'd made from his first visit to the property. He did some more sketches, concentrating on the basement conversion, which would require the most work.

He'd talked with Cessy over the weekend but not with Brad. Mrs. Priebe had safely returned to New York, and the family was settling back into its routine. Cessy, of course, asked about Steve, and wanted to know if a definite date had been set for his gallery showing. He relayed the information he'd received from Steve—that the show would open in three weeks, and that he was awaiting the arrival of a number of paintings his parents were shipping to him from California. He also assured her that Steve would be sending them a formal invitation to the opening, which pleased her.

He rather hoped he might hear from Brad Monday night. While John had withdrawn to the periphery of his consciousness for the weekend, Elliott could sense that he, too, was awaiting the results of Al Collina's DNA analysis, which would officially confirm the identity the circumstances of his death had denied him.

Brad didn't call, and while he realized that something as complex as DNA testing took time, he sensed that John did not. That was confirmed shortly after he fell asleep Monday night.

— *He didn't call.*
— *He'll call as soon as he knows anything.*
— *I don't want Marie to see that photo.*
— *She won't have to see it. The DNA test will prove you're John Collina.*
— *I hope so. But...I feel something's wrong.*
— *What do you mean?*
— *I don't know. But I feel it.*
— *Don't worry. DNA doesn't lie.*
— *No, but it doesn't always tell the truth, either.*
— *What is that supposed to mean?*
— *I don't know, but something's wrong.*

❀

There were times, Elliott thought as he had his coffee Tuesday morning, that John's tendency to be cryptic could be really frustrating. He had no idea what John had been referring to, but knew whatever it was would become clear eventually, and determined not to waste any time worrying about it—which he nevertheless found easier said than done.

He was anxious to have his crew go through the four-flat so that, barring any unforeseen problems, he could get into escrow. Ted, Sam and Arnie had been fairly busy with their own projects and minor upkeep on Elliott's other buildings, but he wouldn't be happy until they could get in and get to work. Once they had gone through the building carefully and had a better idea of just what they'd be doing, he could at least begin the detail work: finalizing the sketches, deciding on the materials, fixtures, appliances they'd need, making the rounds of the various hardware depots. It all took a lot of time, and he loved it.

Despite his impatience to get back to work, he realized that things were going very well in his life. He wasn't quite sure where he and Steve might be headed, but he was comfortable for the moment with just going where the currents would take him. And he had no idea what would become of John once his identity was definitely established. He assumed that once all the issues that had kept John from moving on to wherever it was spirits go had been resolved, he would...well, move on.

Still, Elliott was a little surprised to realize that, in some way, he'd miss having John around. They'd been friends once, when John was alive, and he couldn't help but feel that friendship still spanned their two worlds. That they had found one another after so many years—never mind how, and why—raised thoughts far more profound than he had the ability or desire to pursue.

Once again, his reverie was interrupted by the telephone. John was instantly with him.

"Elliott, it's Brad. I don't know exactly how to tell you this, but we're back to square one...again."

"What do you mean?" he asked, but he was afraid he knew.

"I mean that I just got the DNA report back on Al Collina. It doesn't match our John Doe."

"But it has to!" Elliott realized even as he said it how stupid it sounded. "Al and Johnny had different mothers, but the same father. Surely, that would show."

"It would if they were related. But they're not. Face it, Elliott, I don't know who our John Doe is, but he's not a Collina."

CHAPTER 14

ঞ্জ৯

Sorry, Elliott," Brad continued. "I know how strongly you feel about this, but DNA doesn't lie. Al Collina is sticking to his story that his brother died in Africa eight years ago. He claims he never saw the guy in the photo before in his life, but I wouldn't trust him any farther than I can throw him. I'm going to take the photo over to show it to Sister Marie. We'll see what she has to say. Maybe that will give us an idea of where to look next."

Elliott felt a surge of what he interpreted as sorrow and frustration. He knew John didn't want his sister to see him dead, but there was no choice.

"Okay," he said. "Let me know what she says, will you?"

"You know I will," Brad agreed patiently. "Later."

Elliott managed a goodbye and hung up.

Going to the kitchen for another cup of coffee, he tried to make some sense of what Brad had just told him. He wandered into the guest bedroom and opened the closet, taking down a box of memorabilia from his childhood. Rummaging through it, he found the framed photo of him and Johnny leaning against one another, grinning, his arm over Johnny's shoulder. Carrying it into the den, he got the manilla envelope with John's postmortem photo and compared the two. There was no denying a strong resemblance, though he still couldn't be positive.

Looking again at the photo of the two of them, he remembered how he had been struck by how much Johnny resembled the picture he had once seen of a teenage Vittorio Collina. There was no doubt in his mind that Johnny was Vitto's son. He couldn't comprehend how Al's DNA couldn't match John's.

Unless, he realized in a thunderbolt of thought, unless it was *Al* who wasn't a Collina! Vitto had adopted Marie; perhaps Al was also adopted.

But from what little he knew of Vitto Collina, he found that idea hard to imagine. Vitto was a stereotypical old-country macho Sicilian. He might be willing to adopt the daughter of one of his close friends—by his code, Marie was technically family, and it would be totally in character for him to take on familial responsibility. But to adopt another man's son unless he already had one of his own? And a non-relative? After being married only a couple of years? It was all but inconceivable that Vittorio's pride would allow him to even consider it.

158

And obviously, it wasn't that he wasn't able to have children—Johnny was born four years after Vitto married Sophia.

Shaking his head, he finished his coffee and headed for the shower.

❧

The walk-through of the Elmdale building and going for coffee afterwards with his crew took most of the afternoon. All agreed that the project would be relatively simple, but that the improvements would increase the building's value substantially. Elliott said he'd call the owners and go into escrow as soon as possible; they had been waiting for the sale to be official before finalizing their condo purchase. He would again offer the remaining tenants the option to move into one of his other buildings rather than merely handing them eviction notices, which he always hated to do.

While Elliott was busy with work details, John seemed content to remain on the far periphery of his mind; but once he was in his car on the way home, he could feel John's sense of anticipation—mixed with his own—for Brad's report of his meeting with Marie Collina—Sister Marie.

On his way up from the parking garage his cell phone rang, and he hastily removed it from his pocket.

"Elliott," he said.

"I'm just on my way home from St. Agnes," Brad announced. "I met with Sister Marie right after school."

"And?"

"After being devastated by the idea that her brother John might not have died eight years ago in Africa, you mean? Yeah, she was pretty sure Doe's photo is him."

"Only pretty sure?"

"Well, with the bruising and the fact that she hadn't seen him in nearly nine years, and that she'd never known him to wear any kind of beard or really short hair—as I said, she took it really hard."

"So, what's next?"

"We'll do a check on birth certificates," he said. "Since Sister Marie was adopted, there's an outside chance that maybe she wasn't the only one. We should be able to tell when we see the birth records."

Rather than going through the lobby and trying to talk on the elevator, Elliott paused beneath the building's canopy. He told Brad about John's physical resemblance to Vitto, and his belief that Vitto Collina would not have adopted a son at that particular point in his life.

"So, something has to be wrong somewhere," he concluded.

"Yeah," Brad agreed. "But obviously one of them was not Vitto's son. Let's see what the birth certificates tell us."

❧

—*Marie knows.*

— *Knows what?*

— *The truth. She doesn't want to admit it, but she knows.*

159

— What truth?

— She's too good.

— Too good? I don't understand.

— She refuses to see the bad in people.

— Are you talking about Al?

— He's not a good person.

— She knows something about Al?

— Yes.

— Something about Al and you?

— No. About him and...

Even in sleep, Elliott was more than mildly frustrated by feeling he was constantly playing Twenty Questions with John, having to drag information from him.

— That's not fair. I tell you what I can. There's just so much I don't know yet.

— Oh, great! You're reading my thoughts!

— I'm not reading them. When you're asleep, your mind is wide open. Your thoughts are everywhere. They're hard to avoid. But this is all still so...confusing.

— Yeah, I guess it is. But you say Marie knows something about Al and somebody else. Who?

— About...my father.

— Does she know whether or not Al is your real brother? Whether he's your father's son?

— No. I'm sure she doesn't know that. I never knew that. I still don't know if that's true. These things just...come to me, and I tell you when they do. All I know is that she knows something bad, and she's too good to recognize it.

Elliott woke in the morning still thinking of what it was that Marie might know, and how to find out. Shortly after nine, he received a call from his lawyer telling him that Al Collina's attorneys had notified him Collina was filing suit for the damage done to his property as a result of the explosion.

"Damages? What an asshole!" Elliott exclaimed. "He was tearing the place down anyway!"

"Yes, but he claims the process was made much more expensive because of the dangers created for the demolition crews by the fire damage. However, he says he may be willing to reconsider the suit if you will sell him the property."

"Gee, what a surprise! Tell them to take their offer and shove it."

"I figured that would be your response, but had to pass it by you first."

"Of course. And thanks. I'm sure you'll let me know if he follows through on it."

"I will, but I wouldn't lose too much sleep over it if I were you."

❁

Though he talked to Cessy Thursday afternoon, he didn't hear from Brad until early Friday evening.

"We checked the birth certificates for both John and Al Collina," Brad informed him. "They both show Vittorio Collina as the father. John's certificate shows Sophia Rosa Collina as the mother, but Al's mother was apparently not the woman Vitto Collina was married to at the time."

"Interesting! Who was she?"

"The name on the certificate is Celeste Anna Brusco. No idea who she is or was, but there are a couple interesting possibilities. Vitto was a notorious womanizer—he might very well have gotten one of his mistresses pregnant then took the kid from her. Or maybe his first wife couldn't have kids and this was Vitto's way of getting a son. But just because a man's name appears on a birth certificate doesn't guarantee he's the father. Since one of the boys isn't Vitto's biological son, I can make a pretty sure bet which one that would be."

"Al."

"Al," Brad echoed. "From what I know of Sophia Collina, she was a real class act compared to her husband, and I just can't imagine that she might have played around on him. I think we'll have another talk with Al to see if we can get anything out of him. Even if we can't, it'll be nice to give him something to think about.

"I'd say it's a pretty safe bet Vitto never knew he might not be Al's real father. And I'm also going to check with Chet Green, our unofficial gang historian, to see if he might know anything about what Vitto might have been up to around the time Al was born."

❈

He'd originally intended to get together with Steve Friday night, but Steve called just after Elliott's talk with Brad, saying he had to work late to meet a deadline for an important client, so they rescheduled for Saturday. Elliott spent the night just taking it easy. Idly flipping through the channels just before the ten o'clock news, he saw that *San Francisco* was on one of the movie channels. It was one of his all-time favorite movies, and even though he'd seen it a dozen times or more, he couldn't resist watching Clark Gable, Spencer Tracy and Jeannette MacDonald stumble through the greatest earthquake scenes ever filmed.

It was just before midnight by the time he went to bed, and he had barely closed his eyes when...

— *We're close.*

— *Close to what?*

— *To the end. To having it all come together.*

— *How do you know?*

— *I feel it! When I first came to you, I didn't know anything but my name. It was like having a thousand jigsaw puzzle pieces, all face down, and no picture on the box to be able to compare them to. And then slowly the pieces started to turn over, and fit together. So many pieces. But they're turning over faster now, and I'm beginning to see whole chunks of the puzzle, and pretty soon I know I'll be able to see it all and I'll be free. I feel it!*

— *Do you realize that's just about the most you've ever said at one time?*

161

— Yes. I'm more...me...now. I like it.

Elliott wanted to continue the conversation, but the mind static moved in, and he couldn't resist it.

✽

Steve called at around ten o'clock Saturday morning to announce that the paintings his folks had sent from California had arrived and invited Elliott over for dinner to see them and celebrate. Elliott was definitely in a celebrating mood. He sensed from his conversation with John of the night before that things were beginning to move rapidly to a conclusion. What that conclusion might be he had no idea, but he tried to convince himself it wasn't the destination that mattered so much as the journey.

He stopped on the way over to Steve's to pick up a bottle of champagne.

Steve, too, was in a celebratory mood and, from the smells coming from the kitchen, had apparently spent a lot of effort on preparing dinner. The table was set for two, with fresh flowers in a crystal bowl in the center.

"Too much?" Steve asked as he returned from putting the champagne on ice and saw Elliott taking it all in.

Elliott grinned. "Not at all! I'm just impressed that you went to all the trouble."

"Hey, you're the one who brought the champagne."

He had noticed three or four large, flat cartons of varying sizes leaning against the wall to one side of the door.

"Let's get a drink first, then we'll do the unveiling. What would you like?"

"Bourbon-Seven's fine."

He followed Steve back into the kitchen, where the champagne was cooling in a burled-wood ice bucket. They smalltalked while Steve fixed their drinks, made a quick check of the oven then led Elliott back to the living room.

"I figured I'd wait till you got here to open them up," Steve said, setting his drink on a bookcase beside the cartons and retrieving a utility knife from his pocket. Getting down on one knee, he carefully slit the tape sealing the first carton. He reached in and removed the first bubble-wrapped painting from between layers of protective cardboard.

"Ah," he said holding the canvas by the edges so Elliott could see it, "Manny! I don't do many portraits, but I always liked this one."

The picture was a head-and-bare-shoulders study of a handsome young man, his head turned slightly to one side, looking out of the frame. There was something almost beatific in his calm expression.

"We'd just found out he was positive," Steve said, and for a moment his face reflected a sadness that touched Elliott. As if he'd caught himself, Steve's normal expression returned.

"It's beautiful," Elliott said. "He looks a lot like you."

Steve smiled. "Thanks, but Manny's the good-looking one in the family."

He carefully replaced the bubble-wrap and slid the painting back into the carton, moving it in front of the bookcase.

162

There were six in all—three landscapes; a still-life of a rocking chair in front of a partially opened door; a full-length portrait of a smiling young girl, arms raised toward a brightly colored beach ball partly out of the frame above her head, and Manny's.

"You're not going to sell Manny's portrait, are you?" Elliott asked.

"I don't really want to," Steve replied. "Hell, I don't want to part with any of them—it's like selling a kid. But I did a similar one of him and gave it to him, so this is kind of a spare, and any money I make as a result of the gallery showing will be going into a special fund for...in case Manny ever needs it."

Touched by Steve's obvious love for his brother but not wanting to pursue that particular line of conversation further, Elliott changed the subject.

"I don't mean to be nosy," he said as Steve put the last of the paintings back into its container and the two men moved to the sofa to finish their drinks, "but who sets the price on the paintings, the artist or the gallery?"

Steve shrugged. "It's sort of a collaboration. I told the gallery what I'd like to get for each one, and they though I could get a lot more. So, we mostly went with their recommendations."

"Well, I'm sure you'll do very well. You've got real talent."

Steve grinned. "You wouldn't be slightly prejudiced, would you?"

Elliott returned the grin. "Of course I would. But I'm serious—I really envy you!"

Finishing his drink, Steve reached over and laid a hand on Elliott's thigh. "And on that note," he said, "I think we should see about dinner."

❋

Maybe Cessy was right, Elliott thought as he pulled into the garage late Sunday night. Maybe he should seriously consider settling down, and being with Steve certainly didn't discourage him from that idea. But not just yet. Neither he nor, from what he could gather, Steve was in any hurry.

He always remembered what a friend had told him some time before: "The sooner they say 'I love you', the sooner they forget your name." He didn't want to forget Steve's name, or have Steve forget his, and they really hadn't known one another long enough to be sure if what they were mutually experiencing might not just be, as the song said "too hot not to cool down." Hot, he readily admitted, it certainly was. But, beyond the testosterone, he really liked the guy.

More tired than he realized, he went to bed nearly as soon as he got into the apartment.

— *I do like him.*

— *Yeah, I do, too.*

— *But you're wise not to rush.*

— *Did you ever have a relationship...other than with Cole?*

— *I don't think so. Not really. I guess I never met anyone who could match up to you.*

— *!!!*

— I'm joking, Elliott. I can joke now. I like that. But I do remember you now, from when we were kids.

— How did you ever get hooked up with someone like Cole?

— We're getting into the grey areas here. It's like a fog lifting, and most of my life is still not really clear to me yet. But I know Rob was a disaster, and that I never should have gotten involved with him. Maybe I was just lonely and rushed into something I could only regret later.

— Why did you let your family think you were dead?

— I'm not sure yet, but I think...I think my father disowned me. He was not a nice man. I knew it caused a lot of trouble between my parents, and I think I thought it would be better for everyone if I pretended to be dead. And now I am.

— So, you did it to spare your mother trouble with your father? What about Marie?

— Marie was in the convent. She had God. She didn't need me.

— I won't even ask about Al.

— No, please don't.

❊

The rapid acceleration of John's self-awareness both pleased and disturbed Elliott as he sat in the living room with his coffee, looking out the window at the towers of the Loop in the distance. As John reclaimed his individuality, Elliott was mildly concerned with how two separate people could manage to exist in one mind and body. It hadn't reached the point—and he prayed it never would—of his becoming a classic textbook multiple personality, sharing his body alternately with John. He swore the moment he sensed that happening he would seek professional help. He really liked John, and wanted to help him any way he could, but not to the point of losing part of himself. Still, he had no idea what John's options were, or what would happen when, as John had indicated, he'd be free. Free to do what was the question.

❊

The days passed, filled with busywork. No word from his lawyer, which was fine with Elliott. A few check-in calls from Cessy but nothing from Brad. A meeting with his crew to go over sketches and ideas for the Elmdale building once escrow closed. A call from Steve asking if Elliott could help him take his paintings down to the gallery the following Monday evening after Steve got home from work.

Finally, on Wednesday, just after the evening news, he heard from Brad, who had talked with the department's historian on gang activity.

"Chet did some research," Brad said, "and it seems Vitto was having an affair with Celeste Brusco for about a year before Al was born. The rumor was that his wife wasn't able to have kids. Vitto couldn't divorce her, being a good Catholic, but he was bound and determined to have a son and decided Celeste was going to give him one. He kept her almost a prisoner in her apartment, and he assigned one of his top aides, a guy named Larry Genestra, to keep an eye on her and not

164

let her out of his sight. Celeste apparently wasn't too happy about it, but she didn't have much choice. When Al was born, Vitto paid her off and sent her on her way. No idea what she might have thought about that, but she dropped off the radar. Nobody was supposed to know, but of course, a lot of people did."

"Interesting!"

"Yeah, and it's pretty likely that Genestra might have done a little more than watch over her. The fact that Genestra lived to a ripe old age is a pretty good indication that Vitto never suspected Al wasn't his own."

"You haven't had a chance to get back with Al on this yet, I gather?"

"No, he's put us off a couple of times, but we're through farting around with him. I called his office just before I left work and told him we'll be there tomorrow at two, and that he could talk to us there or we could arrange to have him brought into the station."

"Good luck! Do you think he knows Vitto wasn't his dad?"

"I doubt it. Who would have told him? But we'll definitely check it out when we talk to him. It'll be interesting to see his reaction."

"I'd like to see that, too," Elliott said, and had the distinct impression he was speaking for John as well.

"I'll let you know," Brad said. There was a pause during which Elliott could hear a muffled exchange, then: "Ah, Cessy says dinner's ready. I'll talk to you later."

❊

It occurred to him Thursday morning that John had been very quiet over the course of the past few days—or, rather, nights—and Elliott wondered why. He did recall having some rather peculiar dreams, the details of which he could not remember. Whether they had anything at all to do with John he had no way of knowing.

When the phone rang around six-fifteen Thursday night, he assumed it was Brad, but it was Steve, asking for Cessy and Brad's address so he could send them an invitation to the opening of his gallery showing, which was now only a little more than a week away. He could tell Steve was excited about it, and he couldn't blame him. Though he said nothing, he had every intention of buying the portrait of Steve's brother. He was quite sure Steve would refuse to accept it as a gift, and knew that even offering it might appear that he was flaunting his wealth, not to mention probably being inappropriate at this stage of their relationship. But he really liked the painting and didn't want it to go to strangers. He'd buy it anonymously and not display it until he had a better idea of where he and Steve were headed. Perhaps someday, if anything ever were to develop between them, Steve would accept its return.

They made plans to have dinner and go to a movie Friday night. He was conscious they were easing into an assumption that they'd spend at least part of every weekend together, and he was comfortable with it.

Cessy called at around seven-thirty to update him on everything that had gone on since they'd last talked, which always managed to be a lot despite the fact it had only been two days. Brad, she explained, wasn't home yet, having been delayed as a result of having to follow up on a drive-by shooting.

When Elliott said he had hoped to hear from Brad, Cessy said she'd have him call if it wasn't too late when he got home. He felt a bit guilty about neglecting to tell her not to bother if Brad was tired, but he really was curious about whether Brad had met with Al and, if so, what had come of it.

At around nine-thirty, Brad called. He sounded worn out, and Elliott again felt guilty about making an issue of wanting to talk to him right then.

"Okay," Brad said, "Collina was there and we had a chance to ask him what he knew of his real mother, and the possibility that Vitto Collina wasn't his real father. Now, if someone started questioning me about my parentage, I'd be pretty damned pissed. Al kept his best poker face and flatly denied having any idea what we were talking about, but the rage wasn't there. We couldn't prove he was lying, but I'd bet my bottom dollar he knows more than he wants us to think he does. It's possible he knows about his real mother but not about Vitto not being his real father, and I can't see any way of finding that out."

"I don't suppose Marie would know anything?" Elliott wondered out lout, although he knew from John that while Marie knew something important it apparently wasn't about Al's true paternity.

He could almost see Brad shaking his head. "No, I'd think that would really be unlikely. We could ask, but I'd rather we checked everything else first."

"I understand."

If the purpose of the visit to Al had merely been to rattle his cage, whether it had worked or not was something only Al knew. But at least it let him know he was being watched, and that knowledge just might lead him to do something that could eventually convict him of John's murder.

❈

— *I hope you're wrong.*

— *About what? Al's being responsible for your death?*

— *Yes.*

— *You still can't remember anything about how your...about what happened to you?*

— *No.*

— *What is the last thing you do remember?*

— *Before you and being in your room in the hospital, you mean?*

— *Yes.*

— *I remember being...on a boat. A ferry. Something happened to it.*

— *Yes, it capsized. In Africa.*

— *In Africa. Yes. I was there because...I was...in the Peace Corps! That's interesting! It's all still like being in a thick fog. I'm starting to see some things more clearly now...mostly early things. I remember college pretty well, and dropping out.*

— *Why did you drop out?*

— *My father and I...he disowned me.*

— Do you remember why?

— He found out I was gay.

— How did that happen?

— Al told him.

— Al's a shit.

— Which is why I'm sure he has to be my father's son—they're too much alike for him not to be.

— What about the years between your dropping out of college and joining the Peace Corps. What were you doing then?

— I'm not sure. Moving from place to place. No clear memories. I think that's when I developed an interest in photography, though.

— How did you live, after your father disowned you?

— My...My mother. She sent me money. Until my father found out.

— And that's when you joined the Peace Corps?

— I don't know. But probably. It makes sense.

Reflecting on the conversation the next morning, it struck Elliott again how strange it must be for John, or any amnesiac, to slowly recover lost memories. He couldn't imagine how that must feel. But he knew John was not like other amnesiacs in several major ways, primarily because he was dead but also because he was not only dealing with emerging memories of his past life but with the ability to be aware of things outside himself he could not possibly have known while alive. The body in the basement, for one. His assertion that Marie knew something about Al that John himself couldn't have been aware of while he was alive. for another.

That night, his arm across Steve's chest, he dreamed of water and hills; but they were not the ocean and mountains of his earlier dreams. The water he instinctively knew was a lake, and the hill was more of a large rise, topped with a sprawling Mediterranean-style villa with a green-tiled roof, from which a manicured lawn stretched down to the water's edge. There was a boathouse and a pier, though no boats were visible. Steve emerged from the house and waved.

"I had an interesting dream last night," Steve said as they sat at the kitchen table having breakfast. "You were in it."

Any vestige of sleep vanished instantly. "I was? I'm flattered."

Steve grinned at him. "Don't be," he said. "I don't have any control over my dreams."

Elliott managed to return the grin, though he didn't feel like grinning. "So, what was it about?"

"I'm not sure of all the details. Something about a big fancy mansion on a lake. You came out and waved at me. Are you really that rich, by any chance?"

He hoped his shock didn't show. "Loaded," he said, hoping Steve wouldn't be sure if he was serious. He had never discussed his financial status with Steve because he knew it could be intimidating for some people, and he didn't want to risk its somehow coming between them. But it was Steve's dream—*his* dream, clearly—that disturbed him. This was the second time Steve had inexplicably had a dream that might have been a result of John's experimenting with his ability to reach out to others.

John obviously had made a bridge to Steve, although why he'd done it, Elliott couldn't comprehend—perhaps it had something to do with Steve's having had prior experience with a spirit. But that both he and Steve had seen one another in the same dream setting was downright unnerving.

❧

Though it took him a while to let go of his questions, he and Steve spent a quiet morning listening to CDs, talking about everything and nothing, laughing a lot and, Elliott felt, becoming even more comfortable with each other. At around two-thirty, Steve, who wanted to spend Sunday sending out invitations to his gallery opening and painting, said he'd better think about cleaning up and heading for home. Elliott suggested that, as a water-saving measure, they might consider sharing the shower.

At about four-thiry, totally but happily exhausted, they fell asleep.

— *Sorry about the dream. I was experimenting. It was fun.*

— *I'm glad you think so. So, what does it mean?*

— *I'm not quite sure. It has something to do with the house, though.*

— *Whose house is it? Your family's, I assume.*

— *Yes. You're very perceptive.*

— *I'll overlook the irony in that one.*

— *You're funny, too.*

— *Let's get back to what the dream means.*

— *As I say, I'm not sure.*

— *Why was Steve in my dream? Why was I in Steve's?*

— *That was the fun part. Since I don't know exactly what it means, I thought I'd play with it a little. I really like Steve. He's very open.*

— *Are you trying to pull a Cessy on me?*

— *I don't know what you're talking about...but would it really be so bad to settle down?*

— *Okay, so, back to the dream. No idea of why the house?*

— *It's important. Something's there.*

— *Come on, John! Don't tease.*

— *I'm not teasing. I told you, these things just come to me, and I pass them on to you. If you don't want me to, I won't.*

— *Yes, of course I want you to. It's just that it's really frustrating sometimes.*

— *Try being where I am.*

— *Thanks, but I'm in no rush.*

❧

Returning from taking Steve home after an early dinner, Elliott reflected on the

168

increasing frequency and depth of his exchanges with John, who was reclaiming the distinct personality—including the sense of humor—he remembered from their friendship as kids. While he considered this a major step in John's re-emergence as an individual, it was one thing to have thought of him as a disembodied spirit and quite another to think of him as a real, complete person, someone he actually knew. And, remembering him as a horny teenager, Elliott chose not to speculate on where John was when he and Steve were together. He hoped the adult John's discretion would keep him on the other side of the bedroom door.

He pondered the meaning of the shared dream of John's family home—he assumed it was the one on Lake Geneva to which the Collinas had moved when they left Lake Forest. What might be there, and how could he possibly find out until and unless John remembered something more specific? With Sophia Collina dead and Marie in a convent, that undoubtedly put the property in Al's hands. Since he found it easier to imagine Al in a downtown condo penthouse than on an estate on Lake Geneva, and given the estate's obvious value, he was sure Al would be thinking of ways to cash in on it. For all he knew, it might already have been sold—or perhaps Al was planning to bulldoze it to put up lakeside condos.

But given the nebulous state of John's information, there was really nothing Elliott could do at the moment.

CHAPTER 15

❦

He managed to stay awake about halfway through *Saturday Night Live* and then, finding himself nodding off, he turned off the TV and went to bed.

— *Letters! There are letters! At the house. In a desk, I think.*

— *What letters? To whom? From whom?*

— *To...my father. From a woman. She...wanted money.*

— *Do you know what for?*

— *I'm not sure. I can't read them. But I know they're there, and they're important. If we can find them, you'll know.*

— *How can I find them? Is the house even still there?*

— *Yes. It's there. It's just as...as my mother left it. But it won't be for long.*

— *Al?*

— *Yes. He wants to sell it.*

— *What about Marie? She must have a say in that.*

— *She doesn't need the house. Or the money. But she has gotten much stronger since our moth—recently. She won't let him get away with anything our mother would have objected to. I'm proud of her.*

— *So, what can I do?*

— *Talk to Marie.*

— *She knows about the letters?*

— *No.*

— *You said she knew something about Al and your father.*

— *This isn't what she knows.*

— *And you still don't know what she knows?*

— *No. She keeps it locked inside where she doesn't have to think of it. I can't get to it.*

— *And what can I say to her...that you told me to talk to her?*

— *You can ask Brad to talk to her.*

— *Oh, sure. Even better! He's suspicious enough as it is.*

— *Why? You've been right.*

— *Yes, but one of these days he's going to demand to know how I know what I know. What can I tell him then?*

— Worry about that when the time comes.
— Easy for you to say.
— It is, isn't it? Trust me.
— Do I have a choice?
— I hope not.

✻

He could talk to Marie, he knew. The problem was how to broach the subject of the letters without mentioning John directly. And even if he did tell her of John's presence in his life he, as a confirmed agnostic he didn't know how she, as a woman whose life was devoted to religion, would take hearing he was in communication with her deceased brother. He hoped her concept of an afterlife wasn't limited to the idea of death as being an immediate, nonstop transfer of the soul from the body to either heaven or hell. On the other hand, he was hopeful that, even if she thought he was crazy and rejected his request to search for the letters, she wouldn't tell anyone—especially Cessy—about it.

He'd just have to risk it.

With John becoming more and more a separate and distinct—and stronger—individual, Elliott wanted to do whatever he could to bring the entire matter to a conclusion.

When Cessy called Sunday morning to ask him over for dinner, he accepted without hesitation. He figured he could use the opportunity to ask if she would be willing to set up a meeting with Sister Marie. So that Brad wouldn't object, or think he was trying to interfere with the police investigation, he would explain that, since he and John had been such close friends, he was curious what had happened after they'd lost touch. Whether Brad would buy it or not was another story.

Buy it he did—at least, he didn't express any overt reservations. Cessy said she was sure Sister Marie would be happy to talk with Elliott some day after school, and that she would send a note with Jenny on Monday.

✻

As he'd promised, Monday night he helped take Steve's paintings to the gallery and waited as Steve and the owner discussed various details of the opening. Elliott was impressed by the gallery's support, which included sending invitations to all their regular clients and patrons as well as distributing posters and press releases. Of course, it was in the gallery's own best interests to do everything it could to make the showing a success, but he was impressed, nonetheless.

After spending a couple hours at Steve's helping him unwind, he returned home around ten-thirty to find a message from Cessy that Sister Marie would be happy to talk with him, and that if he wanted to stop by the school Tuesday after classes she would be there.

"Oh," Cessy added, "the invitation to Steve's showing arrived today. I'm so happy for him, and of course, we'll be there. I can imagine how excited he must be. Call me if you get home early enough. Bye."

While he knew she and Brad were probably still up, he decided to hold off until morning to call.

❧

He pulled up at St. Agnes just as the students were pouring out of the doors at the end of their day. He drove around the block to allow time for some of the parked cars with waiting parents to leave then easily found a parking spot.

Jenny had told him Sister Marie's room number was 212, and as he ascended the front steps and entered the building, he was transported back to his own school days. There was an almost palpable aura that emanated from old schools—the faint scent of chalk and books and floor wax; the distinctive echo of footsteps on the hallway's tiled floors; the unmistakable spacing of classroom doors; the glass-fronted display cases along and in the walls; the row on row of identical lockers with identical locks. He knew he could instantly recognize being in a school even if he were led in with his eyes closed.

A large central staircase led up to the second floor, and he took it, noting the worn and pockmarked wood of the dark polished railings, the ever-so-slight indentations along the front edge of each stair where countless feet had slowly worn down the wood.

Most of the doors on the second floor were closed, and the rooms, he could see by looking through the mesh-reinforced windows, were empty and unlighted. He had yet to see another person, and idly wondered where everyone could have gone so quickly.

The door to Room 212 was open, and the lights all on. As he approached, he saw Sister Marie seated at a desk at the front. He paused in the doorway to knock. She looked up at him and smiled, rising to come meet him.

"Elliott," she said with a warm smile. "How nice to see you again!"

"And you, Sister."

"Please, come in," she said, extending her hand.

"I appreciate your seeing me."

She continued smiling as she gestured him to a chair next to her desk. He waited until she had moved around it to take her own seat.

"It's my pleasure," she said. "It's so nice to reconnect with people from the past. I remember how close you and John were and how much fun you had together. I'm grateful to you for that, I'm afraid John didn't have many friends as a child."

He assumed she was alluding to the difficulties inherent in having a wealthy and notorious father and an obnoxious bully for a brother. Either one would make forming normal friendships difficult.

"If it hadn't been for our mother," she continued, "I fear it would have been much worse for him."

"And you," Elliott added.

She smiled again. "Yes, I suppose," she said. "But I always had God to turn to, even as a little girl. And Mother was always there for me. It was harder for

172

John."

He remembered Al's bullying, and while he'd almost never had any contact with Vitto Collina, he could imagine how difficult the combined pressures from his father and brother must have made John's life.

"So, what would you like to know, Elliott?" Marie asked.

He decided the best thing to do would be to try to work into his main purpose gradually. "I've been thinking a lot about John ever since I heard of his death," he began, "and I was wondering what happened to him after your family moved to Lake Geneva."

Marie swiveled her chair slightly toward him and leaned back, her elbows on the arm rests, placing her spread fingertips together as though she were holding an invisible globe.

"Johnny always had a special place in my heart," she said, with yet another small smile that Elliott thought was tinged with sadness. "He had a good, kind, gentle soul, which is one of the things, I'm sure, that led him to join the Peace Corps.

"Alphonso was in every way almost a carbon copy of my father, which made it very difficult for Johnny. His relationship with both of them was never better than strained, and it became more so as we grew up. And then, when Johnny was between his sophomore and junior years in college, my father abruptly disowned him."

Elliott took advantage of her pause to say, "Because he learned of Johnny's sexual orientation?" He was positive Marie had known about her brother's being gay, but he wanted to see if there was any reaction to indicate homophobia on her part. There wasn't.

Marie gave a reluctant shrug. "Yes, I'm afraid so." She did not seem surprised that Elliott knew of John's being gay.

"And what happened to him then?"

"My father threw him out of the house and forbade my mother or me to have any contact with him. But we did, of course, surreptitiously. We'd keep in touch through letters sent through one of my mother's friends, and Mother helped support him financially."

"Until your father found out," Elliott said, remembering John's having mentioned it.

Marie looked at him very strangely. "Yes, but how could you have known that?"

"Sorry, just an assumption," he lied.

"It is hard sometimes to live up to our Lord's teachings," she said with a sigh. "Of course, I loved my father, and I love Alphonso. But even those of us who serve God can admit that there are those who are really not very easy to love, and I've had to struggle with that fact for many years now.

"But anyway, yes, Alphonso somehow found out that our mother had been sending John—he'd stopped being Johnny by then—money and told my father. My father reacted...well, let's just say in a terrible manner. Shortly thereafter, we

173

heard of John's death."

She paused, and Elliott could see her eyes misting.

"And now to find out that he didn't die in Africa, that he was murdered right here in Chicago! It was..." She paused again and quickly wiped her eyes.

"I'm sorry, Sister," he said. "I really didn't intend to bring up painful memories."

She gave a slight wave with one hand. "No, no, that's all right. There are just so many questions. Of course, I can understand now why he pretended to die in Africa—to spare Mother our father's wrath. But to think..."

He regretted having opened doors Marie had obviously chosen to keep closed but decided he had reached the point of no return.

"Were you told," he asked, "that Al's DNA didn't match that of the man you identified as being—and whom I firmly believe is—John?"

She looked surprised. "No, I didn't know that. How could that be? John and Al had different mothers, but..."

"I'm not quite sure, either, Sister. But I was thinking: the police tested Al's DNA, but not your mother's. Do you suppose there might be something at your Lake Geneva home that might have her DNA? A hairbrush, perhaps?"

"A hairbrush, surely," she said. "Mother's rooms are just as she left them."

He was silent a moment, trying to think of how to say what he had to. and when he was unable to come up with anything, he simply began.

"Sister, what I'm about to say may sound very odd, but please believe I am sincere. Ever since I heard of John's death, I've been bothering my brother-in-law Brad, who as you know is one of the detectives on the case, to keep me as informed as he can as to what is going on. And I've been—I told you it would sound odd—having dreams of your home in Lake Geneva. I've never been there, but I get a clear picture of a large Mediterranean-type villa on a rise, with a green-tiled roof and a lawn stretching down to the water. There's a boathouse and a dock..."

Carefully watching for her reaction, he saw her eyes open wide and some of the color fade from her face.

"That's our home," she said. Then, her expression changed to one of mild suspicion. "How could you know?"

"I don't know," he lied again. "But I see it clearly. And I am convinced that there are letters in the house, written to your father shortly before his death, that are somehow important to our finding out who killed John and why."

She was staring at him now.

"So, you think John is telling you this somehow?"

Elliott was extremely uncomfortable but hoped it didn't show. "I really don't know, Sister," he said, chalking up yet another lie. "But I can assure you I'm not delusional, and I have never experienced anything like this before in my entire life. But I'd be willing to bet every penny I have that those letters are there."

He forced himself to keep his eyes on hers.

"And just where in the house are these letters?" she asked finally.

He sighed. "I'm sorry, but I have no idea. Perhaps among your father's papers?"

"Alphonso went through them all within days after our father died and threw out everything that might have been considered personal—though our father was hardly a romantic and probably didn't have many papers that didn't relate in some way to legal or financial matters."

It occurred to Elliott that if Al had found anything incriminating to himself he would have destroyed it or kept it for his own purposes.

"What about your mother's papers?" he asked.

"Mother entrusted all her legal and financial papers to her lawyer—I rather suspect so that Alphonso couldn't go through them. But as to her personal letters and things, she did keep some in a secret compartment in her desk—again, I suspect, to prevent Alphonso's snooping. He may have found them, but I doubt it."

John had mentioned a desk. He could only hope it was the same one. "Have you gone through the desk since your mother's death?"

She sighed. "Not yet. I couldn't bring myself to do so—I suppose I consider it an invasion of her privacy. Silly of me, I know, but..."

"Not at all," Elliott responded. "I understand completely. But with the possibility that there might be something there, would it be too great an imposition to ask you to check?"

Marie looked thoughtful, was quiet a moment, then sighed again. "No, I think it's time I went through them. It would help if I knew what I was looking for."

"I wish I could tell you," he said. "I'm pretty sure they were written to your father, though, just before his death. I don't know how many there might be, but probably not many."

"Frankly, I'd be surprised if there were any at all. As I've said, my father wasn't the type to keep letters. I would imagine he would simply have torn up any personal letters sent him after he'd read them. And how my mother would have come by them if they were written to him, I can't imagine."

"Nor can I, but I believe with all my heart that those letters are there, and that they will be helpful to the police investigation. Would you be willing to look?"

"You really believe they might have something to do with John's death? My father had enemies, but that they might retaliate against John, and so long after my father's death..."

Elliott found the comment interesting, and surprising. That the killer might be someone a little closer to home simply didn't occur to her. Or she wouldn't let it.

"I can't say, but I've seldom felt more certain about anything in my life. The only way to know if I'm right or wrong is to go through the papers. I'm sure you'll recognize them when you see them."

He could only hope that what John was talking about would, indeed, be in that particular desk and not somewhere else in the house.

"If you really feel that strongly about it..."

"Believe me, Sister, I do. I'm sure I could arrange for Cessy to drive you up there at your convenience. Perhaps you could bring the hairbrush back with you."

Marie was silent again for a moment before saying, "I might be able to get away this coming Saturday, if Cessy really wouldn't mind. I've been meaning to get up there to pick up a small box of things my mother kept from my First Communion, and I'm afraid I've been putting it off."

"That would be wonderful, Sister," he said. "I'll check with Cessy tonight and have her get in touch with you." He glanced up at the clock on the wall over the blackboard. "I really shouldn't keep you any longer," he said, starting to get up. "Thank you so much for talking with me."

"One more thing," she said, halting him in mid-rise and making him settle back down. "What do I do with the letters if I find them?"

It was a good question, and one he hadn't considered. "Well," he said extemporaneously, "you might just give the hairbrush to Cessy and ask her to give it to Brad, but as to the letters...I know it's a lot to ask, since you don't really know me all that well, but would it be possible for me to look at them first to confirm what I suspect? If they are what I think they are, I'll turn them immediately over to Brad. If they're not, I'll give them right back to you and promise I will keep anything I read in them in strictest confidence."

She thought that through. "I trust you, Elliott. Whatever they contain—if they do exist—is part of the past and of no real interest to me now, unless you are right in their providing some information on what happened to John."

"I truly appreciate that, Sister," he said as he stood. "Thank you again for your time."

Sister Marie rose at the same time, extending her hand. "You're quite welcome." Her eyes searched his face and her own reflected an odd sadness. "They will catch whoever killed John, won't they?"

"Yes, Sister," he replied. "They will. I promise."

❉

He called Cessy on his cell phone even before he got back to his car, rather surprised at himself for not waiting until he got home. He suspected his impatience might be influenced by John. The experience of John's presence, like John, had been undergoing a subtle change, becoming more an integral part of him, which was mildly disturbing.

If Cessy was surprised by his request, she didn't let it show. He told her that in the course of his conversation with Sister Marie she had mentioned her hopes of getting up to the Lake Geneva house to retrieve some of her things, and that he'd said he'd see if Cessy could take her. Not a lie, but far from the total truth. He did not mention the letters or the hairbrush, though he was sure Marie would say something about it at some point. He fervently hoped it wouldn't be until they were at least on the way—he didn't want to risk Brad's finding out about the letters until he knew for sure they existed.

If Marie found the letters and turned them over to the police, Elliott could not escape being required to provide an explanation of how he knew they existed, let alone where they were; but he wanted to put it off as long as he possibly could.

"BJ has a soccer game Saturday afternoon," Cessy said. "But it's not until three, and I'm sure we could make it up to Lake Geneva and back in time if we could leave early. I'll talk with Sister tomorrow and see what we can work out. It was very nice of you to think of it."

Elliott felt a strong twinge of guilt. "I'd have offered to drive her myself," he said, more by way of justification to himself than Cessy, "but I didn't think it would be appropriate."

He could almost see Cessy grinning. "Well, the church has gotten considerably less rigid about what nuns can and can't do, but you're probably right. And I'll be glad to do it."

"I appreciate it, Sis."

"And we'll see you Friday at the opening? I assume you're going with Steve."

"Actually, I'll be meeting him there. He's probably going to be too busy to care whether I'm there or not."

"Right, Elliott. This is me you're talking to, remember. You can always ride down with us."

"That's okay, Sis, but thanks. I'll sort of leave everything open."

"All right. We'll see you there, then."

As happened with seemingly increasing frequency the older he got, he suddenly found himself at Friday afternoon, the preceding three days little more than a blur. He'd heard nothing from Brad and had no conversations with John. He had talked with Steve a couple of times, noting, despite Steve's outwardly casual attitude, a rising anticipation of the opening. And though Elliott didn't care much for semi-social occasions, he was looking forward to this one for Steve's sake.

He had taken a steak out of the freezer Friday morning, and had it for an early dinner with a baked potato in front of the TV as he watched the news. He'd decided it would be easier to take the el rather than fight traffic and battle for a parking place.

Shortly after seven o'clock, he took another quick shower and got dressed. The weather had turned cool, so as a concession to Steve and the occasion, he wore a tie and his favorite sport jacket. Though he would vehemently deny being even remotely vain, he studied himself closely in the mirror, looking for evidence of any replacements for the grey hairs—seven—he'd discovered and yanked out recently. He was relieved not to find any new offenders. He didn't mind getting older; he just didn't want to look it.

He arrived at the gallery a little after eight and was pleased to see a fair number of people already there. Two red-vested waiters moved among the crowd with trays of champagne and hors d'oeuvres. Cessy and Brad weren't there yet, and it took him several seconds to spot Steve, who was at the far end of the room in front of one of his Calico ghost town paintings, talking with a well-dressed white-haired man.

He looked quickly around the room and spotted the portrait of Steve's brother, and though he did not see the gallery owner, he did see the woman who had been working the first time he had visited the gallery with Steve—Miss Brown, if he remembered correctly. He hadn't gotten her first name. She was talking with a tall, strikingly handsome couple and writing something in a leather portfolio. As he watched, she handed the man a business card, closed the portfolio, smiled and shook hands with them both, then turned to move across the room. Seeing Elliott watching her, she hurried over to him.

"I'm so glad you could make it," she said with a warm smile, and Elliott had no idea of whether she actually recognized him or not. "Have you had a chance to look around?"

"Actually, I'd like to buy the portrait just to the left of the umbrella plant, but I'd like it to be an anonymous purchase."

From her lack of reaction to his stated desire for anonymity, he assumed this was not an unusual request.

"Of course," she said, opening her portfolio. She quickly and expertly went through a number of glossy sheets of paper in a pocket on one side, extracting one with a color photo of Manny's portrait. Beneath the photo was a list of pertinent information ("Oil on canvas, 14 x 24, 2003, Steven Gutierrez") and the price.

Checking to verify that Steve was still engaged in conversation, Elliott took out his checkbook, hoping Steve wouldn't see him or what he was doing. Folding the description sheet, he put it in his inside jacket pocket. There were times when being wealthy came in handy, and this was one of those times.

When he handed Miss Brown the check, she smiled again, slid it into the pocket behind the detail sheets and said, "Would you like to pick it up or have it delivered? We would appreciate your allowing us to keep it on display for the duration of the show, if that's all right with you."

"Of course," he said. "I'll call you to let you know about delivery."

Extracting a business card from her portfolio, she smiled and, as Elliott took the card, extended her hand. It struck him that this was an exact replay of her actions with the couple she'd been talking with when he first spotted her.

"Please do look around," she said, "and if you find something else you'd like, I'm at your service."

He looked up just as Steve noticed him and started over. He excused himself from Miss Brown and went to meet him.

He had never seen Steve in a suit and tie before and he was, to say the least, impressed—and surprised by the unexpected warm flush that swept over him.

178

He was sure it wasn't John this time.

They shook hands, and Steve practically glowed.

"So, what do you think?" he asked, indicating the room and the crowd.

"I think it's fantastic."

"I haven't seen Cessy or Brad," Steve said. "I hope they're coming."

"Cessy wouldn't miss it for the world," Elliott assured him, grinning.

Miss Brown suddenly appeared with a fashionably dressed woman in tow. "Excuse me, Mr. Gutierrez, but when you have a moment this lady would like to talk with you."

"Of course," Steve said with a smile Elliott was sure would make Ebenezer Scrooge grow weak in the knees.

"Go ahead," Elliott said, with a smile and a nod to the woman. "I want to look around some more." He excused himself and moved toward the door, pausing to take a glass of champagne from the waiter. He'd just had his first sip when he saw Cessy come in; he didn't see Brad. She noticed him immediately and came over. She was wearing the same dress she'd worn at dinner with their parents and looked beautiful.

"Where's Brad?" he asked after they exchanged a hug.

"We were three blocks away when he got called in to work. I really hate it when that happens, but after fifteen years of marriage to a policeman, I've gotten used to it it. He dropped me off and said to apologize to you and Steve."

"Well, I'm sorry he had to go in," Elliott said, "but I know he's not wild about this kind of affair anyway."

She smiled and shrugged. "True, but he indulges me shamelessly. Have you talked to Steve yet?"

"Briefly. He's a busy man. He's over there," he said, gesturing toward Steve with his champagne glass. "He's the one about three feet off the floor."

At that same moment, Steve looked over toward him and, seeing Cessy, gave her a big smile and a wave, which she returned.

"He's a very handsome man," Cessy said. "You make a nice couple."

"I don't think we're quite at the couple stage yet."

"But you'd like to be," she said.

He grinned. "Push, push, push."

"So, show me his paintings," she said, taking his arm.

❃

Steve managed to join them after about ten minutes. He offered his hand to Cessy, but she hugged him instead.

"These are absolutely wonderful, Steve," she said. "I had no idea you were so talented. Elliott tried to tell me, but I thought he was just being prejudiced. I can see now he's not."

Steve's expression was a mixture of embarrassment and pleasure. "I'm glad you like them."

"Oh, I do, and I'm going to be sure to tell Mother about you. She and my

179

father are ardent collectors."

"That would be great," Steve said. "I appreciate the recommendation."

"My pleasure."

"Okay," Elliott warned Steve, "I see Miss Brown looking your way. You'd better get back to earning your keep."

He shrugged. "Yeah, I guess you're right. I see my boss from work just came in. I'd better go say hello."

"That you should," Elliott agreed. "In case we don't get a chance to talk again before we leave..."

"No, no, you come find me before you go."

"Okay. Now, go greet your boss."

✾

He rode the el with Cessy to his stop at Thorndale where, despite his insistence that he drive her home from his apartment, she refused with thanks and he got off.

Walking from the el station to his condo, he reflected on the evening and that he'd enjoyed it, as much for Steve as for himself. When he and Cessy had said their brief goodbyes to Steve as they left the gallery, neither Steve nor he mentioned their prearranged agreement to get together Saturday night—Elliott because he didn't want to add any more fuel to Cessy's speculations about their relationship and Steve, Elliott assumed, because he didn't want to give Cessy the idea he was pursuing her brother.

Though he'd had two glasses of champagne at the gallery, he fixed himself a bourbon and Seven and watched a little TV before going to bed.

— *He really is talented.*

— *Yes, I know.*

— *And you do make a nice couple.*

— *Great! First Cessy, now you.*

— *I just calls 'em the way I sees 'em.*

— *You're in a good mood tonight.*

— *Yes. It's almost over. I can tell.*

— *And what will happen then?*

— *Interesting question. I'm not sure.*

— *Will you leave?*

— *Leave you, you mean? Do you want me to?*

— *Well, there's really not room in here for two separate people.*

— *I agree. But once it's over, I'll be free. I'm in no particular hurry to go anywhere. Eternity is a very long time. I can wait a bit. I'd like to see some of the world from my new perspective. But I promise I'm not going to intrude on your individuality or take up too much room in your mind. Still, it would be nice if we could...stay in touch.*

— *What does that mean?*

— *I'm not sure. But we were friends once, and I like to think we've become friends again. I'd like to...well, like I said, stay in touch. I'm not quite sure how it*

180

will work out, and if you ever want me to just go away, I will. I promise. Is that okay with you?

Elliott felt himself rising to the surface of consciousness, but he willed himself back into deeper sleep long enough to complete his thought.

— *Yeah, I think I'd like that.*

CHAPTER 16

✿

Steve called early Saturday morning. Elliott could tell from the tone of his "Good morning, Elliott" that the opening had gone well.

"A success, I assume?"

"Fantastic! I couldn't be happier! I sold four outright—one was anonymous, but who cares, it sold. And several other people expressed interest. Mr. Devereux said they'll probably buy. And I made a lot of contacts. It was great. I'm sorry I couldn't spend more time with you and Cessy, but..."

"Hey, don't worry about it. I'm really glad it was a success. You deserve it."

"Thanks...and thanks for being there."

"I enjoyed it, and Cessy is more convinced than ever that we're a match made in heaven. The girl has to get a life."

Steve laughed. "So, are we still on for tonight?"

"Sure. Seven-thirty okay?"

"Okay, but let me pick you up this time. We're always using your car."

"I don't mind, but sure, if you want. I'll be outside."

"Great. I'm looking forward to it."

❀

He was at the car wash when his cell phone rang.

"Elliott."

"Elliott, it's Cessy. We're back from Lake Geneva, and I just dropped Sister off. She gave me a hairbrush of her mother's and asked me to give it to Brad...and she gave me a letter for you."

"A letter?"

"Yes. She says you asked her for it. What's this all about?"

"Did Sister tell you what was in it?"

"No, she said she didn't read it. She just said she assumes it was what you were looking for. I had no idea what she was talking about, but I took it. It's addressed to Vittorio Collina. Why would you want it? How did you even know about it?"

"Have you read it?"

"No, of course not. But..."

"Can I come over and get it?"

"Now? I'm just going to pick BJ up for his soccer game. Brad had to go in to the office this morning; he's meeting us at the field."

"What time is the game?"

"Three o'clock, and it's nearly two now."

"I can be over at your house in fifteen minutes. Can you wait for me...or leave it somewhere I can find it? It's really important."

"Well, I can put it under the mat if we have to leave before you get here." Her voice reflected her confusion and a certain degree of anxiety. "Can you tell me what's going on?"

"Not right now, Sis, but I will. I promise. I'll see you shortly."

His own level of anticipation was high enough that having it compounded by John's made him feel as though he'd just eaten a box of chocolate-covered donuts and washed them down with two pots of strong black coffee.

Cessy was just strapping Sandy into her carseat and BJ was getting into the SUV when Elliott pulled up in front of their house.

"It's under the mat," Cessy called as he got out of his car and she climbed into the driver's seat. Not seeing Jenny, he assumed she was probably at a friend's house, but he and BJ exchanged casual waves as Cessy backed out of the driveway and turned toward the school and the soccer field.

The letter, which Cessy had slipped into a plastic bag for protection, was addressed to Vittorio Collina at his Lake Geneva estate. It had been roughly torn open, Vitto apparently not being the type to bother looking for a letter opener, and re-closed with a small strip of Scotch tape. He pried the tape loose and took out the letter. A single sheet. It was brief and to the point.

Vitto, you rotten son-of-a-bitch, you took my kid and gave me a lousy twenty-five grand, like that was supposed to last me forever. But I didn't complain, not once in all the years.

But now when I need money for an operation and ask you for help, you don't answer my letters or take my phone calls.

Well, Mr. Asshole, I've got a little bombshell to drop on you as a way of showing my appreciation for your response to my request. Remember Larry Genestra, the guy you paid to watch over me while you kept me prisoner? Well, Larry was ten times the man you'll ever be, and Al is his kid, not yours, you rotten bastard. You don't believe me, they got dna now. Check it out, and then you can go to hell.

Celeste

183

Elliott stood on Cessy's porch, reading the letter several times. So, he was right—Al wasn't Vitto Collina's son. Did Al know it? How could he? Though the knowledge would be ample justification for him to kill John or, more likely, have him killed. Did Sophia Collina know? She'd had the letter. He had no idea how she got it, but he was sure she would have read it. If she knew Al wasn't Vitto's son, why didn't she say anything? Possibly, he reasoned, because she had raised Al since he was two years old and she considered him her own.

He checked the postmark: August 1, 2001. If his trivia file served him right, that was within days of Vitto's death. Had he even read it? If he did, could the letter have killed him? Al was the apple of his eye, his doppleganger, his heir apparent. Did finding out Al wasn't his precipitate his death? The newspaper reports of his death had stated he'd fallen down a flight of steps at his estate; nothing was said about a heart attack or any other cause other than the fall.

So, he had the letter. He wondered briefly if there might have been any others, since both John and the letter had alluded to them in the plural. Vitto had probably destroyed the earlier ones. Why had he kept this one?

All of which was worthy of speculation but still did not prove that Al Collina had been responsible for John's death.

He returned to his car and headed for the soccer field.

✿

The game hadn't yet started when he arrived, and he found Brad and Cessy standing on the sidelines about halfway down the field, waiting. They both looked a little surprised to see him.

"I didn't know you wanted to come to the game," Cessy said, apologetically. "We'd have waited for you and not just driven off."

"No problem," he said. "Actually, I need to talk to Brad for a minute, if I could."

Brad and Cessy exchanged a quick, puzzled glance before Brad said, "Sure. I've got to go to the bathroom before the game starts anyway. Walk with me."

He handed Sandy to Cessy, and the two men headed toward the restrooms.

"So, what's up?" Brad asked.

"I don't know if Cessy's told you yet, but Sister Marie gave her a hairbrush belonging to Sophia Collina—you hadn't tested Sophia's DNA, I assume."

Brad pursed his lips. "Yeah, Cessy said she had the brush, and no, we hadn't thought of getting Sophia's DNA...and we should have. When Al's didn't match our John Doe's we didn't look any further because we were sure Al was Vitto's biological son. Sloppy police work, I'm embarrassed to say, and I'll take responsibility."

"I was sure you'd want something of hers to check for DNA, so I thought I could save you a little time by asking Sister if she could bring something back with her." He handed Brad the letter. "And here's proof that Al Collina isn't Vitto Collina's son, which means that our John Doe is."

They stopped while Brad opened and read the letter. When he'd finished, his gaze moved slowly from the paper to Elliott's face.

"First, while it might prove Al isn't Vitto's son, it still doesn't prove our John Doe is—and where did you get this letter?"

Elliott paused. He was treading on very thin ice, and he knew it. "I asked Marie to get it for me, and I'd wager anything that Sophia's DNA matches John's."

"Which doesn't explain how you knew the letter was there, or how you even knew it existed."

Elliott shook his head. "Look, Brad, I can't tell you how I knew it was there. I just did. I told you that, ever since the accident, I have these over-powering...hunches. And they've all proven to be true."

"So, now you're a psychic?"

"No! It's not like that at all!"

"Then what is it like?"

"Damn it, I don't know! All I know is that I felt I owed it to John to prove who he was. We've come this far—all we have to do is confirm it."

"Which won't tell us who killed him."

"Oh, come on, Brad. If Sophia's DNA proves he *is* John Collina, that gives Al every reason to kill him for the family fortune. What more do we need?"

"Proof would be nice, " Brad pointed out. He was silent a moment, his brows furrowed. "But I'm not arguing with you. I didn't make it to the gallery with Cessy Friday because I was called in on a new murder—a guy named Charlie Cree. Recognize the name?"

Elliott shook his head. "Doesn't ring a bell, no. Who was he?"

"He was the head of C&C Demolition, which by sheer coincidence does all the demolition projects for Evermore Properties. He's a childhood pal of our friend Al Collina. Cree's old man was in the mob with Vitto. The day before Cree was killed, we'd gotten an anonymous tip that he'd been involved in a hit a couple months back. It turns out that Cree had an apartment on Surf not far from where our John Doe was shot. I wouldn't be surprised if, knowing what we know now, the two cases are connected.

"Stretching speculation one step further, if Al knew about the tip, he might have offed his old buddy to keep him quiet, which may well mean Al's starting to make mistakes. But until we can prove it..."

They continued to the restrooms, and Elliott waited outside until Brad returned.

"Would it be possible for me to be there when you talk to Marie?" he asked as they headed back to the field, where the game had just begun.

Brad shook his head. "I don't think that would be a good idea, under the circumstances."

"Me being your brother-in-law, you mean?"

"Yeah, that and the fact that we prefer not to have any sort of distraction when we're interviewing someone."

"Yeah, but this wouldn't exactly be an official interview, would it? More like a conversation?"

"Still not a good idea."

"Could I talk to her before you do?"

Brad stopped short and turned to him. "And why would you want to do that?"

"Well, for one thing, because she doesn't know what's in the letter—Cessy said Marie told her she didn't read it—and I know she's going to be upset by it. So, if you just spring it on her, she'll probably be too upset to be able to think of anything else. But if I tell her what's in it before you do, it might give her time to clear her head and think. Just as I was sure about the letter, I believe she knows something she may not even be aware she knows. The letter might trigger her memory."

Brad hadn't taken his eyes off Elliott. "Well, I can't stop you," he said. "But remember, you're not a cop. Leave the investigation up to us. Understood?"

"Perfectly," Elliott replied. He waited until they were almost back to Cessy before asking, "When do you plan to talk to Marie?"

"It probably won't be until Tuesday at the earliest. We've got a couple leads to follow up on the Cree case Monday." He paused and gave Elliott a small smile. "Subtle question, though."

❊

The more time he and Steve spent together, the more comfortable Elliott was. He was impressed by Steve's down-to-earth attitudes, which were very much like his own.

They drove out to an Old Country Buffet near the Lincolnwood Mall for dinner then took in a movie near the mall. They ended up at Steve's where, as Elliott also thoroughly appreciated, the pleasant casualness of the earlier evening was offset by a Fourth-of-July testosterone fireworks display that left them both seeing stars.

"How in the hell do you do that?" Elliott asked when he finally regained his breath.

Steve rolled over to grin at him. "Well, I'd like to say years of practice, but that's not exactly true. Let's just say it's like ballroom dancing, I just follow my partner."

Elliott took his hand, intertwining their fingers. "Yeah, well, you're not bad at leading, either."

— You're through, I hope? I'll go away if you aren't.

— Well, obviously, since I'm asleep, I'd assume we were through for the moment.

— I just didn't want to intrude.

— I appreciate that.

— So, you're going to see Marie again?

— Yes, to tell her about the letter.

— I wish you didn't have to. She's such a kind soul; knowing Al isn't my father's son will upset her.

186

— *But you said she knows something else, right? Something she isn't aware she knows?*

— *Yes.*

— *Well, perhaps this will somehow get her to remember. You still don't know what it is?*

— *No. As I say, she has it so deep inside her mind I can't see it. But I think it isn't so much that she doesn't know she knows as that she refuses to acknowledge it.*

— *Well, that's certainly obtuse.*

— *The mind is often obtuse.*

— *Now you sound like a fortune cookie.*

Elliott was aware, for the first time, of what he could only describe as a distinctly pleasurable, very slight tickling sensation.

— *Are you laughing?*

— *Yes. Did you think I couldn't? I just haven't had much to laugh about recently.*

— *Point. So, what happens now?*

— *As I've said, we're close. Marie has the key. She'll use it soon. I feel it.*

❉

Monday morning, he called St. Agnes to leave a message for Sister Marie saying he would like to talk to her after school if she was available, and left his number in the event that she wouldn't be. He really wanted to talk to her before Brad did.

He increasingly shared John's feeling that things were moving swiftly to a climax and that Marie held the key. If, as he was now gut-level sure, Al was responsible for John's death, he couldn't really see much direct connection between that and the letter, especially if Al wasn't aware of the letter. If he was, surely he'd have done his best to destroy it. And there was an almost five-year gap between John's presumed first death and the date on the letter.

The afternoon was taken up with a meeting with Ted, Arnie and Sam, going over sketches Sam had done for the conversion of the Elmdale building—specifically, the ground level apartment—and refining earlier estimates of time schedules and labor costs for each aspect of the renovation.

Not having heard anything to the contrary from Marie, he drove to St. Agnes at the close of the school day and made his way to her room. He found her watering one of several plants that hung in front of the windows and lined the bookcases and corner of her desk.

She smiled when she saw him and put down her watering can. "Come in, Elliott," she said. "I was hoping to hear from you. Was the letter what you wanted?"

"Yes, Sister," he said, moving into the room. "Thank you again for giving it to me. I understand you didn't read it yourself?"

She gestured him to a chair and took her own seat behind her desk.

"No," she said. "I know it is terribly un-Christian of me, but I really prefer not to think much about my father's...past, and I assumed the letter had something to do with that part of his life."

"Yes, it did. It was from Al's birth mother, who claims that Vittorio was not, in fact, Al's real father."

While he expected her to be shocked by the news, he didn't expect the intensity of her reaction. She paled and bent her head forward, her hand over her closed eyes.

"Are you all right, Sister?" he asked anxiously, leaning forward in his chair.

Her eyes hidden behind her hand, she shook her head slowly without raising it.

"Yes, yes, I'm fine. I just...I..." She removed her hand and raised her head, visibly pulling herself together. She looked directly at Elliott then slowly rose to her feet.

"Elliott, I'm afraid you'll have to excuse me. I'm not feeling well."

He got up quickly. "Of course," he said. "Is there anything I can do for you?"

She managed a very small smile and the slight wave of a hand. "I'm fine, really. Perhaps I'm coming down with something, but I'm sure it's nothing serious."

She hurried to the door, with Elliott following close behind. Turning toward him, she extended her hand, which when he took it was cold.

"We'll talk soon, I promise," she said, and without another word moved off down the hall, away from the main entrance.

He stood looking after her until she turned down another hallway and disappeared, then left the building.

❈

He didn't know whether to call Brad or not. Based on Marie's reaction to hearing the contents of the letter, it obviously triggered something major. He decided against it, wanting to give her time to calm down sufficiently before Brad talked to her. He sensed that John's anticipation equaled his own.

He deliberately went to bed earlier than usual, assuming John would let him know what was going on. If whatever it was that Marie had kept locked in her mind had been freed, John would be able to access it, and tell him.

He discovered yet again that there are few things worse or more certain to fail than trying to fall asleep. His mind was like a roiling kettle, thoughts, images, ideas rising to the surface only to disappear before he could fully recognize them. Sensations. Emotions. No matter how he tried to hold them down, to force them back, they continued, the turmoil not so much his as John's. What was going on?

He tried yet again to initiate a conversation with John. It had never worked before and it didn't work now.

And then it was morning. If he'd slept, he didn't remember it, and he certainly didn't feel like he had. And there had been no intelligible contact with John.

The morning passed as though time had turned into a stream of molasses. He did not even get dressed but sat groggily in his living room drinking coffee and looking out over the city. The weather was a little too cool to sit out on the balcony, and a brisk wind from the lake lowered the temperature even further. He dozed from time to time, but he never sank fully into sleep.

At ten-thirty, he heard his cell phone ringing and hurried into the bedroom to answer it.

"Elliott, it's Brad. You talked to Sister Marie."

He wondered why, if Brad knew, he found it necessary to say so.

"Yes, I went over there after school yesterday."

"Well, I don't know what the hell went on, but she called me this morning. She wants to talk to me at noon today, and she wants you to be there. Why would she want that? What did you say to her?"

Elliott tried to clear his head. "I just told her about the letter, and she got very pale and excused herself and left. I wasn't there more than five minutes, and I didn't invite myself to your meeting, I swear."

"Well, since she specifically wants you there, I can't keep you away, but I'm not happy about it and I wanted you to know that."

"I'm really sorry, Brad. I'm not trying to butt into your business. I have no idea why she would want me there, but I'd be lying if I said I wasn't glad she does."

"Yeah, well, meet us in front of the school at noon." And with that, he hung up.

Brad's anger was justified on one level, Elliott fully admitted. He couldn't remember ever having that anger aimed at him before, and he felt bad about it. But he *was* glad Marie had asked for him to be present. He hurried into the shower.

Brad and a man Elliott did not recognize were standing in front of the school when he arrived. He assumed the man was Brad's partner, whom he'd never met. Brad did not look happy.

"Elliott, this is my partner, Ken Brown."

They shook hands.

Glancing at his watch, Brad said, "Class will be out in a few minutes. We'll wait out here."

They engaged in awkward smalltalk—he could tell Brad was still less than happy with him—until they heard the bells signal the end of class, the sound instantly replaced by the cacophony of voices as students poured into the halls. The three entered the school against the vortex of milling students and made their way to Sister Marie's room. The second floor hallways were empty of students, which Elliott hoped meant their talk wouldn't be interrupted.

Sister Marie stood at the windows, looking down at the playground below, when Brad rapped on the open door. She turned and gave them a weak smile.

189

"Please, come in," she said.

Brad introduced Ken Brown, and after shaking hands, she indicated the two chairs against the wall and started to pull her own out from behind her desk. "I'm sorry I only have two regular chairs," she said, "but one of you can use mine."

"No, no, Sister," Elliott said. "I can stand. I've been sitting all morning."

"You're sure?" she asked, and he nodded. She moved her chair back behind the desk and she, Brad and Brown sat down. Elliott leaned against the window ledge, being careful not to knock over any of the plants.

"I wanted Elliott here," she began, "because I feel John would want him to be. Without Elliott, I never would have known what happened to my brother, and I never would have allowed myself to accept the truth."

"The truth, Sister?" Detective Brown asked.

Eyes downcast, she nodded. Elliott sensed her hesitation to speak was due to the difficulty of putting words to what she had to say.

"The truth about what, Sister?" Brown prodded.

She raised her head and looked him in the eye. "That my brother Alphonso is a murderer."

If either Brad or Detective Brown had a reaction to her statement, they didn't let it show. Elliott hoped his own surprise hadn't registered on his face.

"You have proof that your brother Al killed your brother John?"

"I can't prove that he killed John, but I can prove that he killed our father."

The two detectives exchanged a quick glance, and Elliott didn't even try to hide his surprise.

"And how can you do that, Sister?" Brown asked.

"Because...I saw him do it. I saw Alphonso push our father down the stairs!" She was trying to remain calm, but the tone and speed of her voice reflected her mounting anxiety.

It was Brad's turn to speak, and he did so as conversationally as he could. "Can you explain exactly what happened?"

Marie clenched her eyes shut and took a long, deep breath. Her arms lay on the chair's, her hands clutching the rounded ends. She released her breath, opened her eyes and began her story.

"Al and I were home for my mother's birthday. Mother and Lucille and Ellen, Alphonso's wife and daughter, had gone into Lake Geneva for some reason. Father was upstairs in his study when I saw the maid coming up the stairs with the mail. I don't know where Alphonso was at the time.

"I went into my room to read. A few minutes later, I heard angry voices, yelling. Although I had my door closed and couldn't hear the words, I recognized Alphonso and my father, and could tell they both were in a terrible temper. Which by itself wasn't at all unusual, they were so very much alike.

"But this time it was even worse than usual. I went to my door and opened it. My room looked out over the landing and the hall to my father's study. Alphonso came storming out of the study, obviously furious. My father was right behind him, waving his arms and shouting something about Alphonso being no son of his, and threatening to disown him. That was a threat he used often, to keep Alphonso in line. I don't think they saw me.

"They reached the landing, and Alphonso suddenly spun around and grabbed my father by the shoulders, turning him so that Father's back was to the stairs. He released him for just a moment as Father continued to yell at him.

"And then Alphonso reached up towards Father's shoulders with both hands. I have convinced myself for five years that Father had begun to fall, and that Alphonso was reaching out to catch him. But all I have to do is close my eyes, and I can see it vividly and know I was wrong. Alphonso wasn't trying to catch him. He hit him on both shoulders with the palms of his hands. Father fell backwards down the stairs.

"I ran out of my room, but by the time I reached him, he was dead. Alphonso just walked down the stairs, passed right by me and went out the front door. He didn't even look at my father—I was sure at the time it was because he was in shock.

"And that's when I convinced myself it had been an accident. I locked what had really happened away in the back of my mind and would never allow myself to let it out...until Elliott told me about the letter. How Mother got the letter, I don't know. And if she read it, she never said a word.

"I didn't say anything to anyone about what I'd seen because I simply could not allow myself to believe it was not an accident or comprehend how or why Alphonso could do such a thing. But of course, he could. I've been in denial about Alphonso most of my life, excusing his cruelties by telling myself I should love him because that's what God wanted me to do.

"But I'm not God. When I found out about the letter I realized that Alphonso killed my father because he knew this time Father was serious about disowning him. If Alphonso could kill my father, he could easily kill John, and I'm convinced that, just as Cain killed Abel, Alphonso killed John."

"Would you be willing to testify against Al in court in the death of your father?" Brad asked.

For some reason, she turned to Elliott and looked him in the eye before she responded.

"Yes," she said. "Yes, I would."

❋

They left about ten minutes later, after Marie agreed to make a formal statement. Elliott, sensing that Brad wasn't willing to discuss anything about the situation while his partner was present, bid his goodbyes and headed for his car. He hoped Brad would call that evening, though if he didn't, he would have to just accept it. He didn't want to alienate his brother-in-law any further than he already had.

That Marie had actually seen Al push her father down the stairs had come as a total surprise, though he immediately realized that was exactly what John had been referring to when he said Marie knew something she refused to admit she knew. He could understand how she would have difficulty acknowledging that

191

Al was a murderer. Al was a thoroughly rotten human being and always had been; but she considered him her brother, and her religious beliefs in goodness and loving one another had made her put reality aside. He could imagine how difficult it must have been for her to finally acknowledge the truth.

As for why Al hadn't destroyed the letter, he suspected Sophia had found it first, probably immediately after Vitto's death, before Al had the chance to go through Vitto's things. He may not even have known Vitto had gotten his information through a letter.

But knowing Al killed his father still was not proof he had also killed John. As someone once said, "Circumstantial evidence is finding a trout in the milk," but it didn't stand up well in court. He could only hope Brad and the police would be able to link Al to Charlie Cree's murder and then somehow to John's.

But if nothing else, Al would finally get at least a part of what was coming to him.

Unlike the previous night, he had no trouble at all going to sleep.

— *I didn't know.*

— *That Al had killed your father?*

— *Yes. I should have known, but I didn't. She kept it so locked up. It must have been terrible for her.*

— *Do you remember everything now?*

— *Almost. I remember that Al knew about me.*

— *I'm sorry?*

— *That I hadn't died in Africa. I'm not sure how he knew, but he did.*

— *So, you were running from Al all this time? Why?*

— *I wasn't really running. I just wanted to stay out of his way. When the ferry capsized and I survived, I thought that if my family believed I was dead, it would be easier on my mother and sister—they could avoid conflict with my father. And after he died, I couldn't go home; I was afraid they wouldn't forgive me for having hurt them.*

— *You don't know that. They loved you.*

— *I know. I was stupid. But it was too late. I thought it was just best to keep things as they were.*

— *So, did you have any contact with Al in those years?*

— *Not directly, but I knew he somehow kept track of where I was. That's one reason I bought the motor home—to make it as hard as I could for him.*

— *Al knew you were coming to Chicago for your mother's funeral?*

— *Yes, I remember now. I called him and told him I was coming. I didn't know how to reach Marie directly, and I didn't want to just show up. It would be too great a shock for her. I'm afraid calling him was a...fatal mistake.*

— *So, you know who...who killed you?*

— *I remember everything up to getting off the plane. Someone met me at the gate. I don't know how they knew I would be on that flight.*

— *Was it Al?*

— No. Not Al. One of Al's friends, I think, from when we were kids.

— Charlie Cree?

— I'm not sure. I think...yes, Charlie...Cree. Brad said Charlie Cree was murdered.

— Yes, and I'll bet anything Al was responsible for that, too.

— I'm sorry. Even now I find it incomprehensible that my own brother...

— He was not your brother. And he killed your father.

— Yes. I just have to get used to the idea.

— Do you remember anything after Charlie Cree picked you up at the airport?

— There was another man. He was in the car.

— Do you know who he was?

— I don't know. Frank? Frank something. I'd never seen him before. He reminded me of the Pillsbury Dough Boy. Very heavy. Very pale. Round face. He was very friendly. He laughed a lot.

— Why did you go with them?

— They said Al wanted me to go right up to Lake Geneva. I told them I had reservations at...at the City Suites on Belmont. I was...going to rent a car and drive up in the morning, then come right back after the funeral, but they said Al had told Marie I was coming, and she was waiting to see me that night.

So I agreed. I told them I'd rent a car there at the airport and drive right up, but Charlie said Al had called while they were on their way to the airport and that he wanted them to pick up something and bring it to Lake Geneva immediately. They said since they had to go up there, too, there was no point in taking two cars. So I called the hotel to cancel.

— And you weren't suspicious?

— Not at first. Frank was cracking jokes and didn't seem to have a care in the world. I remember we took the Diversey exit and went down Diversey to Pine Grove then turned down Surf toward Sheridan. There wasn't any parking available, of course, so Frank pulled into an alley...and...

Elliott was suddenly aware of a powerful wave of emotion pushing him toward consciousness. He fought against it and slowly it subsided.

— We're almost there, John. Go with it.

— I don't know if I can! It's...I can't put it in words!

— Try, John, please.

— Charlie got out of the car to go into a building across the street. Frank kept talking and laughing, and...Charlie came out of the building and came over to the car. He was carrying a small box. He...

Elliott felt cold. He was strangely terrified, and at the same time incredibly sad.

— Go on, John. You have to.

— I know. But it's...I'm going to die, Elliott!

Elliott felt as though he were being battered by a hurricane. He was no longer asleep, but not awake, either. He struggled to form his thoughts.

— It's okay, John. Nothing can hurt you now. What happened? Can you remember?

— Yes. I remember...He came over to my door and opened it. "I've got something you should see, John," he said. "Why don't you step out of the car so you can see it better?" I didn't want to, but I did. He opened the lid of the box with one hand and took out a gun...

The battering of emotions stopped. There was an eerie sense of calm, like entering the eye of the hurricane. Elliott knew John had accepted what he knew came next.

— "This was your father's gun," Charlie said. "Al thought you'd like to see it." I knew what he was going to do. I couldn't run. I couldn't yell for help...no help could come in time. I did manage to ask "Why?" and Charlie said "Al just thought it would be a nice touch." And then I heard...a siren...and he...and then I was sitting in the chair beside your bed wondering who you were.

— Oh, Jesus, John! I'm so very sorry!

— Don't be. It happened. We can't change it. But now I know who I am, and that's all I've wanted from the minute I saw you in the hospital.

— But Al had you killed! He has to pay for it!

— He will. Don't worry. What I've told you should help. And if nothing else, he'll pay for killing our father. Right now, I'm so happy to be free that I really don't care. Now go back to sleep.

Elliott had the sensation of a balloon on a string being released by the hand that held it.

❋

He called Brad and Cessy's at seven a.m. Cessy answered.

"Hi, Sis. Is Brad there?"

"Yes, I'll get him. Is everything all right? You don't usually call this early."

"Sorry about that. But I wanted to catch Brad before he left for work."

"Okay. Hold on."

He heard the muffling of the receiver, Cessy's voice saying something, and a moment later, Brad picked it up.

"Yeah, Elliott. What's up?"

"Is there a way you can check cell phone calls made on G. J. Hill's phone for two or three days before he left for Chicago?"

There was a pause. "Yeah, I think we can do that. Why?"

"Look for a call made to Al Collina. I'm not sure whether it's to his office or to his home. If you find it, we really need to talk."

"Look, Elliott, if this is another one of your psychic moments..."

"Brad, trust me. Please. Just check Hill's phone records."

There was a long sigh, which clearly conveyed Brad's impatience. "Okay. But you'd better be right."

❋

At nine o'clock, his cell phone rang.

"Elliott, what's going on with you and Brad?" Cessy demanded. "I've never seen him this way."

"What way is that?"

"You know perfectly well what I mean. Did you do something to make him angry?"

"Not deliberately, I can assure you. It's about the Collinas, and I really don't want to risk getting him more upset with me by talking about it with you."

"You can't talk to your own sister?"

"Not about this. Not right now. I hope you'll understand."

"Well, I don't, but since I don't have much choice..."

"Thanks, Sis. I appreciate it."

✻

Though he did not hear from Brad for the rest of the day, an article on the second page of Tuesday's *Chicago Tribune* immediately grabbed his attention,

Developer Charged in Father's Death

> Prominent Chicago real estate developer Al Collina was arrested Monday in connection with the 2001 death of his father, Vittorio Collina...

✻

He heard nothing from Brad until Thursday morning. He'd also heard nothing from John, and was mildly surprised to realize he missed their conversations. He wondered whether John, despite what he had said about sticking around, had simply moved on now that the question of his identity and means of death had been resolved; and he had an odd and uncustomary sensation of loneliness.

Just before noon, as he was forcing himself to go through a new catalog of plumbing fixtures, his cell phone rang.

"Are you home?" Brad asked.

"Yes. I—"

"I'll be there in ten minutes."

He responded to a knock at the door fifteen minutes later to find Brad but no sign of his partner. Standing back, he motioned him in.

"You want a cup of coffee?" he asked.

"No time," Brad answered, striding past him into the living room. "Ken's waiting in the car." He went over to the window and looked out at the beach. Without turning around, he said, "The DNA from Sophia Collina's hairbrush matches John's, so that settles that. The San Luis police got a copy of Hill's—John Collina's—cell phone calls. It shows one call to Chicago at seven-fifteen p.m. on March twenty-first, the day before John's murder, to Al Collina's home."

Elliott wanted to say something, but thought it best to let Brad do the talking.

"Al's out on bail, of course," Brad continued, "and he's already lined up a team of the best defense lawyers money can buy. Sister Marie's testimony is the foundation of the prosecution's case, and we've got someone watching out for her in case Al gets any ideas. But the defense will try to rip her story to shreds, since she says herself she convinced herself for five years it was an accident. So, there's a fair chance that Al might walk on it. And unless we can find something solid to enable us to charge him with John's death as well, we're in trouble."

He turned and looked directly at Elliott, and Elliott saw in his face not his brother-in-law but a hardened police homicide detective.

"So, I'm asking you again," he said, "exactly how do you know what you know?"

Again the dreaded question, and again he had no alternative but to lie. "All I can tell you is what I've already told you. I don't know how I know. There's no way I could possibly know from personal experience. I'm not pretending to be psychic, but ever since the accident I just suddenly get these hunches. And you have to admit that, wherever they come from, I've been right."

Brad stood silent, staring at Elliott as though he were a stranger. Finally, he said, "So, do you have any other 'hunches?'"

Elliott, thoroughly uncomfortable, took a deep breath.

"Yes, as a matter of fact. There's a guy named Frank, an associate of Charlie Cree's. He was with Cree the night of the murder."

Brad opened his mouth to speak, but Elliott raised his hand to silence him.

"Please, don't ask. Just hear me out."

Brad closed his mouth but looked at his brother-in-law as though he had never seen him before.

Undeterred, Elliott continued. "They picked John up at the airport. And since Cree was killed and this Frank guy wasn't, I'd say it was possible that Al didn't know Frank was with him."

Another moment of silence, then: "Do you know this Frank person?"

"No. I know he's short and fat and he laughs a lot."

"Hunches don't usually come with names and physical descriptions."

Elliott shrugged. "Mine do," he said. "Do you know who he is?"

"I might. It sounds like one of Charlie's crony's, Frank Rigoni. I'm pretty sure he works for C&C Demolition. I'll check into it. Anything else?"

"Other than that Al's responsible for John's death? No."

"Okay." He walked past Elliott toward the door. He stopped just short of it and turned to him again. "I don't have to tell you not to talk to Cessy about this, do I?"

He shook his head. "No, you don't. It's bad enough that you think I'm crazy. I'm not about to have my sister think it, too."

Brad just gave a curt nod and left.

✽

Steve called to say the gallery had sold a couple more of his paintings, and that the owner had said he'd be willing to keep one or two in the gallery's general displays after the showing ended Friday, alternating them with the others every few weeks. Steve was delighted, and Elliott was happy for him. He offered to take Steve to dinner Friday night, but Steve said he had some business with Devereux, the gallery owner, after the close, and wanted to be there to savor the last couple hours of his first official gallery showing. Elliott understood completely, and they switched their date to Saturday.

He went to bed at his usual time, not particularly anticipating anything from John, and there was nothing.

✿

At four-thirty Friday afternoon, there was a knock at his door. Since there were only a very few people who did not have to have his verbal approval from the front desk before being allowed in, he was puzzled as to who it might be.

He opened the door to find Brad, again alone.

"Hi, Brad. Come on in."

"I'll have that coffee now, if you have some."

"Sure." Brad followed him into the kitchen as he took two cups and the sugar bowl from the cabinet . Luckily, he'd made a fresh pot only an hour or so before. Brad opened the refrigerator and took out the cream, pouring a liberal amount into the two cups. They each added sugar then carried the cups into the living room.

"Coaster?" Elliott asked, breaking the silence..

"No, thanks."

Brad took a seat on the couch. Elliott sat in his favorite chair, swiveling it around to face him.

"So?" he encouraged.

Brad sighed. "You were right," he said. "It was Frank Rigoni. He was with Charlie Cree when Charlie killed John. He was the one who tipped us that Cree was involved in a hit—John's."

"And he just...confessed?"

Brad gave a wry smile. "We didn't pull out the rubber hose, if that's what you mean. We brought him in for questioning on Cree's murder and he denied everything, but when I told him we knew Al didn't know he was with Cree during the hit—which of course we didn't, despite your hunches—and that we were going to tell Al if he didn't come clean, he reconsidered.

"He claims Cree called him to drive the car in case John gave him any trouble. They'd checked the flight schedules and since they didn't know which flight John would be on—there weren't that many—they met them all."

"How did they know which passenger was John?" Elliott asked.

"They had a photo. Al apparently had been keeping tabs on his brother, which had included taking photos of him and his activities." He paused long enough to take a drink of his coffee before continuing. "Anyway, Rigoni swears he had no idea Cree was going to kill John, and that he'd tipped us about Cree as a good citizen when his conscience got the better of him. After a few more

197

questions, it turned out more to be a matter of his being pissed at Cree for a string of grievances, which culminated when Cree refused to pay him what he was promised for driving the car."

"But that still doesn't prove without a shadow of a doubt that Al ordered the hit."

"True, but I think we might have a way. Risky, but Rigoni has agreed to it in exchange for our dropping the accessory-to-murder charge against him. We had him set up a meeting with Al outside the Conservatory in Lincoln Park tonight at seven-thirty. Being in the open like that, we don't have to worry about a drive-by shooting, or Al's trying to get Rigoni into a car. Rigoni doesn't want to wear a wire, so we'll use electronic eavesdropping gear from a distance. We'll have undercovers all over the area, but it's still a risk. But we don't have much other choice."

"Where's Rigoni now?"

"He's with Ken at the precinct. I just wanted to take a few minutes to come over here to let you know what's happening. I figure we owe you. I still don't know how you know what you know, but it doesn't matter, I guess. It's the end result that counts."

"Let me know what happens," Elliott said.

"I will," Brad replied, getting up from the couch with his coffee cup. "Well, I'd better head back. If Cessy calls, don't tell her I was here. I'm not going to be able to make it home for dinner, and she's not going to be happy about that."

"She's used to it," Elliott said, getting out of his chair and following Brad to the door. "Good luck," he said.

Brad nodded without looking back and left.

✤

Elliott returned to the living room. His feeling of anticipation from what Brad had told him was slowly being replaced by one he couldn't quite put his finger on at first. Then, he recognized it—an odd sensation of letdown.

He didn't know what he'd expected. After all this time, after the painstaking piecing together of the puzzle, it was finished. Over. Where, he wondered, was the thundering roll of the tympani and the clash of a cymbal to mark the last notes of the symphony? He'd expected the *1812 Overture* and gotten "Clair de Lune."

He had no sense of John's presence, and he realized he missed him. These had probably been the most unusual several months of his life...but now what?

His spirits didn't lift even when Brad's phone call came in at nine and he said simply, "We got him."

He was relieved, of course, and happy for John that the search was finally over. But even as he drifted off to sleep that night, there was the strong feeling of anticlimax.

— *Anticlimax? Not at all.*

— *You're back!*

— *I haven't really been away. I've just been...exploring. It's great! You'll find out for yourself one day...but don't be any hurry. As I said before, eternity is a long, long time.*

— *Sorry, but I guess I was just expecting, well...more. Something a bit more dramatic after all we've gone through.*

He once again felt that indefinable light tickling sensation he recognized as John laughing.

— *You watch too much TV! From where I stand, all of life is an anticlimax. And what "more" did you expect? You've helped me find myself, and you've found Steve. You've got a family who loves you, and a job you like, and you're young and good-looking and healthy...and rich to boot. What more could you possibly want? Who knows what more is out there, waiting for you? Relax and enjoy it.*

— *So, you do plan to stick around for awhile, then?*

— *Oh, yes! As I told you before, since you're my only direct link to...to where you are, I'd really like to keep in touch. I've never been the type to get lonely, but it is nice to have a conversation with a friend every now and then. I hope you won't mind.*

— *I'd like that.*

— *Good. I'm glad. Oh, and about Steve, you might try listening to Cessy.*

— *I'll think about it.*

— *You do that. Well, I should let you get to sleep, now. I'm going exploring again, but I'll see you soon.*

— *Okay.*

He felt himself floating downward, like a feather. And just before total sleep enveloped him, he was aware of a voice—a real voice he knew was John's.

"Thank you, Elliott."

And then he slept.

END

ABOUT THE AUTHOR

Dorien Grey started out as a pen name, nothing more, for a lifelong book and magazine editor who wanted to write his own novels as a bridge between the gay and straight communities. However, because he was living in a remote and time-warped area of the upper Midwest where gays still feel it necessary to keep a very low profile, he did not feel comfortable using his own name—a sad commentary on our society, he admits.

But as his first book, a detective novel, led to the second and then the third, he found Dorien slowly became much more than a pseudonym, evolving into an alter ego.

"It's reached the point," he says, "where all I have to do is sit down at the computer and let Dorien tell the story."

As for the Dorien's "real person," he's had a not-uninteresting life. Two years into college, he left to join the Naval Aviation Cadet program—he washed out and spent the rest of his brief military career on an aircraft carrier in the Mediterranean. The journal he kept of his time in the military, in the form of letters home, honed his writing skills and provided him with a wealth of experiences to draw from in his future writing.

Returning to college after service, he graduated with a BA in English and embarked on a series of jobs that led him into the editing field. While working for a Los Angeles publishing house, he was instrumental in establishing a division exclusively for the publication of gay paperbacks and magazines, of which he became editor. He moved on to edit a leading LA-based international gay men's magazine.

Tiring of earthquakes, brush fires, mudslides and riots, he returned to the Midwest, where Dorien emerged, full-blown, like Athena from the head of Zeus.

He—and Dorien, of course—recently moved to Chicago, and now devote their energies to writing. After having completed ten books in the popular Dick Hardesty Mystery series, and now Calico, a Western historical romantic suspense, they are currently working on a new mystery with a new protagonist, which may have the potential to become a series.

"Too early to tell," Dorien says. "But stay tuned."

But for a greater insight into the real person behind Dorien Grey, the curious are invited to read The Poems of Dorien Grey, an ebook available from GLB Publishers.

ABOUT THE ARTIST

Martine Jardin has been an artist since she was very small. Her mother guarantees she was born holding a pencil, which for a while, as a toddler, she nicknamed "Zessie"

She won several art competitions with her drawings as a child, ventured into charcoal, watercolors and oils later in life and about 12 years ago started creating digital art.

Since then, she's created hundreds of book covers for Zumaya Publications and eXtasy Books, among others. She welcomes visitors to her website: www.martinejardin.com.

Printed in the United States
117809LV00009B/196-198/P

9 781934 841044